SOUTH

◇ OF THE ◇

BORDER

The Author as a Cowboy Detective

SOUTH

◇ OF THE ◇

BORDER

John Byrne Cooke

BANTAM BOOKS
TORONTO · NEW YORK · LONDON · SYDNEY · AUCKLAND

SOUTH OF THE BORDER

A Bantam Book / March 1989

Book design by Jeffrey L. Ward.
Map copyright © 1988 Anita Karl and Jim Kemp.

Library of Congress Cataloging-in-Publication Data

Cooke, John Byrne.
    South of the border.

    1. Siringo, Charles A., 1855–1928, in
fiction, drama, poetry, etc.   I. Title.
PS3553.O556S66   1989   813'.54   88–7972
ISBN 0-553-05344-2

Published simultaneously in the United States and Canada

Bantam Books are published by Bantam Books, a division of Bantam
Doubleday Dell Publishing Group, Inc. Its trademark, consisting of the
words "Bantam Books" and the portrayal of a rooster, is Registered in
U.S. Patent and Trademark Office and in other countries. Marca Regis-
trada. Bantam Books, 666 Fifth Avenue, New York, New York 10103.

PRINTED IN THE UNITED STATES OF AMERICA

WAK   0 9 8 7 6 5 4 3 2 1

Preface

I INTEND TO hang on to this life just as long as I can. I'm enjoying myself and don't aim to give up the ghost without a fight. But this book will not see the light of day until I have passed from this mortal coil, and so for the first time I am greeting my readers from the other side of Jordan. This is a peculiar situation for me, and perhaps for my readers as well, for as I write these words I am feeling very fit. Full of vim and vinegar, the fact is, as a result of a monthlong journey I recently made to the land south of the border.

I made this jaunt with a picture-show outfit, a lively crew that scares up enough mischief on an ordinary day to fill two or three books. But there chanced to be in our company a man I trailed twenty years ago, and therein lies my tale. Back when I dogged his tracks I never got close enough to set eyes on him, which is just as well for him, for my intention then was to put him behind bars. That was along about the time when the old century shuffled off into the mists to make way for this one, so full of new contraptions and new ideas, and until a few weeks ago I believed my outlaw foe to be long in his grave.

Before I begin my story, I will say a word of introduction about myself, since I and my earlier books may be forgotten when this one is offered to the world.

I was born in Matagorda County, Texas, in 1855. At the age of eleven I commenced a career on the hurricane deck of a Spanish pony, which is to say I was a cowboy. I was more of a boy than some others who entered that lively occupation, although we were on the whole a young lot, hence the term applied to us. I stayed at the job for fifteen years, by which time I felt I had mastered it sufficiently. The cowboy life was rarely a dull one, but with the boldness of youth I wanted greater challenges. In particular, I longed for work that would exercise my gray matter as thoroughly as cowboying had exercised my somewhat spare frame.

For any who wish more details of my cowboy life, I refer you to my very first book, *A Texas Cow Boy,* in which I relate many of the entertaining experiences I enjoyed during those years. Several hundreds of thousands of that volume are at large in the world, but should you not find one at hand, my latest tome, *A Lone Star Cowboy,* covers many of the same events, and includes much history of the cattle business that has never before been published. (You will note that since publishing my first book I have adopted the more modern spelling of cowboy, although I look askance at most things that call themselves "modern." But as a writer I do try to keep up with the times.)

My other reason for abandoning the cowboy trade took the form of a fifteen-year-old black-eyed miss I accidentally met in Caldwell, Kansas, then a booming railhead for the cattle trade. It was a genuine case of love at first sight, and not my first, for I have always had an eye for the pretty women. But when I met Mamie I couldn't bear to be away from her side, so after a three-day courtship and an engagement just as long, we jumped into harness together to trot through a life of wedded bliss. I abandoned the cowboy ranks and settled down to be a two-bit merchant in Caldwell while I pondered where I might find the excitement I longed for. I had happiness aplenty with Mamie, but an unkind fate took her from me after scarcely a handful of years, and long before that tearful day my roaming ways had set me on trails that led far from our happy home.

While settled in Caldwell I wrote and published *A Texas Cow Boy,* and was well pleased with its success. I prospered as a purveyor of cigars and confections too, and soon expanded my emporium to include an oyster and ice cream parlor, but after two years as a gallus-snapping businessman I concluded that Caldwell was too small for my talents, so Mamie and I packed up and took ourselves to the booming city of Chicago to see what opportunities that metropolis might offer. Shortly after our arrival the terrible Haymarket bombing occurred, and like many of that time and place I was swept up in a wave of patriotic fervor against the threat of violent anarchy. I decided that the business life was too tame for a man of my abilities, and I became seized by the notion that for my next work I would pursue those who made bold of flaunting the law.

This may seem a vainglorious hope for one whose only demonstrated skills were punching recalcitrant longhorns and purveying delicacies, but the fact was, I had already chased and nearly captured Billy "the Kid" with some of my cowboy chums. Mr. "Kid" made so bold as to rustle cattle from several outfits in the Texas Panhandle when I was employed by the LX spread in those parts, a trifling enterprise of just over a million acres.

The ranchers in question took offense at such effrontery, as Texans are wont to do when wronged. I was particularly hot under the collar, as the result of the Kid's having passed several months in our panhandle locale some time before appropriating our cattle. I had become intimately acquainted with him and his jovial crowd, and I had become his friend, or so I thought. I was somewhat a defender of his reputation too, for I found him quite different from the cruel-hearted wretch he was often portrayed to be. He had good qualities in fair measure, among them a true kind-heartedness toward the unfortunate. I knew for a fact that he once hired a team and wagon at his own expense in order to haul a total stranger, a sick and destitute man, from Fort Sumner to Las Vegas, New Mexico, to get the man to a doctor. But I soon found that I had been blind to the Kid's meaner side. The panhandle ranches had fed him and given him clean straw to spread his bedroll on, and he repaid us by stealing from us when our backs were turned, which is the act of a scoundrel.

In short order we put together a group of the boys to follow the Kid and our stolen cattle to Hades itself, if that's where he thought to market the beef. Having no such distant goal in mind, Billy and his bunch trailed our steers down to the southern parts of New Mexico, but Pat Garrett put an end to him before we could teach him a Texas lesson or two.

From this experience, I reckoned myself three fourths of the way toward becoming a master manhunter. I was further encouraged by recalling an occasion in Caldwell when I had submitted my head for examination by a blind phrenologist, who proclaimed that I had a large stubborn bump and would surely succeed as a newspaper editor, a stock raiser, or a detective. And so with a brave heart and a face full of brass, I found employment with Pinkerton's National Detective Agency and stayed with the brothers Pinkerton for twenty-two years.

Having been fifteen years in the cowboy school, I intended to remain in the Pinkerton college for an equal period, but I extended my studies because I was eager to learn the ways of the world, and I had in mind that my experiences might offer material for another book. Some may feel twenty-two years is a long time to gather material. I can only say that operating undercover as a cowboy detective proved to be interesting work, and there was always more to learn about the wicked world and its ways.

Soon after joining the Agency I was posted to the Denver office. Apart from an assignment in the Idaho mines, my cowboy skills got plenty of exercise, as much of my time was spent masquerading as an outlaw, trying to get the goods on the notorious cowboy bandits of the old century's closing years. My longest job was pursuing the most daring band of highwaymen the country has ever known, the Hole-in-the-Wall Gang, also known as the Wild Bunch, but there were plenty of other cases just for variety. My work took me across the length and breadth of this land, from New York City to Los Angeles and from my native Texas to Alaska, as well as south of the border where Spanish is the loving tongue.

At last there came a time when I felt that I had exhausted in Pinkerton's employ more lives than a barnful of cats, and had better find more peaceful work before my luck ran out. (Those who wish further details of my exciting detective experiences will find them in my book *A Cowboy Detective*.) Despite being offered the position of superintendent of one of the Agency's western offices, I tendered my resignation, passing up an opportunity for an advance in salary and a chance to swell up with self-importance. I had refused a superintendency once before, feeling there was not enough kick in office work, and I found it even easier the second time around.

Having told the year of my birth, you will see that I am pushing sixty-five now, so I will admit that as the years advance I have found myself more comfortable in the warmer climes. When I left Pinkerton's Denver office for the last time, I therefore turned my pony's head toward Santa Fe, where I had bought a ranch some years before. I dubbed this outfit Sunny Slope, for its pleasant southern exposure, and there, more than twenty years after penning *A Texas Cow Boy*, I sat down to write about my detective adventures, in between milking my blooded Jersey cows and caring for my White Leghorn chickens. But I did not give myself over all at once to the life of a gentleman author. Soon after leaving the Pinkerton employ I did some work for the William J. Burns Detective Agency, and not so long ago I served for two years as a New Mexico Ranger, chasing Mexican cattle thieves. The day came, however, when I was forced to admit that I might be a bit long in the tooth for detective work, and so I have lately given myself wholly over to writing.

As a writer I can live where I wish, which has been my preference since I first jumped off my poor mother's knee and began studying mischief, and so, five months ago, I left Santa Fe and took up residence in southern California. The reasons for this latest removal will be revealed in good time, but suffice it to say that had I remained on my ranch I would never have fallen in with the picture-show crowd, never set eyes at last on my old quarry, never have ridden once more on the deserts of Old Mexico. As it was, the lot of us managed to scare up enough excitement to satisfy the rowdiest of my long-gone friends from the old days, when a man had only his own wits and character to count on when the chips were down.

In the preface to *A Texas Cow Boy*, I said, only partly in jest, "My excuse for writing this book is money—and lots of it." At the time I little dreamt that newsboys would sell my book on every street corner. But inasmuch as I will be safely singing in the heavenly choir when this volume is published, you will see that the expectation of earthly rewards cannot be any part of my reason for writing it. And for those who are familiar with the cowboy practice of stretching a three-foot piece of the truth out to five feet on occasion, I will say no such flings of imagination have been permitted in any of my books. The dewy-eyed dime novelists have produced many fool notions about what life was like back on the wild frontier, but from the start I have tried in my books to set the record straight.

The story I am about to tell is as wild a tale as an old cowboy ever conjured up around a cookfire, but it's the God's honest truth, and I offer it in unvarnished form, because truth, more often than the law, is a thing worthy of respect.

Charles A. Siringo
Hollywood, California
January 1920

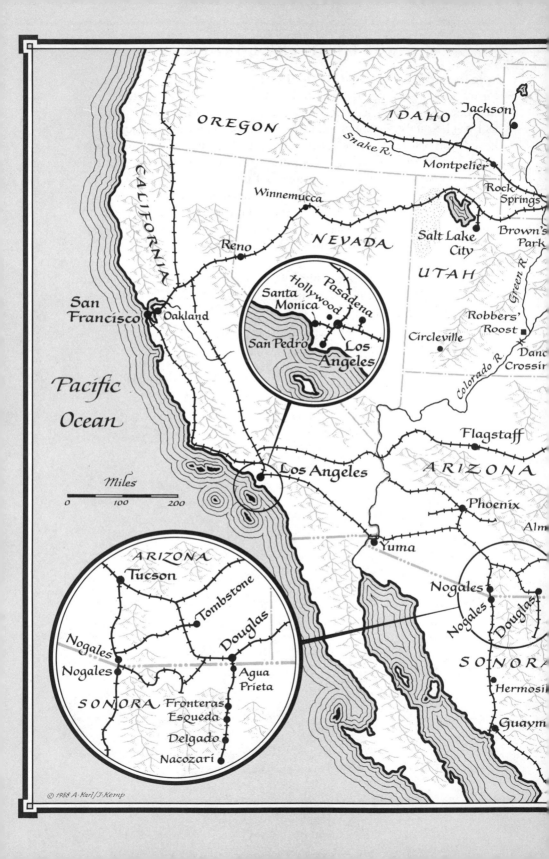

OREGON

IDAHO

Jackson

Snake R.

Montpelier

Rock Springs

Winnemucca

NEVADA

CALIFORNIA

Reno

Salt Lake City

Brown's Park

UTAH

Green R.

San Francisco

Oakland

Hollywood   Pasadena
Santa
Monica

Robbers' Roost

Circleville

Danc Crossir

San Pedro   Los Angeles

Colorado R.

Pacific

Ocean

Flagstaff

Miles

0   100   200

Los Angeles

A R I Z O N A

Phoenix

Alm

Yuma

Nogales

ARIZONA

Tucson

Tombstone

Douglas

Nogales
Nogales

Douglas

Nogales

Agua
Prieta

S O N O R A

Fronteras
Esqueda

SONORA

Hermosi

Delgado

Nacozari

Guaym

© 1988 A. Karl / J. Kemp

Chapter 1

THE THANKSGIVING SEASON just past offered many reasons to be thankful, what with the Great War and the dreaded influenza that followed it both fading into memory. For a time there, it seemed that the apocalypse had truly come to the world's civilized nations, while the three Horsemen of War, Death, and Pestilence rode wantonly across our heavenly sphere. In the ravaged countries of Europe, I imagine many heard the hoofbeats of Famine as well. But by the final months of 1919 the funerals for victims of plague and battle were mostly over, and in southern California flowers bloomed beside the gravestones.

These are booming times on the Pacific shore, particularly this part of it, with emigrants flocking west in numbers exceeding even those of the Gold Rush, bright with the hope of work to be done and fortunes to be made, just like those optimistic fools of seventy years ago. There may be as many fools among the emigrants now, but there is work for all, with oil and the movies both offering pay dirt as rich as any gold. People are happy to forget whatever calamities the recent past may hold and get on with chasing the future. A million new citizens have come to the Golden State since the century began, they say, and Los Angeles, which was a peaceful little Spanish town not so long ago, has grown fivefold in twenty years.

The rains we received early in November were just sufficient to green the Hollywood hills, and the festive Thursday itself was warm and pleasant. By Saturday, before the turkey bones had been turned into soup, I was already looking ahead to Christmas, and I felt that we were truly entering a season of peace for the first time in some years.

It was on that Saturday, the 29th of November, that Leroy rode into our lives.

I passed the morning at my desk to no good end, trying to avoid the blank stare of my writing tablet. *A Lone Star Cowboy* was fresh off the presses, I had mailed the manuscript for my *History of "Billy the Kid"* to the printer, and suddenly that was all she wrote. After giving out a steady flow of stories for years, the well of my imagination had suddenly run dry. I was learning how a calf must feel when he is jerked up short at the end of a rope. This is not to say I had never struggled for a day or two, but always a few hours on horseback would get my thoughts to moving again, and the new pages would follow.

In the week before Thanksgiving I had about worn out my horse Jake on these rides, to no avail. He was sorely tired of my grumbling and I had no more idea what episodes from my life might serve to adorn the as-yet blank pages of my next book than I had a month before. I tell this not by way of complaint, for every occupation has its tribulations, but merely to explain why I kept to the Bunk House on the day Leroy showed up. I was determined to put spurs to my two-by-four brain instead of putting spurs to Jake and riding out to where Victoria and her outfit were finishing up the third and latest "Cimarron Rose" serial.

The Bunk House was full up, as it had been since the day I bought it, just five months earlier. Like the previous owner, I cater to the cowboys and cowgirls of the western movie crowd, who flocked to this land of orange groves in great numbers when they heard they could make twice as much as they made on a cow-calf outfit, and for work that seems like play. Imagine their surprise to discover that the wild stories they have heard are true! I guess these young people like the Bunk House because it's a boardinghouse much like many across the West, and reminds them of home. A cowboy needs a sense of home as much as the next man, however much fun he may be having showing off in front of a moving-picture camera.

Many of my clientele are employed by McQuain & Vickery's Wild West. When the boys and girls are making good money in pictures, some of them will take rooms in the Bunk House. When times are leaner, they'll go back to sleeping in the company's tents and wagons, which are parked on Gerald Ball's land out behind my corrals, just as if they were on the road in summertime.

So long as the weather held fair, the picture outfits were cranking out film as fast as they could, and my cowboys and cowgirls had work aplenty. Like me they were up before dawn. Ordinarily I like to join them at breakfast. Many of those who sleep in the wagons take their meals in the Bunk House, and even though we sit down to a dining room table, the mood reminds me of the chuckwagon breakfasts of my youth. But on this particular Saturday I kept to myself like an old grouch.

I will admit that the failure of my writer's inspiration had put me in a bad temper. I wondered if I was getting too old to call up the creative juices I had taken for granted ever since I was a young man.

Once my roomers were up and gone the Bunk House was quiet. To me it seemed the stillness of a tomb. I strolled through the parlor and the hallways for a time to escape the confines of my study, and so I chanced to see the traveling salesman take his leave. I usually don't cater to drummers, but he caught me in a soft moment the day before. I wouldn't suggest that he thought to depart without paying, but he did appear startled to see me.

"I thought you were staying the week," I said. My tone was a bit sharp, owing to my bad humor.

"When I checked in, I had no idea that you catered to movie people." He raised his nose an inch or two.

I took his money and sent him off with a muttered "good riddance." As if a man who deals in ladies' undergarments has any call to look down his nose at movie people.

When the drummer was gone I removed myself even farther from my writing tablet by going out to walk around the Bunk House grounds and look over our rustic acres just beyond the outer fringes of Hollywood's spreading bungalows. We are somewhat outcasts here, the local pariahs, if you will. My neighbors, except for Gerald Ball, are "old-time" Hollywood residents, mostly retired midwestern farmers who brought with them their churchgoing habits and prohibitionist sentiments. A few years ago the movie people intruded on what had theretofore been a quiet little town, and now they outnumber the old-timers severalfold, to the farmers' horror. Many picture people were formerly in the theater or vaudeville, a class of society decent folks shun. In the view of the hoe-men and their wives, the movie crowd has the morals of rabbits and even less self-restraint. Cowboys don't deserve that reputation, but they are wild, and the locals scorn them just the same. It is a feeling the cowboys reciprocate in spades. We have all seen how the fool hoe-men ruin good cattle range.

On this Saturday morning I was just as glad to keep my distance from my neighbors and everyone else. I ate my noon meal in the kitchen and gave Josefa Acevedo, my Mexican cook, a hard time, generally making a nuisance of myself, when of course I should have abandoned my writing entirely and ridden out to watch Victoria vanquish bad men and Indians alike with a flash of that famous smile and a salvo from her trusty six-shooters.

Victoria, I should say here, is Victoria Hartford, the rising star of the aforementioned Cimarron Rose serials. I have known Victoria all her life and sometimes forget that others need a proper introduction. I met her parents, Jay and Anne Hartford, during my Pinkerton years, and from the day of Victoria's birth I have been her "Uncle" Charlie. Back when she was no more than a fond hope in her mother's breast, I chanced to be staying at the Hartfords' New Mexico ranch when the news of my wife Mamie's death reached me. The comfort of the Hartfords' kindness and hospitality eased that period of mourning greatly. To distract me from my sorrow they took me to see the land adjoining theirs to the south, which was for sale. That land became my Sunny Slope ranch. Between my detective journeys I returned there whenever I could, until Sunny Slope and the Hartfords were at the very center of what I called home.

As fate would have it, I soon had an opportunity to repay the Hartfords' kindness. When Jay was crippled by a falling horse, I became responsible for teaching Victoria the ways of cows and calves and all the ranch work she loved so well.

After the Hartfords sold their spread and moved to California for Jay's health, I felt that I had lost my best friends on earth. It was largely to be near them again that I followed them here. Victoria lives with her parents just a mile or so from the Bunk House, and she and I enjoy many hours together on the movie sets. To the rest of the world ours is the friendship of a stove-up cowboy author and the young picture-show girl who sees him as a colorful relic from the days depicted in her picture-show stories. We are content to let one and all believe our friendship is just that and nothing more.

From the first time I showed up on a western movie location with Victoria, she has seen to it that the director finds out who I am. Learning I am a cowboy author, he will generally ask my advice about the story. These celluloid tales bear less resemblance to my Texas youth than stories from the Arabian Nights, but no matter how nonsensical they may be, I will admit I get caught up in them. As a boy running barefoot on the beaches of the Matagorda peninsula, I rode a stick horse and carried a stick rifle, with which I bedeviled crabs and chickens and anything else that moved. In my advancing years, some of that ability to take delight in make-believe still survives in my addled mind. Having given up the truly dangerous work of my detective years, I guess I am happy to return to the harmless imaginings of my youth.

The directors always swear up, down and sideways that they want to show "the real West in all its glory," and now and again I can swing the story closer to the truth. I had offered a number of suggestions regarding the present travails of Cimarron Rose and went so far as to write scenarios for the early episodes, but from the start I didn't hit it off with Rodney Quillen, Victoria's new director, which was another reason I was not out at the location to witness Leroy's appearance.

A MAN ON a horseback journey takes his time if he cares for his horses and has no pressing business. Leroy had passed a number of weeks on his ride down through Oregon and California, enjoying the feel of being on horseback again and beholden to no one. He rode a big sorrel gelding named Sonny and led a bay mare pack horse. The pack horse carried a complete camp outfit, allowing Leroy to stop for the night wherever the spirit, or the weather, moved him.

After a cool night west of Cajon, Leroy rode down into the broad coastal basin where Los Angeles and her attendant towns are arrayed like an old queen surrounded by her court. He came on the Santa Fe tracks around midday, just in time to see the California Limited sail by. This pleased him considerably, as he has had a lifelong fondness for trains. He gave the engineer a wave and got one in return. What a surprise it must have been for the folks on the train, seeing Leroy sitting there on his horse "like something out of a picture show." Those are Buddy Johnston's words, for by one of those coincidences that make me believe the Lord has a sense of humor, Buddy was on the Limited, coming home at last from France, where the army kept him on after the guns fell silent. Buddy chanced to look up and see Leroy, never dreaming that he and the horse-man would meet before the day was done.

Leroy might have just kept on south. His sights were set on Mexico from the moment he left his home, but he had been to Los Angeles a few times, the first twenty years before. His travels then were by way of mak-ing himself scarce in places where my Pinkerton compatriots and I were taking a lively interest in his whereabouts. Now, the thought that the Limited would be at the Santa Fe's Grande Station before nightfall made him decide to turn west and see what had become of the former Spanish pueblo. Of such idle whims are adventures made and the lives of men altered forever.

He passed through the new towns springing up like weeds in the flat farmland south of the foothills, Alhambra and the rest of them, taking in the houses and the fields, the trolley lines, and the automobiles scaring respectable horses half to death. Now and again he plucked an orange from some farmer's tree to eat on the way. Oranges are all the rage nowa-days, but out that way the hoe-men are reluctant to commit themselves to a single crop, so Leroy rode through orchards of apricots and walnuts, almonds, plums and figs as well as oranges. Being new to the region my-self, I have no idea what may have been ripe enough to add to his luncheon. The seasons are topsy-turvy here, with many crops being harvested when most other American farms are sleeping under a layer of frost and snow.

Leroy soon found that Los Angeles had changed greatly in twenty years. Where once he had fit right in with the crowd, the few horsemen he saw now were dressed in city finery and mounted on thoroughbreds. They looked upon him—covered with dust and leading a pack horse—as an amusing oddity from a bygone era, while the motor cars flew around them every which way. Leaving the clamor behind, Leroy decided to look for a rooming house up by the Hollywood hills.

Late in the afternoon he came on a fair piece of countryside that no enterprising citizen has yet thought to irrigate for crops. He was stopped in the bottom of a wash, watering himself and his horses, when he first heard the whooping and looked up to see what it was all about.

What he saw was Victoria—though at first he couldn't tell she was a woman—with a dozen bloodthirsty Indian braves hot on her heels. She had her matched set of silver-plated, pearl-handled Colt's revolvers in her hands, and every now and then she would turn in the saddle and blaze away at her pursuers. And I'll say one thing for Victoria. If she had live ammunition, she is one of the few people I know, men included, who could put two of Sam Colt's shooting instruments to profitable use against Indians or any other enemy, having been trained in the art of shooting by yours truly. But of course in her present line of work she carries two just for the show.

Feeling at home among the mesquite and sagebrush may have put Leroy to mind of wilder stretches of the West in times gone by. Even so, seeing those Indians must have made him feel a little the way I did when I set eyes on a fully feathered redskin in the middle of New York City, back in my Pinkerton days, when I ran onto Bill Cody's Wild West boys out on a spree.

To give Leroy his due, he didn't stop to wonder what in blazes was going on, not yet. He just grabbed his gun and headed for cover as natural as if he were still a boy back in the Rocky Mountains, where he had imagined such adventures daily throughout his youth, regretting that he came along too late to know such things for real.

If he had been out in the open, Victoria might have seen him, but she was intent on guiding her horse Ranger toward the place where she would jump him into the wash, so whatever part of himself Leroy might have shown as he ran across the river bottom, she missed it clean.

Leroy was leading his two horses along under the rim of the wash, thinking to intercept Victoria and lend her a hand, when a coyote appeared suddenly out of a hole in the bank, running like the hounds of hell were nipping at his heels. He ran between Sonny and the pack horse and pulled his freight for the wide lonesome, leaving two thoroughly spooked broomtails in his wake.

Victoria was almost at the edge of the bank when she saw Leroy trying to hold on to his plunging, rearing horses directly below her. Ranger put on the brakes and tried to head back the other way, but the bank gave way. Before Leroy knew what was happening he had Victoria, Ranger and all, down on top of him. Ranger landed on his feet, shied sideways, lost his footing and went down.

If there is one eventuality Victoria is well-prepared for while on horseback, it's getting out of a horse's way when it falls. Her father's injury was an object lesson about the possible consequences and she never sets her boots too deep in the stirrups. As Ranger went down she threw the reins over the chestnut's head and stepped out of the saddle just as calm as you please, landing on her feet and taking hold of the reins like the whole thing was planned. She was off balance, but a step backward would fix that, or so she thought until she tripped over her own boot heel and fell.

And Leroy was there to catch her. Faced with the choice between letting Victoria fall on her duff and turning his horses loose, Leroy made the chivalrous decision. She looked up, her heart already pounding like a trip-hammer from Ranger's fall, and found herself in the arms of a complete stranger.

Never one to suffer undue familiarity, she righted herself quickly and stepped away from Leroy just as Ranger was preparing to regain his feet. Ever the cool one, she put her foot in the stirrup and swung back aboard as the horse stood up. Ranger was set to buck or run but Victoria held him in, his eyes wide and all atremble, and there she sat, looking down at Leroy.

"That's a neat trick," he offered.

"I just made it up as I went along," she replied, unwilling, even in her moment of triumph, to take credit for a piece of good luck. Just then Leroy spied Redeye Hawk standing ten yards away, a tomahawk in his hand, barefoot from head to toe except for a breechclout, his body decorated with warpaint.

With speed that made Victoria blink, one of Mr. Colt's Indian-killers appeared in Leroy's hand as if he had conjured it out of the air. He carried the gun in his waistband, covered by his coat, so Victoria hadn't even known the stranger was armed. The barrel swung toward Redeye Hawk and there was no mistaking that Leroy meant business.

Redeye Hawk is a genuine Sioux Indian, like most of them with the McQuain & Vickery outfit. The Sioux tribe is noted for the bravery of their warriors, though as a Texan I naturally see the Comanches as the pinnacle of Indian manhood, for every Texas child was raised on stories of their bloodthirsty deeds. But as fearsome tribes of redskins go, the Sioux run a close second to the Comanch', even in my book. At his present age of twenty-one, Redeye would have been in his full glory as a warrior, thirty or forty years ago. Like their southern brethren, the Sioux are tamer nowadays, but even so, Redeye is a wild one. He is forever getting himself into one kind of mischief or another, along with Nate Dicenzo and Karen Valdez, his partners in tomfoolery. Rough and ready would fit the three of them, but there in the wash Redeye was caught off guard and he ought to be forgiven for reacting the way he did, instead of in some manner that might have got him killed.

The poor fellow was only doing his job, after all. He had left the main bunch of Indians, like he was supposed to, and dropped down into the wash, like he was supposed to, and set about creeping up on Victoria in an appropriate manner. So far, everything was going according to the scenario. But between one breath and the next, he found the big eye of a Colt's .44 staring at him, and behind it some fellow he didn't know, and for certain wasn't part of the show, with blood in his eyes.

Redeye let out with an exclamation not fit for polite company and then reverted to proper American in this manner: "Whoa now! I give up!"

Victoria saw Leroy contemplating murder and called out to stop him. "Wait!" she cried, "Don't shoot!"

At the very same moment Leroy told Redeye, "Drop the hatchet!"

All Redeye could see was that cannon staring at him and he froze up like a mule in a mudhole. Whereupon Leroy shot the handle of the tomahawk clean in two.

Chapter 2

LEROY'S MARKSMANSHIP WENT unappreciated by Redeye, who was moved once more to profanity. Victoria was flabbergasted, more by the shooting than Redeye's forgetful speech.

Up to now everything had happened fast enough to startle a hanging judge, but at this point in the proceedings it struck Leroy that this was California in the year of our Lord 1919, and running across an Indian war was about as likely as finding a genuine two-headed calf at a medicine show. He lowered his six-shooter.

Seeing that the danger was past, Victoria demanded—somewhat heatedly—to know where in Satan's hot domain he had sprung from.

"Suppose you tell me what's going on here?" Leroy suggested, unnaturally calm for a man who had just witnessed a dozen Indian braves gallivanting across the California chaparral.

"I'm holding off a bunch of Indians and waiting to be rescued," Victoria said, as if this were an everyday occurrence in her life and none of his concern anyhow. But she realized he would need more than that to make him put up his pistol, so she pointed to where the camera crew was set up by a bunch of live oaks up the wash.

"We're making a movie." The humor in the situation was getting through to her now, and she gave him the beginnings of a smile.

Victoria's smile by itself is enough to pacify a cornered badger, but Leroy didn't lower his pistol until he took a quick look around and saw the rest of the Indians fifty yards off, scratching their heads, and the movie crew beyond. Not far from where the camera was set up, some of the cowboys who were not needed in the present scene were playing a game of sandlot baseball in the sagebrush.

"I'm Victoria Hartford," Victoria said.

"Leroy Roberts," he replied. "Hey, you're that—what's her name?— Cimarron Rose! I've seen your pictures."

He tucked the .44 back into his waistband and smiled like a man who realized he had made a fool of himself but figured he might as well get whatever enjoyment there was to be had from his predicament. He had gone with the demands of the moment, reacting like someone who was used to running up against sudden danger, which told Victoria a good deal about him.

Leroy's horses had stopped not far away, once they were clear of the excitement. Victoria trotted over and recovered them now, and led them back to Leroy. As she handed him the reins she dismounted, bringing herself down to his level, and took the measure of the man before her.

"Today's our last day of filming on this picture," she said, just to make conversation. "We only have a few scenes left to shoot. Maybe you'd like to watch."

She saw a man of medium height with blue eyes and an easygoing manner, so long as you weren't an Indian sneaking up on a damsel in distress. He had a broad face, prominent cheekbones, and a square jaw. His boots and clothes were worn and dusty, and the lines at the corners of his eyes were the sort made by smiling. She found it difficult to calculate his age. There was some gray in his sandy hair, but his eyes were young. She guessed he was about forty-five.

While Victoria was taking in as much as she could about Leroy without appearing to stare, he was appraising her more openly. What he saw was a striking young woman of twenty-eight years, costumed as Cimarron Rose. Her outfit was realistic, in the manner of the times. It would not have been out of place on some of the finer cattle spreads in Texas, if you could find a cowgirl who mounted her horse directly from the haberdasher's window display. Which is to say that she was a very clean cowgirl. There were creases still in her breeches, her fine hair was combed, and the clean bandanna at her throat was held in place with a jasper and silver ring clasp.

Cimarron Rose's breeches have caused some raised eyebrows among the stuffy set. They are hardly the common riding costume for well-brought-up young ladies, but Victoria's serials are based on a New Mexico legend of a woman who rode and dressed like a man, and Victoria has insisted that her costume be true to the old tales. And while most actresses still ride in the split skirts called culottes, some cowgirls in the bigger roundups and stampede shows are wearing pants on occasion. It may be that before long all women will wear pants and their skirts and dresses will be consigned to the trash bin, although I hope I will not be around to see this spectacle if it comes to pass.

The recent excitement had brought a flashing light to Victoria's eyes and a blush to her cheeks. The blush darkened as Leroy looked her up and down, and neither of them paid Redeye Hawk the slightest attention until he stepped between them, holding the two pieces of his tomahawk.

"Where did you learn to shoot like that?" he inquired of the gunman.

"Oh, here and there," said Leroy.

"Did you do that on purpose?" Victoria pointed to the neatly severed handle.

"I don't like to shoot a man until I know what he's up to," Leroy replied. If there was humor in his eyes, his expression was as sober as a Mormon bishop's.

Naturally, Rodney Quillen had called "Cut" when he saw the scene going wrong. Now, seeing his leading lady passing the time of the day with the interloper instead of shooing him off, Rodney strode forward briskly. As usual he was togged out in his jodhpurs and pith helmet, looking for all the world like Stanley on his way to lunch with Livingstone.

"You," he called out to Leroy when he reached the edge of the bank. "What do you think you're doing there? You ruined the shot."

"He thought it was real, Rodney," Redeye said with a grin. "Don't you think that's kind of funny? You're always telling us to make it look real." He gave Leroy a wink. "You've got to admit it was a pretty good scene. Maybe you should write him into the story."

Rodney was not amused. "You, come with me," he said to Leroy. "You two, let's do it over while we've got the light."

"He's got that look you're always talking about, Rodney," said Redeye. "What do you call it? Authentic? He looks authentic. You're missing a bet if you don't keep the shot and write him into the story." It was impossible, of course, the picture being all but finished, but Redeye never passed up a likely chance to needle Rodney.

Maybe Rodney set up the next scene—the last one they needed to complete the episode and the serial—with that in mind. Whether it was on purpose or not, he had never shown the proper respect for the horses, hence my satisfaction in the way Victoria dealt with him.

The scene was part of the final chase, where Victoria and her cowboy pards chase the Indians back to the reservation. The scenario called for Redeye to jump his horse over an arroyo, an addition Rodney had made himself, while keeping most of my ideas for the slam-bang finish.

Redeye opined that the arroyo was somewhat wide, but he didn't want to seem afraid in front of his fellow redskins. Gerald—Sir Gerald Ball, if you please, Victoria's producer, who was on hand for the final day of shooting—said let's get on with it and get home to supper. To convey the outcome in a few words, Redeye's horse did his utmost, but he didn't quite clear the arroyo. When the dust settled, any fool could see that the horse had broken his left foreleg.

That was it for Redeye. He went after Rodney, calling him a number of harsh names and claiming that Rodney set up dangerous shots so something like this would happen and he would get his stunts without paying extra for them. He knocked Rodney to the ground before Nate Dicenzo pulled him off. Redeye was so mad he almost took a swing at Nate, even though Nate is his best friend in the outfit. He had his arm cocked back and ready to fire when he thought better of it, turning on Rodney instead and giving him a few more pieces of his mind.

Rodney never did know when to keep his mouth closed. He said he had no idea the arroyo was too wide. Redeye told him to please go to Halifax or some other hot country, and added that those places would grow cold to the touch before he would do another day's work with Mr. Rodney Quillen. He got himself so worked up saying these things that he lunged for Rodney again, but Nate held him back.

Arrayed around these three were the cowboys and Indians of the McQuain & Vickery Wild West show, which Gerald had hired for the winter, thus acquiring for one—reasonable, it goes without saying—price, everything he needs to make western pictures: men and women, cattle, horses, wagons, the whole shebang. Among the crowd there were more than a few who sided with Redeye and wished Nate would turn him loose.

That's when Victoria stepped in. She knew there was some truth in Redeye's claim, but she saw that the Indian was in danger of getting himself fired. It was her intention to make another serial before spring, while the McQuain & Vickery bunch was still in Gerald's employ, and she had no wish to lose Redeye Hawk.

For those unfamiliar with the world of moving pictures, I will explain that while Victoria's cowboy extras make six dollars a day, a good rider can earn twice that for stunts like making a horse fall on command. Some directors aren't particular about whether or not an animal gets hurt, but Victoria will not tolerate such an attitude on her pictures. She was raised on a ranch and expects others to respect animals as much as she does.

"I told you I won't have a director who endangers the men or the horses," she announced to Gerald. "I want him fired."

Gerald—Sir Gerald, if you please—dresses to the nines for every occasion. I imagine he is quite the dandy stepping into his bath, although I have not been privileged to witness this ceremony. In an age when outlandish riding clothing is becoming the order of the day for moving-picture folk, Gerald keeps his celluloid collars fresh even when filming in rustic locations. His spats are brushed, his shoes polished, and the only concession he makes to rough surroundings is his fine sailcloth motoring duster, which he keeps buttoned whenever the wind threatens to soil his suit with dust. A cloth motoring cap, with goggles perpetually perched on the brim—except when he is actually motoring—completes his outfit. Among the cowboys Gerald looks out of place, and not just because of his costume. He is not fat, but he does tend to be roundish where a cowboy is lean, and too soft in the places that count.

Nose to nose with this spectacle of pampered British nobility was Victoria, with sparks flying from her eyes.

Gerald knows the warning signs and he may have taken a step backward about then. Even I think twice about standing in Victoria's way when she's got her Irish up.

Before Gerald could think how to defuse the ticking bomb before him, Rodney, ever the fool, stuck in his two bits.

"I have a contract to direct your films for another year!"

"That's right," said Victoria. "As long as you're fit to work."

Any sensible man would have kept his distance then, but Rodney never belonged in the company of sensible men.

"I'm fit as a fiddle," he proclaimed. He raised his head a little, like a lamb offering itself up for the slaughter.

"Not for long," said Victoria. She swung from somewhere down around her knee and brought up a haymaker that connected with the point of Rodney's too-proud jaw.

He remained down for the count. Victoria turned her back on him in a dignified manner and walked off. She paused to let her anger cool in the shade of a live oak tree. As it happened, this was the same piece of shade from which Leroy had watched the filming and Victoria's first-round victory over Rodney Quillen.

She rubbed her hand, feeling the pain now. Leroy wet his bandanna— not so clean as hers—from the canteen on his saddle and offered it to her.

"Wrap this around your hand."

She took the bandanna and did as he told her, not sure whether to be grateful for this kindness or angry at him for the amused expression he couldn't quite hide.

"I had no idea it would hurt so much to hit someone," she admitted.

"Yeah, but you've hurt yourself worse doing ranch work."

"How do you know I've done ranch work?"

"By the way you ride a horse, the way you handle yourself. You've had a pole fall on you when you were fixing a gate, or been kicked by a calf, or cut up by barb wire. You've got the look of a cowgirl."

"You can tell all that by seeing me ride a horse?"

Leroy smiled. "I read the newspapers, too. They say you're a New Mexico cowgirl. Isn't it true?"

Victoria nodded. "I was raised near Santa Fe."

"I've been through that country."

She sized him up once more, again noting the two horses, the camp outfit, and the layer of dust that bespoke a long ride. She decided he was a seasoned hand riding the grub line, looking for a place to winter.

"Are you looking for a job?"

"Just passing through."

"We pay six dollars a day for extras. Three more if you help with props. Five dollars for stunts."

"That's a lot of money." His surprise was genuine. Folks are always surprised to learn what picture work pays.

"You'd get more at Essanay. They pay seven fifty a day." Victoria is honest to a fault, which is one reason her crew is so loyal to her.

For the second time that day, Redeye Hawk interrupted their conversation. "I'm sorry to cause a ruckus," he said to Victoria as he joined them under the tree. "It's only that I liked that paint horse so much. I was figuring to buy him off Mr. Vickery when he got back."

Near the camera, the men were clustered about Rodney, who was sitting on the ground holding his jaw. Gerald Ball left the others and walked toward the shady tree, his expression dark.

"You were probably right about Rodney setting you up for a fall," Victoria said.

"Thanks for hitting him," said Redeye.

"Gerald would have fired you." Victoria kept her eyes on the approaching Englishman. "He can't fire me."

"You have broken his jaw," Gerald informed her, nodding in Rodney's direction.

If he expected contriteness from Victoria, he got none. "I won't work with a man who mistreats animals. Besides, he's not right for my feature."

"Victoria! Not that again." Gerald had heard this tune before.

"Serials won't last forever."

"Serials and two-reelers made this business what it is!" Gerald shot back.

"Mr. Griffith and Mr. DeMille don't think so, and neither does Carl Laemmle! Anyway, you said you would meet Brian and listen to his idea. You promised."

"And I keep my promises," he said, not with the greatest will in the world. "In any event, we will need a new director."

He turned and walked back toward the crowd, where Chief John, one of the company's Indian elders, was tying a bandanna around Rodney's head to keep his mouth from hanging open like a half-wit's.

To the west, the sun was dipping into the orange groves off Santa Monica way.

"I was serious about that job," Victoria said to Leroy. "If you stay until after Christmas, I can promise you work."

She already suspected that hauling props and riding as an extra wasn't Leroy's style, but she wanted him to know she hoped he would stay around long enough to get better acquainted.

"By Christmas I'll be in Mexico, lying under some palm tree," he said.

"We've got palm trees here," she observed, but she is not one to beg. She puts her cards on the table, maybe with a bit more brass than is seemly in an unmarried woman, but she'll leave you to raise or fold on your own.

She handed him back his bandanna. "If you want a room for the night, Redeye can give you directions to my uncle's boardinghouse. We're having our cast party there tonight." With that, she turned on her heel and walked off.

Already the boys were loading the horses into a truck and preparing to give the chaparral back to Mr. Coyote and his tribe. A couple of the Indians helped Rodney to Gerald's shiny touring car. Victoria had ridden out to the location with Gerald, but now she climbed into the truck with the cowboys, preferring their company to Rodney Quillen's.

"You ever been to a cast party full of cowboys?" Redeye knew perfectly well that Leroy didn't have the first notion that a cast party was a bust-out shindig picture folks held when they finished up a picture.

"Can't say that I have."

"You want a place to sleep?"

"I'll have to sleep somewhere."

"All right then. We'll load your horses with the rest and you can come with us."

"That's okay. I'll ride."

Redeye shrugged. "Have it your way. Just follow this road until you come to a big bunch of live oaks. Where the road forks, go south."

He continued in this manner, using east and west and the natural features of the country as landmarks, as well as mentioning the roads and houses Leroy would see along the route. From the way Leroy nodded and took it in, Redeye guessed that this was one white man used to seeing the lay of the land like an Indian—like most white men too, a generation earlier. But in this modern age men no longer have a need to notice the lay of the land to get from one place to the next, what with automobiles and streetcars and roads running every which way.

HAD I BEEN present for Leroy's arrival at Victoria's location, I would have seen how she flirted with him and I would have been more on my guard.

As it was, some weeks passed before I pieced together a full picture of that event, but I had my own reasons for taking an interest in him when we met, later on that same day. I will get to these reasons shortly, but it strikes me that my readers may wonder how I can relate these happenings in such detail, in view of the fact that I was not there to see them, and this is a good time to address the point. I intend to tell the rest of my tale in a similar manner and for the most part I shall not stop to say just how I knew of the happenings in question.

First and foremost, I will say that none of the events I have related thus far are mere imaginings pulled out of the air as a writer of dime novels might do. I want to be very clear about this, and so I am going to give away a few secrets of the detective's trade.

The greater part of my work for Pinkerton's was performed under cover, in the criminal element of western society. I got in with anarchist bombers and thieves and killers and cowboy bandits, going by assumed names, making myself out to be anything but what I was—a Pinkerton operative. Naturally in such circumstances I could not ask too many questions openly. I had to keep my ears pricked up to catch whatever I could without appearing nosy. Now and again I could steer some idle talk in a useful direction. And piece by piece I would begin to put together how some nefarious deed was committed.

Sometimes one of my outlaw "friends" would tell me straight out how a robbery was pulled off, but I might get a very different story from someone else. And so it was my job not only to root out facts, but also to reconstruct events based on the various accounts given me by those involved. I had to be a good judge of character, deciding whose word to believe and how far to believe it. I had to see what no one else saw and follow the itch in my detective's nose.

No single skill was more valuable to me in my Pinkerton years than this ability to reconstruct some occurrence I had not witnessed, until I could see the thing happen in my mind's eye. At first I might see it more than one way, with more than one possible outcome. If so, I would follow the several trails until I saw which scenario was borne out by subsequent events, and by and by I would know which was closer to the truth.

Of course when I was collecting my eight dollars a day from the brothers Pinkerton, most of the events I was trying to piece together were crimes of one sort or another. But I have found this skill no less helpful to an author. More than once I have been approached by a participant to some bygone incident I related in a book, and he will say "By God, Charlie, I forgot you were there."

Well, of course I wasn't, but I had succeeded in fooling one who was. Such confirmation that I had seen the true picture sometimes caused my head to swell until my hat wouldn't fit.

In the pages that follow, it is not my intention to fool anyone. The discerning reader will figure out for himself who I've talked to later on to work out what happened when I was somewhere else. From the start I picked up much of the story from Victoria, who knows I like to hear about lively doings. I'd get bits and pieces from Redeye Hawk and Nate Dicenzo and Nate's girl Karen Valdez, mostly without them being aware how much they told me. Chief John was a reliable witness, and later on Leroy himself contributed more than all the rest put together. But he is one who doesn't give away much unless he means to.

Chapter 3

LEROY ARRIVED AT the Bunk House just at dusk. The first to welcome him was my stable boy, George.

"They said I could get a room here," said Leroy. He swung down from the saddle, handing the pack horse's lead rope to George.

There is a particular way a man moves, stretching himself, taking his time, when he knows he has dismounted for the last time after a long day on horseback. Leroy stretched himself in this manner now, taking his time.

"You get a drink here, that's for sure," George replied, sizing him up. "You want a room, that depends on who you know."

"Suppose it was Redeye Hawk."

"That crazy Indian? Man, you out of luck."

I'm afraid I have been unable to curb in young George a tendency to crack wise with the guests, but to give him his due, he is an astute judge of men. Although scarcely ten, George restricts his back talk to those who will take it in the right spirit. With some derby-hatted dude who may chance to mistake the Bunk House for a first class hostelry, George is all sweetness and smiles.

"How about Victoria Hartford?" Leroy offered, raising his ante.

"Huh," George said with a shrug of his small shoulders. "What you think Miss Victoria want with a dusty old cowboy like you?"

Before Leroy could reply, a voice came from the shadows.

"Don't you sass the man. You be polite now, hear?"

Both of them looked around, but saw nothing. The sun was down and the night was thickening. In such circumstances the speaker had a natural advantage. He waited only a moment, then stepped out into the bright glow of the electric lights on the porch.

What Leroy saw was a young Negro man pushing six feet in height and two hundred pounds, wearing an army uniform and carrying a saxophone case in his hand.

What George saw was the older brother he had not set eyes on for more than three years.

It was Buddy Johnston, home from the war at last, over a year after the guns were spiked.

"Buddy," George shouted. In this instance he may be forgiven for neglecting his first duty. Forgetting all about Leroy's horses, George ran to Buddy, who scooped him up in his arms.

"Man, look at you. You sure growed up," Buddy said, laughing. He raised George up at arm's length, then set him back on the ground and pointed to where Leroy was waiting patiently. "You take good care of this gentleman, hear? We'll visit later, when you get off work."

"I'll take good care of him, Buddy!" George scampered back to Leroy's horses as Buddy stepped forward.

"That's my little brother George. Used to be me looked after the horses, before I went into the army."

Buddy worked for me as groom and stable boy before he enlisted, tending to the guests' horses and my own. His parents, Ulysses and Mabel Johnston, tend Gerald Ball's oranges. All this tending was and is topnotch, with no cause for complaint from either employer. Gerald's property adjoins mine, and Buddy had already stopped to have supper with his parents before coming to the Bunk House.

As he stepped close to Leroy now and got a good look at him, Buddy's face suddenly brightened. "Say, I know you! You the picture-show man! You was there by the track when my train went by."

"The train? You were on the Limited?"

"East of here a ways. You looked like a cowboy out of a picture show." Buddy stuck out his hand. "Buddy Johnston. Three-Sixty-Ninth Infantry."

"Leroy Roberts." He took in the ribbons on Buddy's tunic. "You were in France."

"Sure. They kept me on after the Armistice. Up until a couple of months ago I was still parlayvooing with the mademoiselles."

"I was in France once, before the war."

Buddy took interest in this. "What was it like back then?"

"Come on in. We can swap stories over a beer."

Buddy hefted his horn. He could hear music from within and he knew he would be welcome to sit in with the band, as always.

"I ain't never gone in the front door," he said. "Mostly I just came around back to do errands."

He drew himself up. He stood a few inches taller than Leroy and out-weighed him by thirty pounds. Perhaps the comparison bolstered his confidence.

"I reckon it's time I went in the front," he said. They mounted the steps together.

Inside, spirits were running high and flowing freely, to use both meanings of the term. As I write this, Prohibition—a consummate piece of mischief if ever there was one—is the law of the land. If the national Congress deserves any credit in this sorry matter, it is for allowing us a year from the bill's passage to fortify ourselves against the coming drouth. Back in the latter days of 1919 we had only the Gandier no-saloon law to cope with, it having been in force since April of '18. That measure, at least, was voted in by the people. For those unfamiliar with this piece of municipal morality, I will explain that it took its popular name from Dr. D. M. Gandier, California state superintendent of the Anti-Saloon League, and was passed by popular vote shortly after America entered the war. It outlawed both saloons and any liquor stronger than fourteen percent alcohol, and provided that the mild beverages still permitted could be served publicly only in a prescribed zone in the downtown business district. By voting in the law, Angelenos wished to demonstrate their sober patriotism, but cowboys do not take kindly to such governmental meddling in their private habits. The cowboys in the McQuain & Vickery outfit, like those in all the other western film companies in Hollywood and the surrounding communities, had no trouble providing themselves with the robust whiskeys they craved, which were then still legal in Texas and the other native cowboy states, and in many parts of California too.

I was stepping across the boundaries of the law by holding a party at my Hollywood rooming house, which was well outside the Liquor Zone and was a place of "public resort" according to the law. But in those last months before Prohibition the authorities were generally content to bide their time, ignoring minor infractions of the old ordinance until the full force of the federal government could be used to turn America into a parched waste as dry as the Sahara.

The cowboys and cowgirls and their invited guests were working hard at enjoying themselves, and few noticed Leroy and Buddy as they entered the reception hall and approached the door to the parlor. What with the three dozen hands in McQuain & Vickery's employ, together with the rest of the picture crew and boyfriends and girlfriends and acquaintances from the other western film companies, there were more than fifty celebrants in the Bunk House that evening. The double doors between the parlor and dining room were rolled back, and in this expanded public area the party was held.

The rooms were decorated with colored crepe paper and Japanese lanterns, and a banner proclaiming "Cimarron Rose Rides Again" hung above the dining table, which would soon offer a sumptuous buffet supper. The cowboys were already casting hungry glances toward the kitchen door, whence emanated tantalizing smells of the Mexican and American dishes prepared by my cook, Josefa. I brought Josefa with me from Santa Fe, and in a few short months her reputation had spread far and wide among the western picture crowd.

Some wag with an uncertain love of capital letters had pinned a crudely printed sign to the parlor wall. It said "DRink UP—ONLY 48 DayS UNTiL PROHiBitiON," and the partygoers were following this advice wholeheartedly. The clanking of hip flasks against the rims of glasses was a constant accompaniment to the music played by a small version of the McQuain & Vickery band in one corner of the parlor.

From the doorway, Leroy took in the general merriment of the revelers. "I'm going to feel right at home here," he said.

Buddy was still waiting for someone to recognize him.

It was Redeye Hawk who spied the newcomers first. He was drinking with Nate Dicenzo and Karen Valdez, as was his custom, the three of them sitting against the wall in the chairs that had been pushed back to the sides of the room. Chief John Walker had staked out a neighboring seat, but he does not approve of firewater. He was sipping sarsparilla to soothe a nagging cough that plagues him, and was more an observer of the party than a participant.

Redeye Hawk had just tossed back a dose of cowboy's delight when he noticed Leroy.

"Leroy," he cried out, giving a wave of the hand to draw Leroy's eye. "Join us in a snort!"

Hearing this friendly welcome, Leroy stepped into the parlor.

Victoria too heard Redeye's shout. She was at a small table in an out-of-the-way corner, her Cimarron Rose breeches exchanged for a proper dress, her hair combed, looking her prettiest. She had placed herself as a gunfighter might, sitting with her back to the wall so she could keep an eye on the door, precisely in the hope that Leroy might appear. With her were Gerald Ball and a young man half the Englishman's age. At a larger table nearby, a friendly card game was in progress.

"I see your latest conquest found his way," Gerald said, following her gaze.

Victoria gave a shrug as if to suggest that Leroy's comings and goings were of little concern to her. "I just think he would look good on film."

Nate and Karen and Redeye now took note of Leroy's large colored companion, whom they regarded with some curiosity. Buddy still held back, not certain what kind of reception he would get if he entered the parlor like a guest. He had grown an inch or two in the army and filled out considerably, and you had to look closely to see in him the gangly colored boy who had gone off to war.

It was Nate who recognized him first. "Buddy? Buddy Johnston, you sonofabitch!"

Back in Texas in my cowboy youth, a man who spoke profanity in the presence of a decent woman risked being filled with lead by her male relatives, or perhaps just strung up to the roofbeam if the offense was a mild one, but Nate's words were said in a spirit of cowboy exuberance, and not meant to offend.

Buddy stepped forward confidently now as his friends rose from their chairs. There was a round of backslapping and handshaking which ended with Redeye taking Leroy's hand and saying, "Glad you made it."

"You know this crazy Indian?" Buddy asked.

"We've met," Leroy said.

"Until right now, I didn't know was he alive or dead." Buddy grinned at Redeye. "He joined up with some Canuck outfit before I was in uniform and I never set eyes on him through the whole war."

He pounded on Redeye again, knocking the wind out of him. "But you made it after all, and now you back in pictures." He turned to Nate. "Crazy Nate too. What outfit was you with?"

Nate's smile was a bit sheepish. "They wouldn't take me. Bad knees. The doctor said I stove 'em up riding those bucking horses. I guess I'm stuck with buying the beers for you two heroes."

"I'll split the beers with you," Leroy put in. "They wouldn't take me either."

"The way you shoot?" Redeye exclaimed.

"They said I was too old."

Nate laughed. "They missed a bet, I'd say. Where'd you learn to shoot like that, anyway?"

"Here and there."

"I didn't get a chance to say howdy this afternoon," Nate said, offering his hand to Leroy. "Nate Dicenzo. This is Karen Valdez. She's my fiancée."

Karen gave him a dirty look. "I'm not anybody's fiancée until you set the date."

"Hell, we're young yet," Nate said. "You don't want to rush into these things."

He tried to put an arm around her but she shook it off and cocked a fist at him. "I've warned you, Nate Dicenzo. Don't you mess with me."

Karen was in her cowgirl togs, having seen to all the horses once they were trucked back from the location. Even when Karen doesn't pretty herself up she is still an eyeful, with her black hair and black eyes. She is not above mixing it up with a man, when sufficiently provoked, and she might best Nate in a wrestling match. Where Victoria gets her hot temper from the Irish in her, Karen's fire comes from her Mexican blood, with some Apache thrown in for good measure.

Nate sought to prevent an outbreak of war by raising his hands in surrender and turning the talk back to Leroy.

"Just before you come in, I was telling Karen how you got your first job in pictures."

"It wasn't on purpose," Leroy said. "And I didn't take the job."

"Karen's pretty good with a gun herself. A bow and arrow too." Like most cowboys, Nate knows how to pacify a woman with compliments. "She's half Mexican and half Apache."

"Is that true?" Leroy inquired.

"My father was Pancho Villa and my mother was Cochise," Karen said, dead serious.

This unusual claim of parentage is one of Karen's favorite ways to stump strangers, but Leroy wasn't stumped for a minute.

"Cochise wasn't anybody's mother," he said, just as serious.

Karen admired the way he fell right in with the spirit of her brag talk and she gave him a smile that would have warmed Jack Frost himself on a Montana winter's morning.

Chief John had overheard this exchange. He rose now, looking Leroy up and down. "You're pretty smart for a white man," he allowed. "I'm John Walker."

"We call him Chief John, but he's really not a chief. He's an Apache war leader," Redeye said.

"What's the difference?" Leroy asked as he shook John's hand.

"A chief has authority in war and peace both," John said. "It takes a bigger spirit to be a chief."

Common wisdom has it that Apaches are short and squatty while the Sioux are tall and graceful, but the common wisdom did not have Chief John Walker and Redeye Hawk in mind. John stands several inches taller than Redeye and outweighs him by fifty pounds. Redeye is of much the same wiry build as Nate, and the two of them are just about my height. Nate likes to say us Texas cowboys are tough as nails even if we are sometimes packed in a short keg.

When Leroy was informed that the beer was dispensed from an ice-filled washtub in the dining room, he and Nate fetched a round for the war heroes. I will add that I do not use the term lightly. Redeye Hawk was decorated twice, once by the Canadians and once by the Americans, and Buddy Johnston had fought hard to get himself assigned to a combat outfit. While most soldiers of his race spent the war in service units, Buddy's regiment, the all-Negro 369th Infantry, received the Croix de Guerre from the French government, every man jack of them, for gallant and courageous conduct in the fighting. This surprised a good many folks, myself among them. Old attitudes die hard, and among the worst fools they don't die at all. In my earlier books I have sometimes betrayed the attitudes of my Texas upbringing, failing in particular to give Mexicans and Negroes their due, but I have lived long enough to learn that whether a man is a hero or coward depends on matters far more varied than race alone, or the color of his skin.

AT THIS POINT in the celebrations I was ignorant of Leroy's presence. I enjoy a chance to kick up my heels as much as the next man, but that evening I stubbornly kept to my study, as if denying myself a jolt or two of cowboy tonic would somehow open the gates of creation and reveal to me what stories from my younger days would eventually adorn the blank pages of my as-yet unwritten tome. I have stared down or outbluffed more than one hell-bent hardcase in my time, but the cold gaze of my writing tablet was beginning to give me a case of the willies. When a knock sounded at the door, I welcomed it as I might have welcomed Gabriel sounding the call to salvation.

"Come," I said.

Redeye Hawk stepped in. I had pen in hand and my writing pad in my lap. When I get to serious writing, I use the typing machine, but I'm old-fashioned enough to resent all that clatter when I'm trying to think.

"You working on another book?" Redeye asked. From where he stood, he couldn't see that there was nothing on the page in my lap, but I had no reason to fool either him or myself.

"I just can't get going on it," I said. "Maybe I've used up the best parts of my life already."

"I read that one about you being a Pinkerton man. It's a corker."

I feigned surprise. "Why, Mr. Hawk, I thought you were an illiterate redskin of the first water. You never let on you could read."

For all his wildness, Redeye is a good-natured soul and he will tolerate more than his share of cowboy-style ribbing. But there was something serious in his answer to me. "I'm walking the white man's road, Charlie."

His gaze moved to the walls, which I have decorated with wanted fliers I collected during my Pinkerton years, all the men I pursued at one time or another, or most of them anyway. I realized this was the first time Redeye had seen my study. It's down the hall behind the kitchen, a little removed from the boardinghouse bustle. Like many a writer, I guard the privacy of my workbench.

"I heard about this place," he said, with a trace of awe in his tone. I'm afraid I swelled up a little. When the Lord made Texans he must have been short of humility that day, for he certainly doled it out among us with a sparing hand.

Redeye stepped closer and his eyes moved along the wall until they found the picture of Billy the Kid. "He wasn't in that book," he said, tapping the picture with his forefinger.

"I knew the Kid back when I was just a poor cowboy," I said. "And I'll tell you something about that book. Those damned Pinkertons wouldn't let me print half the stories I could tell."

My feud with my former employers is a bitter one. I see no reason why I shouldn't be able to tell the truth about bad men and good, most of whom have gone to the other side of Jordan. But part of the Pinkerton reputation is built on mystery and secrecy, and they have blocked me every step of the way in my desire to tell the whole truth about the twenty-two years I worked in the Pinkerton cause. I was only able to publish *A Cowboy Detective* after making many changes forced upon me by courts friendly to the powerful Pinkertons. No one will be fooled that I wrote "Dickerson" for "Pinkerton," or "Tim Corn" instead of "Tom Horn," but that satisfied the Pinkertons, and lowered them further in my esteem. (I have no wish to endanger this new book by repeating here more details of my disputes with the Agency. They have a long reach and a longer memory. Even years after I am gone, they might seek to suppress any unfavorable mention of Pinkerton's, so I will keep mum, and refer interested readers to my book *Two Evil Isms*.)

Redeye was examining the fliers, unaware of my silent fuming. "You caught all these men?" he asked.

"Not half of them. But I keep track as the years go by. Whenever I hear one of them was arrested somewhere, or died, I put it down." I pointed to the notes I have written on some of the fliers, giving the man's last known whereabouts or the manner in which he met his final reward.

"To tell the truth," I admitted, "I mostly don't bother anymore. The rooming house keeps me busy. Maybe it's time to look ahead, not back. Might be that's why I'm having trouble with the next book."

"What were they like, Charlie, the good old days?"

In that simple question I heard a refrain that runs through the questions all the young fellows ask when they are talking with us old-timers. There is longing in the tone, a sense of having missed out on a time when a man could truly show what stuff he was made of. And how could I answer such a question? Back in the days after Thanksgiving I was at a loss, for I too missed the old days, and judged them finer than the new.

"The old days weren't all good," I finally said. "I've known what it means to be hungry. But there were good times and good men back then. We've lost something getting where we are now."

Redeye looked as if he just woke up from a nap. "Hell, I've been forgetting why I came back here in the first place. We've got a roomer for you. He doesn't go back as far as you do, but I'd say he's seen some of the same country."

Out in the parlor, Buddy Johnston had joined the orchestra, while Nate and Karen were extolling to Leroy the virtues of the McQuain & Vickery Wild West show.

"We got the whole caboodle," Nate said. "Trick riders and ropers and shooters and all. Real Indians and longhorn steers too. We even got a herd of buffalo."

Chief John gave a snort of derision. "They run the buffalo in circles around the camera and make them look like a stampede."

"That's true," Nate said, quieter now. "But a small bunch is all we got. And it looks good on the screen."

Nate never talks back to John. John was a leader among his people, and in the McQuain & Vickery outfit it is he, along with Willie Two Horse and Jack Whistler, who keeps the young whites and Indians alike from stepping out of line.

"It's a good outfit," John said to Leroy. "They been fair with us."

"Good, hell," Nate exclaimed. "We're the best show on the road."

John laughed. "That's 'cause we're damn near the only show on the road anymore."

He spoke the simple truth. It was Tom Ince first had the notion of hiring a wild west show to work in his pictures during the winter months. That was back when the picture people first came to Hollywood. Ince took on the Miller 101 outfit, and before long all the other picture makers picked up the idea. But the Great War stopped the summer tours of the wild west shows dead in their tracks by taking most of the horses and the young men into the army. For the cowgirls and the old-timers like Chief John, picture work was all they had to tide them over until the Armistice, and now it seems that the world prefers new diversions like the movies. Only a handful of wild west shows went back on the road after the Armistice, and half of those failed in the first year. Even while Leroy and his newfound friends were talking in my parlor, Jim McQuain and Walt Vickery were scouring the eastern states for financial backing in the hope of perpetuating for at least another season the proud tradition begun by Buffalo Bill Cody nearly forty years ago.

"You could do worse, if you're looking for work," Nate said to Leroy. "Tour in the summer, make movies in the winter. It ain't a bad life."

"He likes to say it beats real work and pays twice as good," said Karen, getting in a dig at Nate. But she had her arm around him now.

Nate stood up to his full five feet seven and a half inches. "Hell, I've done enough real work for two men. I cowboyed from sunup to sundown and I was champeen bronc rider of Matagorda County, Texas. You ask old Charlie if it isn't so."

This last remark was directed at me as Redeye and I approached the little group. "He was champeen bullshitter of Matagorda County," I corrected him. So much for my lecture on using bad language in front of women. But Karen can raise the paint off a barn door with a few well-chosen phrases when something gets her going, and on occasion I forget that she's not just one of the boys.

"I'm old Charlie," I said, putting out a hand to Leroy. "And not so old I can't tan your hide if you sass me," I told young Nate.

Nate looked sheepish. "I'd sooner rassle a longhorn cow, Charlie."

When I shook Leroy's hand I noticed right away that he was a man to be reckoned with, not the citified sort so prevalent in California. I noticed as well that although he had been in the Bunk House just a short while, he was already welcomed among the rowdiest element in the crew and befriended by Chief John to boot.

Standing beside me, Leroy topped me by a few inches. Where I am slight, and getting slighter as the years wear me down, he was solidly built. But I have never worried about being smaller than other men.

I took special note of his hat and the way it was creased. When westerners speak of a hat's crease we mean the shape of the crown and the brim too. The many styles of crease are highly individual, and a knowledgeable person can tell where a man is from within a few hundred miles by looking at his hat. Leroy's came from somewhere north of Colorado. Western Wyoming, I thought. Like Victoria, I underguessed his age by nearly ten years. His eyes fooled me as they had fooled her. Life interests him and he sees the folly of it, but that doesn't stop him from enjoying himself. It's this interest and amusement in his eyes that makes him look young.

"If you're through with that beer, I'll show you to a room," I said, all the more glad for the departure of the ladies' undergarment specialist.

As we left the parlor, Victoria gave me a wave from where she was sitting with Gerald Ball. She appeared to be excited about something or other, but at the moment I was interested in getting to know my new roomer better. We went to the stables to fetch his saddlebags and bedroll before I led him up to the second floor of the Bunk House.

"We're up to date around here," I said as I turned on the electric light in his room. I don't care for the bright light myself, but coal oil lamps have a way of burning a place down if you knock them over, and I have a country boy's distrust of gaslights.

"We got an attached outhouse too," I told him. "Down the back stairs."

He hung the saddlebags over a chair and tossed his bedroll on the bed, then flexed his left hand and shook his arm loosely, as if it might be tired from holding the reins all day. The bags and roll were like a thousand others I have seen in many a cowboy's traveling outfit over the years. Leroy seemed completely at home with them in a way that was less common nowadays.

"Come far?" I asked without thinking, but I caught myself. "Now you don't have to answer that. I'm enough of an old cowboy to know you don't ask where a man's from or where he's going."

"I don't mind." He gave me a smile. One thing about him, he had a friendly way that wasn't just put on for my entertainment. "I came from up north. Going south. I've been doing my own cooking for the past few weeks. I hope a man can get supper around here."

"You'll hear the bell directly."

Most folks might not have noticed that while he made an appearance of telling me everything I could wish to know about him, he really said very little. But I noticed. Came from up north. Going south. That covered a lot of real estate. I felt a small itch in my detective's nose, and wondered how he came to be traveling horseback. Back in New Mexico or Texas a man on horseback is fairly common, even today. But not in Hollywood, California.

"Your first time in Hollywood?" The question popped out before I could stop it. It's just as well not to ask a lot of questions of a man when you want to learn what he's up to. Better just to wait and watch. It's a game I have played many a time and come up winners. Questions put a man on his guard.

"I was through here a few times," Leroy said, his calm manner unruffled. "Twenty years ago you could blink your eyes riding past Hollywood and miss it clean. It seems like wherever you go anymore, everything's changed from what it was."

"Too much change for me," I said, "but I live in the thick of it now." I felt a sudden pang of homesickness for my Sunny Slope ranch. "Well, I'll let you get settled. You hear a clanging like a blacksmith's set up shop out in the hallway, that's Josefa ringing for supper."

I left him then. He couldn't know it, but he had just ventured across the line that separates my friends from mere acquaintances. There was something familiar about him, not that I thought I knew him. I have a memory for faces that rarely fails me, and was sure I had never seen him before the minute Redeye introduced us. But from men like Leroy my steady companions of a lifetime were drawn and I was kin to the litter he came from. His words told me he shared my memories of the old times and my caution about the new ones. Maybe I was wrong, but I felt that he saw things in general pretty much the way I did.

I decided that before he went on his way I would take the time to know Mr. Leroy Roberts better and see if we might not have some friends in common from our younger days. There weren't so many men who stood out above the crowd back when the West was wild and woolly. I imagined that if we traded stories for a while we would discover our tracks had crossed at one time or another.

As I descended the back stairs I rubbed my nose to quiet a nagging itch, and I wondered if the wind had moved around to the east. Sometimes when it blows off the desert it gives me sneezing fits, even in winter.

Chapter 4

GERALD BALL WAS in a sour humor, which prevented him from enjoying the celebrations. Without giving him any warning, Victoria had invited Brian Hill to the party to tell Gerald about his idea for a "feature" western. Brian was the film director Victoria had spoken of earlier, the one Gerald had promised to meet, and he was the mild-mannered young man who was sitting with Victoria and Gerald at the small table near the poker game. By this maneuver Victoria had taken Gerald off his guard, which was her intention.

Brian was congenial and polite, but Gerald resented being forced into the meeting unprepared. Then too, he detected the trace of an Irish brogue in the lad's speech. Brian had come to America's golden shores when he was five, and a touch of the ould sod still lingered on his tongue, hence Gerald's English disdain. But Gerald knew that despite Brian's youth he had caught the eye of Uncle Carl Laemmle, founder of the Universal Studio. Laemmle saw in Brian a film director, but he was leaving it to Victoria and Gerald to give the boy a trial run.

Gerald paid Brian little attention during the opening pleasantries. At a pause in the conversation he glanced at his gold watch and said, "I promised Rosa I would be home before eight."

"Brian has driven all the way from the Valley, Gerald," Victoria informed him sternly. "The least you can do is hear him out."

Victoria knew his supposed promise to Rosa was only an excuse.

Gerald often tells his wife Rosa that his business affairs have kept him out late when it is often a different sort of affair altogether that keeps him away from home. He fancies himself a Continental gentleman and regards it as proper that he should seek pleasure outside his marriage, but he is discreet.

It was at this juncture that Leroy arrived in the Bunk House, briefly distracting Victoria and causing Gerald to make his remark about her "latest conquest." But she did not forget the business at hand, and as Leroy stepped into the parlor to acquaint himself with her crew, she suggested that Brian tell Gerald the story she and Brian hoped to film.

It was the moment Brian had been waiting for. He knew that the success or failure of his dream depended on how well he told the story. That afternoon he had paced up and down in his rented rooms, practicing the narration so he would leave out nothing.

To cover his nervousness he took out his pack of Pall Malls and offered one to Gerald, who accepted, as he smoked the same brand. Brian lighted both cigarettes and then commenced his pitch.

"You remember three years ago when Pancho Villa raided that New Mexico border town and General Pershing went chasing him into Mexico?"

Brian knew perfectly well that neither Gerald nor anyone else had forgotten Villa's attack on Columbus, New Mexico, in May of 1916. Seventeen Americans had been killed in the fray. The story got banner headlines and set the newspapers to running off extra editions, pushing even the war news from Europe off the front page for a time. Blackjack Pershing's soldiers crossed the border in a blaze of patriotic fervor, certain they would teach the villainous Villa a lesson, but they ran out of steam in the Mexican desert. In the end, the punitive expedition never did come to grips with Villa, although Pershing made up for this failure by distinguishing himself in the late war.

"Good God," Gerald exclaimed. "Do you know what that would cost, a whole army out in the desert?" There is nothing that gets Gerald's dander up quicker than the thought of money being burned.

"Hush, Gerald," Victoria soothed him. "That's not the way we're going to tell it."

"Pershing never caught him, that's the problem," Brian said. "The story had no ending. But it's the starting point for ours. Everyone knows Villa got away scot-free. In our story the time is now, and Villa has come back to the border for another raid. He got away with it once, so why shouldn't he get away with it again?"

He leaned forward in his seat, already caught up in his own tale.

"The name of the picture is *The Trail of Pancho Villa*. We start with a few scenes to establish an unnamed border town and our hero Tom, an all-American cowboy. He wants to marry his Mexican sweetheart, Evangelina—Miss Hartford—but her father is a rich grandee and he doesn't think Tom is worthy of his only daughter. He has forbidden Evangelina to see Tom. But that doesn't stop Evangelina. She's hot-tempered and strong-willed. She sneaks out of her father's house each evening and goes to the cantina, the only place she can meet Tom. When he leaves her there, she joins the musicians to sing of her heartache, knowing that even the worst of the border ruffians who frequent the cantina wouldn't dare to harm a lady."

Brian's enthusiasm was contagious. Victoria had heard the story before, but she found herself hanging on his words. She saw that although Gerald sat back in his chair, his eyes and his attention were on the boy.

"Now Villa and his men ride into town," Brian rushed on. "They're in authentic uniforms, not like the ordinary Mexican bandits with sombreros and serapes that you see in the movies. The time of day is just after sunset. Beautiful light. Villa hears music from a cantina and he looks in the window. There's Evangelina, singing. Tom hasn't arrived yet. Villa is struck by Cupid's arrow. He begins the attack, but in the middle of the fighting he returns to the cantina and carries Evangelina off, and he takes her with him when he and his men flee into Mexico. But this time it isn't an army that chases him, it's Victoria's cowboy fiancé, who will be played by Randall Steele!"

Randall Steele being one of the brightest young western stars in Hollywood's celluloid heavens, this made Gerald sit up and take notice, but not so the untrained eye could see it. He is a master at hiding his interest.

"How, pray tell, are we going to get Randall Steele?" he asked, as if such a thing were as likely as getting Woodrow Wilson to play the part.

But Victoria saw the light in his eyes. "We'll get to that," she said, sinking the hook a little deeper. "Let Brian finish the story first."

Brian took the narrative quickly to its end, telling how Tom and his cowboy companions would follow Villa's trail into Mexico and bring him and his bandit cavalry to their knees despite being outnumbered ten to one. Needless to say, Evangelina is rescued with her honor intact and the picture ends happily.

Gerald looked around, taking in the room, feigning a noble boredom and doing a good job of it. After all, the blood of nobility flows in his veins.

"You would write the scenario yourself?" he asked, getting a nod from young Brian. "And Randall Steele is not just wishful thinking?"

"Mr. Laemmle will not only lend us Brian to direct, he'll give us George Bleumel for a cameraman and Randall Steele into the bargain," Victoria said triumphantly.

Gerald's eyebrows climbed ever so slightly higher. "At what cost?" he inquired in a tone that said whatever the cost might be, it would be too high. George Bleumel's standing among film cameramen was even higher than Randall Steele's among cowboy actors.

"None!" Brian couldn't contain himself. "It won't take a penny out of your pocket, Mr. Ball. All Mr. Laemmle wants is the picture. He wants you to let him distribute it through the Universal Film Exchange. He's very enthusiastic about the idea."

"It seems I am the last to hear of it."

Victoria was barely able to keep her own excitement under control. "It's perfect, Gerald. You have to admit it."

"Except for one thing," Gerald said. "Even without General Pershing and his army, such a picture will cost far more than I can afford."

"More than you want to risk, you mean." Victoria had been expecting this objection. "You've got the money for the next Cimarron Rose serial."

"Cimarron Rose is a proven commodity, not some expensive pipe dream."

"*The Squaw Man* wasn't a pipe dream."

This was her ace in the hole. Cecil DeMille had made *The Squaw Man* for Jesse Lasky and his Famous Players six years before. DeMille brought in the six-reeler for fifteen thousand dollars, and it was a great success. I thought it was poppycock, with its contrived story of an English lord falling in love with an Indian maiden and all, but that English lord bit pleased Gerald no end. He saw the picture four times.

"Like *The Virginian* it was a play before it was a film," Gerald cautioned. "It already had an audience. And DeMille wasn't a novice when he made it. No offense, Mr. Hill, but you are not a proven director." He turned to Victoria. "And you know how I feel about these 'feature' films."

Whether moving pictures will be known to the readers of this book or whether they may prove to be only the passing fancy some people imagine, I cannot say, and so I will offer a few words about the state of the business at this time.

Since the days of the nickelodeons, moving pictures have grown longer with each passing year, but from the start the two-reeler, running twenty minutes or so, has been a mainstay of the young industry. More recently, serials have caught the public fancy. *What Happened to Mary?* was the first, followed a year later by *The Hazards of Helen*, but it was Pearl White's success in *The Perils of Pauline* that proved the "chapter plays," as they were originally called, were here to stay. Now it seems the audience can't get enough of these stories, most of which feature stalwart young women in the leads. Each episode runs one or two reels, with a new episode arriving at the picture houses every week. Gerald was right when he said that two-reelers and serials made the business what it is, and he is not the sort to ignore which side his bread is buttered on.

But Victoria is convinced that longer pictures are here to stay. First there was *Queen Elizabeth* from England at four reels, then *Quo Vadis* from Italy at nine, Thomas Ince's vast *Civilization*, and Griffith's *Birth of a Nation*, which ran a full twelve reels and cost the lordly sum of two dollars to see at a time when top price at even the fanciest picture house in Los Angeles was two bits. After that, Griffith took further leave of his senses and proposed to exhibit *Intolerance* at more than thirty reels, or nearly eight hours! Of course no one would stand for such nonsense and he trimmed it to two and a half hours that put yours truly soundly to sleep along about the middle.

I am not the one to say where this will end, or what sort of picture will be the bread and butter of the business a dozen years from now or a hundred. I am a stove-up cowboy author and such worries are not my concern. But Victoria had her heart set on making a "feature" picture. Back in November this itch of hers was getting so strong she couldn't think of anything else when she wasn't in front of a camera. Luckily for her, Carl Laemmle believes in the longer films. He himself had a huge success with his *Traffic in Souls*, a 1913 feature-length picture upon whose profits Universal City was largely built.

"Brian and I will put up our salaries against completing the picture on time and within your budget," Victoria said. Her cards were all on the table now.

"Your salaries are something we have not yet discussed," Gerald said. "Mr. Hill, I would like to talk with Victoria privately."

Brian had listened intently as the two talked, his head cocked to one side. At Gerald's suggestion he made to rise, more than willing to leave the negotiations to Victoria, who was more experienced than he in business matters, but she held out a hand to detain him.

"The picture is Brian's idea, Gerald. He directs it or it won't be made at all."

"I understand that." Again Gerald directed himself to Brian. "You might enjoy watching the poker game for a time, Mr. Hill. The old gentleman with his back to us is Wyatt Earp. The man on his right is Emmett Dalton."

Brian's eyes fairly popped out of his head. Gerald had correctly guessed that the young man would be flabbergasted to learn that these two famous frontier characters from opposite sides of the law were sitting together quietly in Charlie Siringo's Bunk House playing poker.

"It's all right," Victoria said. "You go on. I can hold my own with Gerald."

Brian left them and moved nearer the poker game, leaning against the wall where he had a good view of Wyatt and Emmett. Emmett was smoking in his customary manner, letting his cigarette dangle from his lips while his hands held the cards. Brian lit a Pall Mall and kept it in his mouth in studied imitation of Emmett, squinting against the smoke that drifted up into his eyes.

Alone now, Gerald and Victoria faced each other across their own table, both wondering if it was an even match.

It may cast some light on these negotiations to reveal that Gerald Ball—Sir Gerald, if you please—was not the producer of the first Cimarron Rose serial, nor did he and Victoria come to be in business together by mutual agreement.

Gerald came to this country as a remittance man. Which is to say he had the bad fortune to be his father's second son. The family lands and title passed to his older brother, who made it plain to Gerald that he was no more use than a saddle on a cow, but if he would entertain himself in the New World, he would receive a remittance sufficient to live upon in the style befitting his station.

When I was a young cowboy I saw many an English dandy making "the tour" of our western plains. Among them were more than a few remittance men. I never met one who wasn't hell-bent on finding a way to stand on his own two feet. Maybe it is running up against our American notions of democracy that lights the fires in them. Whatever the reason, it touched Gerald too, for he had long burned with the same ambition.

He got one foot under him when he married his wife Rosa. Rosa Delgado del Valle Ball is nobility herself, of a sort. There was a time when the Delgados held most of the land east of Los Angeles under a royal grant. When California became part of the United States, the Delgados lost most of their land, like the rest of the Californios. Unlike many, they kept a small piece of theirs. Rosa's dowry was enough to set Gerald up in the orange-growing business.

But it is not Gerald's nature to be contented raising oranges, where his success depends on the vagaries of rain and temperature and an unpredictable growing season. He wants to hold the reins of his fate firmly in his own two hands. When the picture business came to Hollywood, he watched its progress with interest. When he met a producer from the Kalem company who told him of a new serial Kalem felt uncertain about, Gerald made his move. He persuaded Rosa that the new serial, *The Adventures of Cimarron Rose,* was fresh and original. Once more Rosa loosened her purse strings. Gerald bought both Cimarron Rose and Victoria's contract.

Suddenly Victoria found herself obliged to make two more Cimarron Rose serials for a shoestring producer she had never heard of until the day Gerald bought her like chattel from Kalem.

Fortunately Gerald proved to have a sound head for business. He knows you have to spend money to make it. He launched the first serial in a style Kalem could not have matched. Cimarron Rose took her place with Pauline and Helen and the other chapter play heroines, and Gerald has prospered. Because the idea for filming the legend of Cimarron Rose was Victoria's to begin with, her contract guaranteed her a part of the serials' profits and enabled her to share in their prosperity.

But it was only recently, with the further success of the second serial and the imminent release of the third, that Victoria realized it was she, not Gerald, who held the winning hand in any showdown between them. Her contract obliged her to make two more Cimarron Rose serials. Now the terms were fulfilled. Gerald held the financial reins of production, but without Victoria, he had nothing to sell.

This knowledge did much to bolster Victoria's confidence as she sat across the table from Gerald.

"I hadn't planned to discuss our future so soon," he said.

"Now is as good a time as any."

He nodded. "Very well. I expect you will make more serials and I hope you will make them for me. We haven't done too badly, have we?"

Victoria smiled, knowing full well the effect that smile has on any man. "No. We have done very well. That's why I will want a raise in salary and in my share of the profits."

It was Gerald's turn to smile. "I expected nothing less. And I am prepared to discuss some broadening of your participation. But how does young Mr. Hill's picture fit into all this?"

"If you will back our feature, I will make two more Cimarron Rose serials for you. Otherwise I go on my way right now."

"If I back the feature, it seems to me I am taking all the risks. We should have another Cimarron Rose ready in April, when the third one has finished its run. If the feature is delayed in production, the theaters will book someone else's serial, and we could find ourselves with no place to play Cimarron Rose."

"Brian and I have offered our salaries to guarantee we'll finish the feature on time. What more do you want?"

Gerald thought for only a moment. "If I back the feature, will you do three more serials under our present terms?"

Victoria flushed with anger. "Before I do that I'll find someone else to make the feature and the serials as well!"

This did not have the effect on Gerald she had hoped for. He looked at her calmly until she grew nervous under his gaze.

"You realize that the McQuain & Vickery show is under contract to me," he said at last.

Victoria felt a cold knot form in her stomach. "And you would prevent them from working with me if I left you?"

"My dear, I hope and expect that you will continue to work with them, for me."

Victoria's loyalty to the McQuain & Vickery outfit is not just sentimental. To her way of seeing it, she owes them her present career and her parents' well-being, for it was through her work with the show that she got into the picture business. When she was twenty-two, the Hartford Ranch fell on hard times due to a slump in the cattle business. Thinking to take her mind off the ranch and its troubles, I took Victoria to see the McQuain & Vickery show in Santa Fe. To my surprise I discovered my old friend Jack Whistler in the show. Jack was a young sprout of a cowboy who came to work on the LX spread in Texas not long before I left off cowboying and turned to other pursuits. I introduced Victoria to Jack there in Santa Fe, Jack presented us to Jim McQuain and Walt Vickery, and with unaccustomed boldness, Victoria allowed as how she could do anything the cowgirls in the show could do, and better.

To make a long story short, she was hired on the spot. The extra money coming in helped tide the Hartfords' ranch over the bad times, and when the Hartfords moved to southern California they sold it for a good price. By the time the McQuain & Vickery outfit was signed for its first job in pictures, making two-reelers for Kalem, Victoria was one of the show's star cowgirls. From there to Cimarron Rose was only a hop, skip, and a jump.

Because of the debt she owed them, Victoria would no more abandon her wild west friends than she would abandon her own parents. But Gerald didn't know that.

"All right," she said at last, keeping her voice calm. "If the picture is late Brian and I forfeit our salaries and I will make *two* more serials for you under our present terms. But if we finish it on time and within the budget we agree on, you double my salary and my share of the profits."

"Victoria!"

"Those are my terms."

He was quiet for a time, his brow furrowed. Finally he said, "All right, I will think about it."

"Oh, Gerald, you won't regret—" Victoria began, but he saw that she was already counting chickens and he held up a hand to stop her.

"I said I would think about it. I will let you know my decision tomorrow."

As if signaling an end to all business dealings, Josefa rang her hand bell for dinner at that moment, bringing everyone to the serving tables. By the time I served myself there were no seats left in the dining room or the parlor, so I repaired to the kitchen to eat in peace at the kitchen table. A few moments later Victoria joined me there, all bursting to tell me about her talk with Gerald and Brian.

I have often thought that if Gerald Ball had been born into a different station of English society, his rapacious quest for advancing himself might well have earned him a berth on a transport to Australia, but it seemed that on this occasion Victoria had bested him. She was proud of herself for knowing when to stand firm against his demands and she was certain he would come around in the end. In her enthusiasm to tell me all about young Brian and *The Trail of Pancho Villa*, she tried to talk and eat at the same time until I reminded her it wasn't ladylike to talk with her mouth full. But she said nothing about risking her salary, and it was not until many weeks later that I learned of this condition in her agreement with Gerald.

As we were nearing the end of our meal, Leroy came into the kitchen and set his plate on the counter by the sink. This courtesy is a cowboy custom, every good cowboy being eager to get on the right side of the cook.

"Gracias, Josefa," he said. *"No he comido tan bien desde hace muchos años."* For those from Yankeedom, or other parts where Spanish is unknown, this means he hadn't eaten so well for many years.

"Gracias a usted, Señor Roberts," Josefa replied. *"Mucho gusto en servirle. Usted habla español muy bien."* What a pleasure to serve you, and my, don't you speak Spanish well, she told him.

The way they knew each other's names so soon told me something about Leroy's gregarious nature, but what caught my attention by the seat of the pants was the way he spoke Spanish. His accent wasn't Mexican. It had a touch of something farther south.

Victoria noticed the way I froze up with my fork in the air as I watched Leroy leave the kitchen.

"What's wrong?"

"That fellow Roberts speaks Spanish pretty good."

"So? Lots of people speak Spanish. You do. I do. Or I might remember how if you would ever take me to Mexico the way you promised."

"It gets me to wondering, is all. Fella comes along, says he's just passing by. We don't hardly get men on horseback just passing by. Not these days."

"You've known men like that all your life."

"And most of them were running from something," I said. I swear on a Bible, I hadn't thought it until that moment.

"Now don't you start in on him," she said.

"Some reason I shouldn't?"

"It's more than ten years since you quit working for Pinkerton's, and you're still a detective."

"Nope," I said, as if to suggest that detective work appealed to me now about as much as working with sheep. "I've settled down to innkeeping, and glad of it."

I had no wish to let her guess what was going on in my head. It doesn't do for a detective to talk about his suspicions until he has had a chance to follow up on them.

Victoria went back to cutting her baked potato with her fork, the way a cowboy might, if he had a fork, which most did not.

"You've got a knife there," I said.

"Charlie Siringo, I'm twenty-eight years old and it's too late in the day for you to teach me table manners." But she picked up her knife and cut up the potato like her mother taught her to.

"You want to catch the man of your dreams, you eat like a proper lady," I said.

"Oh, Charlie, you're the man of my dreams and you know it."

No matter how many times I heard it, it made me feel good.

By and by I went along to my office, still shying away from the party. I picked up my pen and paper again, but my mind was running at a 2:40 gait. I mulled over what little I knew of Leroy Roberts, looking for one piece that would fit together with the next one to tell me who he was. Even with no evidence to back up the feeling, I was as certain as I could be that he was a man on the dodge.

Chapter 5

WHILE I WAS cogitating, Leroy made himself right at home, drinking with the boys after supper and joining in the talk. Only Redeye noticed how Leroy didn't tell much about his past, and that while the rest were imbibing freely, Leroy held himself to a couple of beers. He doesn't miss much, that Indian, even when he is drinking. And he was drinking that night. The last thing Redeye Hawk will miss is a chance to celebrate. Later on, when we were down in Mexico, Redeye mentioned to me that Leroy seemed a bit spooked to learn that Wyatt Earp and Emmett Dalton were among the players at the nightly poker game that first evening in the Bunk House. But by then I already knew why.

I suppose I should tell how it happened that Wyatt and Emmett were in my rooming house. It was a common enough occurrence, but it set newcomers on their ears to see it. Emmett had served fifteen years in the penitentiary following the Dalton boys' bad day at Coffeyville, Kansas. He came out of prison a changed man. I suppose seeing your brothers killed will do that to a person. I've known men who couldn't wait to raise fresh mischief just as soon as they got out of jail, but Emmett was one of the ones who had learned his lesson good and proper. I don't know just what brought him to Hollywood in the first place, but like a number of old cowboys and frontier sorts, he ended up at the Bunk House whenever there was an evening of western conviviality. All this was before I had even thought of leaving Santa Fe. I never did get this story from Emmett himself, which is why it comes out in odd-shaped bits like this. But it was here in the Bunk House—before it was mine—that he first met some of the picture folks. And before you know it he was acting in *The Last Stand of the Dalton Boys,* filmed back in Oklahoma and Kansas. Since then he has acted in other pictures and written a book about his outlaw years.

If it should occur to some that both Emmett and Victoria got into pictures with a kind of fairy-tale ease, I will say that the same is true for any number of others who are now seen daily on movie screens across the land. This is a come-as-you-are, free-for-all business, and Hollywood is like any other boomtown of days gone by. No one knows what the future will bring in the picture business, but everyone is racing lickety-split to get there before the other fellow.

Mixed in with all the young gold diggers who can't tell a cow from a cartwheel there are a surprising number of us old-timers. I guess we who lived on the wild frontier see in the moving pictures a way of reliving our youthful adventures. As I have said, just being out in the sagebrush with a bunch of young cowboys and a camera crew brings me to mind of the old days and lifts my spirits. Emmett and Wyatt and I aren't the only ones who found our way to the picture sets, but along with Al Jennings we are the top of the heap in Hollywood just now.

Cameras make me nervous and I have avoided putting myself in front of them, but Wyatt stood in a crowd scene in one of Allan Dwan's pictures and proved himself no equal to Emmett Dalton, at least where acting is concerned. Wyatt Earp has stood up to drunks and gunmen of every stripe and all the while stayed as cool as a tall glass of spring water, but in front of a camera he looked so much like the town idiot that after a couple of attempts to immortalize Wyatt on celluloid, Allan asked him please to watch from the sidelines.

In fact, watching from the sidelines is more or less how Wyatt has conducted his life since retiring as a lawman. For the most part he has lived beyond the gaze of the public eye in recent years, although he did draw some brief attention when he refereed the boxing match between Fitzsimmons and Sharkey in San Francisco in '96. I am sorry I didn't see the fight, but I was off on Pinkerton business at the time. I would have liked to see old San Francisco before the fire. Now it is the most modern city in the land, with more than half of this nation's steel and concrete buildings, but scarcely a ghost of the Gold Rush glory remains. Los Angeles suits me better, despite the oil boom. Here at least, the spirit of the old Californios may linger a while yet, in the adobe and the gentle pace of life that prevails outside the towns and the movie lots.

Back in '97 Wyatt was asked to be U.S. Marshal of Arizona Territory but declined the honor, saying he feared his return to the Territory might arouse the bad feelings that still endure from his days in Tombstone.

Since then he and his wife Josie have divided their time between their homes in Oakland and Los Angeles, living in quiet retirement.

Josie is a fine woman, but I will have to state that she is something of a sorehead where good whiskey is concerned. She won't let Wyatt touch a drop around the house. But as these things will do, it all evens out in the end. Josie is given to attending religious gatherings of her Hebrew brethren. (Being born a Catholic myself, I know as much of Hebrew goings-on as I do about Hindus or Zulus, although I have neither confessed my abundant sins nor seen the inside of a church in many years. I guess you could call me a jack Catholic, to use the Mormon parlance for one who has wandered from the fold.) Whenever Josie takes herself off to such an affair, she is scarcely out the door before Wyatt hauls his freight to the Bunk House for a few hands of poker and maybe a glass or two. In Josie's absence he will spend his days at some western movie lot, watching the actors and cowboys at their antics. Evenings he is here. He has a telephone in his home and avails himself of this device to alert Emmett to Josie's plans and notify him when the game is on.

Wyatt is a hard man to beat at cards when he's sober. I have seen him obliged to part the stack of chips before him just to look at his hand, but once in a great while a dark mood takes him. He broods about the old times and drinks more than is good for him, and in this condition he is an easy mark. I think if Josie didn't oppose spirits so vehemently, Wyatt would never take a drink at all, being a sober sort by nature. But on the evening in question, the dark mood was upon him.

He waited until he was about to float away from the table before making his way to the Bunk House's indoor privy to water his horse. The convenience is not far from my study. While Wyatt was in there I heard someone coming down the back stairs. Then the door to the privy banged open. There was some shuffling and an "Excuse me" as whoever it was tried to get around Wyatt, who was probably buttoning his pants right there in the hallway. Then I heard Wyatt speak. I could tell from the sound of his voice that he was already three sheets to the wind and working on his fourth.

"I know you," he said. "It was—" there was a pause, but not long. "Anchorage," with new conviction. "Nineteen and twelve."

The next voice I heard was Leroy's. Maybe he had gone upstairs to get out of Wyatt's line of sight. If so, Lady Luck was bound and determined to bring them together.

"Good to see you again, Wyatt."

"You're—"

"Leroy Roberts," said Leroy, as if to stop Wyatt from saying some other name.

Wyatt laughed his three-sheets-to-the-wind laugh. It's kind of a fizzing sound that escapes past his teeth as if he was trying to bottle it up.

"If you say so," he said. "It was something else then. Bill Something-or-Other, as I recollect, before you said what your real name was. But I told you, didn't I? Told you you wouldn't settle down in one place and stay put. One day you'll find yourself out in the barn saddling your horse, I said. And you have. It's the same with all of us. We can't forget the old life. Not till we get so crippled up with rheumatism we can't sit a saddle." It has been a few years since Wyatt sat in a saddle without pain.

When he spoke again, there was a sadness in his voice. "Everything comes to an end," he said. "Even the old times."

They parted then, Leroy going out to the party and Wyatt coming my way. When he reached the door of my study I was waiting for him.

"Who is he, Wyatt?"

"Say, Charlie, you reckon Josefa's got a little more *flan* for an old law-man?"

"You know that fellow Leroy. Who is he?"

"Leee-Roy?" He gave me a grin, making me wait. "Sure, I know him. Anchorage. Nineteen and twelve. I had a gambling game. He came looking for gold."

"Who is he?"

He made the fizzing noise again. "Oh, he was a wild one back there a ways. A little after my time, of course, and working the other side of the law. But I got to know him in Anchorage. When all's said and done, he's a lot like you and me, Charlie."

"What's his name, Wyatt?"

"Robert Leroy, or whatever he said." He grinned, and I smelled the liquor. Then a change came over him, and for the space of a breath he was as sober as a judge and just as serious.

He looked me straight in the eye. "Let him be, Charlie. The old times are gone. He's one of us now."

He went on his way to the kitchen to hunt down some of Josefa's Mexican custard, leaving me standing in the door to my study. He had confirmed my hunch that Leroy had worked "the other side of the law," but he had told me something more. Leroy Roberts had touched something in Wyatt Earp, way deep inside. Up in Alaska he had won over Arizona Territory's most famous lawman, to where Wyatt now told me to let Leroy be and refused to tell me his name, all in one breath.

I could sift nothing more from what I had heard and what Wyatt had told me, so I went out to join the party at last, where a jolt of cowboy's delight put my mind off Leroy for a time. He wasn't there and I wondered where he might have gone, but I set my wondering aside. It's another trick I developed in my Pinkerton years—not thinking about the thing I most wanted to think about. Often the answer I was searching for would come to me that way, easy and without any fuss.

Things had quietened down by the time I got back to the parlor, mostly on account of Victoria joining the boys in the band. She can shut up a room faster than a shootout at the poker table, although in a far more pleasant manner. Popular songs from the nineties are her favorites and she has made them mine, even over the cowboy songs of my youth. She sings those too, because I taught them to her.

I sat in on the poker game for a few hands, but it had mostly run out of steam as the card players allowed themselves to be distracted by Victoria's singing. Wyatt was down to his last chips. He was nodding off to a gentle love ballad when distant shots sounded somewhere in the night.

Wyatt's head lifted up and his eyes popped open like a cat's—all awake in a second.

"Shotgun," said Emmett, never taking his eyes from his cards.

"Clantons coming," said Wyatt. He was pretty far gone by now.

"There aren't any Clantons left, Wyatt," I said. "You shot half of 'em and the rest died."

"There's always Clantons," he said. "The bastards breed like ground-hogs."

I pricked up my ears but there were no more shots, and it was only later that I learned what had caused the lively doings in Hollywood that night.

It seems that Redeye and Nate and Karen, all having taken on a cargo of cowboy tonic, decided to enjoy the night air by Gerald's corrals, just beyond mine, where the McQuain & Vickery stock is quartered. On their way out of the Bunk House they rounded up Leroy as he came from the back hallway, fresh from his encounter with Wyatt.

Upon reaching the corrals the four of them sat on the split-rail fence to survey the longhorn cattle by light of the moon, and life seemed pretty fine to them. To Redeye in particular, for he had brought along a quart of whiskey, and although he passed it to the others he got the lion's share. Trying to fill that boy with whiskey is like pouring sand down a badger hole with the other end in China. It struck him there was little in the world he couldn't do, and he wanted to do it all.

Just then his eye fell on old Geronimo. I will say straight off that this was not the Apache Indian whose name gave the shivering fits to many an Arizona settler. This Geronimo had four feet and horns, being a buffalo bull of noble breeding, one of McQuain & Vickery's little herd. As an Indian, Redeye has a special feeling for these aboriginal American crea-tures that once darkened the plains. In my own cowboy days, when the hide hunters were already hard at work, I once saw a stream of buffalo from one quarter to half a mile wide that took three days and nights to cross the Canadian River.

As a boy on the Sioux reservation, Redeye had heard the tales of the old hunters, but he himself saw a landscape where nary a buffalo roamed. And so when one of the show's buffalo calves was orphaned by the death of his mother, Redeye took him under his wing. He grafted him to a cow whose calf had died, and although Geronimo now outweighed the biggest longhorn in the McQuain & Vickery herd, Redeye considered him his private pet. He fed him a special diet of corn and cattle feed that he either bought or stole, I wasn't sure which and didn't care to know.

"Tonight's the night," Redeye declared as he sat there on the fence. "I'm going to ride the sonofabitch."

"He's a little spooky at night, isn't he?" said Karen.

"Aw, Geronimo loves me. Anyhow, it's time he was broke to saddle." So saying, Redeye picked a hackamore off the fence and began to make his way through the longhorns on foot.

Why didn't Nate or Karen stop him? For an old cowboy like myself, that's easy to answer. You might think that Nate Dicenzo is hardly a proper cowboy name, but pause to consider Siringo, and you will see that we both had Italian fathers. My mother was Irish, while Nate's was Welsh. The mingling of bloodlines here in these United States is a caution. But there are no rules concerning a cowboy's ancestry. What matters is whether or not he has got what it takes when the chips are down. Redeye had set himself a cowboy challenge and Nate was no more about to stop Redeye riding a buffalo bull, if that's what he had his mind set to do, than I would have.

Nate and Karen, being fond of each other, sat close together to watch the exhibition of cowboy daring, and Leroy wouldn't have missed the show for the world.

But Karen had told the simple truth about Geronimo's nature. That bull, who might have tipped the scales at about a ton of hardpacked bone and meat, had less self-confidence at night than a week-old calf. Even a longhorn cow, who can gut a prairie wolf in a couple of seconds flat, takes on a bad case of the willies by moonlight. Most of the critters in the corral knew Redeye by sight and smell both, but that counted for nothing just now. He was a man afoot in the dark, and few things spook range cattle worse.

They began to mill and bawl, but Redeye kept on toward old Geronimo. The buffalo didn't show any sign he was skittish until Redeye got within about twenty feet from him, whereupon he simply trotted off through the fence.

The fence hasn't been made that can hold a buffalo, not if he's of a mind to ramble. I don't care if it's barb wire or full-round lodgepole pine.

This one was split rails, but to Geronimo it was matchwood. Off he went with every longhorn in that pen right behind him, spreading out and kicking up their heels as they vanished into the shadows.

Even a drunk cowboy knows when he'd best go about his work. Nate and Karen and Redeye lost some time catching their horses and tripping over their own latigos, but Leroy had partaken only sparingly of the bottle. Being of cowboy blood himself, he was saddled and gone before the others.

Soon there were three cowboys and one cowgirl riding the Hollywood back streets for strays, somewhat helped by the weak light of the half moon. In the midst of these proceedings, a retired Indiana farmer named Renshaw awoke to discover a longhorn cow ambling through his rose garden. He responded to this bovine effrontery by letting off two barrels of birdshot at the cow's hindquarters. The birdshot did her no lasting harm, but it caused her some brief discomfort, and she laid waste to a length of picket fence in departing the neighborhood.

It was these salutes that caught our attention in the parlor. To an old cowboy, gunfire on a Saturday night isn't much to take notice of, but California likes to think it's modern and all, and the authorities discourage even cowboys from carrying guns. As a result, random gunfire is a rare occurrence. If the shots had been a bit closer, I would have gone for a looksee. Instead I stayed put to hear the rest of Victoria's song.

When the song was done, Emmett and Wyatt took their leave in Emmett's buckboard. Wyatt had driven himself to the Bunk House in his own automobile, having learned to master these machines a few years ago. Fortunately, in his present state he had completely forgotten how he came to be there, and he allowed Emmett to lead him to the buckboard without complaint. Even before Emmett flipped the reins and started off, Wyatt fell sound asleep slouched over in the seat. But before the buckboard was a hundred yards from the Bunk House, there was a thrashing noise from the bushes beside the road and the sleeping cat came awake in an instant, pulling his hog-leg from the Wes Hardin shoulder rig under his coat even as his eyes opened.

I will mention here that although Mr. Ned Buntline has promoted a good deal of talk about the long-barreled Colt's revolvers he supposedly made for Wyatt, I never saw Wyatt carry any such foolishness. On the night in question it was not even a Colt's that he drew, but a smoky-powder Remington that ought to have been nailed to the wall above his mantelpiece.

"Fill your hand, Ike Clanton," Wyatt roared. Then he let the Remington do his roaring for him, three times. There was a great crash in the bushes, followed by silence.

This commotion was close enough to the Bunk House that we all came running, your humble servant in the lead with a kerosene lamp in one hand and the shotgun I keep beneath the bar in the other. I found Wyatt and Emmett standing in the brush at the side of the road. Wyatt's pistol was still in his hand, still smoking. At his feet was the cooling corpse of old Geronimo. The monarch of the Plains had busted his last fence.

"Wyatt reckoned it was Ike Clanton's ghost," Emmett informed me.

Leroy rode up at a fast clip just as Victoria arrived on the scene, her eyes wide with alarm. She looked from Leroy to me to Wyatt to the buffalo, and back at Leroy again. Seeing that he had taken no part in the shooting, she calmed down as more curiosity seekers arrived from the Bunk House. Leroy dismounted, and before long I saw Victoria find her way over to his part of the crowd as if for a better look at poor Geronimo.

The next horseman to come pell-mell out of the night was Redeye Hawk. When he saw Geronimo lying there on the ground he jumped off his horse and knelt beside the corpse. He patted the buffalo's head like he might of done if his favorite dog had died. After a time he looked up and noticed the Remington in Wyatt's hand.

"You shot Geronimo," Redeye said. His tone was mournful, and I thought I saw a tear in the Indian's eye.

"There's worse things that could happen to a fellow than having his pet buffalo shot dead by Wyatt Earp," I offered. "For starters, you got a top-notch story to tell for the rest of your life."

This gave Redeye pause. He looked at Wyatt.

It finally occurred to Wyatt to put up his hog-leg. "Everything comes to an end, boy," the old lawman said. "An Indian should know that better than most."

He looked at Leroy then, and for a moment he came fully awake. "Everything comes to an end," he said again.

Then the spirit left him and he was just a tired old man. "Take me home, Emmett," he said. "It's time I was in bed."

As Emmett and Wyatt drove off in the buckboard, Nate and Karen came along pushing a bunch of longhorns toward the corrals.

"Wyatt Earp shot my buffalo," Redeye told them when they stopped to see what the excitement was. He said it like it might not be such a bad piece of news.

As he commenced telling the story of what had happened, I drifted away from the crowd. My detective's nose was itching again. I had no idea what Wyatt was trying to tell Leroy, but the old man's interest in this horseback stranger got me to wondering once more, and so I retired to my study to sit in my oak swivel chair and think. I have done all my writing in that chair since I quit chasing bad men for a livelihood, and I do my best thinking in it. It was for this reason that I sat in it that night, not because of the wanted fliers on the walls around me. But the walls were there and a man has to rest his eyes somewhere when he thinks. I lighted the lamp on the desk, completely forgetting the electric light, and maybe the old-time lamplight helped me to see the faces on the fliers more like they were real men instead of photographs.

I looked up and there he was.

Twenty years will change a man, and home life with regular mealtimes will alter both his outlook and appearance. Side by side with the picture, I might have taken Leroy for a different man altogether, but it was the eyes that gave him away. The same amusement at the general folly of life which I had observed that very evening shone bright in his eyes in the old photograph.

Yet I rebelled against what I saw. My mind was reeling, I am not ashamed to admit. To the best of my knowledge this man was dead and gone, dropped in a lonely grave eleven years before.

I knew whose flier it was from the moment I spied the picture, but I rose now and read every word on it. Scrawled in the margins were some words of my own, which reminded me that his death had been rumored but not confirmed. Yet I had accepted it for a fact because I wished to. It suited me to believe that the case was closed, despite conflicting reports stating that the outlaw had died a second and a third time, in different places widely separated by time and geography, or might still be alive.

I heard the sound of horses outside my window. Looking out, I saw that Victoria had joined Leroy and the others in rounding up the last of the cattle. The five of them were moving the bunch toward the corrals, Victoria on her gelding Ranger, riding at Leroy's side.

And I knew he was the man in the photograph. There before my eyes was living proof that he had not died in any of the places where his death was claimed. He had eaten at my table this evening. Tonight he would sleep in one of my beds. And tomorrow?

There has not been another time in my life when I had less idea what tomorrow would bring.

Chapter 6

THE NEXT MORNING at eight o'clock sharp the gong sounded for breakfast and there was a general rush to the dining room. It is Victoria's custom to give her picture crew a picnic at the beach on the day following her cast parties, the idea being that they all feel better working off their hangovers together in pleasant surroundings. These affairs have become as popular as the parties themselves, hence the general willingness to get out of bed bright and early on a day off. By midmorning the crew was shivering on the sands of Santa Monica, hoping the clouds that had rolled in from the sea before dawn would dissipate so the sun might shine upon them.

The customary picnic site was beneath the palisades, midway between the amusement pier to the south and Santa Monica Canyon to the north, where the abandoned Long Wharf jutted into the bay. They situated themselves at some remove from the more populated regions of the strand so they would not frighten the natives unduly with their cowboy antics. As most people nowadays seem to prefer the company of the multitude, Victoria's outfit had a quarter mile of beach more or less to themselves.

In their trucks and cars they had brought all manner of provisions for the barbecue, and the men and women kept themselves warm digging firepits and erecting tents and setting up serving tables. When they were finished, the resulting layout would have suited the Grand Duke Alexis

himself, had he risen from his grave to make another tour of America's
western provinces. Quarters and halves of beef were placed over huge
fires, and the serving tables fairly groaned under their burdens of food-
stuffs.

By the time the preparations for the midday feast were complete, the
sun had evaporated the clouds and the members of the company repaired
to the gaily striped tents to change into their swimming costumes, although in Victoria's outfit it is mainly the easterners who don modern
garb for entering the water. More than one California couple strolling
along the sands that day was taken aback to see red Indians and young
cowboys emerge from the waves clad only in their longhandled undergarments.

Victoria, however, favors the very latest in fashionable swimming costumes. Once attired for the water to her satisfaction, she made certain to
pass by where Leroy was reclining against a log, watching a few of the
young men shoot at a hapless piece of driftwood some thirty yards from
shore. The gunfire disturbed pelicans, terns and gulls, who were unaccustomed to cowboy high jinks.

"I should think you would do well in a shooting contest," Victoria said,
stopping beside him.

"Shooting isn't a game," Leroy said.

"Well, if that shot yesterday was just luck—" she suggested, thinking to
tease him into joining the contest.

"Yesterday you had a bunch of howling Indians after you." She saw that
the lines at the corners of his eyes were wrinkled with amusement. It
seemed he always managed to turn the teasing back on her, but she found
that she didn't mind.

"Aren't you going swimming?" she asked.

"It's a little out of my line."

"You never learned to swim?"

"Oh, I can stay afloat. Back home you can wade most of the rivers. I let
my horse swim the rest."

"My father made sure I could swim. He wanted me to be ready for
anything."

She left him to ponder the unsaid meanings of her words while she
strolled nearer the shooters. By now, the currents had carried the piece of
wood beyond pistol range. Buddy Johnston made it jump with a shot from
his Springfield rifle, which prompted Redeye Hawk to say, "Oh, well,
anyone can hit it with a rifle."

Without a word, Buddy offered Redeye the rifle. Redeye sighted, fired,
and missed. Chief John took the rifle from the young man's hands, threw
it to his shoulder, and made the wood jump again, pushing it still farther
from shore.

"Good rifle," John said as he handed the Springfield back to Buddy.

"Are you boys about done?" Victoria inquired.

"Yes, ma'am," Nate Dicenzo said, putting up his six-shooter. He and his companions watched Victoria as she broke into a run and raced across the sand into the water, where she dove cleanly into a breaking wave. As the shooters dispersed, Leroy got to his feet to see better as Victoria stroked out past the breakers.

Redeye Hawk nudged Nate Dicenzo.

"Hey, Leroy," he called. At the same moment he tossed his pistol to the unsuspecting man. This sort of thing is a common cowboy prank, taking a man off guard to see how he will react, however in this instance Redeye immediately regretted his impulse. Leroy caught the pistol and in the blink of an eye he was in a half crouch, the pistol cocked and leveled at Redeye.

The young Indian felt his heart stop, but before he could make a move to show his harmless intent, Leroy was already straightening out of the crouch, smiling and tossing the pistol back, almost quickly enough to cover the deadly seriousness of his reaction.

"Good thing it was empty," Redeye said, attempting a joke. His voice was strained.

Leroy was still smiling, but he shook his head. "It wasn't empty."

MY OWN MORNING was less hazardous but no less eventful, although it began slowly. Putting my cares aside and getting a good night's rest is another detective's trick that has stood me in good stead over many years, but the night after Victoria's party it failed me. I arose from my rumpled bed at first light in a rank humor, and I kept my mouth shut when I went to the kitchen for a cup of coffee.

I built a small fire in the potbellied stove in my office to ward off the chill of the gray dawn, and while I drank my coffee I glared at Leroy's wanted flier. Finally I worked the tacks out of the wall with my Barlow knife so I could hold the offending document in my hands, thinking perhaps to wrest the truth from it.

I knew that Leroy and the man on the flier were one and the same. Still I wanted proof, as if I were a judge and jury to be convinced by facts and evidence, instead of a cowboy detective whose instincts had kept him alive through twenty-two years of working in false identities among desperate men.

Josefa brought my breakfast to the study, setting the plate and silver on the desk without a word. She knows my moods, and she knows that no matter what his problems of the moment, an old cowboy will eat when food is set before him.

As I ate I looked at the flier again and read all the words, both those printed there and those I had written myself. My mind was running like a thoroughbred on a freshly groomed track, and like that thoroughbred it was running in circles. I knew it was him. But how could it be?

I heard the breakfast gong and the sounds of the picture crew going to breakfast, but I kept to myself, unable to share my dilemma and unwilling to be distracted from wrestling with it. I leaned back in my chair to sip the last of my coffee, and it was then that my eyes fell on the telephone bolted to the wall of my office. I never had a telephone in Santa Fe, and I was still not accustomed to reaching for one whenever I wanted to talk to someone. My habit was to saddle up and go knock on his door. At the moment I wanted to talk to Gerald Ball, but I knew that Rosa made him attend church each and every Sunday morning, he having converted to the Catholic faith in order to marry her. By looking out my window I could see the back side of the Balls' house beyond my corrals and his, but the angle was wrong for me to see if the touring car was parked in the shade of the ancient live oak beside the house. I rang the number to save myself the quarter-mile walk to and fro, and was not surprised when Gerald didn't answer his ring. If he and Rosa had gone to early mass, they would be home by nine-thirty or ten, so I bided my time.

After breakfast there was further bustle as the McQuain & Vickery crowd prepared to set out for the beach. From my study window I could see the corrals, and I saw Leroy with the others, saddling his horse, apparently intending to ride to the beach horseback, as a few of the others would do. This suited me to a T, since I had no wish to come face to face with him just yet.

When everyone was gone and the rooming house was quiet, I tried Gerald again, although it was only a quarter past nine. Again there was no answer, but with the earpiece still in my hand I realized I might be able to speak with my old Pinkerton colleague Frank Dimaio, who had more than a passing acquaintance with the case of "Leroy Roberts."

By good luck it took just a quarter of an hour for the operator to reach San Francisco, where I believed Frank to be living, and to inquire if a Mr. Frank Dimaio had a telephone. He did, and he was at home.

"Hello?" Even through all that wire he sounded like himself.

"Frank? Charlie Siringo."

There was a moment's silence. Then, "Charlie? Where in hell are you?"

"I'm in Hollywood, Frank."

"How are you, you old fox?"

We chatted idly for a few moments, but soon I cut the chatter short and told him why I was calling. Without, I should add, giving any hint of why I was suddenly interested in a case the Pinkertons were content to leave in the "Closed" file.

"I suppose you could call the Denver office," Frank said when I had explained what I wished to know. "They'd have the most up-to-date files. Or maybe your old friend Sayles. He was superintendent right here in San Francisco."

"I can't call the Denver office or any other damn Pinkerton office, Frank," I reminded him. "Not after the trouble they made about my books. As for Sayles, I haven't the first idea where he's living, and he'll be the last man in the world to let one of these infernal devices in his home, wherever it is."

"What are you up to, Charlie? You getting your hand back in detective work? I heard you were working for the Burns Agency there for a while. That sure must of burned the Pinkertons." He chuckled at his little joke.

"Oh, it's nothing like that." I tried to sound casual. "I thought I might do a book on my part in that case if I could turn up anything new. I missed out on the end of it, you'll recall. Anything you can remember might help."

Frank thought for a moment, and then he told me about losing Leroy's trail, and investigating the many rumors of his death.

"You get up this way, you come by, Charlie," he said as we bid each other good-bye. "I'm on Powell Street down behind the Catholic church. You'd feel right at home in this neighborhood. It's full of Italians. Good cooking and good wine." He laughed. "Right across Columbus Avenue it's all Chinese. Who said never the twain shall meet? Anyway, you come by. We'll talk about old times."

I promised that I would. But the truth was, Leroy's appearance in my rooming house made me more certain than ever that I should let the old times be and concern myself with the new ones. Here in the second decade of the new age I had a chance to—do what?

The answer eluded me. This was what had kept me tossing in my bed all through the night, a feeling I couldn't even describe. A ghost from my past had stepped through my door, proving himself to be living flesh and blood and not a ghost at all. And I was filled with a sense of impending— not doom, but some unformed possibility I couldn't get a grip on.

The one thing I was sure of was that I couldn't spend another minute in the Bunk House. It was time for this hound to get out on the trail. But before abandoning my study I tried Gerald once more, and this time I got lucky. Immediately upon hearing Gerald's English voice I bid him good morning, and without breaking stride I asked him for the name of his lawyer. Edgar Fenton? And would Mr. Fenton mind being bothered with a question or two on a Sunday? I hung up without satisfying Gerald's curiosity about why I had called.

I jiggled the hook and a moment later I was speaking with Mr. Edgar

Fenton, counselor-at-law. He confirmed that he would be willing to receive me. A few minutes later I had Jake saddled and I was on my way, dressed in my Sunday-go-to-meeting frock coat and string tie.

Upon arriving at Mr. Fenton's house, I was invited to have a glass of lemonade and accompany him into his library. As I seated myself in the wing chair in front of his desk, I congratulated myself for being a very clever fellow and taking advantage of changing customs in this new age. When I was a youth, making a business call on a Sunday was the height of bad manners among polite folk, although a cowboy might be forgiven such a presumption, seeing as cows did not observe the Sabbath.

But when I explained my business, Edgar Fenton looked at me as if to say I was not so clever as I thought.

"I'm not a criminal lawyer, Mr. Siringo." He was about thirty, I guessed, and he had a nervous habit of tugging at one ear as he spoke.

"You're a lawyer, aren't you?"

"Sure, but we're in the twentieth century now. The law is specialized. Most laymen don't understand that." His smile became condescending. "My specialty is motion picture law. I'm grateful to Sir Gerald for recommending me, but what I know about criminal law you could write on Mary Pickford's left nipple."

He grinned as if to say this was the sort of witticism a man of the world would enjoy, but he guessed from my expression that my opinion of his wit did not match his own.

"Well," he said, hurrying on, "you are a friend of Sir Gerald's. It might be that I can dig up an answer to your question, just as a favor."

Lifting the earpiece from his desk telephone, he spun the dial on its base three times. "I have a colleague who may be able to help us. If anyone knows . . . Nathan? Ed Fenton."

It took me a moment to realize that he was no longer speaking to me but to his party at the other end of the line, and all without so much as a word to an operator. I have just got used to chatting with these unseen ladies and already they are being rendered unnecessary by the new automatic dialing systems.

"Oh, it's booming," Fenton said after a short pause. "I haven't got a free moment . . . Lunch? That would be swell. . . . No, better make it the following week. Any time after Wednesday. . . . Sounds fine. I'll phone you to confirm. Listen, Nathan, I've got a client here with a question about extraditions from California to other states. . . . Armed robbery . . . Well no, not recently. About nineteen or twenty years ago. . . . Nevada, Wyoming . . ."

Here he gave me an inquiring glance.

"Montana and Idaho," I added.

"Montana and Idaho . . . Yes . . . Mmm hmm . . . Okay. But if he was out of the state? . . . All right, Nathan, thanks. And I apologize for calling on Sunday. . . . Oh, of course. Ha, ha. Well, then I'll always call on Sunday but never on Saturday. Thanks again."

He laughed again as he replaced the earpiece in its cradle. "He's Jewish," he explained to me, and then he grew serious. Lawyers are always serious when they speak of the law.

"Nathan used to practice in Denver. He says he'd have to look up the laws for those other states, but he says for armed robbery the statute of limitations is sometimes as short as three to five years."

"So a man who committed a crime twenty years ago would be off the hook."

"Not necessarily," he said. "It would depend on where the criminal has been living in the meantime. See, the way the statutes of limitations generally work, they're suspended if the criminal leaves the state where he committed the crime. In a state with a five-year statute, he would be free if he lived for five years in that state. But if he left the scene-of-the-crime state and hasn't been back, or has spent less than five years there *in toto*, then he'd still be wanted. And as long as a man is wanted by another state, California will extradite him."

Fenton gave his ear an especially hard tug. "You have aroused my interest, Mr. Siringo. What desperate criminal are you pursuing?"

"Oh, I'm not after anyone, Mr. Fenton. I've got an idea for a new book and I want to get my facts straight." This story sounded so polished and convincing, I half believed it myself.

Chapter 7

IN THE SHORT while I had been in Fenton's house the low clouds had rolled back toward the sea and already the sun was pleasantly warm. With my frock coat tied behind my saddle I turned Jake's head toward the west, keeping to the shade of the trees along Sunset Boulevard's winding course. Where the roadway curves before entering Beverly Hills, I stopped at the German's luncheon stand for a hamburger and ate two. If someone had introduced me to these delectable snacks when I was a cowboy, I would have opened the first hamburger parlor in Caldwell and no doubt become rich in short order, instead of wasting my time with oysters and ice cream.

Once through Beverly Hills, Jake and I changed course to the south and entered the farmlands between the hills and Santa Monica. There having been no rain in some time, the many automobiles out for a Sunday drive raised choking clouds of dust on the farm roads, which Jake and I sought to avoid by keeping to bridle paths where we could. More and more, however, bicyclists are taking over the bridle paths, and these energetic young men and women looked at Jake and me as if we were objects from a curio shop.

On reaching the palisades, I reined in Jake and took in the view of the coast, admiring the sweeping curve of Santa Monica Bay and noting the disrepair of the nearly mile-long structure of the Long Wharf. Since ships have taken to docking at San Pedro, the once thriving Port Los Angeles has been abandoned, save by the handful of Japanese fisherfolk who live in tumbledown shacks at the base of the wharf. South of the palisades, by the Santa Monica pier and beyond, hordes of people were taking advantage of the fine weather to enjoy a day at the shore. While I watched, a tiny train climbed the roller coaster trestle on the pier and plunged down again, no doubt providing good value to those who had paid money to be scared out of their wits.

It was a perfect day for a picnic, more like May than late November. In Santa Fe, we might have had snow on the ground.

From my vantage point I had no trouble locating Victoria's picnic site. Among the cluster of motor vehicles parked there was the Model T coupé that Victoria had bought for her parents, and I was gladdened by the thought of seeing Anne and Jay.

I rode down the California Avenue Incline, where the roadway descends the cliffs to the beach. As I crossed the railroad tracks and macadam road that run along the base of the cliffs, nearing the tents and fires of the movie outfit's camp, I began searching among the picnickers for Leroy. The company's cars and trucks were parked on the sand beyond the road. Among the half dozen horses tethered there I recognized Leroy's roan gelding Sonny.

I tied my horse with the others and found myself lingering unnecessarily over loosening Jake's girth to make him comfortable. My ride had been so enjoyable that I had let my mind wander. I still had no idea what I was going to say to Leroy when we came face to face, or if I would say anything at all. From Edgar Fenton I had learned that the law might still take an interest in Leroy Roberts. Unless he had lived for several years in each of four or five western states since committing his latest crimes there, he could still be prosecuted if anyone was so inclined. And I had no doubt that some ambitious attorney general would jump at the chance, if only to puff up his reputation. But I was far from certain that this was the outcome I wanted, and in my uncertainty I welcomed an excuse to put off confronting Leroy. When I spied a sudden commotion by the serving tables I made straight for it to see what the excitement was. The unlikely sight that greeted my eyes was Redeye Hawk tackling Nate Dicenzo and throwing him to the sand, whereupon he began pummeling Nate with his fists.

Just moments before, they had been standing peaceably at the meat table together with Chief John, while Luke Fister, the McQuain & Vickery cook, carved second helpings of barbecued meat from a huge haunch.

"Man, that's good meat," Redeye said.

"It oughta be," said Luke. "You always fed him good."

Redeye was understandably puzzled. "I fed him good?"

Chief John laid a large hand on Redeye's shoulder. "You get a lot of honor, providing a feast like this. We all want to thank you."

"Providing a feast? I didn't provide any—" A nasty suspicion set foot in Redeye's mind. "You mean this is—"

Nate was shamefaced. "I didn't figure to tell you until later."

Redeye threw down his plate and started for Nate, who began backing away. "Now hold on, Hawk. We couldn't let the old fella go to waste."

"You cooked up *Geronimo*? He was my friend!"

Redeye let fly with a blow that nearly knocked Nate off his feet. Seeing that Redeye's anger was genuine, Nate lit out running.

At this point your humble servant made his entrance and witnessed the rest of the proceedings. Redeye pounded on Nate pretty hard once he had him on the sand, but Chief John and Luke hauled him off. They turned him loose again when Nate had a running start. John was laughing, which brought on a fit of coughing, but he didn't mind, he was so tickled by it all. He popped a cough drop into his mouth and kept on laughing and coughing.

I saw that it was just a cowboy squabble not likely to result in anything more serious than a broken tooth or a cracked rib or two and I turned my attention elsewhere, looking around for Leroy. I spied him not far away, sitting on the sand with Karen Valdez, the two of them eating from tin plates and apparently enjoying the spectacle of Nate and Redeye making fools of themselves.

Gerald Ball passed by me on his way to break up the fight. "Come along, Charles," he said. "I will need a hand putting a stop to that."

"Hold on there," I said, taking him by the arm. "You skipped out of that shindig last night before I could corner you. I know Victoria set you down with young Brian Hill. What was your answer?"

At supper the night before, Victoria had asked for my help in case Gerald still balked at making her feature. "Help me persuade him, Charlie," she said. "I know you'll think of something."

I had thought of something, all right. It was something Gerald wanted badly, but I hoped I wouldn't have to offer it.

Redeye and Nate went running off toward the water's edge and Gerald gave up any idea of following. "You're part of this conspiracy too? Victoria's Uncle Charles, always looking out for her interests?"

"She and this Brian fellow, they're bright youngsters. It couldn't hurt to give them a chance."

"You share Victoria's confidence?"

I nodded.

"Enough to share in the risk?"

Right there I should have noticed that Gerald had done nothing but ask questions without giving an answer to mine. It's an old detective's trick, one I have used myself on many occasions, revealing little while learning as much as I could, but I was distracted by keeping an eye on Leroy and wondering what to do about him. Instead of pulling Gerald up short I gave him more rope and then put my own head in the noose.

"I have enough confidence in her to lend a hand with the work, if you give the go-ahead," I said. "I've been to Mexico and I know the border like the back of my hand. Might be I could help Brian with the story."

"We would be grateful for your narrative skills, but I had imagined a more substantial participation."

"Such as?"

"Would you put up your rooming house against the completion of the picture?"

There it was. Gerald had seen it too. The Bunk House was my ace in the hole, only he had played it first.

Here I should explain that I more or less stole the Bunk House out from under Gerald's nose. Before leaving Santa Fe I took out a hefty mortgage on my Sunny Slope ranch, thinking perhaps to buy a house in Hollywood near the Hartfords, where I might retire in my old age. When I arrived in California I had this fresh cash burning a hole in my pocket, looking for a new place to roost. Victoria took me to the Bunk House on my first day in Hollywood, knowing I would like the old-time feel of the place. She introduced me to Wes Larson, the owner. Wes was a Texan who had more than a passing acquaintance with the taste of trail dust, and we soon saw that we were cut from the same cloth. Like me, Wes had a touch of chronic bronchitis from breathing that dust over the course of many years. We toasted each other with cowboy tonic, and I learned that Wes was ready to retire from innkeeping. Before the night was over, the Bunk House was mine. I had owned a boardinghouse once before, in Gem, Idaho, while I was a Pinkerton operative, but never had a single boarder owing to the violence between the striking miners and the owners. Ever since then I had wondered what it would be like to be a real innkeeper, and now I had my chance.

The purchase was completed before I met Gerald, and before I learned he had tried to buy the Bunk House for several years. What especially galled him was that I got it for less than he was willing to pay. But he had kept his offers low, taking Wes for a rube just because he spoke in the Texas manner.

As Wes handed over the deed he told me, "Charlie, I'm just happy to know the place will be in good hands."

That was what mattered to Wes, not the money. But Gerald always figured I robbed him, and he had never stopped looking for a way to get back at me.

"Well?" he demanded now. Off in the distance, Redeye tackled Nate again. They rolled in the sand, but this time Nate ended up on top and started pounding Redeye.

"When you get your mind set on something, you don't let go, do you Gerald?"

"With a rooming house to lodge my actors, I could keep my costs down. It would give me an edge over the shoestring producers."

Gerald was a "shoestring producer" himself, but he fancied himself better than all the others who worked outside the gates of the studios.

"You could manage the place for me," he added. "I have no wish to run it myself. I would give you a free hand."

"But it'd be your place instead of mine." For me, that difference was like night and day. But I could see no way out of giving him some kind of chance at what he wanted, not if Victoria was to get her picture made.

"It might be I could sweeten the pot," I offered.

"You'll do it?"

"I said sweeten the pot, not fold my hand before I'm busted. You give these kids a chance and I'll give you one. If they don't finish the picture in whatever time they agree to, you can buy my place for half off the market value. But it's got to be cash on the barrelhead, and you get a week after the picture's done to come up with the money."

My terms gave him pause for thought, but finally he said, "All right. But if the picture is completed late for any reason, including an act of God, I get the Bunk House."

I nodded my head yes, fighting off an urge to shake it no.

"And no one but we two is to know of our arrangement." Gerald is not stupid. He knew Victoria would never consent to the risk I was taking on her behalf.

I nodded again.

"Done," he said, smiling now, and we shook on it.

I wanted to be there when he told Victoria she could make her picture, so I followed him to where he and Victoria and their invited guests had sat down to eat their picnic luncheon in high-class style. In the shade of a striped awning their table was set with linen and silver. A spray of yellow roses in a crystal vase adorned the center of the table.

Victoria would have been just as happy sitting on the sand with Leroy and Karen and the rest of them, but even as a little girl she liked dressing up in fancy clothes. Today she wore a yellow dress that went well with the roses.

At the table with her were her parents, Jay and Anne Hartford, Brian Hill, Gerald's wife Rosa, and the Ball children, Matthew and Magdalena. Rosa is a handsome woman, and like Victoria she was dressed stylishly for a luncheon at the beach.

The one person I didn't know was a youngish man, prematurely balding, who was introduced to me as George Bleumel. It took me a moment to remember that I had heard the name before. He was the pioneer cameraman Brian had borrowed from Carl Laemmle. For one of the most respected artisans in the business, Bleumel cut an unimposing figure, and I took little notice of him just then.

Victoria was waiting impatiently through the hellos, obviously fit to bust with some excitement or other. "Well," she said as I shook hands with the cameraman, "has Gerald told you? Isn't it wonderful?"

"Isn't what wonderful?" I asked.

"Gerald has agreed to make the feature! He's given us fifteen thousand dollars and a month to make it. It's the same budget DeMille had to make *The Squaw Man*."

I felt like the hayseed who has just been slickered in the shell game at a country carnival. I wanted to strangle a certain British popinjay, but I had given my word to keep our deal secret, and however underhanded Gerald's dealings with me, my word has always been my bond.

Victoria was so thrilled she didn't notice the black looks I gave the Englishman. "We have a surprise for Gerald too," she went on, the words all tumbling out. "Rosa has a wonderful idea!"

"We could make the picture at my family's ranch in Sonora," said Rosa. She seemed very pleased with herself, and by the looks on their faces it was clear that Brian Hill and Victoria were already set on the idea.

"Take my company into Mexico!" Gerald exploded. "Now? With all the recent troubles?"

"The trouble's over in Texas, like always," I said. "They've been taking potshots across the Texas border since the start of the revolution."

"It's not all border troubles," he protested. "Down in Puebla they arrested an American consul!"

"So? That's a thousand miles from Sonora."

"Perhaps, but there is talk of war in the newspapers, and Senator Fall says—"

"Oh, Gerald, honestly," Victoria interrupted him. "Senator Fall would use any excuse to attack President Wilson."

"To hear him talk, he'd like to make Mexico the forty-ninth state," I added. Albert Fall had served in the Congress as senator from New Mexico, and I was well acquainted with his ambitions.

"Mexico is an infant republic not capable of governing itself!" Gerald replied. "As the *Evening Herald* observed the other day, 'Our forbearance is sorely tried. We have been patient long enough!'"

"According to the *Evening Herald*, we should have gone to war with Mexico every day for the last ten years," Victoria said scornfully.

All this talk concerned the recent kidnapping of one William O. Jenkins, the American consular agent in Puebla, who was held for ransom by bandits and delivered back unharmed when the ransom was paid. The Carranza government promptly arrested Jenkins, claiming that he was in cahoots with his kidnappers, had shared in the ransom, and had perjured himself before Carranza's officials who investigated the affair. There was talk that Mexican troops were gathering near the Texas border, preparing to repel the Americans if we tried to intervene, and reports from that section were inflamed, but while the American government had protested Jenkins' detention, it threatened nothing more. Senator Fall, whose committee was in the midst of a long investigation of our relations with Mexico, had seized on the affair as further proof that President Wilson was mollycoddling Carranza.

"Gerald, dearest, please listen to us." Rosa Ball's tone was soft as she sought to cast oil on the troubled waters. "I have telephoned Señor Garza, the stationmaster in Delgado. I spoke with him this morning. He assures me that there has been no trouble in that part of Sonora in a long time."

Gerald made as if to open his mouth but Rosa held up a hand. She turned to Victoria like a society hostess orchestrating a drawing room conversation.

"The revolution has brought hard times to Delgado, but the men are eager to work. They could help with the sets and props, and they could appear as extras too. The money would help the town."

Brian Hill had been listening to the conversation with his head tilted to one side. Now he spoke up for the first time. "Fifteen thousand dollars doesn't go as far as it used to, Sir Gerald. It will buy a lot more in Mexico. We'll have a first-class picture all the way."

Gerald's brow was knitted up like it always is when he is thinking hard.

"I could bring the children down for the holidays," Rosa said sweetly. "We would be together for Christmas."

Having referred once before to Gerald's "affairs," I will add that Rosa is well aware of his occasional infidelities, as Victoria learned when she befriended Rosa not long after Gerald misjudged Victoria and made a pass at her. Victoria brought him up short, of course, not only making it plain that his advances were unwelcome, but warning him never to trifle with any of the women in the McQuain & Vickery show. Because Rosa was a pure young maiden when Gerald married her, he may have thought he was getting a shrinking violet, but Spanish ladies come into their own in marriage and Rosa is no exception. She is too wise to think she can change Gerald's weak nature, but she keeps him on a tight rein both financially and socially, and helping Victoria now was a subtle way of reminding Gerald who the real boss is in their marriage.

Unaware of the marital politics going on around him, George Bleumel stroked the smooth skin on the top of his head with the palm of one hand.

"Shooting in Mexico would give the picture a completely original look," he mused.

"It would be the most authentic picture ever made," Brian added. "And the publicity wouldn't hurt us. 'Filmed at great risk in strife-torn Mexico,' we could say."

Gerald shrugged. "It's your picture. I leave the production decisions up to you."

This brought exclamations of joy from those at the table. They all beamed at Gerald as if he were Santa Claus giving out presents ahead of schedule. I held back from the general celebration, wondering if Gerald had agreed in the end because it had occurred to him, as it had to me, that any delay or disruption of the production while in Mexico would assure that the picture would be finished late. And I still had a bone to pick with Sir Gerald Ball. Before I arrived, he had already given the picture his approval, but I played the greenhorn for him and he hoodwinked me as neat as you please. I was a man of my word and I would keep the bargain, but I made myself a promise that if ever I had a chance to repay Sir Gerald Ball in kind, I wouldn't let it slip by.

"By God, it's old Charlie," Jay Hartford said, noticing me for the first time. "How long has it been, Charlie, a month or two?"

The Sunday previous, I had taken my Sunday dinner with the Hartfords, but that had slipped Jay's mind. He's not the man he used to be. He comes and goes, and it's hard to tell just how much he takes in anymore. But Jay is all wool and a yard wide, and without men like him the West wouldn't be safe today for those like Gerald Ball.

"Howdy, Jay." I took the hand he offered. "It's good to see you."

"Seddown, Charlie. We'll talk over old times."

At that moment shooting broke out not far away and I nearly jumped out of my skin. Being on edge from thinking about Leroy made me nervous, I suppose, but it was only a few of the cowboys down at the water's edge shooting once more at a bit of driftwood offshore. Having been absent during the first such competition, I was unprepared for the second go-round. I calmed myself and took a seat, making sure I placed myself so I could keep an eye on Leroy, where he was picnicking with Karen Valdez.

KAREN HAD BEEN taken with Leroy right from the start. If it hadn't been for her affections for Nate Dicenzo, which she wasn't certain he deserved, she might have made a cowgirl's play for the stranger. But she had noticed the way Leroy's eyes kept seeking out Victoria, first in the Bunk House and now at the beach.

"I suppose about now you're wondering why she's not married," Karen said.

Leroy gave her a grin. "You could quit this hard work and take up mind reading."

Nate and Redeye came along just then and sat down beside them, each carrying two bottles of beer. Nate was nursing a bloody nose, but the fisticuffs and wrestling were over and they were friends again, and old Geronimo could rest in peace. Redeye handed a beer to Leroy while Nate gave one to Karen, who accepted it without acknowledgment of any kind.

"Victoria's like me," Karen said to Leroy. "She won't look twice at the Hollywood dandies. She's waiting for a real man to come along."

This last was a dig at Nate. "You got a real man right here," he reminded her.

"You better marry me while you got the chance, or I'll forget you offered," she told him, and she moved a little closer to Leroy.

Nate took a swig of his beer, and for the first time he noticed that yours truly had joined the privileged few at Victoria's table.

"Damn," he exclaimed, "will you look at Charlie Siringo. Don't he come to a picnic dressed like Sunday-go-to-meeting."

"That's Charlie Siringo?" There was something in Leroy's tone of voice that made the others look at him, wondering what was wrong, but he was quick to cover his surprise. "Everybody just called him Charlie. He's Charlie Siringo the Pinkerton man?"

He made it sound like it was a matter of passing interest.

"Sure," said Redeye. "He trailed every outlaw you ever heard of, from Billy the Kid to the Wild Bunch."

Leroy sipped his beer and took this in. Karen turned the conversation in a new direction, still playing up to Leroy in the hope of getting Nate's goat, and none of the others gave it a moment's thought a short time later when Leroy rose and left them, saying he was going to carry some water to his horse.

I never saw him go. As I sat down with the Hartfords Anne smiled at me, which distracted me as it always does, and Rosa set about serving me up a plate of food. Jay had forgotten what he wanted to say to me, but the rest of them were already halfway to Mexico, planning their picture show, and I got caught up in their conversation.

"What about your crew?" Brian said to Victoria. "I mean with the holidays coming up—"

"Oh, they won't mind working," Victoria said. "So long as they're drawing wages, they're happy. But are you sure a month is enough time?"

"We make two-reelers in a week and you turn out a whole Cimarron Rose serial in two months," Brian said. "If we plan it carefully we can do it."

"They will not accept bank notes in Mexico," Rosa Ball interjected. "You will have to pay for what you need in gold."

Gerald's brow furrowed up again. "That's a considerable risk, carrying the entire budget in gold. We would need at least two men to guard it."

He looked at me. "I don't suppose . . ."

Victoria saw where Gerald was heading and she jumped on his bandwagon quicker than a politician at election time. "Oh, Charlie, do! Come with us!"

The Mexico idea had taken me by surprise. I was still catching up with how quick it had changed from being an idea into a fact. All I knew was, I wouldn't get a thing done here at home, wondering how the picture was going down in Sonora. Not with the Bunk House on the line. Besides, I had offered to help Brian with the story, and now I had an interest in making it both a good one and quick to film.

All eyes were on me. "I imagine Josefa can take care of the Bunk House for a while," I said. "I'll look after your gold."

"And I know just the man to help you!" Victoria exclaimed. She jumped to her feet, but I was just as quick.

"Now hold on there, girl!"

"He can shoot better than any man I ever saw, except maybe you."

"And you don't know a whole heck of a lot about him!"

We stood there nose to nose, the others forgotten.

"I know I trust him, Charlie Siringo." She was simmering just under the boiling point. "That's more than I can say for most men."

About then I started thinking like a detective. When you have lived among outlaws, pretending to be one of them, you learn to think fast. More than once, when I was within a whisker of being found out, only my quick wits had kept me alive. I knew if I fought Victoria over this, she would smell something rotten in Denmark. So I turned the tables on her.

"All right," I said. "He'll do, if he wants the job. It'll give me a chance to get to know him."

She was off and gone like a schoolgirl at recess, running across the sand, then stopping when she saw that Leroy was no longer with Karen and Nate and Redeye. That was when I too noticed his absence for the first time. I looked all around but couldn't spy him anywhere.

"Charles, who on earth . . . ?" It took Gerald a moment to imagine who we were talking about. "Not that drifter?"

"He's right for the job," I said. "Chances are we won't have any trouble down there anyway."

Gerald knew me well enough to trust my judgment in the matter, but he would have had a conniption if he knew who Mr. Leroy Roberts really was.

I wanted to go help Victoria find him, to see how he would react when he heard of our job offer, but before I could leave the table I found myself facing two officers of the law and five sheepish cowboys who were threatened with being slapped in the hoosegow for recklessly endangering the public safety of Santa Monica by discharging firearms within the city limits. As a former cowboy detective I have more than a passing acquaintance with the law and its minions, so I did my best to soothe the officers, and by the time they agreed to let our boys off with a stern warning, Victoria had found Leroy.

If I had known that Leroy was already aware I was Charlie Siringo, I wouldn't have given a Chinaman's chance for her persuading him to stay. But it was neither the first nor the last time that I underestimated her.

Leroy had carried water to his horse, all right, but he wasn't planning on coming back. When Victoria caught up with him he was tightening Sonny's latigo, getting set to mount up.

"Leroy!" she called out, and he turned. "We're going to Mexico!"

"Who's going to Mexico?" he wanted to know, without any hint of a smile.

Victoria noticed the change in him but she wasn't to be denied, not just when everything was going her way.

"We all are!" she told him. "We're going to make a movie in Sonora, at Rosa Ball's family's ranch. You said you were going to Mexico, didn't you?"

Leroy nodded. "I've got a friend down there. The last I heard of him he was in Chihuahua." Something about being around Victoria made him say more than he intended to.

"Well, you can go with us," Victoria announced, as if it were settled.

Leroy hauled on the latigo again, catching Sonny with his wind out. "I'll be going on ahead."

"You'll get there sooner with us. We're leaving by train in just a few days. You could help us make the picture and then find your friend. Chihuahua is right next door to Sonora."

Being a ranch girl, Victoria didn't think much of the distance involved. To her, Arizona is right next door to New Mexico, and if that means riding across a few hundred miles of sand and cactus, it's all in a day's work.

"I wouldn't be any use to you," Leroy said, fastening the cinch snugly to its ring. "I don't know the first thing about making pictures."

Victoria gave him a radiant smile. "You don't have to. You can help Charlie look after our gold."

That stopped him.

"What gold?"

"They won't take paper money down there. We'll pay for everything in gold."

Leroy chewed on that for a minute or two. "What does Charlie think about this?" he said at last.

"He said it would give him a chance to know you better."

Chapter 8

HAVING PROMISED TO be fully truthful in telling this story, I will admit that I had another reason for my decision to go to Mexico, one that had nothing to do with Leroy or Victoria or making moving pictures.

It was a chance for adventure.

Ever since I signed on to be a full-time cowboy at the tender age of eleven, I have had an itch to know what was over the next hill. Trailing beeves to Kansas soothed my restlessness for a while, and when my duties as LX trail boss took me to Chicago I felt that I was halfway round the world from my home. During my Pinkerton years I broadened my horizons further, chasing bad men from Alaska to Mexico and the hills of Kentucky, with whistle stops in New York City and Los Angeles and points in between. Once I settled in my Sunny Slope nest, if I ever felt confined all I had to do was saddle Jake and pick some piece of the wide lonesome to explore. But in the five months I had been in California, that old fenced-in feeling had crept up on me. Wearing out Jake's iron shoes may have quieted it for a day or two, but nothing makes an author squirm worse than losing a staring contest with his writing pad. The notion of a Mexican holiday suited me to a T.

Was I worried that I had hired a renowned outlaw to help me guard Gerald and Victoria's gold? You bet I was. And at the same time I was so pleased with myself I could hardly keep still for the few days it took Brian

Hill and Gerald to organize our supplies and get them loaded aboard a train for Douglas, Arizona, where we would cross the border. I had set up my own little forty-rod piece of excitement in one corner of our Mexican adventure and no one knew it but me. Or so I thought.

I will grant that I was behaving strangely for a former Pinkerton operative. I had a celebrated desperado in my sights. I had gone so far as to ascertain that he could still be prosecuted for his crimes, and I sat by while he prepared to leave the country. Not only sat by, but took a hand in his departure, you might say, by finding him employment for the journey. Once we crossed the border he would be beyond the reach of American law, and getting paid for it to boot.

By way of explanation I can only say that Leroy's crimes seemed like ancient history to me. The money he stole was long since spent. Any passing injury he did to those who had received his professional attention was long since healed by insurance settlements or new profits. Even society's interest in bringing criminals to the bar of justice as an example to others who were contemplating a career at similar pursuits was an empty concern in Leroy's case. His deeds were forgotten by most, his former way of life outdated by rapidly changing times.

By the time we boarded the train for Arizona I realized that I was moved by private concerns, not public ones. Finding Leroy alive and kicking in December 1919 was like coming upon Lazarus sprung fresh from the grave. It was a miracle of sorts, and I guess I was brash enough to think that a mischievous fate had arranged it for my benefit. If there was a purpose to bringing us together now, I wanted to stick around to learn what it was.

BETWEEN LOS ANGELES and Douglas there is a vast lot of dry country. Our company took over one entire passenger car, and for a time we all behaved like tourists, gawking at the passing landscape. But as we left the plots of cultivated land behind us and entered the desert regions where one mile looks very much like the next, most of the men and women became involved in conversations or card games, or took the opportunity to catch forty winks.

Not me. I kept my eyes glued to the window during the whole long day it took us to reach Douglas. To me each passing alkali flat or barrel cactus looked more familiar than the one before. I was going home to the wide open spaces that I loved. As we neared the border the setting sun cast long shadows across the low hills thinly covered with ocotillo and greasewood, and I was in seventh heaven.

We arrived in Douglas at dusk. Then our work began, for we were obliged to spend most of the night loading our outfit off one string of railroad cars and onto another one across the border in the Sonoran town of Agua Prieta. No American company would allow its rolling stock to enter Mexico for fear it would be appropriated by one revolutionary faction or another, or blown to Hades in the fighting. Sonora had been more or less peaceful since Villa's raid of 1915, but even so, we were compelled to transfer everything, lock, stock and barrel, onto ancient cars that bore faded symbols of the Santa Fe and the M. K. & T. and the Southern Pacific, and other American roads that had long ago judged them worn out and sold them to the Sonora line.

Along with our horses and film equipment, we had brought the wild west show wagons, while leaving the cattle and buffalo—the latter tribe still in mourning over the loss of its patriarch—behind. The wagons contained all the equipment and supplies necessary for making pictures and would also provide lodging for the crew while in Sonora. The cowboys and cowgirls preferred the accommodations they knew, however rustic, to the uncertainties of sleeping on the ground in the Mexican desert, which they imagined to be aswarm with hostile wildlife of the small variety.

Our work was performed under the round gaze of an all but full moon and the watchful eyes of American and Mexican border guards, who faced one another across a flimsy barb wire fence. The Mexicans were at first suspicious of such a large group of Americans, many of us armed now that we were entering a strife-torn land. But our papers were in order, and when the guards recognized Victoria as "Rosa Cimarrona," which is Mexican for Cimarron Rose, they dropped their reserve and helped us carry our belongings, and a few even asked for her autograph.

No one got any sleep, but one thing I'll say for the men and women in the picture business, they work like Texas cowboys and they keep at it until the work is done. Now and again you hear some nonsense about regular work hours and more pay for overtime, and other such frippery, but generally these notions get the horse laugh they deserve. A rancher or a farmer learns to make hay when the sun shines and the same attitude prevails in the picture business, both in the making of westerns and every other kind of film. On Victoria's crew they worked day or night, Sundays and holidays included, with a cheerful spirit, knowing that when the work was over there would be time enough to while away the hours in idle frolics.

Luke Fister and his Negro assistant, Hotcakes Talmadge, fixed us a late supper and an early breakfast right there in the rail yards, building fires in the open and cooking out of the outfit's chuckwagon as they would do while we were in Mexico. Luke is a New Mexico boy with a taste for border cuisine. I was pleased to notice a tangy warmth in the beans and eggs he served up just as the light grew bright in the east, although some of our cowboys from the northern states were obliged to reach quickly for orange juice or water to soothe their scorched tongues.

The line running south from Agua Prieta is a spur line built to serve the large cattle ranches along the western foothills of the Sierra Madre mountains. From Los Angeles to Douglas our boxcars and flatcars were attached to a passenger train, but in Mexico it was the other way around. Our sole passenger car became part of a small freight train consisting of three cattle cars hitched to those hauling our wagons and horses. Fortunately the passenger car—a Southern Pacific parlor car whose former splendor was now frayed at the edges—was placed ahead of the slat-sided cattle cars carrying our bovine traveling companions, and hence was upwind once we were under way.

Spirits were high as the train rolled out of Agua Prieta heading south. It rolled somewhat slower than the train that brought us to Douglas, and the ride was rougher than before, owing to the poor condition of the trackbed and the fact that some of the cars had wheels more square than round. But we were all excited to be in a foreign land, and before long some members of the band pulled out their instruments and struck up a tune, with Buddy Johnston chiming in on his saxophone.

Buddy had lost no time finding employment. In addition to playing with the band, his duties also called for helping out with props and sets, but he was a strong lad, not afraid of work, and pleased to find himself with an opportunity to play his horn and forget about the war.

His cohorts in the band were Bob Elderberg, Hotcakes Talmadge, Luke Fister, and Tommy Fear, playing fiddle, clarinet, banjo, and string bass respectively. They were joined by Charlie Noble, the rugged young actor who was to play the hero Tom's best pal. It was a part for which we needed someone almost as good-looking as Randall Steele, but not cast in the mold of a leading man. Charlie fit the bill perfectly with his blond hair and friendly smile. As it happened, he also played the ukulele proficiently, although we couldn't use that talent in the picture.

All in all, it was a fine little orchestra. Of course for the wild west shows there was a big bass drum and some brass horns, but the full band playing inside that railroad car would have deafened the lot of us, so the other musicians sat out this impromptu performance.

Randall Steele himself was seated near the musicians, tapping his elegantly booted foot to the music and smiling. Victoria had introduced me to the actor at the start of the journey. He was amiable enough, although in person he gave no hint of the dashing heroes he portrayed on the screen.

I was with some of the old-timers—Chief John and Willie Two Horse and Jack Whistler—halfway down the car. Working all night in the cool air had brought on a touch of my bronchitis and I was unable to stifle an occasional cough.

"Have a cough drop," said Chief John. He offered me a box of Smith

Brothers drops, which I accepted with alacrity. In no time the sweet lozenge silenced my cough and I sat back to enjoy the music more fully.

"He sucks on that candy like a baby at his mother's tit," Willie Two Horse observed.

"It's not candy, it's medicine," I said.

"Medicine's supposed to taste bad," Willie said. "Those cough drops, they're sweet like candy."

"That's on account of we gave all the bad-tasting medicine to the Indians and saved the sweet stuff for ourselves," said Jack Whistler.

Willie nodded. "That's just like a white man, keeping the best for himself."

"Have one." Chief John offered the box of drops to Willie, which was what Willie had been angling for all along. Willie took two, and sucked on them noisily.

Jack gave me a wink, as if to show how much he enjoyed this sort of banter. He knew Willie Two Horse's father, whose name was simply Two Horse, and it was through Jack that Willie, and Redeye Hawk as well, came to be with McQuain & Vickery. When the railroads pushed into Texas and ranch life no longer offered the excitement of the trail drives, Jack had left the LX Ranch and joined the army to seek adventure. He missed the last of the Indian fights by a whisker, but he learned the sign language and a few Indian dialects, and he had many occasions to interpret for his superior officers, often in the hide teepees of Indian camps.

A stranger meeting Jack for the first time might have taken him for Kit Carson's ghost, or maybe Bill Cody's younger brother. He had the deepset eyes of people who have looked across broad prairies for generations. His tall, lean frame and military bearing gave him an air of nobility—if cowboy nobility were not a contradiction in terms—an impression that was reinforced by his aquiline nose, neatly clipped mustache and chin whiskers, and mane of swept-back gray hair. In the absence of Walt Vickery and Jim McQuain, he was the straw boss of the wild west show. He might easily have been the show's master of ceremonies as well, but there was little of the showman in Jack. Underneath his impressive looks and military bearing, he was still the unassuming west Texas cowboy I knew so long ago, happy, now as then, to be working among good friends.

Willie was holding the box of cough drops up before him, inspecting the likeness of the Smith Brothers depicted there.

"Are these men any relation to President Grant?" he asked.

"Not as I know of," Jack said.

"They look like him," Willie said. "President Grant, he tried to sweettalk the Sioux out of the Black Hills. He'd of done better to offer us a bunch of these cough drops." He took another drop and tossed the box back to Chief John.

Soothed by the little band's lullabies and the sound of the train's wheels, I tilted my hat over my eyes and went to sleep. I awoke greatly refreshed at midday to find the band still playing, the windows open to the air, and the train winding its way along a lush green river bottom.

Jack and Willie and John were all looking at me curiously.

"I didn't know you to be such a napper, Charlie," Jack said.

"Old white men, they need a lot of sleep," Willie said.

Chief John snorted. "Fine thing if somebody walks off with our gold when he's takin' a snooze."

I glanced around and I noticed two things right off. Our gold was fine, but Leroy was gone. I knew John wanted me to show where the gold was hid, but I was too clever for him. I kept my head and eyes moving until I had looked all around the car before I said, "They ain't walked off with it yet."

The gold was in a strongbox hidden within a trunk full of Victoria's costumes. I wanted that trunk within sight at all times, hence my making sure it was loaded into the parlor car along with many other pieces of personal luggage, instead of in the boxcars with the rest of the baggage. Being too large for the overhead racks, the trunk was placed in the aisle. Victoria was sitting on it now, to be close to the music.

Confident that the gold was safe for the time being, I went in search of Leroy. I had glimpsed him often in the rail yards at Douglas, and noticed that he was quick to lend a hand where it was needed. It had crossed my mind that he might saddle Sonny and slip away in the confusion once he was safely past the Mexican border guards. But my detective's nose was calm, with nary a twitch of suspicion, and when we piled aboard the parlor car he took a seat with Redeye and Nate and Karen.

Now, I found him easily enough. As soon as I stepped out on the parlor car's forward platform I saw a pair of legs swinging from the roof overhead. I leaned out over the iron guardrail and looked up. Leroy was sitting atop the car, apparently having a grand time.

"Riding the iron horse?" I inquired, shouting to make myself heard over the clatter of the wheels. The train was making all of about fifteen miles an hour.

Leroy climbed down to the platform. "Just looking over the country-side, Charlie. You get a good view from the top of a train." He peered through the window in the car door. "Who's watching our gold?"

"Victoria's sitting on it."

We leaned on the iron railing and watched the scenery roll by. The train was climbing out of the green river bottom. As it left the watercourse we entered a landscape much like the Arizona desert we had seen the day before, but knowing it was Mexico made it foreign and therefore more interesting.

Leroy wore a bit of a smile. It struck me that he seemed like a man perfectly at peace. In California there had been something guarded about his manner, but now his guard was down.

"I notice you don't carry a gun," I observed as if passing the time of day.

He lifted his pants leg and pulled a Remington over-under derringer out of his boot, offering it for my inspection. I hefted it and gave it back.

"You'll need more than that if some bandido decides to lift our gold," I said.

"I've got a .44 in my bedroll."

"Might be a good idea if you were to wear it once we get where we're going," I said. "Victoria tells me you know how to use it. She says you shot a tomahawk out of Redeye's hand the day you showed up."

Leroy shrugged. "It was a lucky shot."

I pulled my own Peacemaker from the Wes Hardin shoulder scabbard I use when I don't want to be too obvious about my artillery. The piece of Mr. Colt's hardware I carry is a silver-plated, pearl-handled example in size .45. I generally don't carry it in California, but I put the shoulder rig on before we reached Douglas and was already accustomed to the weight again, after less than a day.

Leroy hefted the Peacemaker, sighted along the barrel, pulled the hammer back and lowered it gently back into place, handling the weapon in the manner of a man who has lived with guns since childhood.

"A moving target makes it kind of interesting," I suggested. "How about that cactus?"

I pointed to a young saguaro about the size of a small dog sitting upright, maybe fifty yards from the tracks.

Moving as if he had all the time in the world, Leroy held the sixshooter out at arm's length and fired. A hole the size of a fist appeared in the cactus. He passed the gun to me.

Early in my detective career I once hit a coyote at a hundred yards from a moving stagecoach, impressing my traveling companions considerably and astonishing the poor coyote, but I knew it was a lucky shot. At half the distance, still a fair piece to a moving target, luck had no part in Leroy's marksmanship. I wasn't certain I could do as well.

"That one," I said, aiming at a smaller cactus equally far away. I pulled the trigger and a notch flew out of the edge of the cactus. Not bad for an old man. Feeling my oats, I handed the gun back to Leroy, leaving it to him to pick his next target.

The car door opened and Brian Hill looked out, his eyes wide with alarm. "Mr. Siringo? What's going on?" Behind him some others were gathered, peering around him, trying to see what the excitement was.

"It's all right," I told him. "We're just having a little target practice."

Leroy took aim, I wasn't sure at what. At the sound of his shot, an undernourished palo verde bush toppled over, cut off cleanly just above the ground. I suppose it might have been an inch thick at the base, but I'm a generous fellow and may be fattening it up a bit.

"Lucky shot?" I inquired. Leroy shrugged as if to say maybe so, maybe not.

On the occasion of my long and fatal shot at Mr. Coyote, I had to follow up with a further demonstration of marksmanship to prove that the first shot wasn't just luck. This took place at my destination, where I knocked a knot out of a pine fence at fifty yards. Now I had to prove myself again, but here I couldn't wait until my feet were on solid ground.

I took aim at a rock the size of a fist, maybe a little closer than Leroy's palo verde, and fired. The rock jumped as if stung by a scorpion.

"Bravo, Mr. Siringo," Brian exclaimed. Hearing the sound of applause, I leaned out and saw that many of the picture company were watching from the windows of the car. I stowed my pearl-handled Peacemaker, content to rest on my laurels.

"We're a pretty good match," I offered.

"Yup," Leroy agreed. "Any rough-looking hombres give us the eye, we'll just blow up some rocks and cactus and scare the bejesus out of them."

Seeing that the show was over, Brian and the other gawkers withdrew from the doorway, leaving the two of us alone once more on the platform.

"You been down here before." I said it only half as a question. It was time to get down to business.

"A few times. They're easygoing people."

"Not so easygoing for the past ten years."

"The way I see it, the revolution's about run out of steam."

"That's not how the newspapers tell it," I said.

Leroy shook his head. "The border squabbles have been going on forever and that Jenkins deal's got nothing to do with the revolution. All this hooraw now is just politicians shouting at each other over the back fence. The revolution, that's another story. It's long and sad."

"After thirty years of Porfirio Díaz, the Mexican people were ready for anything else," I said.

"And they got it."

"Madero was all right."

"He didn't have the gumption to keep the hotheads in line and the sense to shoot Huerta before Huerta filled him with lead."

"And Huerta was worse than Díaz," I said.

I was surprised to find Leroy so savvy in political matters. In few words we had summed up years of death and chaos. Reduced to its essentials the balance of the revolution, up to the present day, could be put almost as simply. As soon as Victoriano Huerta took power, he found himself fighting Obregón, Carranza, Zapata and Villa all at once. Huerta held out for just over a year, then decided his health would improve in some other climate. After a few more years, Carranza and Obregón saw that none of the revolutionist factions was likely to win out on its own, so the two men made a back-room deal that gave Carranza the presidency with Obregón's support and left Zapata and Villa out in the cold. Zapata held out in the southern mountains until Carranza got someone to shoot him in the back. But the new president couldn't get near Villa. In his home state of Chihuahua, Villa was untouchable.

"You planning on staying down here for a time, are you?" I asked, turning the talk away from politics.

Leroy gave me a pleasant smile. "What happened to that old cowboy who didn't ask a man where he was going or where he came from?"

"Well, I'll tell you. I set to chasing cows when I was eleven years old and I kept at it until I was a young man. Then I switched jobs and took to chasing men. I don't know if you heard, but I used to work for Pinkerton's."

Leroy nodded. "Charlie Siringo's a name that got around, not too long ago."

That added an inch or two to my height. "Twenty-two years chasing men. Asking questions was a big part of the job. It's a bad habit, I guess."

"You chasing someone now?"

"Oh, I'm retired and plan to stay that way. Most of the men I chased are long dead, anyhow. But now and again I hear something about one of the ones that gave me the slip. It gets my blood up. Sometimes I poke around and find out what I can."

I was throwing my cards on the table one at a time, face up, and it felt good. Not so long ago, my work as a New Mexico Ranger had taken me through this same country in pursuit of rustlers who ventured north of the border to steal fat American cattle. Being back in Sonora brought me alive again. I was standing as tall as my wiry Texas frame would allow, I had a Colt's revolver nestling snugly beneath my left arm, and I was ready for anything.

"I read that book of yours, about being a detective," Leroy said. "Not too many men got away from you."

"Not too many," I agreed. I had never for a moment imagined the man beside me turning the pages of *A Cowboy Detective*. But who would have more interest in reading it than my most notorious quarry, after all, to see what I wrote about him?

"It did happen I'd get called off a case now and again," I said. "Toward the end there, a good number of the cowboy outlaws left the country. Mostly I didn't mind. I was doing a job. I didn't have anything personal against the men I was chasing. But there were some I took a special interest in. The fellows who made the chase interesting. The one that interested me the most, I never set eyes on. That was Butch Cassidy."

Someone without my detective experience might not have noticed how my saying that name caused Leroy to freeze up like a statue. Up came his guard again, but he recovered himself quickly, whereupon I drew a folded paper from inside my coat and handed it to him.

He appeared calm enough as he unfolded the paper and looked it over. As he read it, I saw it in my mind's eye. It was the Pinkerton wanted flier that had adorned my office wall until a few days ago. I knew most of the words by heart, having read and reread them a dozen times since then.

The flier offered a four-thousand-dollar reward for apprehension of the bandits who robbed the First National Bank of Winnemucca, Nevada, on September 19th, 1900. The first name listed was "George Parker, alias 'Butch' Cassidy, alias George Cassidy, alias Ingerfield." The other men were O. C. Hanks and Harry Longabaugh.

Included on the flier were two photographs of Butch, one of Longabaugh—who was called the Sundance Kid, for having been jailed in Sundance, Wyoming, at a tender age—and one of Hanks.

At the bottom of the page I had scrawled in my own hand, "Butch rumored killed with SK in Bolivia, 1908," and the further notation, "(Not confirmed)." For lack of room I hadn't written the other reports of how Butch supposedly died in Green River, Wyoming, in 1906, or in Argentina in 1911, or how one Pinkerton informant had been certain he was in jail in Chile as late as 1913.

I handed Leroy another item about the size of a postcard. It was a photographic copy of Butch's identification card from the Wyoming State Penitentiary, written up when he entered that forbidding institution in July of 1894 to begin his one and only prison term.

"This one's got the name right," I said. "It's the best description, too."

There has been so much confusion over Butch Cassidy's real name that some of it persists to the present day. Most of the fliers and posters, even in the Pinkerton files, give his true name as George Parker, owing to his having used both that name and George Cassidy as aliases at various times. But the penitentiary records were accurate. "Name: Geo. Cassidy, alias Butch Cassidy, alias Ingerfield, right name Robt. Parker." It went on to say he was five feet nine inches, a hundred and sixty-five pounds, with light complexion, flaxen hair, and blue eyes.

The height understated Leroy's by an inch or more, but that was common on prison records. A man entering prison does not stand up straight and tall when he's being measured for a set of prison stripes. The rest of the details fit Leroy Roberts to a T. Even the graying of his sandy hair changed his appearance far less than would have been the case with a dark-haired man.

"If you read my book, you know most of it," I said. "I got put on his case right after the Wild Bunch held up the Union Pacific at Wilcox, Wyoming. June of '99, that was. I stayed on the job for almost four years, chasing Butch and the gang. The whole time I never set eyes on him. He had a nose for trouble sneaking up on him."

Leroy's eyes moved from the card back to the flier. "It says here Butch got himself killed in South America."

"Maybe. Him and the Sundance Kid both, some tell it. But no lawman ever saw the bodies. You follow those stories, they all go back to an American mining engineer named Percy Seibert. He knew Butch and the Kid in Bolivia and I guess he liked them, by what I hear. Some Bolivian soldiers showed Percy a couple of dead Americans and he said 'That's them, all right.' Of course, there were quite a few Americans down there pulling robberies. Some others from the Hole-in-the-Wall crowd."

Leroy looked over the flier once more before refolding it and handing it back to me along with the card. "You think this Seibert made a mistake?"

"Not exactly. He knew Butch and the Kid wanted more than anything to leave their outlaw ways behind. Best thing in the world for them would be if everybody thought they were dead."

The engineer let out a couple of toots on his steam whistle. A moment later we passed two shepherds and a dog holding their flock in a bunch. The dog was standing guard between the sheep and the train so none of the stupid creatures would run over to throw themselves beneath the wheels.

Leroy leaned over the platform railing, looking forward along the train. "It's a nice train," he said.

"You like trains, do you?"

"Always did. It's not the Denver & Rio Grande, but it'll do."

"Old Butch, he had a fondness for trains," I said. "Trains and banks."

I was like a dog with a bone, unwilling to let it go until I chewed on it just a while longer.

Leroy grew serious again, and I was sorry I had distracted him from his boyish enjoyment of the train. There was something about the way he delighted in everyday things that made it a pleasure to be in his company.

"Suppose you're right about this Seibert," he said. "How come we haven't heard anything about Butch in all these years?"

"Oh, I imagine he's been holed up somewhere, going by a different name. If he stayed out of trouble he might make a new start for himself."

"He'd be a fool to go looking for trouble," Leroy said thoughtfully.

"And he wouldn't want to use anything too close to his own name."

Leroy leaned on the railing, his face not only serious but maybe a bit tired. "Unless he figured no one would give a thought to Robert Leroy Parker nowadays. Or unless maybe he was just worn-out going by names that didn't sound anything like his own."

Some may think it strange how we continued to refer to Butch this way, like a third party not present, but it seemed natural to me. Leroy had scarcely spoken that other name for more than ten years. He had trained himself not to speak it. Leroy Roberts was close enough for now.

The train had strayed a mile or so from the tropical lushness of the river bottom and was traveling now across a broad reach of grassland.

"Good cattle country," I said.

Leroy nodded, but remained silent.

"You really read my book?" I tried to imagine him in a rocking chair by a reading lamp, chuckling to himself at how he had outwitted me.

"Two of them," he said. "*A Cowboy Detective* and that other one about you growing up in Texas. I liked that one better. I grew up on a horse myself."

"Victoria said we had a lot in common."

We watched the country slide by.

"I've been down here a couple of dozen times over the years," I said, musing over the memories. "Always on some kind of job. The last time, I was a New Mexico Ranger. Before that it was Pinkerton business, always chasing some bad hombre or other."

"A Pinkerton's got no authority in Mexico," Leroy observed.

"Never had any, never needed any," I said. "I'd watch my man, wait for him to get tired of beans and tequila. When he went home, I'd have the law waiting."

It occurred to me that he might take this personally, which was not my intention. "I'm going to enjoy this trip, not having that kind of worry."

That was where I was headed from the start, although I hadn't known it until I got there. I had no quarrel with this man. From the moment we met I had taken a liking to him. Having him show up at the Bunk House shook me out of my writer's doldrums and set my life in motion. Now here we were launched on a Mexican adventure. Best of all, I was working at something like my old detective's trade, guarding Gerald's gold. With scarcely any effort on my part, it was as if I had found a way to step back in time and take Leroy with me, not as a quarry to chase, but as someone who shared my experiences from the olden times and understood them.

I had been holding the flier in my hand while we talked, but now I tucked it back into the inside pocket of my jacket.

"Those outlaws you chased down here," Leroy said. "If a man didn't figure on going back to the States, he'd have nothing to fear from you or the law."

"That's true," I said. "Of course if a man wronged me or someone I cared for, that would be a personal matter."

I was not so foolish as to forget that his chosen profession had been lifting other people's gold, not guarding it. So long as we were working together, I intended to keep him on a close rein. But my mild warning did nothing to disturb Leroy's calm. He continued to watch the passing country like a tourist who had never set eyes on it before, smiling slightly as if he hadn't a care in the world.

"Siringo, that's Italian, isn't it?" he said after a time, taking me by surprise. "Didn't you say in one of those books that your father was Italian?"

"That's right. He died when I was a baby."

"I was in Italy once."

That surprised me even more.

"I liked the Italians," he said. "They're friendly people."

"So I've heard," I said. "But then I'm not Italian myself. I'm a Texan."

Chapter 9

AS WILL HAPPEN when friends are confined together on a long journey, people moved about often during the day. When Leroy and I reentered the car the band had quit playing for the time being. Redeye was in my former seat, Jack Whistler having gone to sit with Bob Elderberg, the show's head wrangler. Chief John was at the far end of the car with Nate and Karen, and Willie Two Horse had crossed the aisle to sit with his wife Anna, so Redeye and I were alone.

"Hey, Charlie, pull up a chair," he greeted me, as Leroy continued along the crowded aisle.

"I knew the two of you would get along," Redeye said. "I'll bet he was tickled pink when you hired him on for the picture. You should have seen how he sat up and took notice that day at the beach, when he heard who you were."

I felt as if I had been hit in the chest. My heart missed a beat, and it took me a moment to figure out why Redeye's news jolted me so badly. From the minute I recognized Leroy I thought I held all the cards. Finding that he held a full house to my straight disabused me of that notion in a hurry.

"You told him who I was?" My tone was accusing, as if Redeye had given away a sworn secret, and he was taken aback.

"Well, I think it was Nate mentioned it. Something about how Charlie

Siringo sure dresses up like Sunday-go-to-meeting for a picnic at the beach. He didn't mean nothing by it."

"No, son, I'm sure he didn't. Excuse me."

I left him abruptly and made my way to where Victoria was sitting with Brian Hill. I told Brian I would like a word with Victoria, and being a polite lad he left us alone without resenting the interruption. Not far away, Leroy was laughing and joking with Karen and Nate and Chief John, seemingly unconcerned over what had passed between us.

"Last Sunday at the beach," I said, "where was Leroy when you found him?"

The question surprised Victoria. "Near the road, where the horses were tied up. Why?"

"What was he doing?"

"He was getting ready to leave. He said he had to get down to Mexico to find some friend of his. Charlie, what's this about?"

"Did he look spooked to you?"

Victoria thought for a moment, regarding me quizzically. "I suppose he may have, now that you mention it. It was odd the way he left in the middle of everything."

But he hadn't left! He had started to run and then changed his mind. He knew who I was and still he had agreed to take this job when Victoria offered it to him!

That really set my thoughts to dancing. Out on the car platform, he had said, "Charlie Siringo's a name that got around, not so long ago." I didn't know when he had learned my full name, but I imagined it was sometime after we hired him on to guard Gerald's gold. By then we were all on our way to Mexico anyway, and he had little to risk by staying around. Probably he figured I hadn't made him out. It never crossed my mind that he might have known who I was earlier, when he was still within the reach of American law.

Why had he stayed?

"Charlie?" Victoria was looking at me as if she could see the wheels turning in my head. I had aroused her curiosity by being direct, but there was no help for that.

"I'll tell you all about it. Not right away, but I'll tell you."

"I'll hold you to that."

She knew there was no use badgering me with questions while I was working something out, so she rested her head against the stained antimacassar and closed her eyes, leaving me with my thoughts. I picked up a Los Angeles *Evening Herald* someone had left on the seat across the aisle, but catching up on the news was the last thing on my mind.

Knowing I was Charlie Siringo, why had Leroy stuck around?

This time, as soon as I asked myself the question I knew the answer. Back when he was a notorious outlaw and I was a cowboy detective, he had heard me baying over his scent for four long years, while I had known him only by the fleeting trail he left here and there. Running across him now, I had imagined myself the clever bloodhound overtaking his old quarry the bobcat at last, catching him unawares, when the truer picture was the hound and bobcat stock-still in their tracks, taking the measure of each other across some forest glade while we decided which way to jump.

Leroy was just as fascinated to meet me as I was to meet him. And it stood to reason. No doubt he had wondered what sort of fellow I was to stick so doggedly to his trail, while I wanted to know the nature of the man who could stay one jump ahead of me and always out of sight.

Back at the turn of the century, Leroy and his boys had a head start on all the Pinkerton hounds, but now I had the jump on him. And although he had read my books about my cowboy youth and the detective's adventures that followed, I fancied that I knew just as much about him, at least the parts that counted, for I had studied my first lessons about Robert Leroy Parker in his hometown, and my teacher was his own sister.

FOR SOME MONTHS when I was first on the Wild Bunch case, I was certain it was wild geese I was chasing, not flesh and blood cowboy bandits.

At the start, my partner W. O. Sayles and I were on a trail hot enough to scorch the soles of our boots. We were close behind "Kid Curry" himself as he and another man pushed a bunch of the gang's horses down into Utah after the robbery of the Union Pacific Railway at Wilcox, which was the outrage that moved the American Bankers Association and the railroads to hire Pinkerton's National Detective Agency to break up the Wild Bunch.

Sayles and I had a good tip that Curry and his pal had forded the Colorado at Dandy Crossing, in the southeastern part of Utah, but we let the trail go cold as a result of following instructions from our regional office in Denver to proceed on horseback to the Indian reservation at Fort Duchesne. There we would receive "new information" that would aid us in our pursuit, or so we were told. Of course the "information" proved useless, and I learned never to abandon fresh tracks for telegraphed promises from Denver.

Next, we were sent in opposite directions on money trails. Once a band of highwaymen went to ground, there was no surer way of tracking them down than by following the trail of stolen money as they spent it. In the following months I traveled thousands of miles, most of it on horseback, first to Dodge City and thence to points farther south and east, until I became acquainted with the lower reaches of the great Mississippi

River where it flows broad and deep, and where Negroes are thicker than flies on a syrup keg in August, but there the trail petered out.

On returning from the South I was sent to Montana, where I got in with a man named Jim Thompson. He accepted my story of being Charles L. Carter, a Texas cowpuncher turned outlaw, and introduced me as such to some shady characters on the fringes of the Wild Bunch. In time my acquaintance with these men led me so close to Butch Cassidy himself that I could breathe his dust before it had time to settle, but before that day I had other false trails to follow. It was not until the gang struck again, first hitting the Union Pacific once more, this time at Tipton, Wyoming, and then robbing the bank at Winnemucca, Nevada, just three weeks later, that my luck changed. Following those daring holdups I was sent to southern Utah, where Butch Cassidy was born, and within a short time I knew more about him than all the other Wild Bunch wrong-doers put together.

Butch's sister Lula Parker was the assistant postmistress in Circleville at the time. She was a pretty thing, and I had to work hard not to fall in love with her. I remembered a broken heart I had left behind me in Nashville, Tennessee, a town with more pretty girls to the square inch than I had ever seen before, and I vowed to do right by Miss Lula, who was a respectable girl, not one of the sporting house crowd I was more accustomed to.

I introduced myself by my most recent alias, Charles L. Carter, but for Miss Lula's benefit I made myself out to be a cowboy on the chuckline, with maybe a shady spot or two in his past. This story struck a note with pretty Miss Lula. In no time she poured out her heart to me, telling all about her brother Bob, as she called him. It was only his brothers and sisters who used that name, she explained. His parents had addressed their eldest son as Leroy, while outside the family he was known as Roy. Thus at an early age he got used to going by many names, a practice he expanded upon in later years.

Bob was named for his grandfathers, both of whom were Robert. He came into the world on the 13th of April, 1866, a Friday, and was the first child of a large Mormon brood, thirteen in all when the counting was done. Those who are superstitious may wish to attach some significance to these facts. I merely pass them along as they were told to me.

Bob's father, Maximillian, worked hard to make a go of farming and ranching. As the oldest boy, Bob toiled by his side. By Lula's account he was a cheerful and hardworking lad raised in the bosom of a loving, religious family, but that didn't save him from getting a black mark against his name at an early age.

One day, in need of new overalls, Bob went into town, only to find the general store shut up tight. Not wishing to make another trip, he let himself into the store, took a pair of overalls and left a note promising to pay for them the next time he came to town. All over the West such a written IOU was as good as money in the bank, but for some reason the storekeeper was not a trusting soul. He swore out a complaint, which resulted in the sheriff paying a visit to the Parker ranch. Bob did not go to jail, for the sheriff was more understanding than the merchant, but in Lula's view this injustice gave Bob his first push toward the outlaw trail.

Another injustice had farther reaching consequences for Bob and the whole Parker family. In the hope of improving his fortunes, Max Parker homesteaded a second parcel of land, but the title to the land was disputed by another farmer. Miss Lula said straight out that the Parker claim was jumped. As was customary in such matters, the local bishop was called upon to resolve the difference of opinion.

It might be well to say here, for those unfamiliar with Mormondom and its ways, that in Utah as in few other places in these United States, the arm of the church has a long reach. In pioneer days the bishops had some authority in lay matters, in the absence of civil courts, including the power to adjudicate land disputes. In the matter of the Parker homesteads, the bishop ruled against the Parkers.

Miss Lula grew vehement in recounting the affair to me, asserting that the bishop's decision was made not on the merits of the case but on matters of religion. Although Bob and Lula's mother Annie was devout, their father was a "jack" Mormon, less respectful of the church and its dictates than the other farmer. As a Lancashire lad, Max had been compelled to polish the boots of the Mormon missionaries who visited his father, who was even then important in the church. Young Max despised this task, and once in Utah he chafed under the ever-present authority of the church in its new Zion. Perhaps the western notions of a man's freedom and independence strengthened his resentment. But whatever its cause, Miss Lula was certain that the Circleville bishop's decision in the land dispute was intended to punish her father for his erring ways, just as she was certain that some of Max's irreverent attitude toward the church rubbed off on his firstborn son.

With the second homestead lost, many of the Parkers were forced to take jobs to make ends meet. Bob went to work as a cowboy on a neighbor's ranch. There he learned to resent the men Miss Lula called the "greedy land barons" over near Parowan, big ranchers who knew many tricks that made life miserable for the small outfits. And there he met a carefree cowboy named Mike Cassidy. It was Mike who taught young Bob to ride and rope and shoot, how to care for horses and cattle. He gave Bob a pistol and a saddle, and Bob idolized him. And it's just possible that

Mike passed on some tips about rustling too, lessons that Bob applied later in his life.

Here I am reading between the lines of Miss Lula's story. She admitted that some said Mike Cassidy was a two-bit outlaw, but she thought the world of her big brother Bob and she wouldn't hear a word said against the Parkers' ranching neighbors. To her, any "rustling" done was no more than a case of small ranchers whose beef had strayed onto the land of the powerful land barons trying to get their animals back and being falsely accused of stealing. At worst, there might have been a little mavericking going on.

In my own cowboy youth, mavericking—the branding of unbranded animals—was a respectable occupation. Many of Texas's foremost ranches were begun by mavericking on a grand scale after the end of the Rebellion, when five years' increase of wild longhorns were roaming the coastal plains of Texas all as unmarked as the day they were born. I worked for Shanghai Pierce in those days and can testify from personal knowledge that his Rancho Grande would have raised nothing taller than grass if he had been made to show a bill of sale for his stock, which was bought and paid for with nothing more substantial than the long ropes and hot irons wielded by us cowboys. Even to the turn of the century and beyond, most westerners distinguished between mavericking and rustling, applying the latter term only when branded stock was run off for profit. Recently, however, even the long-honored practice of a hungry man killing any handy steer, branded or not, is frowned upon, and men have been put in jail for trying to feed themselves in this manner.

But in the old days as in modern times, once a man had his brand on an animal he did his best to keep that critter to himself. If he was a big rancher, that sometimes meant using fair means or foul to keep the little fellows from living off his herds. In some cases, such as the notorious Johnson County War in Wyoming, the big ranchers sought to drive the little ranchers out of the country altogether, and never dreamed of calling it rustling when they stole a poor man's stock in broad daylight.

There in Circleville in the autumn of 1900, it was not my job to determine whether the Parowan ranchers bent the law to their own purpose, although I knew full well that large landowners often had the law in their pockets. What interested me was the fact that young Bob Parker signed an affidavit saying he had branded some steers claimed by the Parowan land barons. Miss Lula said he did it because those who were truly at fault were married men with homes and families in the Circle Valley. Bob didn't want his friends' lives ruined over a few contested steers, she said, so he took the blame on himself and left the country.

To hear Lula tell it, her brother was pushed to the wrong by the injustices of the world. I had heard such tales before, some told by the most callous outlaws of that day and age, but I must admit that my heart began to soften toward Bob Parker as I saw for myself the love his sister had for him and learned firsthand the good opinion he had left behind among his neighbors in the Circle Valley. Everyone I talked to—the many friends and relatives I chanced to meet in Miss Lula's company—spoke repeatedly of Bob's good nature, his ready smile, and his willingness to help others no matter the cost to himself. These feelings were expressed so often and with such sincerity that I could not discount them as an attempt to whitewash a wayward youth. After all, these people had no idea I was a detective. They saw me as a wandering cowpuncher much like Bob, and it was Miss Lula, not I, who called on their memories of her brother.

Later, I heard many other stories about Lula's brother and the outlaw he became, and except for those told by "greedy land barons" and others who found their chickens plucked by Butch Cassidy's nimble hands, the stories reflected favorably on him. From the start of his life he had been given cause to believe that the rich and powerful cared nothing at all for the fate of the small and weak, and so in his own way he championed the cause of the underdog, earning from that class of men an enduring loyalty.

Of course when I was in Circleville, Butch Cassidy was a name known far and wide. Both his parents were living then, although I did not meet them, and Miss Lula was well aware that Bob had taken Mike Cassidy's last name in order not to cast shame upon his family.

"I know Bob looked up to Mike Cassidy," she told me on the day I bid her adieu and prepared to leave Circleville behind. "And it may be that knowing Mike helped turn Bob toward the bad. But I have never been able to find it in my heart to blame Mike. He left the country before that rustling business came up, you know. Bob wanted to go with him in the worst way, but Mike wouldn't hear of it. 'You're too good a kid to go where I'm going,' he said. 'The place for you is here on the farm.' So you see, that outlaw drifter did more to try and help Bob than his own friends who lived right here in the valley. They let him run away from home to take the blame for them. It broke our mother's heart."

That was not the first time I had heard proof that the cowboy outlaws had a code of their own, nor was it the last. In the years after my Circleville visit, I heard stories time and again of how Butch Cassidy warned many a starry-eyed boy to stay away from the crooked back trails he himself had chosen to ride despite Mike Cassidy's advice. He and his kind were loyal to one another and would risk everything to help a friend, and all in all they were a better breed of men than the low class of modern-day holdups, who kill without warning and make their getaways in motorcars.

I looked up from my newspaper, curious once more to see Lula's brother Bob as he looked now.

"It's him, isn't it?" Victoria was awake beside me. "Whatever you were trying to figure out has something to do with him."

"Leroy? I scarcely know him."

This seemed to satisfy her, perhaps because she sensed that I spoke the truth. For all I had learned about Leroy back in my detective days, there was much more to know. I wanted to know it all, especially the tricks he had used to escape my clutches. And he had been aware of me, just as I had known of him. More than once, when I was going by one of my outlaw names, I heard talk of Charlie Siringo, and how he just wouldn't let Butch and the Wild Bunch alone. I would listen to the plans they had for me if they ever got hold of me, and I would put in a few ideas of my own about what to do with Siringo, just to be one of the boys.

Now here we were at last with a chance to see that the other was no more than flesh and blood after all. Leroy's staying around once he knew who I was proved that he was just as curious about me as I was about him.

As I emerged from these cogitations, I noticed that Leroy was watching me with a look of amusement. I realized that I had not turned a page of my newspaper for some time, so I busied myself with searching for some item of interest, and on the very next page I discovered a report which rumored that Pancho Villa had been taken prisoner by his own men and might be turned over to the Carranza commander at Parral, Chihuahua, for the "standing reward" of fifty thousand pesos. I read the item to Victoria, feigning to be unaware of Leroy's scrutiny.

"If Villa is captured," Victoria said, "that means the revolution would be over, doesn't it?"

"All but the shouting," I said.

"Good," she said. "We won't have to listen to Gerald fretting about bandits and revolutionaries."

With that, she returned to her napping while I glanced through the paper for other news of the Mexican situation. Senator Fall was calling for a break in diplomatic relations with Mexico over the Jenkins affair, while Jenkins himself had said that while he had no wish to stir up trouble between the two countries, he would "like to help string up a few of the 'greasers' who have been active in persecuting him," as the paper put it, which remark was scarcely likely to promote peace and understanding. I was further unsettled to see a report that Carranza was buying arms and ammunition from Spain, and another warning that American citizens were being warned to leave the troubled regions of northern Mexico. I decided to keep these items to myself, judging that Victoria would work better without worrying about Mexican politics.

The next headline I saw put Mexican politics clean out of my head. "Train Robber Carlisle Captured," it said. In recent years, Bill Carlisle, a lone bandit, had been keeping the Old West alive by robbing trains and banks in the former stomping grounds of the Wild Bunch. He was imprisoned for a time, but escaped, and now it appeared that his bandit days were done. He was in the hospital in Douglas, Wyoming, having been shot by the deputies who captured him.

"He may live," the article said, *"but his injuries are very painful. Carlisle's capture was effected yesterday by a small posse led by Sheriff Roach of Platte County, in the mountain cabin of Frank Williams near Estabrook, in the Laramie Peak region, about eighty miles from the scene of his last holdup.*

"The career of the daring bandit has been spectacular since his entry into the West nearly four years ago. His versatility ranged from train robbery without harm to passengers, to doing fancy needlework and leading Liberty Loan campaigns among prisoners while he was in jail. In his whole career as a bandit, he has never shed human blood and he has always been courteous to women and old men and kind to children. For this reason hundreds of citizens of Wyoming and Colorado have been inclined to sympathize with Carlisle in his efforts to escape the law."

It struck me that except for the parts about needlework and Liberty Loans, every word of that last paragraph might have been said twenty years earlier about the man who was sitting not ten feet away from me now.

I found myself looking forward to the coming weeks. It had occurred to me more than once, in the old days, that despite being on opposite sides of the law our lives were much alike. We both went by false names and sought to avoid being found out by the wrong man at the wrong time. We both knew that a misstep could cost us our lives. Now, while Brian and Victoria made their picture, we would have time enough to tell our stories, perhaps even to share some good laughs about our escapades back when I was the hound and he the bobcat.

Chapter 10

FROM AGUA PRIETA to our destination was scarcely a hundred miles, but our little train took nearly all day to cover that distance, due in part to long stops at Fronteras and Esqueda and the other towns along the way, where various articles were loaded on or off the train, and in part to the fact that the revolution had turned the nation's attention away from such tedious chores as maintaining the railroads.

We arrived in the little town of Delgado late in the afternoon and at once set about unloading our belongings from the train and getting ourselves settled for what promised to be a month of fun in the sun, before that sun took his leave for the day.

Delgado was a hacienda town like many I had seen before on my travels into Old Mexico for William and Robert Pinkerton. The hacienda itself was situated above the town at the edge of a broad plateau that stretched away to the eastern mountains, changing from desert to grassland as it rose gently to meet the foothills. Just west of the hacienda the plateau ended abruptly, dropping in a series of steps to the green river valley our train had followed for most of the journey. The town and the railroad were on the first and broadest of these steps, or benches, which was a few hundred yards wide. Across the river the land rose more slowly to the next range of mountains twenty miles to the west.

The town sported only two proper streets, one parallel to the tracks, the other perpendicular to the first, extending from the whitewashed railroad station to the central *plaza*. Together these avenues formed a large T, with the station at the juncture. Small houses, also bright with fresh coats of whitewash, faced the tracks and lined both sides of the *avenida* from station to plaza, while the rest of the town was brown adobe, some of it showing its age. Behind the neat white rows of houses facing the two streets, the homes were scattered higgledy-piggledy among gardens and goat pens and chicken coops and small corrals to hold the livestock.

The poorest of Delgado's two-hundred-odd residents lived west of the tracks, where the land fell toward the river, in shacks that themselves seemed destined to tumble down the hillside in the next stiff breeze.

In olden days there was no town, just the hacienda and its outbuildings, built by Rosa Ball's pioneering ancestors. Over time the Delgados prospered, the hacienda became a focus for the commerce of a small region, and the little town grew up beside the hacienda. You might say such places are the Mexican versions of our "company towns." Judging by the smiling faces of the townspeople, who were out in force to greet us, Delgado had a kinder heart than most company towns I have seen, particularly the mining towns of Idaho, where I got the goods on the anarchist bombers claiming to represent the miners' union and nearly lost my life while I was at it.

The liberal amount of whitewash in evidence surprised me, and I said so to Victoria as I helped her down from the car.

"You'd think they spruced the place up just for us."

"The government did most of it," Victoria said. "Rosa's cousins have supported Carranza all along. Once he became president he repaid them by cleaning up the town."

The train's fireman was refilling the engine's boiler from an enormous water tank beside the tracks. At the base of the tower's framework, a one-cylinder donkey engine putted away noisily, pumping water up from the river. I observed that the tank was large enough to slake the thirst of several dozen engines a day, and Victoria informed me that Rosa's family had persuaded the railroad to put up a water tower big enough to supply water to the town as well as the engines. The Delgados themselves had paid to pipe the water to the plaza, where they built a fountain so the women wouldn't have to go to the river.

Even at first glance, it was obvious that in the four years Carranza had been president of the republic his largesse, and the railroad's, had made life better for Delgado. Of course, better is a relative term in Mexico, especially during hard times. But from what Victoria said, the Delgados were benevolent *hacendados,* and the people in Delgado weren't starving, which put them better off than many others in a land wracked for ten years by bloody revolution.

The railroad station was a sturdy adobe structure, obviously the pride and joy of the uniformed stationmaster, who strutted about like a rooster, calling out commands and instructions that were cheerfully ignored by our cowboys as they began unloading our traveling movie show under the quieter direction of Jack Whistler and Bob Elderberg.

By the look of it, the whole town was on hand to welcome us. As Randall Steele descended from the car he waved to the assemblage as if it was gathered solely to welcome him.

"Well, this looks like a nice place to spend a few weeks," he said. Just then a dozen members of the crowd surged forward when they saw Gerald Ball appear at the other end of our parlor car.

"Geraldo!" a buxom woman shouted.

As they neared the car some of these same people spied Victoria.

"Victoria!" they cried, and the group changed course and made for us. Before I knew it, we were surrounded by Rosa Ball's cousins and aunts and uncles of every variety, all laughing and weeping and embracing Victoria, Gerald, Randall, and me. I gathered that Rafael and Magdalena Delgado were the *patrón* and *patrona* of the hacienda, and forgot the rest of the names as quickly as I learned them. In the absence of Rosa, who was to remain in Hollywood until her two children were let out of school for the Christmas holidays, Victoria and I did our best to translate between Gerald, who spoke only rudimentary Mexican, and the voluble members of his wife's family.

Feeling like a stranger in this congregation, Randall stepped back to remove himself from the crush and tripped over Victoria's valise, which I had set on the platform. He sat down hard, evoking laughter from the Delgado children, who had been regarding him curiously. He joined right in the laughing as he picked himself up. Evidently the children had been told that Randall was a famous film actor, for they clustered around him now, no longer in awe.

When at last the Delgado clan hustled Victoria and Gerald and Randall toward two waiting automobiles, I stayed behind, wishing to keep an eye on Victoria's costume trunk. Off they went, everyone talking at once, the children leading Randall by the hand. They piled into a dusty Dodge touring car and an old Model T Ford coupé and chugged up the hill toward the hacienda with two teenage boys pedaling along beside the cars on a broken-down bicycle built for two, looking for all the world like a scene from a Keystone comedy.

It took some time to unload our prairie schooners from the flatcars, but neither the stationmaster nor the train's engineer nor the townspeople objected to the delay. During this enterprise, in which Leroy and I assisted, *vaqueros* from the Delgado *rancho* unloaded one carful of shorthorn cattle into the stock pens beside the railroad tracks.

There were children and dogs everywhere, enough to populate all of Sonora, it seemed to me. While the grown-up *delgadeños* watched with interest as the cowboys rolled our wagons down improvised ramps and wrangled the horses out of the boxcars, the children amused themselves by running every which way and shouting at the top of their lungs.

The sun was almost down when the unloading was done. As the train rolled out of the station the engineer gave a parting salute with his whistle and we Americans gave a cowboy cheer. Some of the boys fired their pistols into the air, which I am afraid may have upset a few of the towns-folk, who did not know that this sort of thing was normal behavior for high-spirited youths of the cowboy tribe when they are feeling their oats.

This was the last time any of us saw a passenger car on the line, and I later learned that it was only through the influence of the Delgado family that the parlor car was obtained for us from Nogales.

Under the guidance of old Ramón, an aged vaquero now become the hacienda's majordomo, we loaded our baggage into two horse-drawn wagons, and with many of the town's dogs and children escorting our caravan we ascended the gentle slope to the hacienda, where we parked the wagons in a loose array outside the walls, near the corrals. In short order, Willie Two Horse and Chief John set up their teepees among the wagons. Apaches don't live in teepees, but John has adopted the housing style of the northern tribes because wild west show audiences expect an Indian to live in a teepee no matter where he hails from, thanks to the dime novels and now the moving pictures.

Seeing the two elder statesmen erecting their tents moved some of the McQuain & Vickery cowboys to do likewise, as the hacienda grounds appeared to be free of hostile wildlife and using a few of the company's tents as bedrooms would ease the crowding in the wagons.

It was easy to see that defense against attack had been foremost in the minds of Rosa Ball's ancestors when they built their new home in what was then a wild frontier region. The solid adobe buildings commanded a view in all directions and their thick walls contained openings more the size of gun ports than true windows. These outward-facing openings were protected by wrought iron grilles. The high walls of the hacienda's largest building enclosed both the main house and an elegant courtyard, which boasted a well in its center and a bubbling fountain in one corner, set about with flowering plants. Graceful ironwork adorned the tops of the walls and served as railings for the long veranda that ringed three sides of the courtyard, but the courtyard gate, like all the outer doors, was made of solid timbers thick enough to stop a bullet.

"That well was a handy thing to have back in the old days, when they were holding off Indians or bandidos," Jack Whistler said as we looked the place over. He was thinking like a cavalryman.

"They were lucky to find water up here on the bench," Leroy observed.

"Any kind of a problem, we'll be all right if we get everyone in here," Jack said.

"The same thought crossed my mind," I admitted. The Indians tended to keep deeper in the mountains nowadays, but bandits continued to flourish in the border states, thanks to the revolution distracting the nation's attention from minor forms of lawlessness.

These thoughts prompted Leroy and me to search for a safe place to store Victoria's costume trunk and its golden hoard. I learned that Victoria and Gerald and Randall Steele would be accommodated on the upper floor of the hacienda, which was the only building in town equipped with a second story. There being a fourth guest room on that floor, Leroy and I agreed to keep the precious trunk there, with one of us sleeping in the bunk bed to guard it.

"You take the bed, Charlie," Leroy said when we had set the trunk down inside the room. "I slept in a bed for ten years. That's long enough."

He regarded me steadily, as if calculating whether this remark had set my detective's brain to wondering why he left that bed and came to Mexico, and it had. On the train he had intimated that he had come to stay. Maybe that was true, maybe not. What was more certain was that he had recently set his life on a new course, one far removed from what it had been during the ten years he slept on a feather mattress. In time I found I was right, but that first evening in Delgado I had no wish to play detective. I wanted to get to know him, not to pry where my curiosity might be unwelcome, so I was casting about for some way to disarm his wariness when he spoke again.

"Is it true you rode my mule Ikey?"

Talk about taking a man off guard. Ikey was long under the sod, but that was one mule I would never forget. I had met him soon after visiting with Bob Parker's sister Lula in Circleville. "I made Ikey's acquaintance back in 1900," I said.

"Up in the Haystack Mountains," Leroy said.

"Where your friend Jack kept hay and grub for the Wild Bunch in case any of you chanced to pass by," I added. "I told Jack I was a friend of Jim Thompson's from up Montana way, and that worked like 'open sesame.' He hid me out for a week."

"Jack was a good friend."

"That Ikey wasn't a bad mule, either. He could outrun a coyote. I always wondered why you left him behind."

"You Pinkertons ran me out of New Mexico. I rode Ikey clear to Wyoming and he needed a rest."

"He was good and rested when I got there," I said. "I took him out on the prairie to hunt some sage chickens for supper. I got off him to shoot, and at the first shot he lit out like a panther. Didn't stop until he was clear home at Jack's ranch. I had to hoof it all the way back."

"Ikey never would stand still for shooting. But that was his only fault."

"It's a good thing Jack had supper ready when I got back, or I would have tied that mule to a stump and fired off shots next to his head until he quit spooking. All that walking ruined a good pair of boots."

"Yeah, but that story made good reading. I really got a kick out of hearing about old Ikey again after all those years."

An author is always glad to hear that someone enjoyed his writing. Until Leroy recalled it, I clean forgot that I had put the story in *A Cowboy Detective,* but his mention of New Mexico prompted me to remember another event from that time.

"I've got one for you now," I said. "Down there in New Mexico twenty years ago, why'd you save Frank Murray's life?"

Leroy laughed. "Damn, Charlie! Have you been fretting about that for twenty years?"

The fact is, I had. That act of apparent kindness had puzzled me ever since. It didn't seem reasonable to me that Butch Cassidy should save the life of a Pinkerton man who was hot on his trail. And not just any Pinkerton man. Frank Murray, who lived to see the twentieth century solely because of Butch Cassidy's benevolence, was the assistant superintendent of the Agency's Denver office back at the turn of the century, and it was from the Denver office that operatives were dispatched all over the western states on the trail of the Wild Bunch.

The other reason I was interested in those long gone happenings down in the little town of Alma was because that was the one and only time I came close to getting Butch Cassidy in my sights.

Alma, New Mexico, was the southern terminus on the Outlaw Trail, and a favorite hiding place of Butch and his chums. What was known as the "Outlaw Trail" was a fairly well-defined route used by the cowboy bandits as they moved between Montana and New Mexico. It extended from Montana through the Hole-in-the-Wall country of Wyoming, down to Baggs and Dixon and over into Brown's Hole in Utah, on down to Robbers' Roost, and finally into New Mexico. Along the way the outlaws left messages in secret "post office" trees and stumps and rocks, warning one another where the law was hottest and where safe haven could be found. In the worst times they drifted down into Chihuahua to lay low south of the border.

Some of the stolen bank notes from the Wilcox U. P. robbery having turned up in Alma, I was sent down there to meet Frank Murray, who had gone on ahead. But I arrived to find that Murray had departed in great haste just days before. Rumor had it that he was a Pinkerton man.

I made myself known as Charles L. Carter, the same name I had used up in the Montana country. I found that my reputation as a hardcase had preceded me among the shady element, which was a lucky thing, for they suspected everybody from passing drummers to the boy who swept out the town's lone saloon of being Pinkerton spies. Once I was accepted by the outlaws, I had a hard time keeping a straight face as they fell all over themselves to tell me how close they had come to nailing a Pinkerton's hide to the barn.

It seemed that Murray, getting nowhere in uncovering the Wilcox robbers, decided to take one of Alma's citizens into his confidence. Being a shrewd judge of character, he picked one Jim Lowe, owner of a saloon popular with the long riders. Mr. Lowe was a soft-spoken man who permitted no rowdiness in his establishment. Murray was told that Lowe did more to keep the peace in Alma than the sheriff, who spent the nighttimes sleeping and daytimes in his cups.

Scarcely a day after Murray took Lowe into his confidence, Lowe drew Murray aside and warned him urgently to make tracks for the hills. The outlaws were on to him, Lowe said, and the only reason they hadn't already dispatched him to Satan's favorite vacation spot was that they couldn't agree on a means gruesome enough to suit one of the despised Pinkertons. Murray lost no time in following Lowe's advice, adding in his report, which he wrote out once safely back in Denver, that he would need a company of cavalry to carry out the job he had been sent to do in New Mexico.

I thought it curious when I learned that Jim Lowe, the solid citizen who had saved Murray's life, had sold his saloon and left the country too, so recently that his dust was still in the air. Curious, that is, until my outlaw informants let slip that poor old Murray had given himself away to one of the very men he was trying to uncover! Jim Lowe was none other than the mastermind of the Wilcox job, I was told, the one man who could keep Kid Curry and the rest of the Hole-in-the-Wall boys in line, Mr. Butch Cassidy himself. The best joke of all, to the outlaws' minds, was that "Jim Lowe" was camped in the mountains just forty miles to the southeast, where he had established a local robbers' roost.

I should say here that at the time it was widely believed that Kid Curry, whose real name was Harvey Logan, was the boss of the Wild Bunch. He and Cassidy both had their own gangs before they and several lesser collections of cowboy bandits combined in '96 to form the Wild Bunch, Curry having taken over the original Hole-in-the-Wall gang by then. Cassidy and his pals were called the Diamond Mountain Boys among their outlaw friends, but they were known informally as the "wild bunch" around Rock Springs, Wyoming, which was their stomping ground until things became too hot for them there. But while Butch was known as a happy-go-lucky sort who preferred to avoid bloodshed, Curry had no equal as a cold-hearted badman in those days, save perhaps for Blackjack Ketchum of New Mexico fame. More often than not, when Curry took part in a job someone got killed. At Wilcox he showed his colors right at the start when he struck the poor engineer over the head with a pistol just because the man was not obeying orders quick enough. And when Sheriff Hazen's posse caught up with the bandits, it was Curry who fired the fatal shot that sent Sheriff Hazen to boot hill. From this it is easy to see why Pinkertons and lawmen alike credited Curry with running the "Bunch," but what I learned in Alma suggested that we had underestimated Cassidy's importance.

I wrote at once to Denver, acquainting Assistant Superintendent Murray with all I had learned. I begged to be allowed to go to the outlaw camp and get in with the gang, but Murray's dander was up, as he was still red in the face over his failure in New Mexico. He wrote back saying I was quite wrong about Lowe, whom he knew to be a "nice gentleman." He instructed me to return to Denver so I could go to Wyoming, where he had new leads in the case. And on this occasion I broke my recently-made rule about following hot trails.

Perhaps the knowledge that Butch had saved Murray's life made me softhearted, or maybe I just wanted to see Murray squirm when he learned the truth and realized that Butch was still free because he called me back to Denver too soon. In either case, I followed orders, taking the stage for Silver City, there to board the railroad. Later both the Pinkerton brothers and Murray himself admitted to me that Lowe was Cassidy, and the name Jim Lowe entered the Agency's files as one of Butch's aliases.

"You're right," I said to Leroy, "it has bothered me. I don't know whether you heard, but a friend of yours was on the stage with me when I left town."

Leroy nodded. "Blake Graham. He said what a nice fellow Charlie Carter was. He couldn't figure why you left in such a hurry. You were a sly one, Charlie."

"I got lucky that time. If you hadn't let Murray go, your pals wouldn't have had such a good time crowing about it, and I might never have figured out who was the real boss of the Wild Bunch."

This caught Leroy's interest. "You didn't know before that?"

"Up to then we all figured it was Kid Curry. After what I heard about Jim Lowe in Alma, I began to think we were on the wrong trail. From then on, I followed up every clue that might lead me to Butch Cassidy, but I never got close again."

Night was falling fast, the way it does in the southern latitudes. The room was so dark I could scarcely make out Leroy's features.

"What I'd like to know is, was your friend Graham right? He said Jim

Lowe just didn't have the heart to let a poor unsuspecting fool like Frank Murray get himself killed, even if he was a Pinkerton. Did you take pity on old Frank just because he was such a fool?"

There was enough light for me to see Leroy shake his head.

"That wasn't it. It wasn't all of it, anyway. Your friend Murray told me who he was because he trusted me, Charlie. I've always tried to do right by people who trusted me."

Chapter 11

BRIGHT AND EARLY the next morning the entire company was raring to start on *The Trail of Pancho Villa*, but before the first scene could be filmed, a dispute arose that threatened the picture, Victoria's dream, and the fate of the Bunk House as well. The seeds were sown at breakfast, which was eaten before dawn.

"Say Brian," Nate Dicenzo happened to ask, "what outfit were you with in the war?"

"I wasn't in the war," Brian replied as he got up from the table. His voice was soft and conveyed some embarrassment.

Nothing further was said at the time, and by half an hour after sunrise everyone was out in the chaparral east of the hacienda, swinging their arms against the morning chill. I remained in the hacienda, leaving Leroy free to watch the filming, which was all new to him. My instincts told me I could trust him, but I wasn't sure how far I wanted to risk Victoria's gold if I happened to be wrong this once.

When Brian tried to call Randall Steele and his cowboy pals into position, only Randall and Charlie Noble were front and center. In the background, the McQuain & Vickery boys who were to play the hero's pals in the picture lingered by their horses, talking among themselves as if they hadn't heard a thing.

Brian was the very picture of a veteran film director, clad in riding breeches and khaki shirt, but in place of the pith helmets favored by DeMille and his imitators he sported a brand new John B. Stetson hat more in keeping with the spirit of our story, and instead of English riding boots he wore the cowboy variety. To complete the picture, a Pall Mall dangled from his lips in perfect imitation of Emmett Dalton. Removing the cigarette now, he called again through his megaphone.

"Gentlemen, if you please. Let's get this show on the road."

Still Bob Elderberg and Nate and the rest of the cowboys didn't budge.

"Orville," Brian said, "see if you can find out what's the matter."

Orville Hintz was Brian's assistant, a willing Indiana lad built along the lines of a tall fencepost, who served Brian as an extra pair of hands and legs for any task a busy director didn't have time to do himself. He had exchanged dim hopes back home in Indiana for the bright promise of California, and was all agog to find himself in Mexico.

When Orville returned from speaking with the cowboys, he shuffled his feet in the dirt and wouldn't look Brian in the eye.

"Well, what's the problem?" Brian demanded.

"What is it, Orville?" Victoria encouraged the lad.

Naturally she was on hand, along with just about everyone else and half the town to boot, mostly women and children. No one wanted to miss being in on the start of things. The Americans all knew we had a month to make the picture, starting today, and Victoria knew a good deal more than the others about what the consequences would be in her own life if the film wasn't finished on time.

"Oh, hell," said Orville. He shuffled his feet in another direction, trying out some new footwork. "Dammit, Miss Hartford, I'm sorry, but those lunkheads—" He ran out of words and shook his head, looking blackly at the cowboys, who still refused to acknowledge the existence of anything in the world but themselves and their horses.

"Spit it out, boy," said George Bleumel.

"Okay. Okay." Orville glanced from Victoria to Brian, then planted himself squarely in front of George, unwilling to say what he had to say to anyone else.

"Those lunkheads say they're not about to take orders from any chicken-hearted college boy who didn't have the gumption to fight for his country."

"I'll put a stop to that," said Jack Whistler. When Jack sets his jaw in a certain way those around tend to back up and make room, but Victoria put a hand on his arm.

"Let me go, Jack."

"It's my job," said Brian. He started for the cowboys, but George blocked his way.

"No, Boss," he said. "You stay here. I'll take care of this."

Something in his voice stopped Brian in his tracks, but he called out as George stomped off, "There's no need to tell them everything!"

"It happened, didn't it?" George threw back over his shoulder. "There's no sense to hide it."

When George reached the cowboys he addressed himself to Bob Elderberg. "Bob," he said, "I've only known you for a few days, but I'll admit I may have misjudged you. I gave you credit for good sense, and I may have been wrong."

"Now, George, you've got no call to talk to me like that." Bob did not rise to be head wrangler of the McQuain & Vickery show at the age of thirty-five by taking guff from anyone. He and George were about the same height, but Bob was twenty pounds heavier and tough as baling wire. He could have knocked George flat without half trying, but like some men who are truly tough, Bob had a gentle temperament. In this instance he was trying to calm George down, not dispute him.

"We ain't working for no slacker," said Tommy Fear, a pint-sized Colorado cowboy with a five-gallon portion of pride.

"What regiment was you in, Tommy?" Jim Ray Thompson said with a grin.

Tommy smacked Jim Ray in the mouth, hard enough to knock Jim Ray to the ground and cause him to swallow his chewing gum. He stood over Jim Ray like a bantam rooster, ready to tear his innards out if Jim looked at him sideways.

"They wouldn't let me in because I ain't tall enough! But at least I ain't afraid!"

Jim Ray wiped his mouth with the back of his hand and saw blood, but he didn't say anything. Jim Ray and Tommy were partners the same way Nate and Redeye were, and Jim Ray hoped that friendship hadn't just come to an end because of a casual jest.

"Easy, boys," Bob Elderberg said.

"Yeah, you all take it easy," George agreed. "And you listen good. You too, Bob, because I'm going to say this once and that's it. Brian Hill has been in this business almost as long as I have. He started with Reliance Pictures in 1910 as a prop boy and he worked on my first picture."

"That don't mean—" Nate Dicenzo began, but Bob Elderberg cut him off.

"Shut up, Nate."

Nate looked hurt, but he shut up, and George went on with what he had to say.

From a distance, the sight of George lecturing the band of cowboys must have seemed incongruous. As a genuine film pioneer, George felt no need to keep up with the flamboyant fashions in clothing that were affected by many picture folk, and he was about as un-western as a man could get. He wore a little porkpie hat and low-heeled brogan shoes, corduroy pants and a checked flannel shirt. When he was embarrassed, or thinking hard, he would remove the little hat and stroke the top of his bald head with his free hand. As he was embarrassed now, he had been stroking his head all the while as he talked. He cut an almost comical figure, but those cowboys listened to him as respectfully as they might have listened to the boss man of any big outfit they ever worked on, for George's reputation had spread among the cowboys as well as the other members of the crew.

By chance, Redeye Hawk had heard of an American cameraman named George Bleumel who went through the war with a frontline Canadian unit, armed with nothing but a movie camera. Redeye mentioned this to the other veterans, and on the train ride from Los Angeles to Delgado Bob Elderberg had learned the rest from Brian. By now just about everyone knew that our George was that very same frontline cameraman. And they knew that long before the Great War George had been sent to Mexico at the start of the revolution, by the Mutual Film Corporation, to cover Pancho Villa's army. They had heard how he lugged his camera around on horseback for almost a year, right in the thick of the fighting, and how one morning Villa was getting set to attack Huerta's army at dawn, but George made him wait half an hour until the light was just the way he liked it. "All right, General," he told Pancho. "You can start now." The cowboys got a kick out of that one.

At the age of thirty, George had seen more of battle and death than any two men in the outfit put together, including the veterans. In their eyes, his courage was beyond question, and although this was the only time he laid down the law during our stay in Mexico, they would have listened just as attentively on any other occasion, no doubt with similar results.

"After that first picture I didn't see Brian for a few years," George told them. "I was working down here in Mexico for a while. The next time Brian and I worked together it was on a Civil War picture. We were shooting a scene where a house gets blown up by cannon fire. Brian was the effects man by then. See, he figured he'd learn every job there was behind the camera and then maybe he'd know enough to be a director, which is what he wanted from the beginning. He had this charge of black powder set to blow up half the house, only it didn't go off. He used black powder instead of dynamite because it looked better on film. It makes more smoke and a slower kind of explosion that films better. Even then he was a stickler for authenticity, see? Now meantime, one of the horses got loose from where they were tied up and wandered over near the house.

Brian figured maybe the fuse was just a sleeper, burning real slow, but when he saw that horse right by the house he ran down to chase it off, and he just got close when the charge blew up the house and Brian with it."

"What happened to the horse?" Jim Ray asked.

"The horse started off when Brian came running up. The explosion scared the daylights out of him, but he was all right, which is more than you could say for Brian. He was in the hospital for two months, but they can't fix a busted eardrum. You notice how he turns his right ear toward you? He only hears on that side. When the war came he tried to enlist, never said anything about the ear, but the doctor spotted it. So Brian did what he was good at. He made movies. Began writing them, too. He worked on the war pictures mostly. Some say they helped in the war effort. All I know is, he did what he could."

By now the cowboys looked like a dozen imitations of Orville Hintz, all shuffling their feet and looking at the ground. The fact that Brian was nearly killed saving a horse no doubt helped to raise him high in their estimation. Bob Elderberg had his sack of Bull Durham out and was concentrating hard on the smoke he was rolling.

"Now the way I see it," George said, "Brian's the boss of this crew while we're down here, just like the captain of a ship. I don't know what kind of a captain he'll be, but I figure to give him a chance. As for how brave he is, well, we'll all find out how brave we are when the time comes. Until then, I don't see the point of talking about it."

When George fell silent, the matter was closed.

"Well, boys," Bob Elderberg said, "we made fools of ourselves. Let's get to work."

And that was that. Ten minutes later the cowboys were mounted up and galloping through the chaparral behind Randall Steele and Charlie Noble, with George back behind his camera and Brian Hill calling directions through his megaphone. Whereupon the next impediment to the day's filming appeared in the form of a mongrel dog, its spirits raised by the general excitement, that chased after the horses, nipping at their heels and causing those in the rear to shy and kick.

Back went Randall and the cowboys to their starting point, down came Orville's arm when Brian called "Action," and once again Tom and his chums rode past the camera, chased now by three dogs instead of one.

"Cut!" shouted Brian. "Can't someone get rid of these dogs?"

The problem was not the dogs themselves, of course, but the children of Delgado, whom the dogs accompanied everywhere. It being a Saturday, there was no school, so the town's younger citizens were present in force, ready to be entertained by the doings of the *yanquis* from the fabled golden city of Hollywood. As a consequence, most of the canine population of Delgado was on hand as well.

Fortunately the urchins were already growing bored with the slow pace of picture making. They didn't want to see a movie being made, they wanted to see a *movie,* the whole story unfolding before them just as if they were sitting in a darkened picture house. It mattered not a whit that none of them had ever seen the inside of a picture house or that only the older ones had ever seen a moving picture at all, when a traveling movie show passed through Delgado three years before and set up its projector and screen in the town's church to show one of Hollywood's religious epics. Even in this remote Sonoran cattle town, the children had been touched by the magic of the silver screen, but they saw none of it in the disjointed activities played out for their benefit thus far.

It was Leroy who hit upon a way to get the children and dogs out from underfoot, thereby saving our company many hours of frustration in the following weeks.

"¡Hola, muchachos!" Leroy called to the children. *"Vengan conmigo."*

He left Victoria's side, from where he had been watching the filming once the cowboys' short-lived strike was over, spoke briefly to Jack Whistler, and took a lasso from one of the equipment wagons that had been driven to the site. Twirling the lasso over his head he spread a large loop which he allowed to drop around himself, then caused to rise back up over his head.

The *muchachos* were ready for any sort of entertainment. They followed Leroy willingly as he led them away from the picture crew to a fenced pasture north of the hacienda, where Jack joined them shortly, carrying several items he had fetched from the company's wagons. The pasture was empty of livestock, but the horses and cattle sometimes held there had cropped the sparse grass short, which suited Leroy's purpose perfectly. He performed a few more simple rope tricks until all the children were gathered around him, then hung the lasso on the fence and took from Jack's hands a baseball and bat.

"¿Quién sabe jugar béisbol?" Leroy inquired. Who knows how to play baseball?

A few tentative voices spoke out from among the children, but it was apparent that any knowledge they might have of the game was rudimentary.

"Bueno," said Leroy, undeterred. *"Vamos a aprender."* Okay, let's learn.

Jack had also brought four empty feed bags, which Leroy dropped on the ground at the corners of a rough square about forty feet on a side. He divided the children into two groups, and thus the Delgado Baseball League was founded. It may be that Leroy was inspired by reports in the States that a third league might soon be formed with the backing of Harry Sinclair, the oil tycoon, and Edsel Ford. Perhaps he hoped to get the Mexican franchise, before subsequent events led him to remove himself from a direct managerial role. At last report, Delgado is supporting four teams that compete fiercely for the town championship, so far without recognition from the big leagues up north.

With the children now enrolled in Leroy's baseball class and the dogs watching from the bleachers, the filming resumed and the pace picked up. By the end of the morning the crew was no longer encumbered by any onlookers whatever, for the grown-up *delgadeños,* like the children, couldn't understand why a simple scene sometimes had to be done over and over to get it right. They were further disappointed when they learned that the story would not be filmed from beginning to end the way it would appear on the screen. When they could make no sense of the unconnected scenes played out before them, they drifted away.

For those unacquainted with the reality of making moving pictures, I will explain that it is more practical to film scenes requiring a certain sort of location all in a row than to start at the beginning of the scenario and proceed page by page to the end. Scenes requiring no sets are often the first to be done while the sets are built, and such was the case in filming *The Trail of Pancho Villa.* The scenario, which Brian and George and I had worked on almost around the clock during the three days between Victoria's picnic and our departure for Delgado, called for the dastardly Villa to burn the American border town at the conclusion of his attack. Imagining that Delgado's inhabitants would take dim view of our burning their homes, we planned to construct a false-front town to burn. That first morning in Delgado, Gerald Ball was in town, assisted by Rafael Delgado, hiring workers to begin the construction. The word was out that the Americans were hiring, which is why the onlookers at the filming were mostly women and children.

THE SET BUILDING proceeded rapidly in the following days, after a short delay in getting lumber. This obstacle was removed following a flurry of telephone calls from the railroad station, which contained the town's only telephone as well as the telegraph. The next train brought a load of lumber from Nacozari, the southern terminus of the line, and soon we were employing most of the able-bodied men in Delgado at one task or another. They built false fronts and slathered them with mud to resemble adobe and erected these flimsy structures on the plateau southeast of the hacienda to create the town Pancho Villa would attack. Other men hauled our props and equipment hither and yon, while many of their wives and children were employed in a variety of capacities, including helping to prepare and serve our meals.

Even the local vaqueros got some work right at the start, providing cattle for the scenes of Tom and his pals. Our American cowboys watched their Mexican counterparts with interest, for they knew it was from Mexican vaqueros such as these that the first Texans had learned the skills of cowboyography a century before. They marveled at the ease with which the vaqueros handled their seventy-five foot rawhide *reatas*, and even awarded them passing grades in horsemanship. Before long, our boys were swapping stories and tricks of the trade with the vaqueros during breaks in the filming, unimpeded by the lack of a common language.

The head vaquero, Eugenio Ortiz, quickly became a favorite among our crew. He was scarcely taller than Tommy Fear and swaggered just as boldly to make up for it. Gene, as he was quickly dubbed by the Americans, was part *indio* and all cowboy, and consequently fell into company with Redeye Hawk and Nate Dicenzo, judging himself related by blood to one and by calling to the other. Gene introduced his newfound friends to *pulque*, the Mexican workingman's national beverage, which resulted in some lively antics during the evenings. Even so, the celebrants were front and center each morning, however much they may have regretted their excesses of the night before.

In short, as the production hit its stride a jolly time was had by all. Had it been summertime, we would have roasted like chiggers on a griddle, but we were fortunate with the weather and our patch of the Sonora cattle country was a garden spot even more pleasant than southern California.

Our crew made the most of it, working hard and playing hard. Laughter makes work seem easier, and our crew was provided with much to laugh about from an unexpected source, for they soon learned a fact unknown to the fans of western pictures: left on his own, Randall Steele will find a way to trip over his own shoelaces.

Such a man might have become the butt of many jokes in a rough-and-ready outfit like ours, but Randall was saved by his good nature. He has never got over his surprise at discovering that he can get paid for having fun, and he treats the whole business of picture making like a holiday. When he fell on his face, he laughed at himself right along with the rest of us. From the start he got up early in the morning, he hit his mark, and he did what was required of him. Nothing earns the respect of picture people quicker than that.

And then the word began to get around that when Randall Steele was in front of a camera, a miracle took place. Suddenly he could do no wrong. He was at home on a horse, and he knew how to handle both pistol and rifle. He could not do fancy shooting to save his soul, and from the outset Brian refused to let him attempt stunts that might get him killed and thus delay the picture, but what mattered to the crew was that he was game, and he was good at his job. So long as the camera was rolling he was nimble of foot and dexterous of hand. He performed the less dangerous stunts flawlessly. He never tripped, never fell, never ruined a take by any sort of clumsiness. But when Brian said "Cut," it was Mabel, grab the crockery before he broke it.

Pretty soon the boys were looking out for him between takes, catching him before he fell and picking him up if he managed to stumble over a pebble while they weren't looking.

To put the icing on the cake, it soon became apparent that Victoria had picked a winner in Brian Hill. As George had pointed out, a film director has all the authority of a ship's captain once he and his crew are on location. But it was not Brian's way to lord that authority over those in his command. Being fresh-faced and wet behind the ears, it is just as well he didn't try. Instead he showed his respect for crew and actors alike, asking their advice and offering suggestions in ways that made them feel important. He knew nothing about animals, and depended on those with cowboy skills to do the right thing when horses were in the scene. But he knew what he wanted, and in getting it his soft-spoken, respectful manner often inspired the actors to give performances beyond their previous abilities.

"I've got to hand it to you, my dear," Gerald said to Victoria on our third day in Delgado, while Brian was directing Randall Steele in a horseback scene. "Young Mr. Hill knows his business."

Victoria smiled like the Cheshire Cat. Since we arrived in Delgado she had been as happy as a child in summer camp. She was making her feature film at last, the initial difficulties were quickly overcome, and now even Gerald had to admit that Brian Hill had the makings of a first-rate director. Victoria had watched Gerald closely from the first, wary that he might try to delay the production somehow. But he seemed willing to let events take their natural course. He even volunteered to oversee the production accounts to free Brian from that task. Gerald's unexpected compliment convinced Victoria that he would give her a fair chance to finish the picture on time, and her last worry evaporated.

Chapter 12

EACH EVENING AFTER supper I sat down with Brian and George to go over the scenario, looking for ways to improve it, but apart from that I generally left the picture-making to others and took most of the gold-guarding on myself, especially once I learned how Leroy was keeping the children out from underfoot. His small-fry baseball games became a regular feature of the afternoons. Jack Whistler was the umpire and Leroy coached all the players impartially. The games were often chaotic due to the participation of the dogs, who grew as excited as the children and frequently bowled over the runners by darting between their legs. Jack suggested, only half in fun, that this problem could be alleviated by shooting sufficient of the dogs each day to serve as bases and foul posts.

"They'd stay put better than those gunny sacks," he told Leroy, trying to make himself heard above the barking and shouting occasioned by a home run.

When I first heard how the children took to Leroy, I remembered stories I had heard about Butch Cassidy, and how he would make friends with the children within moments of entering a strange town. This was one more reason why he had kept a jump ahead of me for four long years. After all, who will turn in a man beloved by the children?

Even the children of Delgado sometimes became exhausted after a few dozen innings of baseball. On those occasions Leroy entertained them with rope tricks or turned them over to Dusty Clark. Dusty is McQuain

& Vickery's bullwhip artist and elder sharpshooter, although his pistol shooting skills diminished as a result of losing his right eye some years ago when a gun blew up in his face. But he can still split a bullet on an axe blade with a rifle, and his feats with a bullwhip are a sight to behold. Any of our crew who were not working when Dusty gave his little performances always joined the crowd to watch.

I learned all about these goings-on from Victoria, who brought me the baseball scores and glowing reports of the day's filming each evening when her work was done.

On our tenth morning in Delgado, Gerald sat down at the small table in my bedroom to go over the company's accounts. With the gold safely in his care, I took the opportunity to stroll downtown, where the picture crew was at work. They were using the town's small cantina for the scene where Pancho Villa first sets eyes on the beautiful Evangelina. Several scenes would be filmed in the real town, including some of Villa's attack.

As with so many small Mexican towns, most public activity in Delgado centered on the central plaza. The cantina was there, and the church, and the small fountain built by the Delgados bubbled cheerfully in the center of the square. Because the cantina was on the west side of the plaza Brian wanted to film while the sun was low in the east, so the early morning light would illuminate the front of the building. In the movie the scene would appear to take place at sunset, not sunrise. By the magic of editing, the cantina would seem to be part of the false-front town our workers had now completed, and both the cantina scene and those of Villa's attack would appear to take place at sundown. The burning of the false town would take place after dusk, for the most dramatic effect, and also so it would be harder for an audience to see that only false fronts were going up in flames.

Of course, when filming in the morning, everything had to be done in reverse order, the "sunset" scenes done first, then those that took place earlier in the "afternoon."

Leroy was helping keep the townspeople back from the cantina. Now that Hollywood and "Villa" himself had moved right into their town, the *delgadeños* were taking renewed interest. Before the camera, Villa, played by Chief John, crept up on the cantina and peered in the window. The light was beautiful, as Brian had promised it would be when he first told Gerald the story back in the Bunk House. Across the plaza, more townspeople looked on from the steps of the town's *tienda*, or general store, and three women who entered the plaza just then paused to watch the *yanquis* at their antics before filling their water jugs at the fountain.

"All right, now you see her," Brian coached John through his megaphone. "Wow, what a dish! Right away you want her. But now the music gets to you. And before you know it, you're falling in love."

John played his part with gusto. In response to Brian's coaching, his emotions passed from pure love to thoughts less noble, and back again. Within the cantina, Victoria sang a plaintive love ballad, although she was not in sight of the camera, to help John summon up the required sentiments. The strains of the music floated through the cantina's open door, casting a spell over crew and onlookers alike.

Calling upon an Apache Indian to play Pancho Villa might seem an odd choice, but the decision was an added testimonial to young Brian's genius. We take it for granted that the Mexicans are a dark-skinned people, but we never stop to think that this is because the Spanish invaders, unlike the more northerly Europeans who settled the U.S. of A., married freely with the natives they conquered. And who were these natives? None other than the Indian tribes of Mexico. You take an Apache or a Sioux Indian, or a Comanche, for that matter, dress him in a Villista uniform, and you would never dream that his father used to pass the afternoon lifting white men's scalps in Arizona or Texas or Montana.

"Cut!" Brian said. "Let's get a close-up of John by the window. You boys stick around. We'll do your approach to town next."

This last remark was addressed to Redeye Hawk and the rest of our wild west Indians, who were enlisted in Villa's band along with some of the cowboys. They were sitting horseback behind the camera, all togged up as revolutionists, armed to the teeth and wearing heavy cartridge belts across their chests.

Most of the factions in the Mexican revolution wore uniforms much like American Army field uniforms of the day, but Brian guessed that by now, long past Villa's heyday, his army would be a ragtag outfit. As a result, our boys wore only partial uniforms mixed with odd pants and jackets, and of course the broad-brimmed slouch hats or sombreros favored by the Mexican irregulars over proper uniform hats.

Brian's attention to detail was evident in the layer of dust worn by both men and horses, and the dark makeup around the actors' eyes, which made them appear both weary and cruel. Let me tell you, if you saw that outfit pounding across the desert toward your New Mexico border town, you would dig a hole quick as a badger and pull it in after you. Give them live cartridges, and I would have thought twice before tangling with them myself.

When the camera was in position for John's close-up, I entered the cantina to pass the time with Victoria as she sang another verse of her song for the next take. She was costumed as Evangelina, having begun the day's work with the scene where she runs from the cantina in alarm when Villa begins his attack. As I listened to the heartbreaking Mexican love song I may have grown a trifle damp about the eyes, for Victoria put every pretty saloon girl I ever fell in love with to shame. Her skin was darkened with makeup and she wore the sort of Mexican skirt that cantina girls wear, brightly colored, the kind that swirls as they dance. Her blouse was one I would not think proper for a well-brought-up young woman to wear in California, but in pictures the common notions of decency are often set aside. The effect, even for me, was to make it difficult to remember that underneath it all she was still Victoria Hartford.

In short order the close-up of Chief John was completed, and the cast and crew prepared at once to depart for the plateau, where they would film Villa's band approaching the town.

"Thanks, Victoria," Brian said as we emerged from the cantina into the light of day. "We'll be working with John and the boys the rest of the morning."

"You mean I have the morning off?"

"Free as a lark. Enjoy yourself. We'll see you at lunchtime."

As Victoria stood amidst the bustle, I noticed how the crew moved around her at a respectful distance, the men glancing at her often when she wasn't looking. Buddy Johnston nearly bumped into her as he moved past carrying one of the silver panels used to reflect sunlight on the actors' faces. He excused himself profusely and backed away, still apologizing.

I had noticed a similar effect before, on other picture sets. When Victoria is made up as one of her characters, the men and women around her treat her differently, more like the character than herself. As Cimarron Rose, the McQuain & Vickery fellows found it easier to joke with her and treat her like one of the boys. In *The Trail of Pancho Villa*, Evangelina was noble and proud, miles above the low-life sorts that frequented the cantina. It was plain to see that she set the crew's hearts on fire with her sultry beauty, and yet they kept their distance, so complete was her transformation.

"I don't know what to do with a whole morning free." Victoria was looking about like a schoolgirl whose playmates have abandoned her. "Come on, Charlie. Let's see the town."

"I best get back to the hacienda. I left Gerald counting your gold. He'll be done by now."

She put a hand to her brow and feigned a heartache worthy of Evangelina. "I'll go alone then."

As she walked off, it seemed to me that she was still caught in the mood of her love song. Like the Americans, the townspeople fell back before her, unwilling to intrude on her privacy. Even the children left her alone. But when she stepped out to cross the broad Avenida Central, she jumped back as Leroy careened into sight on a bicycle, nearly colliding with her. His vehicle was the rickety bicycle built for two that I had seen the teenage boys riding on the day of our arrival.

Victoria's mood changed in an instant. She jumped up and down, calling after Leroy. He wheeled around the small fountain in the center of the plaza and returned to her side. In a twinkling she was aboard the second seat and together they pedaled twice around the plaza, Victoria laughing gaily, before they picked up speed and shot off down the avenida toward the railroad station.

Something about the quick shift in her spirits caused a small itch in my detective's nose, but before I could give it much thought Brian and George pulled up beside me in the Delgados' Model T, which was on loan to our picture crew for running about town.

"Charlie? You want a ride to the hacienda?" Brian offered. "We're going that way."

"I'd be obliged," I said. As I squeezed in beside them a train whistle sounded not far away.

"Damn!" George exclaimed. "The train's early. Orville!"

"Orville!" Brian echoed, looking all around.

The gangly youth appeared at a run from inside the cantina, carrying the shawl Victoria had worn earlier that morning.

"Get in the back!" George said. The train whistled again, much nearer.

Brian threw the flivver into motion as Orville leapt into the rumble seat.

All this rush was because Orville was scheduled to board the train that was even now puffing to a stop at the station. Naturally we had to send our film to Hollywood to be developed, and neither Brian nor George nor anyone else was going to risk sending the film home unattended. Orville would carry it back and forth by hand, bringing a working print of each lot of film back with him. He was to depart with the first batch on today's train, which had caught us all by surprise, being early. More often it was late.

Brian glanced at the sky as we tore down the avenida. "George and I better get up to the location before the sun gets any higher. Would you see Orville onto the train, Charlie?"

"He's got the film in back there," George said as we skidded to a stop by the station, raising a cloud of dust.

"You go on," I said. "We'll manage."

Orville handed me two large round film tins from the rumble seat. He grabbed two more tins and a small carpetbag before slamming the seat closed.

As the Ford sputtered away, Victoria and Leroy pedaled past, waving cheerily.

"*¡Por favor, señores, apúrense!*" the stationmaster called from the platform, asking us to hurry in getting Orville aboard. He was looking at his big railroad watch and pacing back and forth as if the cattle train were the

California Limited. After ten days in Delgado, we knew that the trains to and from the border ran more according to when the engineer felt like making the run than by any printed schedule. The whole arrangement offended Gerald's British sense of order. He said you could set your watch by the trains in olde England. To the stationmaster's explanation that it was *la revolución* which caused the uncertain schedules, Gerald replied that when the revolution was finally over, the Mexicans would find a new excuse.

"You take care now," I said as I handed the film tins up to Orville once he was aboard the caboose, where he would ride with the brakeman. "We've all got a lot riding on this picture."

"Don't worry, Mr. Siringo, it'll be a crackerjack picture. I'll guard the film with my life."

I hoped such drastic measures wouldn't be needed, but I felt some genuine concern as the train pulled out of the station. From now on, Orville would make the trip regularly, spending just a day or two at the ends of his journey. After this first lot of film reached Hollywood, it was Brian's hope that never more than a week's worth of celluloid would be undeveloped. Even so, the scheme contained a considerable risk. If any of the film should prove defective, many days of work would have to be repeated and our hope of completing the picture in the allotted month would go up in smoke.

Aboard their bicycle, Victoria and Leroy entertained no such trifling concerns. They were off on a lark, and the train's departure offered a chance for adventure. When it overtook them north of town they pedaled for all they were worth and even managed to keep pace with the engine for a brief time, tearing hell-bent for leather along the road—barely a wagon track, really—that ran alongside the tracks. But soon they fell behind and gave up the unequal contest, coasting to a stop to catch their breath.

Leroy, being a gentleman, offered to let Victoria take the front seat, the one with the handlebars that worked. Once in charge of the vehicle's direction, she became daring, venturing off the beaten track and turning toward the gentle slope that led to the green banks of the river.

"Careful now," Leroy cautioned her. "We've got no brakes."

"What!" Victoria screamed, but it was too late.

Moments later she and Leroy were sitting in a foot of water having themselves a good laugh, once it was apparent that neither of them was hurt.

"Women drivers," Leroy said, shaking his head.

"You could have told me we didn't have any brakes!" Victoria seized him by the shoulders and pulled him over backwards, like a Baptist minister dunking a convert. She is stronger than a man suspects, what with a lifetime of handling horses and wrestling calves, and she held him under until he nearly drowned.

The morning sun was bright and warm and they sat on the riverbank to dry their clothes while Leroy struggled to straighten the bicycle's bent handlebars. Victoria shook her hair to help it dry, doing her best to look pretty and making a good job of it.

"Next time I'll stick to a horse," Leroy said, clamping the front wheel between his legs and giving the handlebars a twist. "When I was growing up in Utah, it was horses or nothing. No bicycles or automobiles. We didn't know how good we had it."

"You make it sound like a hundred years ago."

"Sometimes it feels like it."

After a final heave at the handlebars he decided they were as straight as he could get them without tools, and he laid the bicycle aside.

"Tell me about your friend," Victoria said. "The one you came to find."

"I don't really know where he is. Harry moves around a lot, like me. He could be long gone."

"What if you don't find him?"

"Then I'll move along, I guess."

"I'm grateful to you for staying on to help us."

He was embarrassed to be thanked outright. "It's a grubstake. Enough for a man to live a long time in Mexico."

"Or in California."

To this he made no reply.

"You've worked a miracle with the children," Victoria said.

"I always took to kids."

"But you never had any."

"Not yet." He looked at her in a new way and it was Victoria's turn to be embarrassed.

"The thing about kids is, they see the world all fresh and simple, the way it ought to be," he said. "They trust everybody. If you don't treat a kid wrong, he'll trust you with his life. I don't see why we've got to lose that."

"A lot of people aren't trustworthy."

"I guess that's so, but I never saw why it had to be that way."

Victoria stretched out in the grass, enjoying the warmth of the sun. "It's heaven to be away from the work, just for a while." She swatted at a fly that was taking an interest in her left arm.

Leroy stretched out beside her. "Oh, I don't know. This picture business is more entertaining than I thought it would be. I always wondered what it was like to be a movie star."

"We're just ordinary people."

"Ordinary people don't get their names in the newspapers and their pictures in *Photoplay* magazine."

Victoria made a face. One of the qualities she admired in Leroy was that once he had revealed a familiarity with the doings of Cimarron Rose, he made no more of it. She does not suffer gracefully the fawning of the motion picture public. She is a ranch girl, brought up on the frontier virtues of common sense and hard work. To her, making pictures is a job of work. She collects her pay and goes home at night like ordinary folk, and she has no patience with those who bow and scrape and generally behave like simpletons in her presence.

She closed her eyes and appeared to be sleeping. "What I like most about acting is playing other people. It's interesting to be someone else for a while. You can learn a lot about people, if you take it seriously."

Leroy was propped up on one elbow, looking at her, a stalk of grass in his mouth. "You can see other people as they are, without them seeing you."

"That's right. When I'm in costume I can forget about Victoria Hartford for a time. Today I'm Evangelina. I even begin to feel Mexican sometimes." She opened her eyes. "I look at you and think 'There's a handsome *gringo*.'"

She was enjoying the fantasy, but Leroy was serious. "The trouble is, the ordinary people think you're really Evangelina, or Cimarron Rose. They expect you to be like the characters you play."

"That's right," she said. "How did you know?"

"And sometimes you get tired of people thinking you're someone else. You want to be yourself. You want people to know who you really are."

Victoria sat up and wrapped her arms around herself. She was not cold, for the day was growing steadily warmer, but she felt that Leroy could see straight through her clothing and flesh to her very bones.

"How do you know all those things about my life?" she asked.

It was not her life he was speaking about, but his own.

LONG AFTERWARD, VICTORIA told me of what passed between them on that Sonora riverbank. I felt like something of a fool for not having noticed sooner what was going on between them. I have related here several scenes to which I was not privy, about which I had no knowledge as yet, but even so, I know Victoria well and I should have noticed the signs. Instead, it was on the day of their bicycle ride that I got my first inkling that something was afoot.

They arrived back at the hacienda just in time for Leroy to help me watch over the gold while Brian and Gerald passed out bright American double eagles to our Mexican workers. These paydays were held often, as seeing the fruits of their labor raised the workers' spirits and encouraged them to work without complaint during the long hours of picture-making.

Since our first day in Delgado, Leroy had followed my suggestion, wearing a gun whenever he was overseeing the gold. He wore it now, a well-cared-for Colt's Frontier model that he carried stuck in the waistband of his trousers so as not to be too conspicuous. For my own part, I carried a cut-down American Arms shotgun of the twin-barrel variety, it having long been my experience that nothing serves to keep bold men on the straight and narrow so well as the dark-eyed stare of two twelve-gauge eyes.

We were a mean-looking pair, I have no doubt. The workers regarded us with proper deference as they stood in line, and they grew noticeably more nervous as they reached the table and received their gold. Some threw worried glances our way, as if we were two bad men from a western movie who might decide to switch sides of the law and rob them of their precious coins.

But Leroy got no such respect from Victoria when she strolled through the courtyard. She was costumed in another of Evangelina's outfits, in expectation of scenes to be filmed after the noonday meal. The workers' heads swiveled as she passed, but Victoria had eyes only for Leroy. She took one look at his feet and put a hand to her mouth to contain a girlish giggle.

I looked down and saw that his boots were wet, and I recalled that Leroy had walked a little gingerly as we fetched the strongbox from Victoria's trunk. Like Victoria, he had changed into fresh clothes when he returned from the eventful bicycle ride, but he had only one set of boots and no time to dry them before standing guard duty with me. As yet I had no idea how his footgear became watersoaked, but while observing this scene played out silently between them I recalled how Victoria had smiled with pure delight and hopped aboard the bicycle down in the plaza, and I realized that she and Leroy were no longer strangers.

They had become friends, and maybe something more.

At once I searched my memory for other clues, and had no trouble turning them up. When a man of cowboy upbringing washes his face every day and puts on a clean shirt every two, he is either working in a bank or courting his best girl. There was no bank in Delgado, Sonora, but I had ignored Leroy's shiny visage and clean wardrobe because I was so interested in getting to know him. Meanwhile, he had gotten to know Victoria. How well, I didn't know, and I decided to find out directly. If there was any courting going on, I intended to nip it in the bud.

When the workers were gone and Leroy and I had returned the strongbox to my bedroom, I cast about for a way to bring up what was on my mind.

"You want to eat lunch first?" I asked him, just to say something.

"You go on," he said, as agreeable as ever. "I'll eat later."

"It crossed my mind you might take a powder once we got here." At the moment I tended to favor the notion.

"I signed on to do a job, Charlie. I don't run out on a job."

His manner changed as he sensed my mood. He was quieter, more serious, but still friendly. It was plain that he had no idea what had me on edge. Still I kept circling, like the old hound stalking the bobcat.

"It would be a shame if anything was to happen to the gold," I said. "This picture means a lot to Victoria."

"I don't want to see her get hurt any more than you do."

"I'll count on that." I felt fairly certain that Victoria's gold was safe in his hands, but I was still concerned for her heart.

"Anybody hurts her, he'll answer to me," I added for good measure.

"He'll answer to both of us, Charlie," he said, just as if he agreed with everything I said and didn't see the warning at all.

Chapter 13

"HELLO? HELLO!" GERALD shouted into the telephone. Getting no response, he looked inquiringly at Señor Garza, the stationmaster, who urged him to speak again.

"*Sí, el está allá, señor. Hable otra vez.*"

Victoria and Brian and I were gathered around Gerald in the railroad station, all of us with a stake in *The Trail of Pancho Villa* having come down to learn whether the first batch of film turned out all right. Of course only Gerald knew just how much each of us had risked to get the production under way in the first place.

"Hello?" Gerald said tentatively. "Ah, there you are, Hintz. This is Sir Gerald Ball speaking. What on earth is causing all the delay . . . No, the delay! What is taking so long? . . . Good God, you're not serious! . . . Yes . . . It is? . . . All of it?"

A smile replaced Gerald's frown and he made encouraging gestures to the rest of us while he listened to Orville on the other end of the line clear up in Hollywood.

"He says it all came out and it looks splendid!" Gerald said. "What's that? . . . Speak up, can't you!"

"I can just imagine Orville Hintz saying it looks splendid," Victoria said.

Brian grinned. "I'll bet he said it was all crackerjack."

"For heaven's sakes, hush!" Gerald exclaimed. He listened to Orville a moment longer, then exploded. "Monday afternoon! But . . . Minter! Oh, for God's sake!" He fell silent, listening intently, now and then saying "Yes," or "All right." When it appeared he was about to end the conversation, Victoria made gestures to indicate that she wanted to speak with Orville when Gerald was done.

"That's the train my wife will be on," Gerald said to Orville. "All right . . . yes. It's worth waiting for." He offered the earpiece to Brian. "He wants to speak with you."

Brian grabbed it and put it to his good ear. "Orville! How's that morning shot at the cantina? . . . The cantina! . . . It is? Great! . . . Never mind. So long as the light's about the same, it'll work fine!"

"Damn all the Wobblies and Bolshevists!" Gerald proclaimed to the room at large, taking everyone aback. Victoria looked at him as if he had lost his senses.

"*Yo soy carranzista, señor,*" the stationmaster protested, but Gerald ignored him.

"It took Hintz three days to get to Los Angeles," he explained. "Passenger service on all the western lines is cut back because of a coal strike in the East. Imagine those agitators managing to delay our picture from thousands of miles away! Then there was a mix-up at the laboratory. They have a new Mary Miles Minter picture on rush. And Arbuckle is pounding on the door as usual, always in a hurry. They developed our film but didn't print it. Now they will do the print over the weekend. Hintz should have it on Monday. He will leave Los Angeles the next day, on the same train as Rosa and the children."

Brian was hearing roughly the same news from Orville, without the political tirades.

"All right," he said. "We'll see you then. But listen, that means you'll have to turn around and go right back. We've got to be sure all the exteriors of the phony town come out before we burn it. . . . Okay . . . No, you'll get your Christmas dinner. I promise."

"Wait!" Victoria snatched the telephone from Brian's hand as he made to hang up the earpiece. "Orville? Hold on a moment."

She turned to us. "Would you gentlemen excuse me?"

The gentlemen left the lady to her private conversation and stepped outside into the noonday sun. Gene Ortiz and a few of his vaqueros were hazing a small bunch of cows down the road, heading for the stockyards.

Brian glanced impatiently at his wristwatch as he paced back and forth. "Come on, Victoria," he muttered.

"You're ahead of schedule," Gerald said.

"And I'd like to stay that way," Brian replied. When Victoria emerged from the station, looking very pleased with herself, he hustled her into the Model T coupé and rattled off.

Gerald and I having ridden to the station on horseback, we mounted up. Gerald rode competently enough, as a result of wasting his young manhood chasing defenseless foxes across the Surrey countryside.

"Two and a half weeks to go and more than half the picture done," I said as we started off. "Looks like you'll have to get into the hotel business some other way."

"The film isn't in the can yet, Charles," Gerald said.

He was telling me not to count my chickens, but I was feeling carefree that day. Since Orville left Delgado the pace of production had picked up. Brian was keeping everyone hopping from sunup to sundown, and when night fell they were too tired to get into mischief. The picture was two days ahead of schedule, and my concerns for Victoria's heart were growing smaller into the bargain.

Since my little chat with Leroy he had volunteered to spend more time with the gold. Naturally I accepted his offer, and without making much of it I scheduled our shifts in a way that kept him busy when Victoria was free, and vice versa. I ate my meals with Victoria and the crew, leaving Leroy to eat alone in the kitchen when we were done, and I kept him watching over Victoria's trunk until everyone was asleep at night. He accepted the new state of affairs without complaint, passing his time upstairs by reading the handful of English books in Rafael Delgado's library, while Victoria's high spirits continued undiminished as she devoted herself wholeheartedly to doing her best work ever in *The Trail of Pancho Villa*.

I had done some detective work too, which consisted mainly in chatting with Redeye and Chief John and Victoria herself about the day Leroy showed up on the company's location in Hollywood. Judging by what John and Redeye told me, and Victoria's reticence, I guessed that she had taken an interest in Leroy from the start, but seeing the two of them just as merry even while their work kept them apart, I began to feel that I had been too quick to imagine the sparks of romance flying between them. This is such a fine example of wishful thinking, I would frame it if I could, and hang it on the wall.

Gerald and I trotted past a pretty young señorita and her mother, who were walking down to the river carrying bundles of washing on their heads. Gerald tipped his hat, which caused the señora to frown and hustle her daughter along. Gerald glanced at me a trifle guiltily. He had been on his best behavior since we arrived in Delgado, unwilling to risk an indiscretion in his wife's family's hometown.

"Is that horse of yours up to a faster pace?" I asked. He was riding Jack Whistler's iron-gray stallion, Buck. Gerald was posting to Buck's trot in the lordly British manner. I knew Buck to be a fine horse, but more suited to the long haul than short sprints.

Gerald smiled, sensing a dare. "Buck will be glad to teach any pace you like to that animal of yours."

I would not stand for Jake being insulted, so I socked spurs to his flanks and gave him to understand that he could sprout wings and fly, if he had a mind to. We jumped out a length ahead of Gerald right at the start.

"Last one to the hacienda's a rotten egg!" I called back over my shoulder.

Jake was hogfat and raring to go after having little exercise for nearly two weeks. By the look of him, he had put on some weight, doing justice to his namesake, Eat-em-up-Jake, a Russian wolfhound I owned for many years and loved dearly. Naming a horse after a dead dog might seem strange to some people, but I have known more than one horse named for a man, and many named for women. Shortly after Eat 'Em Up Jake went to dog heaven, a colt was born on my Sunny Slope ranch, and as he took his first steps something about the gleam in his eye reminded me of Jake, so I gave him Jake's name. In the mysterious Orient, philosophers believe that every spirit, even those of animals, returns to live many lives on the earth. I scoffed at this foreign notion in my youth, but I may have gained some shreds of wisdom in surviving to my present age. My wolfhound Jake was always sad at being forced to remain at Sunny Slope while I was away on detective business, and I think it is entirely reasonable that he might have come back as a horse so he could accompany me on my travels, instead of staying home.

Jake and I beat Gerald and Buck to the hacienda by at least a furlong, and to make Gerald's day complete Jack Whistler gave him a good dressing-down for riding Buck without asking first. Jack told Gerald in no uncertain terms that among the cowboy set a man might be horse-whipped for riding another's horse without permission, but seeing as how Gerald was an ignorant city fellow, Jack said he would let him off this once with a good scolding.

BACK IN TEXAS where I was raised, Old Saint Nick sometimes rode into the Christmas holidays on a Texas blue norther and left looking the worse for wear, but December in Sonora can be like spring in California. As we entered Christmas week of 1919, the good weather held. We all worked like Turks while George cranked out film by the tinful, and blue northers were the farthest thing from my mind.

Because we couldn't burn the false town until the film that showed those sets still standing had been safely developed and printed in Hollywood, Brian picked scenes from throughout the scenario to work on while we awaited Orville's return. Two days before Christmas he surprised everyone by announcing that we would film the next section of the story in its proper order, which caused Victoria to remark that she would know where she was for the first time in days.

The sequence of scenes began with Villa returning triumphantly to his bandit's lair, bringing with him the booty from his raid.

This lair, as it happened, bore a startling resemblance to the Delgado hacienda. For these scenes, several dozen townspeople were enlisted as "extras" and dressed up like the families of the revolutionists. Dressed down would be putting it more accurately, as even the poorest Mexicans do their best to keep their homes and their persons clean. The *delgadeños* made camp outside the walls and even within the courtyard, with babies and dogs and cookfires everywhere, and the hullabaloo they set up when Chief John and his *muchachos* returned with the captive Evangelina could have roused the dead. It's a pity movies don't have sound.

John rode through it all with a dignity befitting the bandit king of northern Mexico, and it struck me that the modern age has created more than one set of strange bedfellows. Cowboys and Indians working together in the McQuain & Vickery show are all very well, but there have been no more bitter enemies on this earth than Apaches and Mexicans. In his youth Chief John spent a good deal of time dealing out death and destruction south of the border. Seeing John playing a Mexican now, riding through the cheering throng of "his" people, I felt a sudden hope that perhaps the Great War will truly prove to be the cataclysm that ended war, and this new age may be a time of peacemaking among all peoples who have heretofore been enemies.

I suppose the approach of Christmas had something to do with this woolgathering, which is not like me.

With the bandits' return successfully captured on film, everyone looked forward to the next morning's work. Naturally the burning question on the audience's mind at this point in the story is what the dastardly Villa will do to Evangelina once he has her alone in his impregnable stronghold. Never ones to disappoint our public, we scenarists have Villa do just what the audience hopes for: he takes Evangelina to his boudoir—if a Mexican bandit can be said to have a boudoir—and there he intends to pitch her a little woo.

At our daily conference after supper, Brian and George and I scrutinized the scene long and hard, looking for some way to improve upon it.

"Villa can't be just another leering barbarian ravishing the poor helpless damsel," Brian said. "We saw enough of that kind of thing in the war. Drooling Huns plucking the flower of French womanhood, and all that."

"Evangelina's no helpless damsel," George observed. "Miss Hartford would walk off the set if you tried to make her play it like that."

Women who can handle themselves in a fix, much like the hardy women of the true frontier, are the style of the times in western films, and Victoria wouldn't have it any other way.

"The audience will be watching for Evangelina to try something," Brian said.

"They know what to expect from Evangelina," I said. "The fellow we don't know is Villa."

Brian seemed to have the glimmer of an idea. "What was he like?" he asked George. "I mean really. Beyond what you've already told us."

Of course the minute I learned that George Bleumel knew the real Pancho Villa, I had joined Brian in pumping him for everything he could remember, so as to learn what qualities of the original we might wish to use in our movie play. The American newspapers portrayed Villa as an unwashed ruffian, but George had soon corrected that impression.

"He's very serious," he had told us as we hunched over a table in the parlor of the Bunk House. "He's quite dignified, actually. He never gets tired, and he oversees everything that goes on in his army. He has a great capacity for organization. He was just thirty or so, when I was with him, but he handled that army as well as any general officer I saw later on in Europe."

Now we were looking for something more.

"What was he like with women?" Brian asked.

"Oh, he's a Mexican all right," George said, stroking his shiny dome with his fingertips. "I mean he has an eye for the women, and they just about faint dead away when he looks at them. They competed for his favors, you might say."

My brain was up to a trot by now. "We need to show the man beneath the bandit."

Brian was way ahead of me. "We need to show his soft spot. He really *loves* the women. We need to show the quality that wins over all those ladies."

"There weren't that many ladies, Boss," George said. "But there were a few."

"Up to now we've shown old Pancho as a disreputable hooligan," I said.

"That's fine," said Brian. "That's just what the public expects. But now we surprise them."

Half an hour later we had the revisions to the scene all worked out. Brian pounded away furiously at his portable typewriter for another half hour, and the next morning at breakfast the actors looked over the revised pages of the scenario.

For Villa's "boudoir" we borrowed Rafael and Magdalena Delgado's bedchamber, which was redecorated in a fashion appropriate to a revolutionist leader. To achieve this look, Buddy Johnston stood by with an armful of guns and knives and whatnot while Brian selected the items he wanted and placed them artfully about. As filming commenced I kept guard on the bedroom door, admitting only those with a job to perform, lest the room get so crowded we couldn't get any work done at all.

Although the scene would run less than five minutes in the theater, it took all morning to film, what with master shots and close-ups and Brian's insistence that we get it just right.

In a nutshell, it goes like this: Villa enters the room, hauling Evangelina roughly behind him. He throws her on the four-poster bed, where she cowers in terror. But then Pancho undergoes a change. As he unbuckles his cartridge belts he sees how afraid she is. He smiles and says, "Do not fear me, my beauty. I am a gentle man."

At this point there is a close-up in which Chief John gives the camera a look guaranteed to melt the hearts of the women in the audience, it being our intention to engender some sympathy for old Pancho.

Now Evangelina dares to hope that she may call on the revolutionist's mercy to save her from a fate worse than death.

Villa's line, and the close-up, and Evangelina's hopeful reaction, were the changes we had made in the scenario the night before. Sure, Tom and his boys are going to whip Villa's men to a frazzle in the next ten minutes, but it was our idea to make Pancho a gentlemanly adversary who concedes that he has been beaten by a better man and gives a parting wave of blessing to the happy couple at the end of the picture. That would set female hearts to pounding all across the U.S. of A., or we missed our bet, such romantic twaddle being like milk and honey to the poor souls who live ordinary lives.

Naturally we could not allow Pancho to show Evangelina just how gentle he could be. After some further interplay between them, mostly consisting of impassioned looks, Villa turns his back on Evangelina to undress. Whereupon she grabs a vase full of flowers from beside the bed and knocks him colder than a mackerel. To save Chief John from a fractured skull, we had a number of these vases specially made by the local pot maker. They were very thin, and unfired, which made them break easily. Still, Victoria played both her fear and her revenge to the hilt, and by the time Brian had redone the knockout three times, old John looked a little woozy.

"I hope you're not figuring on having me ride a horse today," he said to Brian after the third take. John was sitting on the bed, holding his head.

"Half the picture is horseback. I was figuring we'd get started on the chase this afternoon." Brian was very serious.

"Can't we give everyone a few hours off?" Victoria ventured. "It's Christmas Eve."

Brian looked surprised. "Is it? I guess that means we can only work half a day tomorrow."

"We can't ask these people to work on Christmas Day!" Victoria protested. "I don't care if it puts us behind schedule or not."

Brian grinned, letting down his false front. "Actually, we've gained another day on the schedule since Orville left. I thought we'd give the crew this afternoon off and all of tomorrow."

This brought hurrahs from all present, and as the crew ate their midday meal Victoria came up with a novel way to celebrate the holiday. She conferred briefly with Jack Whistler, then stood on the tongue of the chuckwagon to address them.

"What would you think of giving a show for the town, by way of saying thanks for all their help?"

THE *DELGADEÑOS* HAD never seen a wild west show before, but they took to it as readily as any audience of Americans. The performance was held on the street by the railroad, with the townspeople lining both sides of the roadway. Chairs for the Delgados and their children were placed in front of the railroad station, right in the center of things. *Patrón* and *peón* alike cheered the trick riding and roping, and everyone went wild when our red Indians attacked the wagon train, forcing it to circle in front of the railroad station. There the besieged "pioneers"—which included all the women of the company, dressed in gingham dresses and sunbonnets— fought off the howling savages, burning enough black powder to cloud the street with acrid smoke, until Jack Whistler led a detachment of cavalry "scouts" to the rescue. Willie Two Horse's wife Anna was among the pioneers as always, reliving the scene she had played for real while only an infant. (Although she was as white as any person in the McQuain & Vickery outfit, Anna was more at home speaking Sioux than English, having been captured when she was just five years old and raised among that tribe. When peace came between the whites and the Sioux she was offered a chance to return to her own people, but she replied simply, "These are my people now.")

In between acts, Dusty Clark entertained the crowd with his bullwhip, and partway through the performance he took center stage to render the "drunken cowboy" stunt that is so well-known to wild west show audiences.

When it came time for our boys to demonstrate their cowboy skills on bucking horses, the local vaqueros couldn't wait to get into the act, and before we knew it we had an impromptu stampede going on, using the chutes of the railroad stockyards to hold the bucking horses before they were turned loose. When the bucking events were done, Gene Ortiz rode off with a few of his lads and came back a short time later pushing a bunch of steers for roping and bulldogging. I was glad to see Leroy among the vaqueros. I was caught up in the good will of the season, and felt I had been unjustly harsh in keeping Leroy bottled up with the gold in recent days.

"Brian and Gerald are counting the gold and going over the books," he said, reining Sonny in next to where I was sitting on the stockyard fence. "I thought I'd come down and see the show."

"You're just in time to see the girls do their stuff."

He had arrived in the middle of the cowgirls' trick-riding act, put on by Victoria and Karen Valdez and Dottie Thompson. Even when Victoria became a picture star she insisted on keeping her place in the act, much to her directors' horror. But she said if she hurt herself performing with the show, at least it would be doing what she loved to do. There is no arguing with her when she puts her foot down.

The cowgirls shook out their ropes and built their loops, spinning them above their heads and letting them drop until each rider was encircled by her own lariat as she raced along the street.

"I haven't seen that stunt before," I said.

"I gave them the idea for that one," said Leroy, looking pleased with himself.

At the far end of the street, the cowgirls dropped their ropes and came back with the three horses racing neck and neck. One by one they stood up in the saddles. Karen, the smallest of the three, jumped from her paint horse Apache to join Victoria on Ranger's back, then climbed atop Victoria's and Dottie's shoulders, where she stood triumphantly, her legs steadied by their free hands. As she passed the stockyards, she removed her hat and sailed it toward me and Leroy, who caught the hat and sailed it back to her when the cowgirls trotted along the street one last time to accept the applause of the crowd. Dottie gave a wave to her husband Jim Ray, who was sitting nearby with Tommy Fear. Of the two Thompsons, Dottie was top hand without a doubt, but Jim Ray never let it bother him. Just now he was shouting himself hoarse for the cowgirls to show his appreciation of their skills.

"Come on, Charlie," Leroy said. "Let's get in on this steer roping. We can't let these young fellows show us up."

That was a cowboy challenge I couldn't refuse. In a twinkling I was astraddle Jake's hurricane deck. "I'll have to borrow a rope somewhere," I said.

Leroy didn't seem to hear me. He was looking toward the south end of town where a small bunch of riders was approaching at a trot. There were seven men in the group, and they were armed. They slowed to a walk when they reached the edges of the crowd. Their manner was utterly different from that of the carefree vaqueros, who rode in and out of town as if they owned it. The *delgadeños* fell back before the newcomers, and I saw mothers gathering their children around them.

"*Rurales*," Leroy said. A moment later I heard the same word whispered among the townspeople.

The little patrol stopped briefly as the leader spoke with a few of the onlookers. Just then a steer was turned loose from one of the stockyard chutes, with Gene Ortiz close behind him. Gene shook out his rawhide riata in a jiffy, cast it perfectly over the steer's horns, flipped a coil down the rope to snare the steer's front feet, and before the poor animal knew what had happened, he was on the ground with the wind knocked out of him, trussed up so he couldn't move.

"We ain't gonna beat that time," I observed.

"Speak for yourself, Charlie," Leroy said. He was still watching the *rurales*. They joined in applauding Gene's dexterity, and they appeared more relaxed as they continued down the street.

"Good thing there's only seven of them," Leroy said.

"Good thing our boys have got their hardware on," I said.

The McQuain & Vickery crew were all armed to the teeth for the show, but I had left my Peacemaker at the hacienda. I felt naked without it, and was just as glad that the *rurales* had no way of knowing our boys' guns were loaded with blank cartridges.

The *rurales* have often behaved like loose cannons lurching about the Mexican deck, uncontrolled and dangerous. The people, no matter whether they support the government or the revolution, generally fear them, and with good reason. But with just seven of them, this patrol would think twice before starting any trouble around a bunch of armed *gringos*.

"They take out a patrol that small, they're sure not expecting any trouble in this part of the country," Leroy observed.

The *rurales* dismounted to watch the show, chatting with the crowd. The *delgadeños* responded cautiously at first, then more warmly as they saw that the *rurales* meant them no harm.

Leroy and I joined the ropers waiting their turn, and we acquitted ourselves well enough, both throwing our steers. As soon as mine was turned loose from the chute I let out a Comanche yell, terrifying the poor brute so badly he could do nothing but run in a straight line, right into my loop. But I was right about no one beating Gene Ortiz's time. He walked away with that event. You've got to get up early in the morning to beat a real vaquero at his own game.

Our boys fared better at the bulldogging, which is an American art, having been originated by the famed Negro cowboy Bill Pickett. Nate Dicenzo's dun mustang Buster was born to work cattle and he delivered Nate neatly onto his steer's horns not thirty feet from the gate, which gained Nate a time that proved to be the day's best in this event.

I took no part in the bulldogging. When a man is past sixty and has

eaten as much trail dust as I have, he has earned the right to watch younger men risk life and limb for the sheer joy of it. But Leroy was determined to have a go. He drew the last steer of the afternoon, a sturdy beast
that had already been roped twice and bulldogged once. I hazed for him,
keeping the steer running straight when he made his jump for the horns.
He brought the steer down right in front of Victoria, where she was
watching from the railroad station platform in the company of the Delgados.

As Leroy turned the steer loose and got to his feet, a distant whistle
heralded the arrival of the cattle train.

"It's Orville's train!" someone shouted.

Leroy's steer, determined to suffer no further abuse, bolted straight
down the street, scattering the crowd that was already flocking to the
station to welcome the train.

Leroy dabbed at his nose, which he had bashed against the steer's head
in bringing the animal down. He found a trickle of blood.

"Hold still," said Victoria. She used the corner of his bandanna to wipe
the blood away.

"You two are a fine pair," she said. She made out that she was scolding,
but we could see she was secretly pleased that we had held our own with
the younger men, and we swelled up to about twice our normal size as the
train pulled into the station.

Seeing Gene Ortiz trot past us on the trail of Leroy's fugitive steer, I
called out to him above the puffing of the engine and the squeal of brakes.

"Hey, Gene, you might have one of your boys keep an eye on those
rurales and let me know if they bed down in town or head on out." Or
words to that effect, since I spoke in Mexican. He gave me a wave and
went on his way.

Inasmuch as many Sonorans were traveling up and down the line to
join other members of their families for Christmas, we had expected that
there might be a passenger car on the train, but what the railroad had
provided instead was a boxcar fitted with rough wooden seats. Despite
these rude accommodations, Rosa Ball and her children were the very
picture of holiday cheer as they stepped down to the platform. Rosa was
astonished to find us all on hand to greet her, and even as the Delgados
flocked around her, re-enacting the scene that had welcomed our company to Delgado with even more tears and laughter, the Dodge touring
car arrived from the hacienda with old Ramón at the wheel to carry her
thither in style.

A cheer greeted Orville Hintz as he appeared with a stack of film tins in
his arms. He earned an even louder one when he returned to the car and
emerged again, this time carrying a small Christmas tree. Relieved of this
burden in turn, he went back a last time for two large shopping bags that

contained many small items he had bought for members of the company at their request. There were cough drops for Chief John, Wrigley's gum for Jim Ray Thompson, newspapers for me, and Pall Malls for Brian and Gerald. I saw him hand one parcel to Victoria, which no doubt explained her private conversation with him on the telephone.

With the sun setting in the west, we escorted the car up to the hacienda, feeling the pleasurable exhaustion that comes from hard play, which is so different from being just plain tired. I was unsaddling Jake out by the corrals when Gene Ortiz found me to say that the *rurales* had gone on their way.

"They bought some things at the *tienda*," he told me. "Then they rode out of town, going to the north along the railroad."

As long as the *rurales* were around I felt like there was a wild card in the deck, and I didn't like the feeling. Knowing they were gone was all it took to put me back in the Christmas mood.

Seeing the film Orville brought back was the picture crew's Christmas present. Brian had a projector and a screen, and as dusk fell on Christmas afternoon, we saw some of the best picture footage any of us ever set eyes on. Not even Griffith and Bitzer could top Brian Hill and George Bleumel's work on *The Trail of Pancho Villa*.

There is nothing that makes a writer feel more important than seeing his ideas brought to life in black and white on the silver screen, and that first look at our handiwork pleased me no end. George had a painter's eye for beauty, both in the natural world and in the faces of the actors. I have never seen Victoria look better, and George had a knack for making the scenes look *real*. Maybe his time with Villa, and with the Canadians in France, accustomed him to the look of real life as seen through the camera lens. Even when he was shooting the lighthearted tale of Tom and Evangelina, he managed to make it appear like a depiction of true happenings rather than a story acted out for the camera.

When the lights came on, everyone was all smiles. Gerald gave Brian a nod of approval. "Most impressive," was all he said, but coming from him, that was a lot.

In no time, Orville's tree was set up in the hacienda's main hall and decorated with improvised ornaments, including a large star made of cardboard and tin foil. Just about everyone in the company assisted in this project. When it was done we all stood back to admire our handiwork. However much fun we were having, we were strangers in a foreign land, and the tree made us feel at home. The hacienda had electricity—the only dwelling in town so equipped—but the growing American fad for electric Christmas tree lights has not yet reached into Mexico, and the tree was decorated with the more traditional candles, to everyone's delight.

"Now it's a real Christmas," said Katie Elderberg, speaking for all of us.

Speaking just for myself, it was a Christmas I will never forget, in part for a reason none of the others could guess.

When I was a small boy in Texas, during the Rebellion, a Spanish ship wrecked on the Matagorda peninsula, not far from the humble home I shared with my dear mother and sister. Life was hard for us in those days, my father having died when I was too young to remember. My idea of a feast was three bowls of mush and milk, and maybe a couple of hard-boiled eggs.

Naturally we were off to the beach as soon as we heard of the wreck. I ran as fast as my bare feet could carry me and got there ahead of my female relations, hoping to find a treasure of Spanish gold washed up on the sands. Never mind that gold couldn't float. I would swim for it if I had to. The main thing was that I should find some treasure. But what I found instead was crate upon crate of fancy tableware, some of the crates broken open on the beach. The stuff was blue with gold trim around the edges, and some sort of picture in the middle of each piece. I was considerably put out, this not being the sort of booty that appealed to a lad of my tender years and lively imagination. But my mother's eyes grew wide and she set us at once to carrying the plates and saucers back to our little shanty. To her, having more than two plates of the same pattern was more treasure than she ever hoped to see, and I will admit that when next we sat down to supper, I felt that I had risen a notch or two in the world to see my mother setting out our modest fare with such pride.

Some years later Mother sold her fine china in Illinois, having been lured thither by her second husband, the no-good Mr. Carrier, whose main talents were imbibing corn liquor and wheedling my poor trusting mother out of her meager savings. When the small cache of gold she had set aside before the war against "hard times" was gone, Mr. Carrier pulled his carcass for parts unknown, and Mother was forced to pawn most of our belongings to make ends meet.

Imagine my pleasure when I came to dinner down there in Sonora on Christmas Eve and saw the very same brand of china adorning the long tables set for the movie crew and Delgado family in the hacienda's spacious hall. There were not just three or four plates that matched, but three dozen or more, with saucers and butter plates too.

Of course the hacienda had a proper dining room, which was off the main hall through a broad archway. Hospitality being as important a tradition here as on American ranches, the Delgados' dining room could seat a couple of dozen guests in regal style. But as the guest list for our Christmas banquet exceeded that number, the dining tables—along with several others—had been moved into the great hall, which made the front parlor of an American cattle baron's ranch house look like a two-hole outhouse by comparison. The McQuain & Vickery cowboys, all scrubbed down and dressed up, stood around somewhat self-consciously until Magdalena Delgado, assisted by Rosa Ball, herded them toward their seats.

Victoria came to dinner in her best dress, with a silk bandanna around her neck, her hair combed and shining, and laughter in her eyes. If she had ever appeared more contented, I could not recall the time.

"Oh, Charlie, this is the best Christmas ever," she said as she took her seat beside me. "And it's going to be a wonderful new year, too. Brian thinks we'll finish the picture early."

I opened my mouth, but she put a finger to my lips. "If you say 'Don't count your chickens,' Charlie Siringo, I will never speak to you again."

"Why, Miss Hartford, you're pretty as a picture," Leroy said as he sat down opposite Victoria. In his new dungarees, clean shirt and string tie, he was the very picture of an old-time cowboy dressed for a fancy supper.

As Rafael Delgado asked the Lord's blessing on our gathering, the festive moment and the sight of those plates took me back to my boyhood and the sound of my mother's voice saying grace. She being Irish and my father Italian, I was Catholic on both sides, so Señor Delgado's words were familiar to me, even though spoken in another language. I will admit that there may have been a small tear in the corner of my eye, but no one noticed an old cowboy's tender memories.

This sentimentality was soon banished by the arrival of the first course, and from start to finish the victuals were first-rate. Mexicans have their big meal on Christmas Eve, while most Americans wait until the holy day itself, but here, just as in the States, a fat turkey is the centerpiece of the feast. In Texas the bird is accompanied by cranberry sauce and sweet potatoes and pumpkin pie, with eggnog to wash it down. In the Delgado hacienda the side dishes were different, and the cranberry is unknown to them, that being one of the better products of Yankeedom, but the smell of the turkey made us all think of home once more.

Perhaps it was the Mexicans who brought the turkey custom to Texas, but no one of my generation would admit that our Christmas feast came to us from south of the border, as we were still too burned up about Santa Ana and his butchery of our forefathers at the Alamo and Goliad.

But recriminations were the farthest thing from my mind at our Christmas dinner in Delgado. This holiday is a time for joyful family reunions in Mexico. In the Delgado hacienda Rosa was reunited with her relations and they in turn made us all feel like family. I have said little enough about our hosts, but we had come to know them well, Rafael and Magdalena and their four children. They had extended us every sort of hospitality during our stay, up to and including inviting us all into the hacienda for a proper Christmas dinner. I had developed a soft spot in my heart for Magdalena Delgado as soon as I met her, for I had once been in love with a Mexican girl named Magdalena in Las Cruces, New Mexico, and Magdalena Delgado's sparkling eyes reminded me of my former sweetheart. I should add that the rest of her person bore no resemblance to my own slender Magdalena, as Señora Delgado tipped the scales at around two hundred pounds before breakfast.

Wine and *pulque* flowed freely throughout the meal, and before long the fermented juice of grape and cactus began to do its work. Brian Hill rose to propose a toast to our hosts, which prompted other toasts. As the feast drew to a close some of the boys were growing boisterous. Nothing would do but that we should have music provided by our picture-show band, and of course where there was music there was bound to be dancing.

So long as everyone was at the tables, Leroy and I could watch the stairs and eat in peace, knowing the gold in my bedroom was safe. Now, with people moving about the hacienda, one of us would have to keep a closer watch. As we rose from the table Leroy volunteered to stand guard so I could dance for a while, but I was warmed by the wine and feeling benevolent, and I assigned myself to stand the first watch.

"I'll leave the dancing to you younger folks, for now," I told him. "Later on, when things settle down, maybe I'll sit at the foot of the stairs and listen to the music."

The truth was, my taking part in the steer roping that afternoon had aggravated an old shoulder injury that was inflicted during my detective years when a team of horses ran away with me and threw me from a buggy. The wine had soothed the pain somewhat and I thought that a short rest would fix me up just right, and so, full of my own goodness and the charity of the season, I retired to my room to peruse the Los Angeles newspapers Orville had brought me.

The headlines were full of a sensational murder trial concerning one Harry New, who was supposed to have killed his girlfriend because she was in a family way and he did not want to marry her. This was just the sort of story the newspapers love, full of scandal and gossip, but it was not the hope of reading such juicy items that had prompted me to ask Orville for the papers. With Victoria and her film crew in Sonora, the threat of American intervention in Mexico was much on my mind, and so I dug deeper in the paper to ferret out the Mexican news.

I was relieved to find it heartening. President Wilson had taken a direct hand in the Jenkins affair, overriding a blustery ultimatum issued by Secretary of State Lansing. Jenkins, the American consular agent, was out of jail, and it appeared that tempers were cooling on both sides of the border. I learned too that the rumor Pancho Villa had been taken prisoner by his own men was decidedly false. He was apparently as free as ever, off raiding into Coahuila, the Mexican state on the eastern side of Chihuahua, where he and his army were said to be retreating into the northern mountains with President Carranza's *federales* closing in on him from three sides. On the fourth side lay the Texas border, and the *Evening Herald* assured its readers that should Villa attempt to retreat into the U.S., he would be arrested by American troops and brought to trial for the murders he committed in his 1916 raid on Columbus, New Mexico.

Reassured, I set the papers aside and lay back to rest, feeling pleasantly lightheaded from the wine. When the music started up in the hall below, the strains floated gently to my resting place and I dropped off for a short siesta.

Chapter 14

AS THE COWBOYS and the Delgados' servants moved the tables aside to make room for dancing, Victoria already felt like the belle of the ball. She moved among the men, twirling slowly to imaginary music, as if she were dancing on air. There was no particular reason for her joyful spirits that evening, or at least no one reason among the several that cheered her almost to the point of laughter. Christmas was her favorite holiday, she had her eye set on a handsome fellow who had his eye set on her, and on top of that her picture was going better than she had any right to expect.

But when the music began and she looked around for her fellow, he had disappeared. With me out of the way, she was free to track him down directly, without pussyfooting around the way she had been doing for the past week or more, ever since Leroy mentioned to her that Charlie didn't seem too happy the two of them were keeping company.

The first place she looked was out among the wagons, where Chief John and Willie Two Horse were stoking Luke Fister's cookfire into a bonfire near the chuckwagon. Both John and Willie were Christianized enough to appreciate the meaning of Christmas, but Christianity for them is like an extra overcoat they have donned to comfort them in the hard times they have seen, without ever abandoning entirely their older, more primitive ways. On this night, as on some others, they had brought out their drums. As Victoria moved beyond the adobe walls of the hacienda and nearer to John and Willie's fire, she left behind the lively melodies of

1919 and entered a scene that, but for the wagons, might have been taking place a thousand years before. On many another night out on the road with McQuain & Vickery, she had passed the evening sitting by just such a campfire, but tonight she had other things on her mind. Her eye was out for Leroy, but she saw Nate and Karen first, just as sparks began to fly between them.

"Aw, now Karen, don't spoil everything tonight," Nate said.

Until a moment before, he had been holding Karen in his arms, but he made the mistake of asking her what she wanted for Christmas and her answer was, a wedding date. Now he saw the fire in her eyes and took a step back. "Come on, now, honey."

"Don't you honey me, Nate Dicenzo. You got until New Year's Day to set a date for our wedding or all you'll get from me is the toe of my boot!"

Christmas was one of the two or three times in the year when Karen Valdez wore a dress. Prettied up, she could break Barrymore's heart. Even when she was angry, some men would be so taken by her looks that they wouldn't see the danger until it was too late.

She advanced on Nate like a mother cow going for a prairie wolf, circling slowly, then charging in for the kill when she was within striking range. But Nate knew what to expect. He dodged the kick Karen aimed at him and took off into the dark, nearly knocking Victoria down in his haste to escape.

Karen started after him, but stopped when she saw Victoria.

"You've got to run at a man or away from him," she said. "You stand still, they won't give you the time of day. Me, I'm going to leave that one in the dust." She turned on her heel and strode off toward the hacienda, ready to take the dance floor with any man there except Nate Dicenzo.

With Karen's advice fresh in her mind, Victoria continued on her way, searching among the wagons. She found Leroy standing at the tailgate of the wagon where he slept, doing something with his hands. He pushed a small object quickly out of sight in the wagon when he saw Victoria approaching.

"Have you got plans for the evening?" she asked for openers.

"I hear there's a dance hall full of movie stars holding a shindig."

"You got a special girl?"

"Could be."

She changed course then, the way a woman will do to keep a man off balance. "In your family, do you open your presents on Christmas Eve or Christmas morning?"

"Christmas morning."

"In ours, we open them Christmas Eve."

Before leaving the hacienda she had fetched a shawl from her room to keep her warm, and one other item, which she kept behind her back until now. It was the parcel Orville Hintz had handed her when he got off the train, only now it was wrapped in colored paper and tied up with a red ribbon.

Leroy was plainly delighted to find within the package the very latest model in men's bathing costumes.

"Now I'll have to learn to swim properly," he said.

"You get a free lesson with it," said Victoria.

That sobered him. "It might be a while before I take you up on that."

Reaching into the wagon he brought forth a small packet and placed it in her hand. It was wrapped in white tissue paper and tied with a piece of the same rough twine the Mexicans use for just about everything under the sun. But if the wrapping was crude, what lay within took Victoria's breath away.

"Oh," was all she could say when she saw the two small silver pistols the village silversmith had crafted to Leroy's order. They were crossed as if on a coat of arms, fastened to a silver ring. On the butt of one pistol was the letter *V*, on the other an *H*.

Victoria guessed right away what it was for, and was glad she had worn her best silk bandanna. She removed the ring that fastened the bandanna at her throat and replaced it with Leroy's gift.

"It's beautiful. Thank you," she managed to say.

Neither one of them spoke for a short span of time.

"You might ask a girl to dance," Victoria said at last.

"I dance worse than I swim," Leroy said.

"Then I'm fresh out of ideas."

"Ideas about what?"

"How to get you to put your arms around me."

WHEN I AWOKE from my rest and came downstairs, the Delgados and the servants had gone off to mass, along with a few of our company who kept the Catholic faith. A dozen couples were dancing, Leroy and Victoria among them. In a quiet corner Charlie Noble was instructing Katie Elderberg in the tango, and I could see from the way the other women kept an eye on him that he was a sought-after partner.

I hauled a chair close to the stairway so nobody could go up or down without my knowing it, and settled back to watch the goings-on. The music from the band and the twinkling candles on the Christmas tree made the big room very festive, but my cheerful mood dimmed as I noticed how Leroy and Victoria held each other close like sweethearts. After a few more tunes, when I saw that neither of them had any intention of dancing with another partner, I made my way across the floor, coming up behind Leroy.

"Suppose we swap partners," I said, offering him my shotgun when he turned.

As he took it, I noticed the new ring clasp on Victoria's bandanna. Gone was the piece of New Mexico jasper in a silver setting that I gave her for her eighteenth birthday, and I guessed at once who had given her the crossed silver pistols that took its place.

Just then, Karen Valdez stepped up to me. "I've been waiting all night for a dance with you, Charlie," she said.

Before I could protest she took me in her arms and off we went, she doing the leading, guiding me away from poor Nate just as he caught up with her. All evening she had kept one jump ahead of him. While she made bold with the other boys, Nate had consoled himself with the fermented juice of the maguey cactus. By the time I came downstairs he was red of eye and unsteady afoot. He looked like an old longhorn bull and he had the disposition to match, but Victoria took him in hand.

"Come on, Nate, let's talk about your future." She held out her arms and he accepted her offer, grateful for any port in a storm.

Leroy took my chair by the stairs. From there he kept an eye on Victoria and Nate, while Nate kept an eye on Karen even as he guided Victoria around the floor.

"You ought not to give that boy such a hard time," I told Karen. "He's devoted to you. You take it from an old hand at this business. Since I've known you two, I haven't seen him look twice at another woman. Well, maybe twice, but that's the limit."

"I know, Charlie. But he's got this damn fool notion he's wild and free and can't be happy any other way. If those old cattle trails of yours were still in business, he'd be gone."

"He's got the spirit of adventure, that's sure."

"I've got my own sense of adventure," Karen said. "No decent woman would speak to me if she knew all I've done or what I've given Nate in the past two years. But I've got my own notion of what's proper, too. I want that man to marry me. I've wanted it from the start."

"Nate'll settle down," I said. "Give him time."

"Dammit, Charlie, he takes every minute I give him and always wants more." She shot Nate a dirty look and spun me around so her back was to him.

It struck me that I was counseling one young couple to bury the hatchet and get hitched up for life while at the same time hoping to prevent another couple from doing the same thing. I thought I had nipped that romance in the bud, but now I was sure it had gone well beyond the early pruning stage. As I danced with Karen I wondered if there was any chance I might still stop it, and if I could, whether or not I had the right.

As soon as our dance was done, Karen was off again, her sights set on Randall Steele as Nate made for her from across the floor. Randall bowed to Katie Elderberg, who had favored him with the last dance, turned away, and stumbled into a small table, knocking glasses and bottles every which way. Nate tripped on a beer bottle and fell sideways into the table, breaking one of its legs to complete the destruction. When he looked up, Karen and Randall were dancing away.

Somehow in the commotion Victoria had disappeared, and then I saw that Leroy too was gone. At the foot of the stairs my shotgun leaned against the wall and the chair was empty.

I stopped Jack Whistler as he headed for Dottie Thompson to ask her for a dance. "Say, Jack, you didn't happen to see where Victoria went to?"

"Why, I believe she and Leroy just left," he said.

"Which way'd they go?"

"Off out back. You'd likely find them sitting on the pasture fence, just like every night."

"What do you mean, like every night?"

"The last week, Victoria's been waiting up till you turn Leroy loose from looking after that gold. They go off and set on the fence and talk."

"That's it? They just talk?"

"So far as I know." He saw that didn't reassure me. "Hell, Charlie, these things happen. They're both of age. What's got you so hot and bothered, anyhow? Leroy seems like a nice fellow."

"I'd take it kindly if you would keep an eye on the upstairs for a while," I said.

"Why, all right, Charlie. I was going to turn in early anyway."

"You sleep in my bed, then. I'll bunk out by the wagons."

The fat crescent moon lingered in the western sky, and as I moved past the corrals toward the pasture where Leroy held his small-fry baseball games I could see there was no one sitting on the fence. I turned toward the bonfire, keeping to the shadows, but Leroy and Victoria were not with the Indians, nor did I see anyone else afoot among the wagons. I slowed my pace then, beginning to have second thoughts about chasing after the missing couple. After all, what could I say if I found them together? But I kept moving all the same, circling around the hacienda, passing through the courtyard, and finally walking down the road to town.

So much for Mr. Leroy Roberts doing right by people who trusted him, I thought. I had trusted him. I had offered him my own personal amnesty and I had extended the hand of friendship to boot. I had given him a free rein. But I had also warned him once about trifling with Victoria, although I hadn't put it in so many words. The next time I got him alone I would speak more plainly.

The town of Delgado was magically transformed for Christmas Eve. Set on the ground along the sides of the railroad avenue were dozens of small lanterns, each containing a candle. *Luminarias*, they are called. When I reached the station and turned up the Avenida Central, I found it similarly illuminated. The streets were deserted, and I felt that the lanterns might have been set out just for me, to guide me along the candle-lit pathway to the plaza. It too was ringed with lanterns, and more stood on the steps of the church.

The whole town was crowded into the little church. I stepped inside the door and that was as far as I could go, but it was far enough to feel like part of the fold, although the mass was nearing its end. The church was lit by hundreds of candles, bathing the celebrants in a warm glow. I had not been inside of a church in years, but there is nothing like Christmas to get a lapsed Catholic in the proper mood for reverence. I found myself murmuring the responses along with the townsfolk even as I looked around, standing on tiptoe to peer over the heads of the crowd.

Fortunately for me, Mexicans tend to be shorter than Americans. Leroy and Victoria were among those standing at the end of the pews, along the wall. Victoria had her shawl over her head, and the way she held Leroy's arm made them appear to be just another couple who had come to observe the Christmas Eve ritual. Seeing how they seemed to belong together did nothing to calm my fears, but finding them in church made me feel like a spy. When the mass was over, I was the first one out the door. I didn't have the heart for further snooping, so I left the plaza by an alley and took a short cut to the hacienda, making my way up the slope to the plateau and alarming a few dozen dogs as I went.

I approached the hacienda from the back side so no one would know I had gone to town. Around the bonfire the drums had fallen silent and the voices raised there were singing the final verse of "Good King Wenceslas."

"Hey there, Charlie," Willie Two Horse greeted me as I stepped into the firelight. "Have a cup of coffee and set a spell."

Anna Two Horse, Willie's wife, was in charge of the coffee. She liked it strong enough to float a rock. "You drink this," she said as she handed me a tin cup of the stuff. "Make you strong, you bet."

We sat and chatted, and before long we were joined by the young people, who came from the hacienda in twos and threes. The gathering took me back to the trail drives of my youth, when my chums and I would enjoy some company and talk around the cookfire after a long day of breathing dust and cursing the obstinate nature of the longhorn tribe. Just to make me feel fully at home, a coyote howled somewhere out in the grassland.

At a lull in the conversation, Bob Elderberg said, "Spin us a yarn, Charlie."

This was not an unusual request. Of a quiet evening at the Bunk House the cowboys often asked me for a story. Among themselves they sometimes indulged in the cowboy diversion of telling tall tales and stretching the truth hither and yon like an india-rubber poncho, but from me they wanted the unvarnished stories of my eventful life, and I often obliged, sometimes choosing an adventure I had written about in one of my books, sometimes trying out a new one on my audience to see how it might fare with my readers.

"Victoria says you were down here before, when you were a detective," Dottie Thompson said, by way of steering my thoughts to our Mexican surroundings. Jim Ray had his arm around her and her head rested on his shoulder.

"I been to Mexico a bunch of times," I began. "Growing up in south Texas I knew some of the lingo, so the Pinkertons figured I was just the man to send south of the border. The first time I was chasing an Atchison, Topeka brakeman who was in a train wreck not far from the border. The express car got busted open in the wreck and there was money blowing away on the breeze. This fellow gathered up about ten thousand dollars and set out to retire in Mexico City. My job was to keep an eye on him until he went back to the States, so I had some time on my hands. I saw the sights and even managed to get some revenge for the Alamo."

"The Alamo? How'd you do that?" Nate wanted to know. Like any full-blooded Texan, Nate sat up a little straighter at the mention of the name. He was across the fire from Karen, apparently having failed in his efforts to make peace with her.

"I knew an engineer on the Mexican railroad. He took me to the Church of Guadalupe, where Santa Ana is buried. They have an iron fence around his grave and the mound is covered with bits of broken crockery and all sorts of relics. Some kind of Mexican custom, my friend said. There was an armed guard there too, but I had to have some of that crockery, so I hopped over the fence and grabbed a piece while my friend talked with the guard. Later on, he told me the penalty for tampering with Santa Ana's grave would be death, or life in prison. If I'd known that, I might not have done it, but I've always felt like I struck a blow for Texas that day. You come to my office when we get home, and I'll show you that piece of china."

Nate might have been the only one there who understood what my prank meant to me, him and the Indians, who place great stock in the things put on a man's grave.

"Another time I was down here with Joe LaFors, the U.S. Marshal from Cheyenne. We ran around most of Chihuahua hunting some of the Wild Bunch, but it turned out it was a false trail. Old Joe, he spent nearly as much time as I did trailing Butch and the boys, but he came up empty, just like me."

"Was Butch the toughest outlaw you ever knew?" Bob Elderberg asked. Bob was from Lander, Wyoming, right in the heart of Butch's outlaw stomping grounds, and he took a lively interest in the Wild Bunch stories.

"First off," I said, choosing my words with care, "I didn't set eyes on Butch in all the years I worked for Pinkerton's. I learned so much about him I felt like I knew him all the same, but I wouldn't say tough was the right word for him. I don't mean he was soft. But he wasn't mean like some of them, and he wasn't a killer. The Sundance Kid was a cold one, I heard tell, and Kid Curry would shoot you soon as look at you. I'd say he was the toughest."

"What sort of Christmas do you suppose those men had?" Katie Elderberg wondered. She moved closer to Bob and put her arm around him, as if thinking of an outlaw's lonely Christmas made her cold.

"They got their share of turkey and pumpkin pie," I said. "They pulled off most of their robberies in spring and summer, when the grass was up and the horses were strong. Wintertime, they laid low. They tried to find some place like home, even if the company they found was men on the dodge. They had some lively times in Brown's Hole, and I heard tell that one winter Butch Cassidy played Santa Claus to a family of nesters."

I poured myself some more coffee, then resettled myself so I could lean back against the hind wheel of Bob and Katie's wagon.

"I got this from the nesters themselves, when I was on Butch's trail. It was a family named Hargrove, or Hancock, or something of that nature. They'd been hoodwinked by some crooked land speculators and were living pretty low, trying to get by farming. Out of this December blizzard comes a man on horseback, three-quarters froze to death. So they rub him down with snow and thaw him out and feed him as best they can on what they've got. When he's up and around, it's a day or so before Christmas. He borrows a buckboard and team and goes into town, buys clothes and food and presents for the whole family. When he's unloading this stuff at the nesters' shack, three men stop by, a sheriff and two deputies."

By now, my listeners were hanging on my words. At the mention of the sheriff, Bob Elderberg stopped in the act of rolling a smoke, the drawstring to his Durham sack held in his teeth.

"Well, Butch figures they've got him cold," I went on, "so he keeps on lifting boxes and sacks out of the buckboard, and the nester kids are jumping up and down with joy. Finally, when everything is on the porch, Butch says, 'You folks saved my life, so here's a merry Christmas to you.' About then the sheriff speaks up and says, 'We're looking for a man called George Leroy Parker? Any of you people run across someone who answers to that name?' 'No,' says the nesters, and naturally Butch says 'no' too, so the sheriff says 'Merry Christmas,' and gives Butch a smile, and they ride away."

"Good thing they didn't recognize him," said Jim Ray Thompson.

"Of course they recognized him, boy," Bob said. "That's the whole point of the story." He licked his smoke and took a stick from the fire to light it. "You hear a lot of stories like that around Lander. You can't get anyone to say a bad word about Butch. It seems like he helped more people than he hurt."

Something moved in the darkness across the fire from where I was sitting, and I made out Leroy standing by a wagon there, just at the edge of the light. I wondered how long he had been there.

"If he was such a nice fellow, it's too bad he didn't quit when he was ahead," said Redeye Hawk.

"He tried," I told him. "He offered to give up the holdup life if the Union Pacific would drop the charges against him. He offered to serve as an express guard."

"Boy, that'd put a quick stop to train robberies," Jim Ray said.

"What happened, Charlie?" Buddy Johnston asked. He was sitting back from the fire.

"A lawyer friend of Butch's went to Heber Wells, the governor of Utah. Wells helped set up a meeting between Butch and the Union Pacific, at an old stage stop in Wyoming. Butch waited all day but the U.P. men didn't show. Their train was late, if that doesn't beat all. Butch thought they stood him up, so he left a note telling them to please go to Hades, and the next job he pulled was to hit the U.P. again. Right after that, him and the Sundance Kid and Will Carver took the bank at Winnemucca, and the next summer they robbed the Great Northern Coast Flyer up in Montana. Three big robberies in less than a year. That was their last hurrah."

"And you never got close to Butch?" Tommy Fear wanted to know.

"I was waiting for him to make a mistake, but he never tripped up once. Even so, we busted up the gang. When the going got too hot, Butch skipped to Argentina with the Sundance Kid."

"Things'd have to get mighty hot before I'd run to Argentina," Tommy said.

"Oh, it wasn't too bad," I said. "It's beef country, full of cowboys. They call them *gauchos* down there, but I hear they rope pretty good. Some two-bit outlaw named Bill McChesney hid out down there back in '87 or so. By the time Butch and Sundance got there, it was just another stop on the Outlaw Trail. But they didn't go there to hide out. It was Butch's second try at going straight. They bought some land and ranched peaceably for a few years, Butch and Sundance and Etta Place. She was the Sundance Kid's woman and she was a looker. They raised horses and cattle and sheep too. It's good sheep country, by what I hear."

"But they pulled robberies there," Bob said.

"That was later. There were plenty of Americans down there, and not all of them outlaws. As it happened, a former Wyoming lawman was traveling through the country buying stock. He recognized Butch and figured there might still be some reward money up for grabs back in the States, so he told the local law where they could find Butch Cassidy. Butch and Sundance and Etta got chased off their land and they went to robbing banks."

"So if that stock buyer hadn't come along, they might of kept on ranching there instead of getting themselves killed?" Tommy Fear wondered.

"I couldn't say," I told him. "It's possible."

I had my eyes on Leroy as I said this. No one else had noticed him, but I wanted him to see that I knew he was there, and I wanted him to remember our conversation on the train. I had related Butch's attempts to go straight to remind him that he might stay clear of trouble so long as he kept to the straight and narrow way. But I knew who he was, and I still had that Pinkerton flier. It was a weapon I held in reserve, like his derringer. I didn't want to use it, but while we were together I was dealing the cards and I figured to keep the aces to myself.

"South America was the last stop for Butch," Bob Elderberg said, getting to his feet. "And this here's the last stop for me. Katie and I are gonna turn in."

The hour was late. Seeing that I had run out of stories for the moment, some others got to their feet. This became a general movement toward the bedrolls, as no one wanted to waste a day off by sleeping the morning away.

As I left the fire, Leroy was nowhere to be seen, but once I was off in the dark a voice said, "There's an extra bedroll in my wagon, Charlie," and I found him at my side.

"Where's Victoria?" I demanded.

"Sound asleep, by now." He was taken aback by my harsh tone. "We went down to church. I brought her back to the hacienda a while ago and found you gone, so I checked on the gold. I woke Jack Whistler out of a sound sleep. Say, you're one hell of a storyteller, Charlie. I was listening to most of that. I'd of sat down, but I didn't trust myself to keep a straight face."

"I trusted you. I took you at your word."

He was thoroughly confused now. "What word was that?"

"You promised me you'd let Victoria be."

"I said I didn't want her to get hurt any more than you do, and that's the God's honest truth. I've done nothing to hurt her."

"Our deal didn't include trifling with her affections."

"Is that what's bothering you? Damn, Charlie, you take one hell of an interest in her welfare, for an uncle who isn't even a real uncle."

"Victoria is my daughter."

He wasn't expecting that. He looked at me long and hard. "You might have said something before now," he said at last.

"We've all got our secrets," I told him. "There's not a soul on God's green earth knows this one, except Victoria and her mother. Up until now."

With that, I left him. I borrowed a bedroll and laid it out by the fire, where I spent much of the night watching the stars drift across the sky.

Chapter 15

IT IS NOT easy to write about what happened between me and Anne Hartford, and this revelation may cost me the good reputation my friends and readers have granted me. If such is the case, so be it, but my promise to tell the whole truth demands explaining the circumstances of Victoria's birth. Victoria herself will be the one to decide if and when this book is published—for I plan to give it to her before I climb aboard a heaven-bound cayuse—and that helps some.

As I have related, the Hartfords comforted me in my sorrow over the death of my wife Mamie. I suppose this made it easy for me to feel close to Anne. But I never said a word that might be thought improper until she let me know, in the ways women have, that she returned my affections. In brief, we fell in love. These things happen. Sometimes they lead to violence and bloodshed. Almost always they bring some heartache with them. I will not make excuses, but for what it's worth, Anne and I swore an oath that no one would suffer because of our indiscretion. Above all, we vowed that we would endure the fires of purgatory before we would allow Jay to be hurt by what we did. If a stove-up old cowboy has any right to call on the Lord's attention, it is to thank Him for helping us keep that vow.

After years of childless marriage, it happened that the Hartfords were blessed with a baby girl, and no one was more tickled than Jay. Of course, Victoria grew up believing Jay to be her father. A child is not equipped to comprehend the follies of the grown-up world. But as Victoria left child-hood behind, Anne saw how fond of each other Victoria and I were, and she decided that the girl should know the truth. Without forewarning me, she told Victoria the facts of her parentage on her eighteenth birthday. Later that day I arrived with my own present in hand, the aforementioned ring clasp for Victoria's bandanna. Victoria opened the gift and I was sur-prised to see her eyes fill with tears. "Thank you, Father," she said.

Well, my heart almost stopped, but when she told me that Anne had revealed our secret, that calmed me somewhat. Soon I saw that Victoria accepted her unconventional origins with a wisdom beyond her years. She treated Jay with more tenderness and understanding than ever be-fore, while for my part, the joy of knowing that my daughter accepted me grew until I was fair to bursting with pride.

Over the years I tried marrying again a time or two, but those unions failed due to my continuing love for Anne and my unwillingness to live far from Victoria. Even so, my detective work kept me away much of the time, and my recent move to California was prompted in large measure by my wish to make up somewhat for my long absences in my daughter's formative years. As I have said, my own father died before I earned my first spanking, and my mother's second husband was good only for imbib-ing corn "likker" and absconding with her nest egg, so you will understand if I say it was my foremost hope, and one I expected easily to fulfill, to be a better father to my daughter than the men who had failed to play that role for me. Where I had no father, I was determined that Victoria would now have two, with all the comforts and protection Jay and I might provide.

Protecting her was much on my mind on Christmas Day of 1919. No visions of sugarplums danced in my head the night before, and by Leroy's appearance that morning, his rest was no better than mine. He was al-ready up and about when Victoria came to fetch me into the hacienda bright and early to watch the Delgado and Ball children open their presents. He took a cup of coffee and a book up to the second floor when Jack Whistler came down to breakfast, and he got none of the bacon and flapjacks enjoyed by the rest of the crew, so far as I could tell.

When he came down at noontime, Victoria couldn't get two words out of him, although she tried. He was pleasant enough, but as soon as she turned him loose he was gone. This change in attitude hurt her, and, as always, seeing her unhappy pained me, but I could think of no way to ease her troubles until the picture was done and we were safely back in California.

For the rest of our company it was a cheery holiday, and a welcome day of rest. The next morning, Orville was off again on the train, which passed through Delgado just after sunrise, and we were back at work with a vengeance. Within the film tins Orville carried was all the footage we had shot since his first departure, including the scenes taken among the false fronts of the "border town" Villa would attack. As soon as we knew the scenes had turned out, we could burn the set. The fact that Orville would arrive in Los Angeles on a weekend meant that the laboratory costs would once again be high, but we were within budget, and Brian judged that time was more important than money at this point in the production.

In the days that followed, Leroy and I walked carefully around each other, never saying anything about what passed between us on Christmas Eve. But it stood there like a barb wire fence, and I was sorry for that. At times I found myself wishing he would get angry, or offer to fight me, or even call me out with a gun, anything to end the stalking game between us. We had made a start at laying to rest that long pursuit of twenty years before, but because of Victoria we were still on opposite sides of an invisible fence, where I was still the watchdog and he the bobcat.

The fact that Leroy no longer kept company with Victoria occasioned some comment among the crew, but there was little opportunity for idle tongues to wag as we worked straight through the weekend, dawn to dusk. Twice I saw Victoria coming downstairs after carrying meals to Leroy in my bedroom, and other times I observed her attempting to engage him in conversation. By the sober look on her face after these episodes, I judged he was refusing her advances, but that did little to reassure me. She was doing the courting now, and I knew full well that she was accustomed to getting what she went after. She was twenty-eight and unmarried, and more than once she had vowed that while she intended to hold out for true love, she would not become an old maid.

In Hollywood, Victoria had bad luck with men, enough to make her swear off the local crowd. I didn't know all the details of her courtships, but in the short time I had been in California, I had met two gentlemen callers she thought enough of to introduce to me, without, of course, letting them know why she was presenting them to a stove-up cowboy innkeeper.

The first was the son of an "old" Hollywood family. His parents came to California ten years before the picture people, and you would think they came on the Mayflower, to hear them talk. Victoria's young swain allowed as how he might offer his hand in marriage if she would agree to abandon pictures and never again set foot in my disreputable rooming house. That was the end of him.

The next man Victoria brought by was a well-known actor. He thought the Bunk House was a swell place. So grand, in fact, that he took to coming by without Victoria and sparking the McQuain & Vickery cowgirls when he thought I was not looking. Victoria caught him at it, and after this incident she swore off Hollywood dandies from either side of the silver screen, saying she would wait for a man who could take care of himself and knew how to behave with a lady, even if she had to go back to New Mexico to find him.

She had not been back to New Mexico since, and in the days after Christmas it struck me that Leroy was the first likely candidate to come within range. I thought about having a word with Victoria, but I could think of nothing to say to her. The last thing I wanted to do was tell her who Leroy really was. She grew up hearing my stories of Butch Cassidy and the Wild Bunch. Like my listeners around the campfire on Christmas Eve, she was inclined to see him more as a misunderstood hero than as a villain, so I kept my fingers crossed and held my tongue. Her eyes still sought out Leroy whenever he was near her, but I saw no sign that he encouraged her in any way, and I was grateful for the hard pace that Brian set for his leading lady.

On Monday morning, four days after Christmas, Señor Garza, the stationmaster, ran up to the hacienda at lunchtime to inform Gerald and Brian, between huffing and puffing, that "Señor Orville" was on the telephone and wished urgently to speak with them. This caused some brief alarm, but the news was all good. Orville had arrived in Los Angeles in record time, the laboratory had developed and printed the film, and Orville was at that moment in Union Station in Los Angeles, preparing to return with the print. The scenes involving the false-front town were all crackerjack, Orville reported.

With that, preparations for burning the "town" got under way. For the rest of the day, Brian rehearsed the entire company and half the townsfolk in the roles they would play during the complicated scene. Once the fires were lit, there would be no going back. We had to get it right the first time. Brian would man the tripod camera himself, while George would film the action simultaneously with a portable Aeroscope, the same camera he had used in the war. This ingenious contrivance was operated by air pumped into the camera beforehand, relieving the operator of the need to crank the film. George could hold the camera with both hands and move about freely, and he assured us that the resulting film would make the viewer feel he was in the thick of battle.

Monday evening we filmed Villa's raiders in the real town, in a dozen small scenes that would be edited into the footage of the burning sets. The Villistas galloped among the houses carrying flaming brands and threw them at the houses while men stood by with pails of water beyond the camera's view, lest anything actually catch fire.

On Tuesday, the company was charged with repressed excitement as rehearsals continued throughout the day. To everyone's surprise Orville returned in midafternoon, barely twenty-seven hours after leaving Los

Angeles, thanks to his having arrived in Agua Prieta moments before the cattle train departed for points south.

As the sun neared the horizon, a hundred actors and extras were put in position in and around the false fronts. The townspeople who were not employed in the scene were gathered in a crowd behind the cameras. Just before sunset, Brian raised his hand. A hush fell over the multitude.

"Start the fires!" Brian gave the order, and then it was every man for himself.

Chief John and his raiders galloped hither and yon while the rest of us, including some of Delgado's most peaceful citizens, returned fire from among the burning sets. Naturally, all this shooting was done with blank cartridges, or there would have been more dead than Texas suffered at the Alamo. When it was over, George expressed his satisfaction by giving a whoop and throwing his porkpie hat in the air, while keeping his precious Aeroscope clutched safely to his breast.

That evening we looked at the new pictures Orville had brought back. Once again, seeing the product of our work raised everyone's spirits, if that was possible following the excitement of the day. Afterward, as the company and the Delgados mingled, commenting on their favorite scenes, Victoria drifted through the crowd and came up on Leroy before he saw her coming. To prevent his moving away, she took his arm and stood close beside him as she had done in the church on Christmas Eve. When I started in their direction she guided him off, leading him through the French doors onto the long veranda that overlooked the courtyard, and there she turned to face him.

"I'm not used to being treated like this," she said.

"How's a movie star used to being treated?"

That took the wind out of her sails. She has never asked for special treatment because of her celebrity, and has refused it when it was offered. "It has nothing to do with being a movie star," she said in a smaller voice. "It's just that for a while there I thought you were courting me."

"For a while there I forgot why I was here."

"Finding your friend won't take the rest of your life."

"Whether I find him or not, I'm staying in Mexico."

Something in his voice made Victoria feel cold. She wrapped her arms around herself against the sudden chill. "Why?" she asked.

"There's nothing for me in the States. Not anymore."

She misunderstood him, thinking he included her in his dismissal of America and everything within its borders, forgetting that she was standing right beside him in the middle of Sonora. He sounded so firm in his resolve that she could think of nothing further to say.

Watching this exchange from within the hall, I saw Leroy tip his hat and leave her, and I saw how forlorn she looked as she watched him walk through the courtyard and out the gate. My heart went out to her and I stepped out to join her. When she turned to me, plainly glad to see me, I loved her more than ever before.

"I don't understand him, Charlie."

"I don't need to ask if he knows you're sweet on him."

"Mama taught me not to reveal my feelings to a man until I was sure of his," she said. "I guess I'm not doing a very good job of it."

"It's not like you to throw yourself at a man."

"Throw myself! We've been here for weeks and all I've gotten out of it is a bicycle ride and a few dances."

This would have made me feel better, but for the fact that it was said more as a lament than a claim of virtuous innocence.

"It might be best if it stopped right there," I told her.

"Have you forgotten how you felt when you first met Mama?"

"Your mother and me, that's different."

"How? How is it different?" Her dander was up now. She faced me squarely and stood her ground. She has got the Irish in her, and I have only myself to blame. With my Italian father in his grave before I reached my second birthday, my Irish mother had ample opportunity to instill her hot-tempered ways in me, and I have passed this trait on to my daughter.

"You don't know a whole lot about Leroy Roberts," I said.

"I know he's everything you told me to hold out for! Don't go falling for some Hollywood dandy, you said. Wait for a man who can take care of himself, you said. Well I haven't, and he can!"

She had me there. I had said just those words to her. She had tried the Hollywood dandies and found them wanting. Now she was after a man made of sterner stuff. But she didn't know all there was to know.

"He's not the sort of man to stick around for long."

"What about you, running off to chase outlaws right after you met Mama?"

"That was my job."

"You took that job because it suited who you *were*! But you settled down in the end."

"Leroy didn't come down here to make pictures."

"I know all about why he came down here. He came to find a friend of his, someone named Harry."

"He isn't the man for you."

A thought struck her and she looked at me reprovingly. "Oh, Charlie, you didn't! You warned him to stay away from me!"

I have never been good at lying to her, so I kept quiet, and she took my silence as an admission that what she suspected was true.

"Have you told him the truth about us?" she demanded.

"Yes."

"Dammit, Charlie! Then tell me the truth about him! You know more than you're saying."

"I can't do that."

On Christmas Eve I had offered Leroy our secret in exchange for keeping his, and by his behavior it seemed he understood my terms. By stopping his courting he had acknowledged my rights as Victoria's father. He had behaved honorably, and I was bound to keep my part of the bargain.

Victoria touched my arm. "You know how long I've been waiting for the right man to come along and carry me off."

"He isn't the one, girl. You get that through your head."

I don't tell her what to do very often. Not in terms as blunt as that. When I try, she usually lets me have it, but not this time. Instead she gave me a look that showed me just how much I had hurt her, and she slipped away into the house, leaving me there to count the stars.

It was my turn to stand alone on the veranda, wondering how I could protect my daughter without breaking her heart. But I was more certain than ever that I had to protect her, for hearing that Leroy had come to Mexico to find "Harry" had set my head to spinning. The minute I heard the name, I was sure the Harry in question was Harry Longabaugh, otherwise known as the Sundance Kid. And what reason could Leroy have for finding his former friend, if not to hit the outlaw trail again?

Butch Cassidy tried to quit his life of crime not twice, as I had told the boys around the campfire, but three times. The first two attempts had failed through no fault of his own, some might say, but Butch had returned from South America, and his third try at going straight had worked. By his own account, he had slept ten years in a bed, and by the look of him he had led a comfortable life. But to succeed in escaping his past, he had almost certainly found it necessary to cut himself off from friends and family, from everyone who knew him. Even if he had started a new family, he could trust no one completely, not even those closest to him. In short, he had to give up who he was.

For a murderer or a sneak thief that might be no great sacrifice, but Robert Leroy Parker *enjoyed* being Butch Cassidy. He had been liked and admired by friends and family, even by strangers. Finally, after years of pretending to be a different sort of man, he had decided to go back to being his own self, no matter the cost. Leroy Roberts was just a stop along the way. Down here in Mexico he figured to live as Butch Cassidy again, and the devil take the hindmost.

If I was right, then all my notions about how alike Leroy and I might be were no more than foolish daydreams. In his wild youth he had turned to the bad, and I had not. Twenty years later, that was still the difference between us. If he went on his way without a fuss, I would let him go in peace. But if I was right about the road he was on, I would do whatever it took to prevent Victoria from going with him.

Chapter 16

THE NEXT MORNING Victoria kept silent around me. I sometimes saw anger in her eyes, but more often I saw the hurt, and it was not easy for me to maintain a stony silence. I had not counted on losing her affections in the very act of protecting her.

The rest of the company was oblivious to our low spirits, for they were feeling a growing euphoria. It was the last day of the year. A week remained in the month allotted to make the picture, and Brian was more confident than ever that we would finish ahead of schedule.

"I know you all want to celebrate the new year," he announced at lunchtime. "If we finish with Randall and his boys in front of the ruins this afternoon, we'll quit early."

He raised a hand to silence an incipient cheer. "First thing tomorrow it's back to work. You might keep that in mind this evening. Once we're back in Hollywood, you can celebrate all you want."

After lunch we set up in front of the still-smoking ruins of the false-front town, where Randall and Charlie Noble and their cowboy chums were to learn for the first time that Villa had kidnapped Evangelina. As assistant scenarist, I was on hand in case we needed to make any last-minute changes, and I was glad to see that Victoria was among the onlookers instead of taking this opportunity to visit with Leroy in the hacienda while I was not around.

Orville Hintz stayed close to the Model T, ready to depart for the

railroad station at a moment's notice. He had been unable to learn when
the train might arrive, the telephone at the station being out of order
today, so he kept an eye on the tracks to the south and stood by to take
with him whatever film George might complete before the train made its
appearance.

The scene was simple enough. Tom and his friends ride into the ravaged town, not having learned of Villa's attack until the next morning.
Naturally they are horrified by the devastation wrought by the dastardly
Villa. There are bodies lying about and women crying over the corpses of
their men. Karen Valdez plays a poor girl Evangelina has befriended. She
tells Tom that Evangelina was carried off by Villa. Tom is shocked, but in
a jiffy his shock is replaced by iron-jawed determination. "You know what
she can expect at the hands of that brigand," he says to the cowboys. "I'm
going after her!" He vaults from a hitching rail onto his horse and rides off
at a gallop. Naturally his stalwart chums can't let him face Villa alone.
Charlie Noble says so in a few choice words, and then the cowboys jump
aboard *their* horses—less dramatically—and go after him.

As always, Brian and George filmed the scene from several angles.
When they had a shot of the cowboys racing out of the "town" away from
the camera, they withdrew some fifty yards so the cowboys could repeat
their departure, this time racing toward the camera.

"Roll camera, and action!" Brian called. The cowboys rode straight for
the camera, missing it as closely as they dared, and thundered off into the
chaparral.

"Cut!" Brian called, when the dust from their passing had rolled over
him and George and the camera. George loved filming from downwind to
get just such an effect.

"Are you happy with that, George?" Brian asked, as the cowboys reined
in. The question was mostly a formality, as George rarely needed more
than one take of such a simple shot unless one of the cowboys forgot
himself and grinned at the camera as he rode past.

"That's a take, Boss," George would usually reply. But this time he said
nothing. He had his head cocked to one side, apparently listening to
some faint or distant sound. I pricked up my ears and then I heard it too,
a pounding of hoofbeats, as if the cowboys had kept on going and had
somehow increased their number tenfold.

Brian could see we were listening to something, but he couldn't make
out the sound. He cupped his good ear with his hand.

"Look there," someone said, as the riders came into sight. They came
from the south in a column, rising from the benchland to the plateau.
There were seventy or eighty in all and they rode along the western edge
of the plateau at an easy canter, coming straight for us. A one-eyed man
could see at a glance that they were cavalry.

"More *rurales?*" Redeye Hawk wondered aloud.

"*Federales,* maybe," Jack Whistler said.

"Or bandits," said Randall, who had watched with the rest of us as the cowboys acted out their several departures for the camera.

"If that outfit is bandits, we'll all be belly-up by nightfall," Bob Elderberg said.

I took Brian's megaphone from his hand and spoke through it. "Put your hands above your heads," I told Charlie Noble and his men. "I'm not kidding, boys. You want to live through the next five minutes, raise 'em high."

The cowboys were the only ones among us who were armed. Whoever the approaching riders might be, I wanted them to know we were not their enemies. We might get time to explain ourselves if they were *federales,* but a force of *rurales* that large would cut down the lot of us without stopping to hear explanations if they thought we posed a threat to them.

I moved close to Victoria and kept her by my side as the rest of our company drew into a tight group, the way sheep will do when the shepherd and his dog come into sight.

The column drew near, and then, without any command we could see or hear, it split into three groups. The largest force veered off down the slope, making for the town. The other two bunches, each made up of about twenty horsemen, continued in our direction. As they drew near, one bunch kept going straight for the hacienda while the other fanned out to surround us with guns leveled. The cavalrymen wore a varied assortment of uniform pieces and other clothing, and almost every man had two cartridge belts, or *banderillas,* crossed over his chest. While some of the men disarmed the cowboys, the officer in charge looked us over.

"*¿Quienes son ustedes?*" he demanded. Who are you? He was a slender man with cruel eyes.

"*Somos americanos,*" I said. "*Somos una compañía de cine. ¿Quienes son ustedes?*" I told him we were an American film company, and asked who he and his soldiers might be, but he paid no attention to my questions. Instead, he ordered us to leave our equipment where it was and walk toward the hacienda. Our cowboys were forced to dismount, abandoning their horses to our captors.

"I hope they don't touch the camera," George said as we started off.

"It's all the film back in the hacienda I'm worried about," Brian said under his breath.

"Oh my God, Boss, if they open the cans—" George fell silent, unable to voice the consequences. If the film was exposed to daylight, we would lose the burning of the false-front town and everything else filmed in the past week.

As we approached the edge of the plateau we could hear screams and

shouting from the town. All those found in and around the hacienda—
including the members of our company who had not been needed for this
afternoon's work—were gathered in a group against the outer wall near
the courtyard gate.

In a handful of minutes, the column of cavalry had taken control of the
town without, so far as I could tell, a single act of resistance. There were
soldiers everywhere. The officers spoke, and they obeyed.

By order of the cruel-eyed officer we were halted at some distance from
the hacienda and held under guard. The officer called out to a subordi-
nate, demanding to know if any Americans were among the other captives, whereupon Chief John and Redeye and the others were separated
from the Mexican prisoners and allowed to join us, but Gerald Ball
refused to leave his wife and children.

"Charlie, where's Leroy?" Victoria said.

He was nowhere to be seen. How he had evaded the roundup, I
couldn't imagine. On the second floor of the hacienda there was a ladder
that led to the roof, which had been used as a lookout in past times. He
might be hiding there, but it would do no good. Even if he and I and all
the cowboys were armed, we would be no match for the soldiers.

A trio of officers galloped up on horseback from the town. Our officer
joined them as they reined in. He saluted the man in the center, and
spoke rapidly, obviously reporting to his superior.

The commander was about forty years of age, solidly built, with small
eyes and a thick black mustache. He was unshaven and tired-looking, but
his dusty uniform was neatly buttoned and like the rest of his officers he
wore a proper campaign hat. He was light-skinned for a Mexican and had
a pleasant face, and he listened attentively as the officer who had taken
the hacienda spoke to him. When the officer had finished, the commander spoke briefly, gesturing toward the captives by the hacienda wall.
The cruel-eyed officer saluted, then turned and shouted orders.

Soldiers moved among the Delgados and their household staff, lining
them against the wall in single file. One of the kitchen maids screamed
and some of the other women began to sob quietly.

I felt a chill deep in my bones as a squad of soldiers formed a line facing
the wall.

"Oh my God," said Brian.

"They're going to shoot them!" said Victoria.

I took her arm and held it tightly. "Hush, girl."

Just then there was a large explosion north of town. The ground shook
and a puff of dirty smoke rose into the air.

"Blowing the railroad tracks, I'd say," Bob Elderberg muttered.

"You see any way we can take a hand in this thing, Charlie?" Jack Whistler said.

I shook my head. I have never felt so helpless.

Chief John gave a small nod of his head toward the soldiers guarding us. "We jump quick, we might get a few of those guns."

"At least we'd take some of them with us," Willie Two Horse said.

"We can't let them shoot the Delgados and Sir Gerald!" Brian exclaimed, but when the cruel-eyed officer looked in our direction, he dropped his eyes.

"What's he waiting for?" Nate Dicenzo wondered. A moment later his question was answered as more soldiers approached from town, driving the entire population of Delgado before them. The *delgadeños* were herded into a line facing the hacienda, apparently to witness the execution of the Delgados and their household.

But now Gerald Ball stepped away from the group by the hacienda wall. A soldier raised his carbine to club the upstart gringo to the ground, but Gerald's confident manner was so impressive that the soldier hesitated, giving Gerald time to speak his piece.

"I am Gerald Ball," he said, addressing the commander. "*Sir* Gerald Ball. Those people are members of my motion picture company, this is my wife, and these are her family." He gestured imperiously toward our group, then to Rosa and the prisoners around him. "I demand to know who you are and by what right you treat us like this."

By his tone, he might have been asking a chimney sweep for directions to Buckingham Palace.

"You demand?" the cruel-eyed officer said in English. He drew his pistol. It was a Colt's .45 automatic, not as accurate as the worthy gentleman's revolvers, but still capable of putting a hole in a man big enough for a cat to crawl through.

The commander said a few words to the officer, who acknowledged the order with a curt nod before lowering his pistol and returning his attention to Gerald.

"I am Coronel Ortega," said the officer. "You have the honor to address General Francisco Villa."

This announcement brought an outburst of surprise from the *hacenda- dos* and Americans alike. Among those by the wall there were moans of dismay, but old Ramón, the majordomo, cried "*¡Viva Villa!*" He saluted Villa smartly and shouted again, "*¡Viva el General Villa!*"

From the crowd of townspeople there were a few tentative cheers, but those who voiced support for Villa received black looks from the others.

"Aren't you going to say hello to your long-lost father?" Nate Dicenzo muttered to Karen, but she made no move to do so.

"I demand to know why we are being held prisoner," Gerald said once the excited murmuring had died down. He was less self-assured now that he knew who he was speaking to.

"Dígale a este inglés que los Delgados han mantenido a Carranza desde el principio de la revolución," General Villa said. *"Serán todos fusilados, con excepción de este viejo. Toda la propiedad será confiscado."*

At the hacienda wall, there was a new outbreak of wailing from the women.

"General Villa says that the Delgado family has supported President Carranza since the early days of the revolution," Ortega translated for Gerald. "Their property is confiscated and you will all be shot, except for the old one there." He pointed to Ramón, whose Villista fervor had earned him a pardon.

Gerald swallowed hard and took a step back.

"No, you can't!" Victoria cried out.

Villa glanced in our direction.

"Hush, girl!" I hissed, tightening my grip on Victoria's arm. The last thing I wanted was for Villa or any of his men to take an interest in my daughter.

"Si muere mi patrón, yo muero a su lado," Ramón declared, vowing his intention to die by the side of his employers, General Villa's pardon notwithstanding.

But Villa cared nothing for Ramón's brave loyalty to the Delgados. He got off his horse and handed the reins to an orderly who followed him everywhere like a shadow. Moving like a man who spent most of his waking hours on horseback, he approached us with his eyes on Victoria. I stepped in front of her, but his gaze passed on, taking in the rest of us. They stopped on George Bleumel, and Villa smiled.

"¿Jorge, por qué no le da la bienvenida a este viejo amigo?" Why don't you say hello to an old friend? he wanted to know.

George managed a halfhearted grin, like he wasn't sure he was glad Villa recognized him, but he said, "Hello, General."

With that, Villa opened his arms. George knew what was expected of him, so he stepped up to get hugged. Mexicans, men included, are very big on hugging and kissing. Villa's embrace made George uncomfortable, but he put up with it.

When Villa let go of George he gave Ortega a good tonguelashing, demanding to know why he hadn't recognized their old friend Jorge Bleumel, and if he had, why he hadn't told Villa. Without waiting for an answer, he turned back to George and switched to English.

"Jorge, because it is you, I will permit you to film the execution." He said it like he was awarding George some kind of prize at a state fair.

"Uh, General, if there's any way you could call this thing off—"

"Think of it! How many? Twenty, twenty-five, all at once. We never have filmed so many all at once."

Brian was aghast. "George? You filmed executions?"

"I filmed whatever happened, Boss. I didn't have any say in it." Poor George must have wished the ground would open up and swallow him.

Villa turned to Ortega, all business. "*Coronel Ortega, prepare el pelotón.* Jorge, make your camera ready."

"I had to leave my camera back where we were filming, General. Colonel Ortega's orders."

Villa shouted an order. Three men leaped aboard their horses and galloped off to retrieve George's camera.

Ortega called out to the firing squad to present arms.

"I absolutely forbid you to harm these people," Gerald said in a voice that was now tremulous. "I am an American citizen. They are my family."

Ortega was delighted. "You forbid it?" He aimed his pistol at Gerald's head, and without taking his eyes from Gerald, he said, "*Jefe, déjeme matar a este cabrón inglés.*" Let me kill this obscenity of an Englishman.

Villa regarded Gerald with a slight smile. "*Bueno,*" he said at last, giving his consent. "*Pero mátalo despacito.*"

Which meant to kill him slowly.

"It's now or never, boys," I said to the cowboys under my breath. I tensed myself to rush one of our guards, but at that moment a sergeant appeared at the gateway to the courtyard, and Leroy was with him.

"*Jefe,*" said the sergeant. "*Creo que usted conoce a este hombre.*"

Leroy stepped forward alone. Ortega's pistol swung in Leroy's direction, but he let it drop to his side when he saw the expression on Villa's face, which was a combination of wonder and delight.

Leroy stopped twenty feet from Villa.

"*No lo creo,*" Villa finally said. "*Después de tantos años has regresado.*"

I don't believe it. After all these years you've come back.

He strode forward, took Leroy in his arms, and hugged him with even more Latin abandon than he had shown George. When he turned him loose at last, he put his arm around Leroy's shoulders and they strolled off together, beyond the hearing of soldiers and captives.

"The American newspapers say you're over in Coahuila," was the first thing Leroy said.

Villa smiled. "It is true, some of my army is there."

"And while they're making a lot of noise in Coahuila, no one would think of looking for you in Sonora."

"Let us hope not."

"But Harry isn't with you."

"Neither in Coahuila nor here," Villa said. "He is gone, Roberto. Two years ago, three years ago. It seems a long time. The woman went with him, as always. Your friend Harry, he said he will start a new life. He and the woman were married by one of my priests."

Leroy was sorry to hear Harry was gone, but the news tickled him. "Sundance and Etta? That's great. Where were they going?"

"He did not say. Someplace where they are not known, as you have done."

They stopped walking and Pancho looked Leroy up and down. "You said you would come back."

"I've come back."

"But for your old friend Harry, not for me."

"For you too."

The soldiers sent after George's camera returned. Villa waved them toward the Americans, where they delivered the camera to George. The firing squad had grounded the butts of their carbines and Ortega's pistol was back in its holster.

"I'd appreciate it if you could call off the firing squad," Leroy said.

Villa looked upon the soldiers who awaited his orders and the captives who would live or die by his whim.

"The Delgados are traitors to the revolution. *Carranzistas*," he declared.

"If they back you, they're traitors to Carranza. He's the one who's president," Leroy said.

"Carranza is like Díaz and Huerta and all the rest! He loves power. But I love *Méjico*! Soon the people will see this and they will come back to me! Stay with me, my friend. We will fight together again. This time we will win."

"We'll fight together and this time I'll stick with you. If you'll forget about shooting the Delgados."

"They mean so much to you?"

"They mean a lot to my friends," Leroy said.

"And the woman, she is yours?"

"She's Victoria Hartford, the picture star. Cimarron Rose."

"*¡Rosa Cimarrona! ¡Qué tonto soy! ¡Ahora la reconozco!* I have seen her movie pictures sometimes when I am in El Paso! She is very beautiful. Is she in love with you?"

All he got from Leroy was a shrug of the shoulders, but Villa grinned. "I think she is in love with you. See how she watches you. Oh, my friend, you are like me. You need excitement, and you need a beautiful woman!"

"This one's different."

"And she does not know you are married?"

This got him a shake of the head.

"Your marriage, how does it go?"

"One day I told her who I was, just like you said I would. After that, it was like she was married to someone else."

"She wanted the man she married."

"Hell, the man she married was someone I made up out of thin air."

"You have children?"

"She couldn't have children. We adopted a son. He's not much like me."

"Of course. It is a matter of *sangre*. He does not have your blood. You should have children of your own. Marry this woman. I will get a priest for you."

"She'd get mad as hell if she found out. And she'd find out, because I'd have to tell her."

"All of my wives know about the others! Sometimes they complain, but I cannot stay all the time in one place! You and I, what we can give a woman in one month is enough to last them a lifetime!" Once again he put a companionable arm around Leroy's shoulders. "We will find a way. But your friends do not know who you are?"

"Just the old gent by the girl."

Had the old gent heard what passed between Leroy and Villa that day, he would have been reaching for a buggy whip or a gun. As it was, just seeing the two of them chatting like long-lost brothers was enough to set me cogitating so hard that I almost didn't hear Victoria when she spoke to me.

"Charlie, I want to know what's going on here," she said.

"I don't know any more about it than you do, girl," I told her.

That was a flat lie. I was dead certain I knew what was going on here, and I was thunderstruck by the conviction that threatened to overwhelm me. Somehow Leroy knew Pancho Villa, and my guess was that he had expected to find Harry Longabaugh in Villa's company. He had come to Mexico to hook up with these two. Maybe to take up the outlaw trail, maybe to fight with the revolutionists. Maybe both. But that wasn't the half of it.

He had come to die.

He had tried a new name and a new life and he had found them wanting. Like other men before him, he had grown tired of living a lie. And so he had emerged from hiding to enter the fray once more, and if that meant going out in a blaze of glory, so much the better.

But something unexpected had entered his plans. He had met Victoria. *What if he had reached out to her in an effort to save himself?*

I had got this far in my thinking and no farther when Leroy and Villa finished their reminiscing and strolled back in our direction. While Villa stopped to speak privately with Ortega, Leroy continued on toward our group.

"Unless I miss my guess, we're about to find out how good you and old Pancho get along," George Bleumel said to him when he reached us.

"You're not going to believe what he wants," Leroy said, but Ortega wasn't going to let anyone steal his thunder.

"*¡Señores y señoras! ¡Amigos!*" he announced. "By the great generosity of General Francisco Villa, in recognition of his friendship for Señor Leroy Roberts and Señor Jorge Bleumel, there will be no execution."

The townspeople raised a cheer on hearing that their *patrón* would be spared. Over by the wall, Señora Delgado fainted dead away. Gerald Ball sat down on the ground and took his children in his arms, while Rosa sobbed openly.

"He wants to play himself in the picture," Leroy said.

"He what?" said Victoria.

Brian wasn't sure he had heard Leroy correctly. He turned his good ear toward him. "I beg your pardon?"

Leroy repeated himself.

Brian's eyebrows climbed up a notch. "General Villa? He wants to play himself? In our picture?"

Ortega frowned and rushed on with his pronouncement. "General Villa wishes to welcome the most beautiful movie picture star Victoria Hartford and the great movie picture director Señor Brian Hill to *Méjico*. By his great generosity, he has agreed to appear in the movie picture as himself."

Brian was quick to see the commercial possibilities. "The real Pancho Villa? In our movie? Imagine the publicity! Quick, George, how many close-ups do we need of Villa?"

George totted up the scenes on his fingers. "Outside the cantina. The bedroom scene with Victoria. A couple during the raid, at his headquarters, and the chase at the end. It's not much, Boss. It wouldn't take long. Maybe a couple of days."

"Are you willing to give it a try?" Brian asked Victoria.

Victoria had scarcely taken her eyes off Leroy since he joined our group, but now she looked at Brian.

"What if he's no good?"

It was Leroy who answered. "Simple," he said. "You shoot the film, or pretend to shoot it, until he gets tired of playing movie star and goes on his way. Then you use the scenes of Chief John just as if Villa never came along."

"All right," Victoria said. "I'm willing if he is."

Brian's eyes were bright and he spoke rapidly, the way he does when he's excited about something. "Okay, we'll do the scenes in the hacienda first. Orville, have a few of the boys set up the cantina in the meantime. If we can do that first thing in the morning, we may be able to cover the rest tomorrow and we'll still be ahead of schedule."

Ortega beamed at us. "Señores. General Francisco Villa awaits your orders."

Villa is not a large man, no taller than Brian, but on sheer force of personality he stood head and shoulders over the American youth. Faced with the mustachioed revolutionist, Brian was suddenly tongue-tied.

"Go to it, boy," I told him. "You won't hear those words again. Not in this lifetime."

Brian swallowed hard. "General, if you'll follow me please. Victoria, everyone, we'll start as soon as you're ready."

Off they went, Brian leading the way to the hacienda and Mexico's most famous general following in his footsteps.

As soon as they started off, George touched Leroy's arm. "Did you see what happened to the film cans? They were stacked in Sir Gerald's bedroom."

Leroy grinned. "They're right where you left them. You'll find two very nervous guards looking after them. I told the Villistas they were full of dynamite and nitroglycerine for the special effects."

This news turned George into a Mexican. He embraced Leroy fervently and kissed him on both cheeks before grabbing his camera and racing after Brian and Villa.

"What about the gold?" I asked Leroy.

"When I saw them coming, I stuffed it into the mattress. There's not much left, anyway."

It was true. We were supposed to pay our Mexican workers this evening and there would be just one more payday after that, when the picture was done.

Nearby, Ortega was issuing orders right and left, instructing his subordinates to get the soldiers bivouacked near the hacienda, while Orville collared a few of our boys and sent them to restore the cantina to its celluloid glory. The rest of us began a general movement toward the hacienda to help out however we could in the filming. As Leroy and Victoria and I passed near Ortega, a young officer—a lieutenant, if I read his insignia right—ran up to report to his colonel.

"*Los vecinos tienen oro, Coronel. Lo hemos encontrado en casi todas las casas.*" The townspeople have gold, he said. We have found it in almost every house. He opened his hand and showed Ortega a few shining coins.

"*Águilas americanas,*" said Ortega, recognizing them as American double eagles.

I glanced at Leroy. He gave me a small shrug as if to say it couldn't be helped. Victoria was watching him too, but she had other matters on her mind.

"I'm grateful to you for saving the Delgados," she said.

Her gratitude was genuine, but there was something more in her manner. She was after something, and Leroy knew it.

"I told Villa I'd join up with him if he let them go."

"You must mean a lot to him," Victoria said coldly.

"I fought with him back at the start of the revolution when he was one of Madero's generals," Leroy said. "I came down here to join up with him."

Something in the way he said it confirmed everything I had guessed about his intentions.

"What about your friend Harry?" Victoria said.

"Harry's gone."

We were in the courtyard now. As we reached the veranda Victoria turned to face Leroy.

"When were you going to tell me about all this?" Beneath her quiet tone the steel was beginning to show.

"Soon," he said. "I should have done it before now."

"Miss Hartford," Orville called to her from the French doors. "We'll be ready for you in five minutes."

Victoria's jaw was set like her mother's, on those rare times when Anne feels she has been crossed. Her eyes met mine, then moved back to Leroy. When she spoke again, it was no louder than before.

"You and Charlie Siringo can go straight to hell."

Chapter 17

THE HACIENDA WAS full of people, curious soldiers mixing with the more daring townsfolk, while the Delgados and their servants tried to keep some order. Having wished Leroy and yours truly a speedy journey to the netherworld, Victoria commenced to pretend we did not exist. Without another word she slipped away through the crowd toward where Orville was beckoning her.

"Let's have a look at that mattress," Leroy said.

Amidst the confusion, we had no trouble slipping upstairs undetected. In my small bedroom, Victoria's trunk had been rifled, her costumes thrown every which way and the empty strongbox cast aside, but the bed was undisturbed. Leroy showed me the thin slit he had cut in the horsehair mattress, and we could feel the coins nestled within.

"It's safe enough here," Leroy said as he tucked the blankets back around the mattress. "Villa will squeeze as much gold as he can out of the townspeople, but my guess is he'll leave the hacienda alone. Once he sets out to make friends with a town he cultivates the prominent citizens."

"You and Harry Longabaugh, you were with Villa together?"

Leroy's surprise told me I had guessed right about "Harry." He nodded grudgingly, wondering how much more I knew.

"That's a story I'd like to hear sometime," I said.

"Maybe later."

"You said yourself the revolution's about run out of steam," I reminded him. "You go with Villa now, you're joining a lost cause."

"It's still a good fight, even if he's losing. Anyway, I gave him my word. He let the Delgados live and he trusts me to keep my word."

I had occasion once again to remember what Leroy had said about trying to do right by men who trusted him. I could think of nothing that might change his mind just then, so I said, "We stick too close to this room, they might figure we've got something to hide."

We went downstairs together. As soon as we stepped into the big hall again, Orville spotted us and corralled us as guards to help keep the set clear of curious onlookers.

Once again the set was the Delgados' bedroom, transformed into Pancho Villa's boudoir. Only now the real Pancho Villa was on hand, which prompted everyone and his cousin to try to push inside the room and watch the filming. Villa was garbed in Chief John's Villa costume, lending those tattered items a new dignity, and Victoria was properly dazzling as Evangelina. When Leroy and I entered the room, we might as well have been two peons for all the attention she paid us.

Assisted by Buddy Johnston and Jack Whistler, we got the bedroom cleared out except for Colonel Ortega and a few of Villa's staff officers. We drew the line at ranks below major, and civilians were plumb out of luck.

With peace restored, Brian patiently explained the scene and its purpose to Villa. Our director had chosen to do the bedroom scene first for a particular reason. Should his new actor prove to be a talentless amateur, Brian had no wish to embarrass General Francisco Villa in public.

But from the first run-through of the scene, it was clear that Brian's caution was unnecessary. Villa showed a natural talent for playing himself in front of the camera. Some might think this requires no talent at all. To those I would say, you step in front of a moving-picture camera with a director and crew and a dozen of your best friends looking on, and see if you can behave like anything more than a feebleminded imitation of yourself.

None of these considerations fazed Villa, who performed with the aplomb of a seasoned thespian.

Brian was quick to recognize his good fortune. Without making much of it, he interrupted the run-through to say, "We might as well film the rehearsal in case we get something we can use. George?"

George nodded and commenced to crank on Brian's command. He knew Brian hoped to get a more natural performance from Villa by calling the first take a rehearsal.

Picking up the action at the beginning of the scene, Villa threw Victoria on the bed with just the right amount of bravado, then told her in a thoroughly believable manner that he was a gentle man.

"All right, General," Brian said. "Now turn away from her and take off your guns. That's it." He spoke softly through his megaphone, encouraging Villa every step of the way. Even indoors, Brian always used his megaphone when giving directions. It gave his voice a quality that commanded attention.

When Villa turns away from Evangelina, that's her cue to knock him out, but now Victoria turned to Brian.

"Brian, couldn't I do something to put him off guard?"

As always, Brian was willing to hear a new idea. "Keep rolling, George. What did you have in mind, Victoria?"

"I could play up to him."

She rose from the bed and approached Villa like Cleopatra closing in on Marc Antony. She helped Villa remove his gunbelts, all the time gazing into his eyes with a look that would have aroused indecent thoughts in a corpse. With a glance at Leroy, who was standing beside me in the doorway, she threw the gunbelts on the bed and wrapped her arms around Villa's neck, pulling him toward her until their lips met.

Not even Barrymore has received a kiss like that on film. Villa staggered slightly when Victoria let go of him, like a man who has been knocked half silly by a blow to the head. She turned away, unbuttoning the top button of her blouse, then the next, all the while glancing at him steamily over her shoulder. In the fashion of Mexican peasant women she wore no undergarments, a fact that soon became apparent to those in the room.

Brian was quick to follow Victoria's lead. "All right, General," he told Villa, "you start to undress too. But you're a modest man, so you turn your back on her."

Victoria unfastened another button. One more and she would have overstepped my notions of decency. I had seen her play love scenes before, of course, and I knew they were part of the job, but this one was different. The passion behind Victoria's actions was not feigned for the camera, it was genuine.

And then she looked again at Leroy and I saw what she was doing. Having consigned him to Satan's care, she was stoking the fires to make his stay in that hot place as uncomfortable as possible.

She fingered the fourth button, playing the moment for all it was worth, before at last returning to the scenario. Seeing that Villa's back was to her, she seized the large vase from the table beside the bed and smashed it over Villa's head. He dropped like a steer in a slaughterhouse as Victoria fled from the room to an outburst of applause from all present.

"Cut!" cried Brian. "That was great, both of you. Absolutely great."

Villa didn't move.

"General?" Brian stepped in front of the camera, but Colonel Ortega beat him to Villa's side. He shook Villa by the shoulder and called his name, and when he got no response he drew his .45 automatic pistol and waved it about, trying to decide who to shoot first, sending George and Brian and all the onlookers diving for cover, which was small and scarce.

Just then, Villa raised his head.

"So, I can get up? Ortega, what is the matter with you? I am acting! I must do a good job."

Brian pulled himself to a sitting position on the floor, where he had been trying to dig a hole. "Whenever I say 'cut,' General, you can stop acting."

There was no need to film the scene again. Brian and George agreed that it could not be improved upon, but George had an idea about how to prepare Villa for the next day's work.

"Say, Boss," he said, "we could show him the print from last week's film. It's got the cantina scene."

Brian concurred at once, and Villa was delighted by the idea. Dusk was already falling, and in no time the big hall became a movie theater again. Villa and his officers enjoyed the film enormously, even though the scenes were not yet edited into their proper order, and they applauded loudly when the screen went blank. But I had been struck by something about the scenes of Tom and his cowboy friends that I had not noticed before. As Villa chatted amiably with Randall Steele and Victoria, complimenting them on their performances, I took Brian and George aside.

"There's one thing missing here and it's been staring us in the face all along," I said. "You expect Randall and his boys to go up against Pancho Villa, you've got to make me believe they stand a snowball's chance. So far, we're showing them as a bunch of carefree cowboys."

Brian lit a Pall Mall. "You're right. How do we make them dangerous?"

"Well," I said, "a cowboy always wants to be top man in front of his friends, even when it's just in fun. He'll try to rope a prairie dog, maybe even show off with a six-shooter, if there's a bunch of the boys watching."

By now we were accustomed to thinking out loud over such matters. The first one of us to get any sort of half-baked notion would throw it out in the hope that one of the others would come up with a way to make it work.

"Like you and Leroy," George said. "Shooting from the train."

"Something like that," I admitted.

"Maybe that's it," Brian said, as much to himself as to us. "Some kind of shooting exhibition . . ."

I had set him going and that was all he needed. I left him there to work out the details with George, and I took the opportunity to seek out

Gerald Ball in the crowd and congratulate him for the gumption he had shown that afternoon by standing up to Villa and Ortega.

"You've got more grit than I gave you credit for," I admitted. "Hadn't of been for you, they might have shot the whole bunch of us before Leroy showed up to stop it."

"One must never kowtow to these beggars." He was once again the British lion. "You must keep them in their place. I mean, it is all very well to use General Villa in the picture, but this business of sitting at the same table with him is quite the limit."

"The same table?" I didn't know what he was talking about.

"Haven't you heard? Señor Delgado has extended the hospitality of the hacienda to General Villa and his staff. There is to be a dinner in his honor tonight! Good Lord, what a way to begin the new year. The man's a bloody revolutionary."

"And I'm a Texan," I said. "My granddaddy fought one Mexican government, old Pancho's fighting another. It comes down to it, I guess I see things from his side when it comes to politics."

Gerald took this as a personal affront. He shared no further political insights with me and left me to my own devices, so I went outside to look around and discovered that the rest of Villa's small army had arrived while we were filming in the bedroom. There were women and children, even revolutionist dogs, who were quick to establish a perimeter beyond which they would not permit the town dogs to pass. Among the women, a few were armed, the famed *soldaderas* of the revolution. The camp followers were cooking for their men, and some had set up a few small tents and other rude shelters near our wagons, but most would sleep on the ground. By one of the campfires, where a large pot of beans was bubbling, a young soldier strummed a guitar and sang a Villista *corrido*.

On the west side of the hacienda, the evening was quiet. I stood for a time at the crest of the slope looking over the town, marveling at how easily the little settlement had become a Villista camp in just a few hours. When Villa was gone, the town would be Carranzista once more, the townspeople bending like trees in the winds of revolution, simply trying to stay alive.

Chapter 18

AT DINNER THAT evening General Villa was given Señor Delgado's place at the head of the table, where he presided over the carving of a lamb slaughtered in his honor. The town elders—the heads of the little village's prominent families—were present for the banquet. They were nervous at first, no doubt feeling like lambs themselves, dining among the wolves.

Perhaps Villa saw their fears, for he chose a pause between courses to deliver a short speech. In it he demonstrated how he has won the support that has kept him safe for ten years in Chihuahua, where the peasants and townspeople send the *federales* chasing after wild geese when they come to seek out the Villistas. And he confirmed Leroy's prediction that he would court the town's favor, having decided not to fill its leading citizens full of holes. In plain but adequate English and then in flowery Spanish, Villa granted a complete pardon to the Delgados and all their retainers for what he called their "Carranzista crimes." He rescinded his order confiscating their property, and he swore by his God and the revolution that no Villistas would threaten the hacienda or the town again.

With this pronouncement, Villa revealed himself to be a shrewd politician as well as an able general. His men having already scoured the town for American gold, he had nothing more to gain by frightening the townsfolk, but much to gain by granting them amnesty. Just as the condemned prisoner will feel a debt of gratitude to the governor who pardons him, no doubt some of the *delgadeños* swung their allegiance from Carranza to

Villa on that festive New Year's Eve, never stopping to think that the man who granted the reprieve was the same man who had scared them out of their wits in the first place.

The first to be transformed by Villa's clemency was Señora Delgado. At the conclusion of dinner some of the town's musicians entered the big hall on tiptoes and began to play a gentle peasant tune. Villa rose and offered his hand to the *patrona,* who rose, blushing violently, curtsied, and allowed Villa to escort her out onto the floor. In that moment she became the town's most ardent Villista, and to the best of my knowledge has not allowed her allegiance to sway from that newly found path to this day.

Word of the amnesty was quickly carried from the hacienda to the town, and within a very short time all the Mexicans, townsfolk and Villista soldiers alike, demonstrated the sort of general merriment typical of a New Year's celebration south of the border, complete with music and dancing in the streets. When the town was first taken, General Villa had closed the cantina and forbidden the *tienda* to sell liquor—these precautions being taken to curb rowdy behavior on the part of the soldiers and thus to reassure the populace—but the revolutionists managed to enjoy themselves nonetheless. They made friends with the town's dark-eyed young girls, perhaps gaining by their rough charms what some had thought to gain by force only hours before, and as 1919 gave way to 1920, the town of Delgado put on a nightlong fiesta befitting a village twice its size.

In the hacienda, the musicians, who had not known what to expect when they received the command to perform, saw that they had been summoned to give life to a general celebration. They began to smile and to play tunes more suited to lively dancing. Naturally our picture company entered into the swing of things wholeheartedly from the start, being no strangers to after-hours revelry. Some of the Villista officers sought out Randall Steele, having recognized him from his pictures, and Randall introduced them to Charlie Noble, who was awestruck to find himself hobnobbing with Pancho Villa and his staff. How these men found time in the midst of their revolution to keep up on the latest Hollywood movies I couldn't imagine, but it was proof of the far-reaching power of this new entertainment.

Seeing the Villistas so lighthearted, the town fathers grew positively jovial. Señor Garza, the stationmaster, was foremost among the elders by virtue of his important position. Even he, the avowed Carranza supporter, entered into genial conversation with the Villistas, eventually settling down with Colonel Ortega over a flask of tequila. He became quite drunk before long, laughing too loudly at Ortega's jests.

Villa himself took to the sidelines as the festivities grew boisterous.

After two dances with Señora Delgado, he delivered her back to her husband and retired to a corner of the hall, beckoning Leroy to join him there and ordering a bottle to be brought. When it arrived, he poured three fingers of *mezcal* for each of them, and raised his glass.

"*La revolución, y la victoria*," he said.

They touched glasses and drank, and then Villa shook a finger at Leroy like a stern schoolmaster. "You did not tell me everything, Roberto," he said. "We have found the gold you paid the workers. I think you have more somewhere."

"We paid most of it out already," said Leroy. "What's left belongs to Victoria. It's for the movie."

Villa put a hand over his heart. "Then I would not touch it even if it meant my own death. We have the rest of it. That is enough."

Then a crafty look came over Villa's face and he fixed Leroy with his gaze. "Tell me, Roberto, was it the woman or the gold that brought you here with these people?"

Leroy smiled. "A little bit of both, I guess."

"But now you love the woman more than gold. You are truly romantic, my friend. It is unusual in a *gringo, sabes*? You should have been born *mejicano*." He sipped his mescal, his eyes bright. "What a woman, Roberto! You are a fool if you don't marry her. But I think she is angry with you."

He looked where Victoria was dancing with Nate Dicenzo, who was having no luck in his campaign to win Karen back to him.

"I told her I was going with you when the movie's finished."

"So? Bring her with us! She has the spirit of a revolutionary! She can cook for you and mend your clothes. Perhaps she will even fight with us. We will make her a *soldadera*!"

"That's no life for her. She's a movie star."

But Pancho had already seen the truth about Victoria.

"She lives a life of make-believe, but she longs for something real! Why do you think she loves you? She sees a real man, and the rest mean nothing!"

The tune ended and the dancers released their partners. For the moment, Victoria was unattended.

"Look at her fire!" Villa said. "She almost burns me up! Be careful, my friend, or I will steal her from you." He rose to his feet and strode toward her.

Victoria's eyes lit up when she saw Pancho coming for her, the way they had lit up to see Leroy just a day earlier. She let Villa take her in his arms and dance away with her, chatting with him about everything under the sun and only gradually working around to what was really on her mind.

"Will you grant me a wish, General?" she said at last.

"Anything at all, señorita. Providing it does not endanger the revolution."

"The people here have worked hard for us. Return the money we paid them."

Villa looked genuinely sad. "Señorita, a revolutionary needs three things: guns, horses, and money. And women, of course. These people have no guns, they have few horses, and I am sure you would not have me take their women, so I must keep the money." His sad expression became a charming smile. "But because I have the gold, I will not steal your fine American horses. The truth is, I have already stolen enough horses from the *ranchos* to the south."

The thought of losing our horses quieted Victoria. Villa twirled her past Leroy and gave his friend a grin. Victoria feigned not to notice Leroy at all, but when they were beyond his hearing she said, "Then grant me a different wish. Tell me who he is."

"He is my good friend Leroy Roberts."

"But that isn't his real name." She stated it as a fact, using the detective's trick of pretending to know more than she really did in the hope that Villa would tell her what she wished to learn. But Villa was nobody's fool.

"Nor is Francisco Villa mine," he said. "I was born Doroteo Arango. A man may change his name, but in his heart he is still the same man."

"To know that man, I need to know who he is."

"You have touched his heart. You know all that matters."

She got nothing more from him, but during the dances that followed, her eyes sought out Leroy often.

I was sitting in a wing chair not too far from my customary guard post by the foot of the stairs, watching them dance and idly reading a newspaper Orville had brought with him the day before. At my age, whenever I have a chance to see a new decade come in I figure I'm entitled to celebrate, hence I had a glass of *pulque* beside me from which I sipped now and again. When the glass was empty, old Ramón was generally quick to refill it, but it had been dry for some time now. I was about to go looking for the bottle when George Bleumel sat down beside me.

"I've never seen him drink on campaign before," he said, nodding in Villa's direction. "Not even one glass. He must think a lot of our friend Leroy."

"Leroy fought beside him back in the early days of the revolution." I saw no harm in telling George that much, but he had something more on his mind than Villa sharing a glass of mescal with Leroy. He stroked his bald pate and appeared embarrassed.

"Listen, Charlie, Villa—well, there has been a lot of talk about his conquests—girls taken against their will. There's always plenty who are willing to share his bed with him, but he often prefers the ones who play hard to get. It's just that he seems to have taken an interest in Victoria. I thought I should say something."

"I'm keeping an eye on her," I said. But George's words made more of an impression on me than I let on. The celebrations in the hacienda were so congenial, I had almost forgotten that so long as Villa and his men remained, we were all still in danger.

As soon as Villa turned Victoria loose and returned to his corner table with Leroy, I moved to her side and took her in my arms.

"You and Pancho hit it off pretty good," I said as we danced away.

"He's a perfect gentleman," she said.

"He's got a way with the ladies, all right. That doesn't mean you should go walking in the moonlight with him."

"Oh, Charlie, I wouldn't do that."

"You had some nighttime strolls with Leroy, I hear."

She was quiet for a moment. "You know him, don't you? You know him from the old days."

Her guesses were getting too close to the mark and I tried to head her off. "I never set eyes on him until he first set foot in the Bunk House, and that's the Lord's truth."

"But you're still keeping something from me."

"I only want what's best for you, girl."

Sensing that she would get nothing more out of me, she left me when the dance ended and sat down near the musicians to lose herself in the music. Soon after this, the Villista officers sent for their balladeer, the same guitar player I had observed early in the evening. He arrived in the company of his sweetheart, one of the fighting *soldaderas,* and treated us all to a few dozen verses of "Adelita," which is the Villistas' unofficial marching song, followed by other *corridos.* Whenever he hesitated, Victoria asked for her favorite songs by name, which caused the *soldadera's* eyes to flame with jealousy, but like the officers she was awed to find herself in the presence of "Rosa Cimarrona," and she contented herself with shooting dark glances at the singer when he looked in Victoria's direction.

When he sang an especially beautiful love song, Victoria added her voice to his, for the song was one of those she had learned in New Mexico as a young girl.

Ya me voy par' el Laredo, mi bien,
Te vengo a decir adios.
Ya me voy par' el Laredo, mi bien,
Te vengo a decir adios.
De allá te mando decir, mi bien
cómo se mancuernan dos.

As she sang, she looked toward where Villa and Leroy were drinking. Villa was listening raptly and she made as though she sang for the general, but I knew that she was singing for Leroy. "Take this little golden key, my love," said the final verse. "Open my breast and you will see how much I love you."

If Leroy understood the words he gave no sign, and when the song was over Victoria excused herself, despite the pleas of the Villistas, and went up to her bed.

As soon as Victoria left, Villa too rose from his seat and took himself off to his camp, where he would sleep on the ground like his men. Alone now, Leroy strolled to the dining room off the big hall, where the cowboys had established an informal cantina around the dining table. Nate was there, along with Redeye and Chief John and Tommy Fear and Jim Ray Thompson and the rest. Jack Whistler and Willie Two Horse sat apart from the others, talking softly, with a few Indian hand signs thrown in now and then for good measure.

As on Christmas Eve, Nate Dicenzo's mood was dark and his thirst mighty. Karen was amusing herself by flirting on the dance floor with one of Villa's officers, a bright lad who should have been in university, batting her eyes the hardest when she was within Nate's sight. From where I sat I could see both of them, and there were moments when I thought there might be bloodshed before the night was out, but none of the drinkers shared my concern, their own concerns being to see who could take on board the largest cargo of *pulque* or some other kill-me-quick Mexican beverage.

Nate had pulled at a bottle of mescal throughout the evening, until the little *gusano* that lived in the bottle had scarcely a thimbleful of liquor to swim in. A *gusano* is a worm, and it is said that the most intoxicating essences of the mescal are concentrated in his tiny body. As Karen waltzed by within Nate's view once more, he lifted the bottle and drained it dry, *gusano* and all, and started to rise from his seat with blood in his eye.

Just then there was such an outbreak of gunfire from the direction of town that we thought the whole federal army must be attacking, but it proved to be no more than the revolutionists' way of marking the stroke of midnight. As time went on there were further volleys, the town's few clocks being in considerable disagreement. There would be a period of quiet, then a new salvo of shots as yet another timepiece announced the arrival of the new year.

The initial barrage distracted Nate from his violent impulse, which he had clean forgotten when it ended. He looked puzzled, wondering why he was on his feet. As he looked toward the hall, where Karen was fortunately not in view at the moment, Leroy appeared in the wide archway which joined the dining room to the hall.

"Hey, Leroy," Nate greeted him. "Seddown and lemme buy you a drink."

"Buying" here consisted of calling to one of the servants and pointing out that a fresh glass was needed, for the drinks were on the hacienda.

"If you don't mind my askin', how's it come to be you know Pancho Villa so good?" Nate blurted out once Leroy had a beer.

"I was kind of wondering about that myself," said Bob Elderberg, as if the thought hadn't come to him until Nate brought it up.

"Oh, back at the start of the revolution there were a lot of Americans down here," said Leroy. "Me and a friend of mine, we thought we'd give it a try."

He threw a glance in my direction and I dropped my eyes to the newspaper in my lap, not wanting to appear to be taking a great interest in the conversation. As at Christmastime, the news was full of the Harry New murder trial while reporting all quiet along the Mexican border, but although my eyes rested on the paper, my attention was on the conversation in the dining room.

Leroy told the cowboys as much as he had told Victoria and me about his time with Villa, and then some. He related stories of a few lively battles, just enough to take the edge off the boys' curiosity, before adding that he had been with Villa for only a few months and bringing his account of those days to a close. They asked more questions then, about his younger days and all the things he had seen and done. These too he answered, in a general sort of way, seeming to tell them more than he really was.

Having made some mention of a cowboy's reticence at asking personal questions about a man's past, I will add that there are some circumstances when such restraints are loosened, and this was one of them. These men had known Leroy for a few weeks now and they had kept their curiosity in check. But in the way of western men they had been getting to know him, and he them. As Leroy grew more outgoing once we were in Mexico, the boys on the crew felt more at liberty to approach him with small questions about horses or guns or any of the other things one man might ask another, either because he valued that man's opinion or just as a way of passing the time. This evening's celebration and the attendant thirst quenching had filled our cowboys with good fellowship they all wished to share with Leroy. Learning that he knew Pancho Villa was the last straw. They could hold back their questions no longer, and so they gave in at last to their curiosity about this man who had actually lived the life they were acting out before the cameras and in the wild west show arena.

Leroy kept as close to the truth as he dared. He told of leaving his home to see the world, and how he had raised horses and cattle east of the Big Horns not long before the Johnson County War.

"So you were right there in the thick of it," Redeye Hawk said. "The war, I mean." Unlike some of the others he was still bright-eyed, having nursed a single bottle of beer for over an hour.

Leroy shook his head. "The Stock Growers Association was making it hard for a man to earn a living. I moved back over to the Wind River before that all broke out."

For those with short memories, the so-called Johnson County War of 1892 was one of the livelier episodes in the history of Wyoming. I will not attempt to give all the details, but at the heart of the matter it was a dispute between small ranchers and the big landowners in Johnson County, Wyoming, and in the surrounding country. By highhanded means, the big ranchers tried to force out the small ones in order to keep the vast tracts of public land on which they grazed their herds. The worst offenses against western decency were the regulations passed by the Wyoming legislature in support of the Wyoming Stock Growers Association, which stated that a man could not legally participate in a roundup or brand any "slick" or unbranded calves unless he belonged to the Association and had his brand registered with it. Naturally, the Association did not admit the small ranchers to membership. This meant that a man could be arrested for branding his own calves.

It is easy to see that such a state of affairs could not go on for long. The small ranchers began to band together and conduct their own roundups, sometimes boldly including Association calves in their branding. The "war" took place when the Association hired a bunch of Texas gunmen to come into the country and wipe out the small fry, but the small fry did not cooperate. They bottled up the gunmen at the TA Ranch in Johnson County and were just about to teach the vigilantes a good Wyoming lesson when a troop of bluecoat soldiers arrived and saved the Texans' bacon.

My own feelings in the matter are intricate, but despite my Texas blood I tend to see things from the little fellow's point of view, having been just a working cowboy myself and never more than a straw boss. There is nothing wrong with a man grazing his stock over a million acres of public land, but if he uses his position to squash the little fellow who is just trying to make an honest living, then I'll have to side with the underdog.

As it happened, about the time the war clouds were gathering over Johnson County, the law was closing in on Butch Cassidy. In 1889 he had pulled a bank robbery in Telluride, Colorado, with Matt Warner and Tom McCarty. It was the first serious crime attributed to him, and done before the Pinkerton brothers were called on to track him down. Colorado officers followed him into Wyoming, where he had bought a small ranch on Blue Creek, but just before Christmas of that year he sold his ranch and skipped out. Whereupon the officers went home, he not being a famous outlaw yet.

But in April of '92, the same month when the Johnson County War finally caught fire, Butch's luck failed him. Already blacklisted by the Stock Growers Association and therefore a marked man, he was charged with horse theft by one of the Big Horn "land barons" he so despised. Now it was Wyoming officers who were after him, and they caught him napping. He was arrested, tried, and served a year and a half in the Wyoming Penitentiary. Actually he was tried twice. The first jury found him not guilty, but on a second charge he wasn't so lucky. It was the only time Butch was ever put behind prison walls, and from the day he entered the pen until the day he left, he maintained his innocence.

Leroy told Victoria's cowboys none of this, of course. He made out that he felt lucky to have departed the Big Horn country before the real war broke out, and he passed along to other tales of his cowboy youth, keeping thereafter to safer ground. He drew his listeners along with him, suggesting in many small ways that they had no doubt done many of the very same things.

At a pause in the talk, Nate slapped his knee. "I knew it," he said. "I knew you were a cowboy just like us, back then."

Nate intended this as the highest praise, but Leroy just smiled and shrugged off the accolade. "Oh, I did my share of cowboying," he said, "but there wasn't much future in it. I traded in horseflesh for a while and I saved my money. When I got the chance I moved on to the world of finance."

"Finance?" Nate had no idea where such a world was located.

"Banking and railroads mostly. I held executive positions." Leroy threw a look my way. His expression was sober, but there was a twinkle in his eye.

Nate was suspicious. "How come you ain't rich?"

"It was a high-pressure life, always on the go. I retired to take it easy," he said, smiling that friendly smile.

"I never would have took you for a businessman," Chief John allowed.

"A man's got to better himself every chance he gets," Leroy said. "Look at you," he went on, directing himself to Nate. "You were a cowboy. Now you're a movie star."

"Aw, I ain't a star," Nate said. "Not yet anyway."

"You were a star bronc rider back in Texas."

Ordinarily when Nate Dicenzo is given a chance to wax eloquent on the subject of his own accomplishments he is like a six-eight wheeler at full throttle—full of steam and hard to stop—but on this particular evening something restrained him. A bashful look came over him and he said, "The truth is, I never was champeen of Matagorda County. I did place second once. Dottie there, she took a first in women's saddle bronc, up in Cheyenne. Karen's done her share too."

Leroy turned to Dottie Thompson, who was sitting with Jim Ray, and with a couple of questions he got her talking about her bronc-riding exploits, but she became embarrassed with all the attention.

"Every time I get in that chute, I'm still scared," she said, and she fell silent.

"A person would never know it to see you ride," said Jim.

This prompted a chorus of agreement from the cowboys, and as it died away Leroy mentioned how well Tommy Fear had done at the steer roping in our makeshift stampede the day before Christmas, and before you knew it Tommy was telling him the story of his young life. When Tommy was done, Jim Ray was next, then Chief John. One at a time, Leroy drew them out, listening to whoever was talking like he had never heard anything so interesting before. Those at the table may not have noticed how he always turned to the person who had been left out of the conversation so far, but I did, and I no longer paid any attention to the newspaper in my lap.

The big hall was almost empty now. Once Villa was gone, some of his officers had a beer or a glass of *pulque*, but they were constantly looking over their shoulders as if afraid their *jefe* might return to catch them having a drop of holiday cheer, and before long they went off to their bedrolls lest he decide to rouse them before dawn, as was often his custom. With the Villistas gone, the Delgados retired, along with most of the servants, but in the dining room no one was aware of the time and no one thought of leaving.

Buddy Johnston was the last to be drawn out, and for the first time I heard him speak of the Great War. He told of Champagne and the Argonne, and he managed to convey something of the fearsome nature of modern mechanized war, in which individual human lives are no more significant than the lives of fleas on a dog's back.

There was pride in Buddy's voice, pride in himself and pride in how the colored troops had comported themselves in combat. But there was a sadness there, and something more, which came out at the end of his story.

"After the Armistice, I stayed on," he said. "Even thought I might make a twenty-year man. But then it was back to washin' dishes and diggin' trenches. I wouldn't of minded if all the troops was washin' and diggin', but the white boys had it easy. They got the marchin' and garrison duty while us colored boys washed and dug and learned how to say 'yassuh' to white boys again. Back in the fightin' they needed us. 'You boys are good as any other soldiers,' they told us. 'The way for you to prove it is fight.' So we fought. Yes sir, we fought. Got the Croix de Guerre to prove it. But when the fightin' was done, it was the same old story all over again. And after what we went through."

There was a bitterness in his voice, and suddenly I knew why. On his return to Hollywood and the Bunk House he had been welcomed as the conquering hero. But as a member of our picture show outfit in Mexico, Buddy had soon been relegated to doing just the sort of jobs he had quit the army to avoid. I myself had accepted this as only natural. He was the same boy who went off to war, I imagined, come back all filled-out and grown-up, but otherwise the same. Had I stopped to think, I would have realized that war changes a man. Now I saw how much it had changed Buddy.

But he hadn't meant to complain, and when he sensed that his listeners were uncomfortable, he got to his feet. "I guess I'll turn in," he said.

Brian Hill was quick to follow Buddy's example. "Nine o'clock call to-morrow, boys," he said as he rose. "That's the best I can do for you."

There was a general scraping of chair legs on the floor and a round of good nights. But while the others rose to go to bed, I was rooted to my chair, transfixed by the wondrous thing I had witnessed.

Right before my eyes, Leroy had formed the men and women of the McQuain & Vickery show into an even more tightly-knit bunch than they had been before, with himself at the center. He drew them not by wielding authority, but by making each person look into his own heart and understand himself better. When this evening's talk was done, each one there had shared some confidence with the others, as Nate and Dottie and Buddy had done. People I had known for months had revealed small things about themselves that they had never told me, or anyone else, so far as I knew, and that sharing became a new bond among them.

Seeing him work his sorcery, I understood how Butch Cassidy had formed the Wild Bunch into the most dauntless bunch of outlaws ever to ride the West and how they had eluded the combined efforts of the Pinkertons and lawmen from a dozen states to bring them to justice. Only when the gang members were beyond Butch's counsel had they come to grief. Butch himself had survived, along with the Sundance Kid and his consort, Etta Place, who had the good sense to stick by Butch's side.

The men and women I have known all my life, western folk, are often people of few words and fewer confidences. When they share those confidences, it means they trust the one they are confiding in and would stick with him through thick and thin. And I knew that if I asked each person who had sat around that dining table tonight who was the boss of our picture crew, they might say "Brian is," or maybe "Sir Gerald, I suppose," but I was just as certain as I could be that if any one of them should suddenly find himself in a tight spot while we remained in Sonora, he would look to Leroy to get him out of it.

Chapter 19

"I DIDN'T KNOW you to be such a night owl, Charlie," Jack Whistler said as he passed through the hall on his way out of the hacienda.

"Old white men, they like to sit up all night thinkin'," Willie Two Horse said. He was supporting Anna with some difficulty. The afternoon's experience at the hands of the Villistas had upset her considerably and she had calmed herself with a flagon of *pulque*.

"Used to be they'd think about how to steal the Indian's land," Willie said. "I don't know what they think about now."

"Happy New Year," Anna called out as he hauled her away.

With their departure, Leroy and I had the hacienda's public rooms to ourselves, save for old Ramón, who was dozing in a chair by the kitchen door, snoring loudly. Leroy shook his shoulder and said a few words to him, and the venerable servant ambled gratefully off to his bed.

Leroy searched among the bottles on the sideboard until he found one with some liquor remaining. He filled two small glasses which he carried in one hand while he picked up a chair with the other and brought it to where I sat. The contents of the glass he offered me smelled like sheep-dip.

"What the hell is this?" I asked.

"*Sotol*," he said. "It's a poor man's drink."

"You feeling poorly, are you?"

"Drink up, Charlie. Happy New Year." He tossed off most of what was in his glass.

I had already downed half a dozen glasses of *pulque* and mescal and I was feeling their effects, but I was not to be outdone in a New Year's toast, so I followed suit. The *sotol* tasted even worse than it smelled. As I set the glass on the lamp stand beside my chair, I noticed that Leroy was watching me with an amused expression.

"How about you. Don't you have any questions you want to ask me?" he said.

I thought for a moment. "Well, yes," I said. "How long were you and Harry Longabaugh with Villa?"

"Just six months or so."

"Seems like you made quite an impression on him, for such a short time."

"Pancho and me are a lot alike, Charlie. He got his start in life stealing horses from the land barons, just like me. Later on I went after the banks and railroads and he took on the whole Mexican government, but it's all the same thing in the end. We both want a fair shake for the little guy."

This told me a good deal about why Leroy had come to help his old friend now: as he saw it, the two of them had fought the same fight all their lives. Now Villa was fighting alone, and Leroy had come to side with the underdog one last time.

"I've got another one for you then," I said. "Back there in the Big Horn country, did you steal those horses?"

He shook his head. "Like I said at the time, I bought them fair and square."

"From a fellow who maybe stole them."

"Maybe. It was Billy Nutcher sold them to me. I knew Billy carried a spare saddle ring, but he told me he got those horses by trading for them over in Johnson County. A lot of men stepped across the law in those days, Charlie. Cowboys and stockmen both. The big fellows most of all. There were cowboys lynched for mavericking and nesters shot down in the middle of their own pasture."

As I have said, before the turn of the century mavericking was still an accepted recourse for a hungry man. But a cinch ring heated in a fire was often used by rustlers to alter brands, and when Leroy said Billy Nutcher carried a spare saddle ring he had this purpose in mind.

"I'd like to hear the whole story," I said.

"There's not much to it. Al Hainer and I bought those horses in the summer of '91. The next spring we were arrested on a complaint sworn by Otto Franc. He was the biggest land baron in the Big Horn basin, and when he barked the law jumped, even though he waited ten months before he reported the horses stolen. When the case came to trial, we were found not guilty because the jury believed we didn't know the horses were stolen."

For a moment he seemed weighted down by the memory. "Franc saw which way the wind was blowing. Even before the verdict was in, he swore out another complaint on the same charge."

"The law says he can't do that," I said.

"The first complaint only mentioned one of the horses. The next one mentioned a different horse. There were three of them, Charlie. Three horses and the man couldn't let it drop."

Hearing this, I felt some of the anger he must have felt upon being freed by one jury only to know he would have to go through the whole ordeal again. Apparently Otto Franc had wanted Butch Cassidy badly enough to ride roughshod over the niceties of the law.

"That time around, the jury found me guilty but they let Al Hainer off. That's when I figured maybe he was in on the whole setup. Him and Franc together. That's what some of the boys told me later on." He shook his head. "The one thing I never could figure was why Franc had it in for me. Jack Bliss and his whole gang were up in the Owl Creek Mountains, taking all the cattle and horses they could find. Why didn't he go after them?"

He stretched his left hand wide, clenched it, then stretched it wide again. It was a mannerism I had noticed a few times before. He shook his arm as if to rid himself of Otto Franc's tenacious grip.

"I got a year and a half in the penitentiary. When I got out, I couldn't find a job anywhere in the Big Horn or Wind River country. Franc had me blacklisted worse than before. And that's not all. The next thing I knew, he swore out a new complaint saying I stole fifty head of his horses five years earlier, when I wasn't even in Wyoming! That got me mad. I rounded up a few of the boys and I figured I'd teach Otto Franc a lesson. He claimed I stole fifty of his horses, so that's what I did. We drove them down into Utah and turned them loose. Scattered them all over the mountains around Brown's Hole. I guess over the next few years those horses helped a lot of my friends stay clear of the law."

The memory made him smile. "Hell, it could have been worse. Franc could have hired someone to shoot me." He rose and returned to the sideboard in the dining room, taking our empty glasses.

I thought it noteworthy that in telling his story Leroy had not mentioned two points in his favor. First, that he was out on bond while awaiting his trials and he never tried to run. Each time he showed up on schedule to stand at the bar of justice. Second, that he was released from the penitentiary early on a pardon from the Wyoming governor, who apparently felt that a bit too much justice had been done in his case. The pardon was an attempt to set the record straight, but Otto Franc would not let matters rest there. And by his single-minded persistence in beleaguering one footloose cowboy then perched on the fence between the straight and narrow and a more winding path, that Big Horn land baron had a hand in providing the Wild Bunch with the leader they needed to become the last great gang of western outlaws.

I already knew some of the story from when I followed Butch Cassidy's trail through Johnson County and the Big Horn basin at the turn of the century, just a few years after the Johnson County War, but hearing Leroy tell it made me fully appreciate the importance of that prison term. I saw now that Butch Cassidy was just as surely a casualty of the Johnson County War as any of the others whose lives were caught up in the conflict. He was not quite thirty when he was released from the Wyoming Penitentiary, yet it must have seemed to him that from his earliest years men in authority had stacked the deck against him. From the storekeeper who set the sheriff on him to the Mormon bishop who took his father's land, and right down to Otto Franc, these men had treated Butch as untrustworthy. They had questioned his honor. In the end they did it one too many times.

It is said there is honor among thieves, and it was among that class of men that Butch sought friendship and loyalty, having failed to find it elsewhere. There, among the roughest outlaws the West could offer, his natural abilities as a leader were recognized, and men far more bloodthirsty than he entrusted him with their lives.

Seeing him in this light made me take a new look at myself. I had long believed that what separated me from the outlaw element of western society was strength of character, and perhaps some noble breeding back in my Italian father's bloodline. To put it neatly, I thought I was better than those who rode the crooked trail. In my cowboy youth I had spent much time among outlaws, but I had not succumbed to evil ways, if you leave aside a penchant for drinking poison whiskey and bucking at three-card monte. Now, comparing myself with Leroy, I saw the difference between us, and it had nothing to do with strong character or noble breeding. By good fortune I had run onto the sort of western men who will treat a fellow as worthy of confidence until he proves himself otherwise. In the employ of the LX Ranch I had been entrusted at various times with longhorns and dollars both counted in the thousands, and charged with conveying those articles across great distances. Sometimes I was gone from the ranch for months on end, but I always tried my best to do the job required of me no matter how long it took. In short, because I was trusted, I behaved in a trustworthy manner. Because Butch was not trusted, he vowed to live by his own law.

It was as simple as that. All that separated us was a small nudge from fortune, good on one hand and bad on the other.

Leroy returned, handing me my glass and resuming his seat beside me.

"I'm not proud of my life," he said. Apparently he too had been looking back and summing up as he poured us another drink. "When you get right down to it, what I did for a living was take other people's money. But that wasn't the worst of it. I had a good family and I caused them nothing but grief. I'm sorry for that."

He downed a swallow of *sotol*. "Did you ever do something you were ashamed of, Charlie?"

I hesitated before I answered. "I've always regretted working against the miners when I was a Pinkerton," I said.

This was the one blot on my conscience from my detective years. "I got a lot of men arrested. I reported the facts and let the law take its course, and they were all guilty of one thing or another, from salting mines to stealing high-grade ore, right on up to murder. Catching the murderers I don't mind, but as for the rest, I wish I had never set foot below ground."

"You just told the truth," he said.

"Sometimes the truth isn't the same as justice. What the miners needed was justice. They were paid dirt poor in those days. They took their lives in their hands every time they went down in a mine, and the owners treated them like slaves."

"It doesn't sound like the kind of life a cowboy would enjoy."

"No," I said. "That's a fact." I drank off the rest of my glass.

"So what's it all been for, then, Charlie?" he asked.

"Damned if I know. I figured you did it for the money."

"Hell, we'd spend it all quick as we got it, or give it away."

This improved my spirits and brought a smile to my face. "I heard you were a regular Robin Hood there sometimes, when you weren't shooting chickens."

Leroy lit up as he recalled the incident I had in mind. "You heard about that?"

"Baggs, Wyoming, after you cleaned out the bank at Montpelier."

"Yeah. Well, it's true. I shot that lady's chickens."

"Shot the heads off 'em, I heard. The story was, you did it just to hear her cuss."

"She was a first-class cusser. She could put you or me to shame."

"They say you gave her a twenty-dollar gold piece for every chicken you killed."

Leroy grinned. "Later on, I heard she bought a first-class flock of Rhode Island Reds."

"I also heard you and your boys spread enough gold around Baggs in two days to help the town make it through a cold winter. That wasn't the only time I heard about you helping folks along the way."

I was thinking of him playing Santa Claus to the nesters, and the other stories I had heard while on his trail, but he made no effort to claim credit for those deeds.

"There was a practical side to that deal," he said. "We made a lot of friends when we were flush. Later on, they'd hide us out and feed us when we were on the run."

"And you never stashed anything away against your old age?"

"Maybe a little here and there."

His eyes sparked with some mischievous thought. Whatever it was, it made him think of his present employment. He glanced toward the stairs. "Who's looking after our gold, Charlie?"

"I've kept an eye on who goes up or down."

"Well, you go sleep on it now. I'm done for the day." With that, he rose and left me.

Chapter 20

WHEN I AWOKE in the morning, the sun was already up, the movie crew was off at work, and demons were dancing in my skull. Without a word to anyone, I crept from the hacienda like a thief and walked downtown in search of some aspirin, my hat pulled low over my eyes to protect me from the fiery ball that shone mercilessly from a cool blue sky.

A number of Villa's soldiers were lounging about the railroad tracks, apparently suffering from the same malady that affected me, and I judged that Villa's efforts to keep his men away from the Demon Rum were less than wholly successful. But the village was quiet and there was no evidence of violence to the houses or their occupants.

In the plaza, I discovered that the cantina scene had already been completed, with the real Pancho Villa leering through the window at Evangelina this time. Even now the crew was packing the last of the equipment and moving back to the vicinity of the hacienda, where further scenes involving General Villa would be filmed. I was relieved to see that the doors to the little *tienda* stood open. Holiday or not, the proprietor knew which side his bread was buttered on. With all the Villistas and *yanquis* in town, he stood ready to serve our needs, however trifling.

My own needs were far from trifling. When the storekeeper offered me a bottle of Bayer tablets, I felt profound gratitude. Fortified by three aspirins and a long-necked bottle of cool beer I wheedled out of him, I returned to the hacienda to find the picture crew set up beside the horse

pasture fence, and Leroy and Pancho eating a late breakfast by Luke
Fister's cookfire.

"Pull up a cactus, Charlie," Leroy greeted me. "We'll call for another
plate."

"No food," I murmured. "Just coffee."

"You oughta eat something," Leroy advised me. "You put enough of this
sauce on it, it'll fix you up brand new."

As if to demonstrate the truth of what he said, he spooned gobs of an
evil-looking red sauce from a small dish onto his plate, where several fried
eggs already swam in the stuff. Pancho nodded and smiled and he too
added some of the *salsa* to his food.

Normally I enjoy Luke Fister's spicy cooking, but on this particular
morning the sight of food threatened to turn my stomach. Taking my
coffee in hand, I went to watch Brian and Victoria and the boys do whatever it was they were doing. Later, I wondered if perhaps I should have
taken Leroy's advice. He and Villa both seemed fit as fiddles, while I
spent the morning earnestly contemplating the virtues of a sober life.

The scene being filmed by the horse pasture fence was a small one
Brian was trying to get out of the way while Villa was eating. It was a direct
result of our talk the evening before, about how to make our audience
believe that our hero Tom and his cowboys stood a chance against the
bloodthirsty Villa in our story.

What Brian had come up with was much like some of the frolics I had
played out in my Texas youth. Tom and his pals, whiling away the hours
out on the range, decide to have their own little shooting spree. The idea
was to have the men ride lickety-split along the fence line and shoot as
many tin cans and bottles as they could from atop the posts, where Buddy
Johnston would set them up between riders. Watching this, the picture
audience would see that these were not only fine young American boys,
but deadly shots to boot. Thus the notion of their chasing down Pancho
Villa and fighting him to a standstill might hold water.

There were all sorts of movie tricks Brian might have pulled. The cowboys really didn't need to hit any of the targets at all. They could ride
along the fence, firing to beat the band, and then George could film the
fence while Dusty Clark or Jack or just about anyone else shot the targets
off the posts one by one. But Brian said a scene always played better if it
was done for real. If more picture directors had Brian's attitude, many of
the stunts you see in the movies would be more convincing.

The plan was to have one of the boys clear off the fence while wearing
Randall's hat and coat, so it would appear that Randall was the sharpshooter. Afterwards, Brian would film Tom's pals in their own gear, but the
one shot he had to have to make the scene work was the hero Tom showing his stuff.

Jack Whistler went first. He is a deadeye shot with a rifle, and handy with Mr. Colt's pistols too, when he's standing on solid ground, but he has never got the hang of shooting from horseback. Oh, he could knock down a line of men like tenpins, if they would stand still for him. But those tin cans and bottles were a good deal smaller than men and they dodged Jack's bullets nimbly. He got two with six shots.

Of course only a fool carries six bullets in a six-shooter, not for real. Fully loaded, the hammer rests on a live cartridge. Dropping the pistol can have loud results, sometimes fatal. Any old cowboy or soldier will tell you that you load five and keep the hammer on the empty chamber. But such details are too frivolous to bother the moviegoing populace with. If they see Tom fire off five shots, they're holding their breaths waiting for the sixth. So Jack and those that followed him loaded a sixth cartridge before making their rides.

Bob Elderberg went next, then Nate Dicenzo. Bob got three cans. Nate got one bottle and one can. Jim Ray Thompson made a run, with Redeye Hawk right behind him. Even Redeye only got three targets.

The Villista soldiers, who were gathered in force to watch the *gringos'* shooting prowess, howled in derision. By now Leroy and Villa were done eating and had joined the crowd.

"Three out of six isn't good enough," Brian said, shaking his head.

"We can cut out the misses," said George Bleumel.

"You could let Leroy try," Victoria said.

Villa clapped Leroy on the back. "*Ande,* Roberto. Show him how it is done."

Leroy looked around for some way to get out of it. "I'll have to get my horse," he said.

"Use Buster," Nate offered, holding out his horse's reins. "He'll run straight for you."

"Give him Randall's hat and coat," Victoria said to Redeye.

There was no getting out of it now. Leroy put on Randall's hat and coat and got into position. When Brian called "Action," he socked spurs to the mustang and pulled his Colt's Frontier. And he showed one and all how to pacify that fence line. With each shot, a bottle shattered or a can flew off its post. Leroy took his time, spacing his shots. For the last two bottles he leaned out of the saddle and fired from under Buster's neck.

When the shooting was over there wasn't a target left standing, and Leroy was grinning like he hadn't had more fun in a month of Sundays.

"If you could teach me to do that, I'd be the envy of every man in Hollywood!" Randall Steele exclaimed.

"All it takes is practice," said Leroy.

Chief John thought different. He was standing near Victoria, a little back from the camera. "That don't come just from practice," he said. "A man learns to shoot like that, it's because he needs to shoot like that."

Brian kept everyone hopping throughout the morning, working fast to reshoot the scenes he needed if there was to be any hope of making it seem that the real Pancho Villa appeared as himself in the picture. By editing Pancho's close-ups with the long shots of Chief John and his men, no one would know it wasn't Pancho all the while. This would reduce Chief John's prominence in the picture, which disappointed John, but he had long since learned to take the white man's world with a grain of salt.

After a short lunch of red sausage meat, beans and tortillas, of which I partook cautiously, we were back at it, filming Pancho and our movie Mexicans galloping over the sage after Evangelina. We were only a few hundred yards from the hacienda, but by aiming the camera away from the buildings and toward the foothills it would seem to be miles from civilization. The scene in question took place after Evangelina has conked Villa with the vase. She gets away by stealing a horse from Villa's corral in the middle of the night, but Villa and his boys are hot on her trail. Only the timely arrival of Tom and his pals keeps Villa from overtaking her, and now he's hopping mad. To simulate a nighttime look, George was shooting with smoked glass over his lens.

Colonel Ortega rode in Villa's band, and a few other genuine Villista soldiers were included at Villa's request. "Never have I ridden with fewer than thirty men," he explained to Brian, "not even before the revolution."

For the rest of the insurgents, this New Year's Day was a real holiday. While their *jefe* disported himself in front of the camera they engaged in all the pursuits normally denied them on campaign. Some watched the filming while others dozed in the sun, but most were gathered around the horse pasture, where Leroy and the children were playing baseball. Many of the Villistas were familiar with the game, and before long they asked to be included in the fun. The children were about worn out for the day so they took to the sidelines, and from that point the game became rougher.

Naturally the wild west show cowboys and Indians got into the act, those who weren't required for the filming. At first Leroy tried to mix revolutionists and Americans evenly on the two teams, but before long the sides were dubbed Gringos and Insurgentes, and divided along those lines. When three *soldaderas* joined the Villista side, Dottie Thompson and Katie Elderberg were added to the Gringos, bringing the number of players on each team to fifteen. Karen Valdez was itching to play, but she was dressed in an Evangelina outfit just like Victoria's, standing by to double for Victoria when Evangelina's horse was required to take a fall as Villa's men closed in on her and the cowboys. Victoria had protested this arrangement, as she often did, wishing to do the simple fall herself, but we couldn't risk having the picture come in late just because she got hurt doing her own stunt, so she swallowed her pride. As Brian and George filmed a series of shots featuring Pancho and his gang, Victoria and Karen divided their attention between the filming and the game, occasionally shouting their support for the Gringos.

Leroy was forced to umpire, he being the only man both sides trusted to be evenhanded, but even so, disputes in this unofficial World Series were frequent and the play became lively. The Americans were determined not to be bested at their own national game, but the Villistas gave the contest a new twist or two, as they preferred not to be troubled with the fine points of big league rules or strategy. Every revolutionist on the field tore after the ball when it was hit, which resulted in some bone-jarring collisions, and they were not above obstructing the base runners in a harsh manner. At one point I saw a Villista tackling Tommy Fear to prevent him from gaining third base.

I was content to observe both the filming and this spirited competition from where I sat against a fencepost, letting the sunshine banish the last of the demons from my pickled brain. Nearby, Villa and his gang thundered past the camera, their faces showing them to be bent on murder and mayhem when they caught up with Evangelina, even though she was now protected by Tom and his cowboys, having met them in the desert in the middle of the night. Of such coincidences are our picture romances contrived. I will add that this lucky meeting was one of Brian's contributions to the scenario. I once arranged to meet my partner W. O. Sayles at night by a certain tree that grew near a spring in the Big Horn basin, just north of the Owl Creek Mountains. Neither one of us could find the tree or the spring, let alone the other man, but there in Delgado I kept this intelligence to myself, preferring to believe that true lovers would find each other in the Mexican desert even if blindfolded.

When I saw a group of riders approaching from the north, I took them to be some of the local vaqueros and thought no more of them until one of Villa's officers, a Lieutenant Alarcón, I later learned, rose from the shade of a saguaro. He peered hard at the riders, then sauntered in front of the camera just as Villa and his band galloped past, brandishing their pistols as all good bandits must do throughout a movie chase.

"Cut!" Brian hollered as soon as he noticed Alarcón.

"¡Idiota!" Villa shouted, reining in beside the lieutenant. "¡Arruiniste la escena!" He was winding himself up to curse Alarcón roundly for ruining the scene, when Alarcón waved a hand toward the riders.

"Mire, jefe. Me parecen rurales." Look, Chief. I think they're rurales.

Villa looked at the riders.

"Son siete, jefe. Creen que somos vecinos o gringos." Alarcón added in the same mild tone. There are seven of them. They must think we're towns-people or Americans.

It was the same squad of *rurales* who had passed through Delgado the day before Christmas. They had spied the film crew at work and the base-ball game in the pasture, but they had failed to distinguish the revolution-ist soldiers among the picture folk and the *delgadeños*.

A change came over Villa. Without raising his voice he said, "Jorge, please make the camera go around. Señor Brian, you will direct the scene as before." He turned to Ortega and spoke a few words to him. Ortega dismounted, handed his reins to one of the soldiers, and strolled off with-out apparent purpose toward the baseball game.

For twenty-four hours, Villa had meekly taken Brian's orders, but in a moment he was in charge again. His resumption of command was so natural that no one thought to question him. Brian called directions through his megaphone and George prepared the camera. At the baseball pasture, Ortega spoke to the soldiers watching the game and they moved nearer their guns, which were never far from their sides even on a day of rest.

I was on my feet now, moving toward Victoria. Bob Elderberg and Jack Whistler sensed the danger brewing. They looked back and forth from the approaching *rurales* to Villa's men and they drew closer to me and Victoria.

"What's going on, Charlie?" Randall asked. He and Charlie Noble and the cowboys were holding their horses near the camera. They too sensed a charge in the air, but they hadn't worked out what caused it.

"Just get ready to hit the ground when I holler," I said. I repeated the same thing in Spanish to a bunch of the Mexican kids who were nearby. They had come to watch Pancho Villa play picture star once the grown-ups took over the baseball diamond, and they had understood Alarcón's warning to Villa. In the excitement of the moment my Spanish was less than perfect, but their eyes grew wide and I hoped they had got the idea.

"Action!" Brian called out.

Villa and his men were back at their starting point for the scene. At Brian's command, they whipped their horses into a gallop and charged straight toward the camera. Following the scenario, they split into two bunches and rode on either side of George and his camera. When they were safely past him, the band reunited and kept going. George swung the camera around to follow them as they bore down on the *rurales*, who reined their horses aside in an attempt to get out of the way.

"Now!" I shouted. I had thought to push Victoria to the ground and protect her by placing myself atop her, but she was too quick for me. She gathered the children like a mother hen defending her brood, forcing them to the ground and making them keep their heads down. All I could do was hit the dirt beside her and unlimber a few rusty prayers. Around us, the rest of the crew were hugging the earth like a long-lost mother, but curiosity has always held a ringside seat in my imperfect character, and I raised my head just enough to see what happened next.

Villa and the soldiers in his band opened fire from thirty feet away as they swept by the *rurales,* and unlike our picture company bandidos they were armed with live ammunition. Four of the *rurales* fell in the first volley. The rest raised their rifles or tried frantically to draw pistols, but they never had a chance. So intent were they on the moviemaking, they had not noticed when the revolutionists in the baseball pasture picked up their guns. Villa and his bunch kept going, and when they were a dozen yards past the *rurales* every Villista soldier within range opened fire.

It was over in thirty seconds. When the gunfire stopped, the *rurales* were all on the ground, along with four of their horses.

As I got to my feet a handful of people came running from the hacienda, Gerald and Rosa and the Delgados among them. When Rosa saw the dead *rurales* she ran about frantically, calling for her children, and she broke out in tears when she saw them safe in Victoria's care, together with the Delgado children and the urchins of the town. Moments later, a crowd arrived from town to see what the excitement was. They thought they had missed a lively piece of picture making and hoped it might be repeated for their benefit, but they too gathered their offspring when they saw what had happened.

Colonel Ortega was walking among the fallen *rurales,* prodding the bodies with his booted toe. When he found a man alive, he pulled his pistol and shot him in the head. A moment later he dispatched a second man who had been merely wounded by the Villista fusillade. Once he was satisfied that all the men were dead, he put the wounded horses out of their misery.

Villa himself was issuing orders calmly. These were swiftly carried out by his officers and men while we Americans stood about numbly, shocked by the sudden appearance of death in what had heretofore been a pleasant Mexican holiday. The unfortunate *rurales* were stripped of their guns and ammunition, and their horses, those that survived, were enlisted in the Villista cause. Villa's soldiers were gathered from every quarter, their camp was struck, and in less than a quarter of an hour they were forming up in a column.

The picture folk and townspeople alike kept clear of the Villistas now, hanging back in close-knit bunches, watching silently. Where the *rurales* had fallen, dogs were sniffing at the bodies.

"Even the *chingados rurales* will miss a patrol," Villa told Leroy. "We must go, my friend. Come with us now. I need you."

"We'll be done here in a few days," Leroy said. "I'll be along then."

Villa looked to where Victoria was comforting Magdalena Delgado. "You see the hold this woman has on you?" He took his place beside Ortega at the head of the column, but he turned to call back to Leroy.

"We will camp in the foothills, Roberto. Look for a mountain with two peaks like a gunsight. We will be in the valley below. Three days, no more. Then we return to Chihuahua."

Chapter 21

As SOON AS the Villistas were gone, Leroy suggested that we should have a look around, and we learned plenty. While Chief John and Redeye scouted south of town, he and I rode to the north. Half a mile beyond the edge of town we discovered what had caused the explosion when the Villistas arrived. As Bob Elderberg guessed at the time, they had dynamited the tracks. By the look of things they had used enough TNT to start a new branch line. The rails were twisted like pretzels on either side of a gaping hole. Beside the tracks the telegraph poles stood naked. The wires were stripped for three hundred yards.

Apart from this destruction the countryside was peaceful, so we returned to town along the railroad. As we neared the station we saw a crowd gathered there. It appeared that everyone in our picture company was trying to fit inside the little adobe building, while a few *delgadeños* looked on. We made our way through the crowd to the stationmaster's office, where Gerald Ball was shouting into the telephone. "Hello? Operator? *¡Oiga! ¡Dígame, por favor!* Operator? Damnation!"

Leroy took the earpiece out of Gerald's hand and hung it up. "The wires are cut," he informed the Englishman.

"Then we will patch them," Gerald said.

"Not unless you've got a lot of wire handy," I said. "They wrapped up a few hundred yards of it and hauled it off. Probably cut it half a dozen other places up and down the line too."

Gerald stiffened his upper lip like a general on parade and stepped into the waiting room to address the assembled company. "I want everyone ready to board the next train."

"There won't be any train for a while," Leroy told him. "Villa blew up the tracks."

Just then Chief John and Redeye Hawk bulled their way into the station as we had done, back from their reconnaissance to the south of town.

"The telegraph wire's cut, stripped, and gone," John announced tersely. "The spikes are pulled from half a dozen lengths of track. The first train that comes along will roll in the ditch, unless they're fixed."

Señor Garza assured me in rapid Mexican that as no train had approached Delgado in two days, this meant someone was surely aware of the revolutionist activity in the region. Soon the *federales* would come, he said, and crews to repair the tracks, but Gerald scoffed at these assurances when I translated them.

"I have no intention of waiting for nonexistent track crews while the revolution comes down on our heads. We will travel to the border in the wagons. We will load them this evening and leave first thing in the morning."

"The picture's almost done!" Victoria protested.

"We will have to finish it in California."

Victoria turned to Brian Hill. "Can we finish it without General Villa?"

Brian gave it some thought. "I think so. If we print some of his horseback shots dark, we can use them for night scenes. We could shoot the battle scene with Chief John and intercut Villa in close-up. It will take a few days."

"Can we finish on time?" Victoria asked.

"If we work hard, yes, I think so."

"You mean stay here?" Gerald exclaimed. "It's out of the question! There is no telling when that bandit might return."

George Bleumel looked worried. He lifted his porkpie hat and smoothed the nonexistent hair back over his bald dome. "We've got a lot of undeveloped film here, Boss," he said to Brian, "including everything we shot with Villa."

"And burning the town," Orville added. "If anything happens to that film—"

"Precisely," Gerald said. "The entire picture is at risk."

Victoria turned to me. "Charlie, how much trouble can we get into if we stay here?"

I looked to Leroy. "You reckon there's any chance old Pancho will come back?"

He shrugged. "He got gold from the townspeople, horses from the ranches down south, even a few guns from those *rurales*. He'll probably go back to Chihuahua, like he said. He stays here, he'll have half the federal army down on him, once the word gets out."

Victoria had heard enough. "Randall, will you take a chance?"

Randall's face lit up as if someone had just asked him to a party. "It seems too bad to leave before we're done. Besides, I've never had so much fun on a picture."

"Fun!" Gerald exclaimed. "Is that what you think this is?" He swelled up and faced Victoria. "We're in a country at war with itself! I won't have you and the rest of this company in that kind of danger!"

Victoria was calm in the face of this outburst. "Let's leave it up to them." To the others, she said, "I'm asking you to stay."

"So am I," said Brian.

"You're the boss," Bob Elderberg said. There were murmurs of assent from the crowd.

"It's still light," Victoria said to Brian.

Brian shook his head, once more the director, all business and thinking hard. "We'd barely get ready by sunset. I'll get together with George and Charlie this evening and we'll block it out shot by shot. We might get it done in two days."

"This isn't some kind of democracy!" Gerald was shouting now. "This is my film company and I order you all to load the wagons!"

He didn't have a prayer. The people by the door were moving outside and nobody paid Gerald the slightest mind. He saw he had lost them and the wind went out of his sails. He looked so forlorn, I had to offer a word of comfort.

"Nobody hates taking orders worse than a cowboy," I said. "Except maybe an Indian."

He took me by the arm and spoke urgently for my ears alone. "Help me change Victoria's mind and I'll waive the time limit. You can keep the Bunk House."

It was a measure of how desperate he was. But I knew there would be no changing the outfit's mind, and in my heart I didn't want to try. I had made a bargain, putting my faith in Victoria and Brian to get their picture made on time. I wouldn't try to crawfish out of it now.

"I guess I'm just an old cowboy myself, Gerald," I told him. "I'll take my chances with the rest of them."

As I stepped out the door I heard him say to the stationmaster, "Where is your President Carranza now that we need him?"

"¡Viva el Presidente Carranza!" Señor Garza replied cheerily.

While Leroy went with Chief John and Redeye to inspect the lesser damage to the rails south of town, I climbed back aboard Jake and rode out on the plateau a mile or two east of the hacienda just to be certain everything was quiet. On my way back I circled around to the north end of town again, where I found several men working in the little graveyard that overlooked the river. As the town's priest and a few of his flock buried the *rurales*, George Bleumel was filming them with his portable Aeroscope.

The evening was calm and the sunset just as beautiful as the one before it, but the seven *rurales* had been snuffed out while the earth turned. Their deaths made my own continued living seem like a miracle, although I had been in no real danger. It is often the same with me when I see someone put to rest. As I reined in beside George, I breathed deeply and shifted about in the saddle to savor the simple sensations of being alive.

"The light's going fast," George said by way of greeting. He looked up at the sky, then moved closer to where two young men were digging a grave. He aimed the camera and ran off a little film.

"Look at it, Charlie," he said. "It's beautiful, isn't it? You couldn't set up a shot like this if you tried. See how they move? Real slow and steady, taking their time. They've seen it all before."

It struck me that George had seen it all before too, in Flanders' fields. He had known the horrors of a far greater war, and still he could see that even in death there is beauty. I too was struck by the majesty of the scene, the graveyard ritual played out against that red desert sunset, as if the Maker Himself was giving those luckless *rurales* a special send-off.

The black-clad padre floated like a cloud among the stones, directing the men in the digging of graves and the lowering of bodies, pausing to read a prayer over each one before the diggers began filling in the grave. Throughout the digging and the prayers, the gravediggers kept silent. When the Mexicans bury a young child they are joyful, even to the point of playing music on the way back from the graveside, believing as they do that a child who has not yet attained his seventh year cannot have committed any sin and so will go straight to heaven. For the sinners they are silent, in respect of the soul's tortured way to purgatory, or possibly along the rugged path to the warmer regions below.

For my own part, fear of hellfire and damnation faded right along with my Catholic faith. I believe we live our lives as best we can and when our day is done we get planted. Ashes to ashes and dust to dust, as the Good Book says. I expect no afterlife, neither punishment nor reward. But if I should wake up to find Satan playing host to my departed spirit, I trust there will be a corner of his domain not much hotter than Texas in summertime, where I can pass the time with my cowboy friends in cussing and brag talk, and making don't-pass-me-up eyes at fallen women.

Consoled by this thought, I watched the sun go down, the gravediggers working all the while, and I saw that George was right. The priest and his helpers had seen it all before. They could have buried an army in their sleep. For ten years the Mexican people have seen the ebb and flow of war across their country, with no end in sight. I wondered how many more graves would be dug before peace would descend on all the battle-fields of this troubled land.

THAT EVENING THE cowboys were quieter than usual. They made small jokes about still feeling some pain from their overindulgence of the night before, and they went early to their bedrolls or sat around the fire talking softly. But it wasn't the aftereffects of the *pulque* that toned down their high spirits. Something had changed that day. Our playacting had been interrupted by the apocalyptic Horseman of War, and while we remained in Mexico we could never be so carefree again.

George and Brian and I ate supper together to begin planning the filming we would do on the morrow, but George couldn't get his mind off the scene at the graveyard.

"It's beautiful footage, Boss," he told Brian. "I wish we could find a way to use it."

Brian rubbed his forehead with the tips of his fingers. "Maybe the showdown between Tom's cowboys and Villa's men takes place near a town," he offered.

"They might run for a town because they're outnumbered," I said, without really knowing where I was headed. "Or maybe they just stumble on it and Villa traps them there."

Brian sat up straight. "And the townspeople help them! The cowboys don't beat Villa because they're better shots or braver men! They beat him because they're smarter!"

George caught Brian's enthusiasm. "We can use the real town and shoot from new angles! I can make it look completely different from the opening scenes. No one will know it's the same town."

While we were figuring out how to change the story, Victoria was doing some figuring of her own. Maybe some people have got following a trail in their blood, like a good breed of hound dog. If so, I must have passed on my bloodhound abilities to Victoria, because not even the massacre of the *rurales* and Pancho's leaving threw her off Leroy's trail.

She prowled the hacienda and found him upstairs, recovering the gold coins he had stuffed into my horsehair mattress when Villa showed up. He was on his knees when she came in, reaching into the slit he had cut in the side of the mattress to recover the last coins.

He stood up and dropped the gold on the bed. "It's all there," he said.

"There's not enough to repay these people for what your friend General Villa stole from them."

"They'll have something," he said. "That's better than nothing."

Victoria hadn't followed him this far just to scold him about Pancho stealing the townspeople's gold. She closed the door behind her and stood in front of it.

"In New Mexico when I was a little girl, if a man vanished without a trace, people said he went south of the border," she said. "It meant he went to Mexico to disappear. Is that why you came here?"

"Something like that."

"General Villa called you Roberto. Is that your name? Robert?"

"One of them."

"Why can't you trust me?" He didn't answer. "I know you have feelings for me."

"A man ought to be able to offer a woman something before he gets on courting terms with her," he said.

"And you've got nothing to offer?"

"Not much of a future."

"Not much of a past either. There's a hole in it twenty years long and before that it could belong to anybody. But Charlie knows who you are."

"Did he tell you that?"

"Oh, Charlie's keeping your secrets. That's just the trouble. He's keeping them too well. The only reason he would do that is because you're an outlaw."

For days she had been biding her time, picking up clues, but it was Chief John's remark about Leroy's shooting that had led her to the truth. *A man learns to shoot like that, it's because he needs to shoot like that.*

Leroy didn't quite cover his surprise, and Victoria knew that she had guessed right, but that didn't make her feel any better. She wanted to see him smile and hear him laugh the way he had laughed when the two of them fell off the bicycle into the creek. She wanted him to tell her that what lay in the past didn't matter and what lay in the future could be anything she dreamed. But what you want and what you get in this life are often two different things.

"I should have guessed the truth sooner," she said. "If you were a Pinkerton or a lawman, or anybody else, Charlie would have told me who you were, but he kept quiet and that gave him away."

She regarded him steadily, holding him with her eyes. "Do you know what he used to say? 'Half the men I chased just got off on the wrong foot. You give them a chance at a new start and most of them would turn out like you and me.' Don't you see? He'll give you a chance. You could come back and live in California. I would help you, if you let me. He would too."

"I wouldn't be too sure about Charlie."

"I can handle him. He won't turn you in."

"It's got nothing to do with you and Charlie. It's just the way things are."

It was Victoria's turn to keep silent now, and Leroy's to wish she would smile and tell him nothing in the past mattered.

"For ten years now I've lived under a name that's not my own." He said it as if living under a false name might be a hanging offense. He waited, hoping that might be enough, but she said nothing, so he told her the rest.

"I left a wife back in the States, and an adopted son."

Victoria was struck speechless. This piece of news was the one thing she had never imagined. Ever since Villa showed up she had been harboring a righteous indignation that was directed at Leroy, for holding out on her, for not trusting her enough to tell her everything there was to know about himself. If only he would come clean, she thought, she would show him that her feelings for him could surmount any obstacle and the two of them could find a way to ride off into the sunset, just like in the movies. So she had believed until this moment. But he had raised the one obstacle she could not overcome with a wave of her magic wand. His simple words, so painfully spoken, seemed to close the door on her dreams.

All she could think of was getting away from Leroy, away from the hacienda, away from everything. If she could just get far enough fast enough, she thought she might get away from those words, so it would be as if she never heard them.

Without another word she slipped out of the room, leaving Leroy silently cursing the necessity that had compelled him to tell her that particular piece of the truth. She changed into her riding clothes and got out of the house without anyone seeing her, and no one noticed when she saddled up Ranger and took off into the night.

Redeye said she was riding at a fair clip when she nearly ran him down out in the chaparral. Chief John had posted Redeye and the other young Indians in a circle around the town just to keep an eye on things. He sent them out on foot and told them to keep out of sight. Redeye stood up when he heard Victoria coming, and Ranger spooked a little to see a man rise out of the brush, but he is a steady kind of horse and Victoria calmed him down when she recognized Redeye.

"Redeye! You frightened me." She wiped the tears from her cheeks with the back of her hand.

"Chief John figured we ought to keep a watch," Redeye said. "I'm not supposed to let you go out past the picket line."

"I won't go far. It's such a beautiful night for a ride."

Something in her voice told Redeye she wasn't just taking the night air, but he couldn't think of a good reason to stop her or a way to do it if she wanted to keep going. After all, Victoria was the one who paid his wages, no matter what Chief John said.

"It's been real quiet. I guess it'll be all right. You come back this way, if you would, so I'll know."

She said she would do as he asked, and that was the last he saw of her.

Chief John and Redeye woke me a little after midnight, John carrying a lantern. My old detective's caution had been kindled by the day's events and I had gone to bed with my Peacemaker under the blankets. When I woke up, it came to bear on Chief John's midsection of its own accord.

"Good, you may need that." John turned to Redeye. "Tell him what you told me. Tell it the way a scout tells important news."

Redeye related his story, all serious and a little ashamed of himself, ending up with "It's my fault if anything happened to her."

John would have none of that. "We'll talk about responsibility later. Just tell him what you know."

"I followed her tracks," Redeye said. "They went off toward the hills. None of the other scouts heard or seen nothing. I looked in the corrals in case she come back some other way. Ranger ain't there and no one's seen Miss Hartford."

By this time I was fully dressed and pulling on my boots. I could hear footsteps and voices throughout the hacienda, and other voices from outside my window. It's a good thing John and Redeye woke me when they did, or I might not have been able to take charge before things got out of hand.

When I got to where the men were gathering among the wagons, I found Gerald Ball in his silk pajamas, giving orders like Tecumseh Sherman getting ready to take Atlanta.

"I want every man armed and mounted in five minutes. One of you saddle a horse for me while I get dressed."

Someone had built up the fire. The men were warming themselves around it as they pulled on boots and overcoats.

"Hold on there," I said, putting myself between Gerald and the others. "We don't need an army out there."

"If Villa has her, we'll need every man who can ride," Gerald said. "Chief John, can you follow a trail at night?"

"I'd like to hear what Charlie's got to say."

Good old John. That got everyone looking at me, and I set about pouring oil on the troubled waters. "If Villa's got her, all of us together couldn't take him in a fight," I said. "But a handful of men who know what they're doing might get Victoria back, and that's what counts. Besides, we don't know that anybody's got her. For all we know, Victoria's just gone and got herself lost."

That story was poorer than skimmed milk, but I'd stick by it if it would keep some of the eager beavers home. Victoria could find the Hartfords'

New Mexico ranch in the middle of a blizzard, and she would have no trouble retracing her steps to Delgado with the moon half as bright as day. Either she didn't want to come back, or something was preventing her.

"I'll take Chief John and Redeye and you, Nate. Maybe one or two more," I added, trying not to reveal my own uncertainties.

"I do all right on night patrol," said Buddy Johnston. He was mounted up and dressed to ride, with his Springfield rifle slung over his shoulder. The firelight sparked in his eyes, but the rest of his face blended with the shadow cast by the brim of his hat.

"He's got a point there," Leroy said. He was standing at the edge of the crowd holding Sonny's reins. It made me feel better to know that he was on my side with his sense of humor intact.

"You'll do the most good right here, Gerald," I told the Englishman. "You see that the rest of them stay put and keep out of trouble."

But he still tried to make out that I was a troublesome schoolboy. "You're overstepping yourself, Charles. Now listen to me, all of you. I want to find every man mounted and ready in five minutes."

With that, he turned to go, and found Leroy standing in his way. Leroy smiled pleasantly, said "Sorry, Sir Gerald," and dropped Mr. Silk Pajamas in his tracks with a right to the jaw, as neat and clean as Victoria had dropped Rodney Quillen on the day Leroy rode into our lives.

"You boys listen to Charlie," Leroy said. "He's running the show."

"I appreciate how you all feel," I told the gathering. "But you go rushing out there in a mob, you'll be like city boys on a duck hunt, all noise and no help."

Brian Hill stepped forward. "I'm going with you."

"You might get us all killed, and Victoria too." I tried to put it as gently as I could, but he was crestfallen.

At Leroy's feet, Gerald moaned softly and began to stir.

"You sit on him until we get back," I told Brian.

That perked him up. "Bob, Charlie, I'll need a hand with him. We'll take him into the hacienda."

Bob Elderberg and Charlie Noble moved to do as he asked, and Brian was in charge of his crew once more.

I gave the others chores to do as well, fetching things for those of us who were going. I wanted every man armed, clothed against the chill desert night, and carrying a little food in his pockets. All the while part of me wanted to jump on Jake and take off at a gallop, but I knew from long experience that a successful pursuit begins with good preparation. With my daughter's life maybe at stake, it was a hard rule to follow.

The whole hacienda was awake by now, the Delgados and vaqueros as well as the Americans. The vaqueros wanted to go along with us, but I put a stop to that by asking Gene Ortiz to guide us and leaving it up to him to order his *compadres* to stay at home.

"You be careful," Karen said to Nate as he mounted Buster, his dun mustang. By the way Nate smiled, he was glad not to set out with her still mad at him.

"Don't worry about us," Willie Two Horse said to Chief John. "I'll keep an eye on things here."

Jack Whistler stood next to Willie. They waved as we started out, the old Indian and the cavalryman side by side, ready to guard the fort until we returned.

Chapter 22

REDEYE LED US straight to the place where he had quit following Victoria's tracks and turned back to fetch some help. On the open desert in the moonlight even a greenhorn could follow Ranger's hoofprints, but when we reached the grassland, where the sandy patches were fewer, Chief John got off his horse and walked along with Redeye right behind him. Now and then John would say something to the younger man, pointing out the trail of bent grass left by Ranger's passing, teaching Redeye even as we moved along. It wasn't John's teaching I noticed so much as Redeye's eagerness to learn. Since Villa showed up there had been a change in Redeye Hawk. He was quieter, listening more instead of talking. On New Year's Eve he had been clear-eyed when he went to his bed, for all his part in the boisterous celebration, and when Villa left, Redeye had joined Chief John without anyone asking him to when we rode off to scout around the town.

Before we had been an hour on Victoria's trail, we fell into an order of march we were all comfortable with, as men will do when they ride together with a common purpose. Leroy and I rode twenty yards or so behind Gene Ortiz and the two Indians, while Buddy and Nate dropped back to watch our rear, just keeping us in sight. Strung out like that, it was less likely we could be taken by surprise.

Some may wonder why we felt such precautions were needed. I can only say I have not lived to my present age by being careless. We had no reason to suppose that any calamity had befallen Victoria, apart from her unexplained absence, but I have seen what a man doesn't know rise up and strike him dead before he suspects he's in trouble. The fact that a lack of care had led seven *rurales* to an untimely end was fresh in our minds and no doubt contributed to our watchfulness.

Before long I noticed how naturally I had fallen in beside Leroy. There is something in the way one man rides beside another that tells whether they are partners or strangers, or something in between. Leroy and I rode close, our horses in step. While we both kept an eye peeled for anything that might happen around us, we trusted the other to guard his near side. In short, we rode as if we had ridden together for years, and I felt at home in his company. The feeling of being on a fresh trail settled back over me like a familiar and comfortable garment and some of my concern for Victoria left me. We were a small group, but up to whatever might lie in store.

Occasionally we passed bunches of cattle grazing. Sometimes Ranger's tracks were lost among theirs, but Victoria was making no effort to hide her trail and we always found it again after a short search.

"*Mira*, Charlie. *Ven aquí*," Gene Ortiz called to me during one such instance. We were spread out and moving through a few dozen steers at a slow walk so we would not alarm them and reveal our presence to anyone who might be watching the grassland from a distance. Gene was in a shallow basin where water would gather once the rains came. The ground was cracked and dry. When I reached Gene's side he pointed to where Ranger's tracks joined a swath of hoofprints that had pounded the dry mud of the basin's bottom into dust.

"Could be Villa's trail," I said.

"It's Villa all right," Chief John said as he knelt in the dust. "I had a look at their tracks back at the ranch. Some of them horses are barefoot. The rest got a kind of military shoe. Probably stole from the army."

"*Eso es*," Gene agreed. "*Señorita Victoria sigue a Villa.*" Señorita Victoria is following Villa.

Leroy took one look at the new tracks and started off at once parallel to their course, forcing the rest of us into a canter to overtake him.

A blind man could have followed the trail of such a mob, moon or no moon, and we made better time after that. John and Redeye kept watch at the sides of the trail in case Victoria's tracks branched off, but somehow I knew Gene was right. Victoria was following Villa. I didn't know why, and I didn't know whether to worry more or less, so I tried to persuade myself that until we found where the tracks led us, there was no good worrying at all.

A while after we left the dry catch basin, Buddy Johnston rode up beside me and Leroy.

"You all go on," he said. "I'm gonna drop back a bit."

"You hear something?" I asked.

"More like I feel something. I'll catch up later on."

I didn't think twice about letting him go off on his own. From the moment he volunteered to come along with us, Buddy was a new man, self-possessed and confident in everything he did. He was a soldier now, not an errand boy.

He had scarcely left us when Leroy turned to me and broke his long silence.

"I better tell you why Victoria took off," he said. And he related what had passed between himself and Victoria that evening, including the part about his wife and child.

Learning that my daughter had been courted by a married man, I felt a surge of hot anger in my breast, but I knew that Victoria had done her share of the courting.

To his credit, he made no excuses for not telling Victoria sooner about his family. No doubt knowing I was Victoria's father moved him to unburden himself now, but he told me more, and as he talked my anger cooled.

It surprised me to learn he had studied engineering and even owned a small machine shop. I couldn't picture the man beside me bending over a drafting table. He told me the name he had used and where he made his home, and he told me what he had told Pancho, about his wife wanting the man she had married, the man who was not Butch Cassidy. Once she knew who he was, she behaved as if he had married her under false pretenses, he told me, although he had not meant it that way at the time, and she was not sorry to see him go, leaving her to run the business.

It took him less time to say his piece than it has taken me to write it down. He said what he had to say, using only the necessary number of words and no more, because he thought I had a right to know, but it was not a confession. As a jack Catholic I know a confession when I hear one. I was never comfortable on the few occasions I confessed my sins to a priest. I have always felt that a man is responsible for his actions, good and bad. Counting a string of beads or saying a few prayers won't get him off the hook for the bad ones. If the Lord has any quarrel with something I've done, I'll be pleased to take the matter up with Him directly when the time comes, and I judged by his forthright manner that Leroy shared my sense of a man's accountability for his deeds.

When he fell silent we rode for a time without speaking, paying more attention to our surroundings. We were passing through gently rolling country dotted with live oaks, which resembled southern California more than a little, but soon we left the grassland behind and entered the more rugged terrain of the foothills. Where the tracks lay in the shadows, Chief John dismounted to follow them on foot.

The trail led to a narrow wash with straight sides that Gene Ortiz knew well. It offered a path through the foothills to the valleys higher in the mountains, and Delgado cattle used it to find summer pasture, Gene told us. There was barely a trickle of water in the wash, but when the rains came it would be impassable, and cattle often drowned in flash floods where we now rode so easily.

"I wouldn't want you to think badly of Victoria's mother," I said to Leroy once we were strung out again along the dry bottom. As he had done, I spoke as if picking up an ongoing conversation.

"It's not my business, Charlie," he replied.

"Even so, you know part of it. You should hear the rest." I told him of my wife Mamie's death and how I came to know the Hartfords, and how I had belatedly resolved to be a good father to Victoria.

"I may be too protective of her," I said. "I don't imagine I'd be the first father guilty of that. The fact is, I warned her to stay away from you. I should have known that would only make her chase you harder." After a moment I added, "I suppose I shouldn't worry about her. She's old enough to take care of herself."

I said this by way of reassuring myself, silently adding a fervent hope that wherever she was, she was doing a good job of taking care of herself tonight.

"I'm not going to send her away again, Charlie," Leroy said. "Not if she'll still have me. She knows who I am."

"You told her?"

"She doesn't know my name. Not yet. But she knows who I am."

By the way he spoke I could tell that he was sure of himself, and equally sure of Victoria, and at least until the night was over and Victoria safe and sound, I couldn't find it in me to oppose him.

Leroy moved Sonny closer to me and put a hand on my arm. For a moment I thought he was comforting a father's fears, but I soon learned different.

"Hold up and keep still," he said. We were beneath a tall cutbank, deep in the shadows. Leroy made a low whistle like a night bird's call. Up ahead, Chief John and Redeye stopped where they were and turned into rocks.

Leroy had been glancing back now and then, keeping an eye on young Nate. I thought he was only waiting for Nate to catch up, but when the cowboy drew even with us, Leroy motioned him to join us in the shadows and keep quiet.

It wasn't long before we heard a hoof strike a rock.

"You always did know when somebody was dogging your tracks," I said under my breath, just as three riders came into sight down the wash.

At first the riders didn't seem to see us, but as they drew abreast of us we heard a soft chuckle from the largest figure.

"You gonna speak up, or you gonna let us ride on by?" It was Buddy Johnston.

"How'd you see us?" Nate wanted to know.

Buddy laughed again, but not too loud. "You boys as bad as the Germans. White folks just cain't hide at night."

We couldn't recognize the other two horsemen beneath the hats and overgarments they wore against the nighttime chill, but we knew their horses. One was a McQuain & Vickery mount whose rider was cloaked in a long canvas duster such as many with the show wore. The other figure was covered to the knees by a Mexican serape, which is a blanket with a slit in the middle. Gene Ortiz wore a serape too, and for a moment I thought the newcomer was another vaquero, but the paint mustang was Karen Valdez's horse Apache.

"Dammit, I told you to stay put," Nate said when he recognized the paint.

"Some thanks we get," said Karen.

"It was my idea," said Brian Hill, for it was he who wore the duster. "I figured we'd help out if you got into trouble."

"And never once thought about the trouble you might get into," I said. "Who's looking after Gerald?"

"As soon as you left, he tried to talk all the boys into following you," Brian said. "We had to tie him up. Bob and Charlie and Jack are watching him."

Karen grinned. "Gerald ordered Jack to let him go or he'd fire the whole show. Jack said, 'You can hire me or fire me, Gerald, but you can't tell me what to do.'"

"That was sort of a new concept to Gerald," Brian added.

"Well now you've had your fun, you can go right on back," Nate said.

"You send us back, we'll just turn around and follow you again," Karen told him defiantly.

"We better keep them with us where they can't get into trouble," Leroy said.

"All right," I said, "but you stick close and do what I tell you."

Our little party increased by two, we resumed the trail, following it higher into the mountains where the northern slopes were wooded with small pine trees. The wash broadened as we emerged into a narrow valley. The tracks of Villa's band made a dark path we could follow at a fast lope, but soon the wash became a ravine and the trail turned off to ascend a steep ridge where the going was slower.

"When old Pancho says he's going to camp in the mountains, he means it," Nate said, but I hushed him as Chief John motioned urgently for silence. He had reached the crest of the ridge, and as we joined him we saw a mountain dead ahead of us, its peak notched like a gunsight. In the small valley below the mountain, the lights of a dozen fires glowed beside a running stream whose waters flashed in the moonlight.

Chapter 23

WHILE WE WERE following hoofprints through the night, Victoria was having herself a grand old time. When she left Redeye behind and rode off across the plateau, she had no destination in mind. She thought only to ride until she could bear the burden of her sorrow. That might have been a considerable journey, but as she rode, her sadness turned gradually to anger and then to understanding. She knew Leroy as well as I did, although she knew less of his past and more about what kind of man he was in the present. She guessed that by warning her off, he was trying to do the honorable thing by her. That made her even madder for a time. She cursed Leroy and me for not telling her all we knew, cursed herself for falling for him in the first place, and then cursed herself again for giving up on him too easily. How much more was there that she didn't know about him, she wondered. And then she remembered that in the foothills to the east of her there was a man who seemed to know a good deal about Señor Leroy Roberts.

As soon as the idea came to her, she turned Ranger's head toward the hills and never looked back. For a girl raised to follow the tracks of straying cattle in any kind of weather, day or night, picking up Villa's trail and following it to his camp was a simple matter.

She rode bravely up the trail and announced herself in perfect Spanish to the sentry, and Pancho welcomed her with open arms. He gave her a big Mexican embrace and kissed her on both cheeks, saying she did him a great honor by visiting his camp.

Victoria, as should be plain by now, is no fool. Having failed once before to get information about Leroy from Villa, she took a different approach on this occasion. When she found herself received like visiting royalty, she straightaway made the most of it, batting her eyes and smiling and accepting his invitation to dine with him. Never mind that it was after eleven o'clock in the evening. A Mexican will sit down to supper at midnight and eat until dawn if he feels like it.

The camp was somewhat more elaborate than the rough bivouac the insurgents had made by the Delgado hacienda. Most of the soldiers had fashioned shelters to protect themselves against the cold mountain nights. Villa himself had a command tent large enough to stand upright in, outfitted with a proper table and two chairs.

Villa ordered food and wine, and Victoria found that the ride had made her hungry. As she ate she gave no hint that there was anything on her mind except a pleasant moonlight ride and supping with Mexico's most renowned revolutionist since Benito Juarez. She accepted Villa's hospitality as if it were no more than her due, chatting about everything under the sun except Mr. Leroy Roberts. At a pause in the conversation, her eyes fell on the tent's single decoration, a small framed oil painting hung from one of the tent poles. The subject was a Latin sort in full-dress military uniform.

"Who is that man?" she asked, offering her glass for more wine. She found that the rough red wine went well with the spicy food.

Villa refilled her glass with a flourish. "General Antonio Lopez de Santa Ana, a founder of the republic and a great leader of the Mexican people," he said with pride.

Although she was born in New Mexico, Victoria has taken a Texan's pride in the history of our great state since learning that I am her father. Hearing the name of the man in the portrait sent hot blood coursing through her veins.

"Santa Ana? The butcher of the Alamo?"

"That is all you Americans know!" Villa protested.

"My father is a Texan!" she shot back at him. "We know about Santa Ana!"

"He was much more than a soldier! Five times president of *Méjico*. The Napoleon of the West, we called him." Villa looked hopefully at Victoria as he spoke. So far she was not pacified, but at least she was letting him make his point.

"I will tell you a story about him. Do you know why it took him twelve days to conquer the Alamo?"

"Because the Texans fought bravely!"

"Yes, they were brave, but Santa Ana had thousands of men! He could have won the battle any time, but he delayed because he was in love. He was courting a señorita in the town and she would not yield to his desires. Finally he married her, although he already had a wife. Of course, the señorita did not know that. Santa Ana had one of his captains pose as a priest. It is amusing, no?"

"I don't find deception amusing."

"It makes you angry?"

"Yes, it does."

"I agree. Deception is unworthy of such a man. I admire many things about Santa Ana, but this I despise. Naturally, each of my own wives knows about the others."

Victoria's eyebrows shot up. "You have more than one wife?"

Villa thought hard, counted on his fingers, and abandoned the effort with a shrug. "Fifteen. Sixteen. They are all wonderful women."

"But you're Catholic!"

"Believe me, señorita, God understands more about love than my church does."

"You're as bad as he is!" she said, throwing a dark look at Santa Ana's likeness.

"Without me the revolution will die!" Villa protested. "I must be with my army! First we are in Chihuahua, then we are here. First in the south, then the north. When I am near one of my wives, I go to see her. And each tells me that one week with me is worth a year with any other man!" He pointed his fork at her, forgetting his manners for the moment. "Listen to me. It is a very lucky thing for a man and a woman to find that their lives walk hand in hand, even for a time."

Victoria gave him a hard look. "You only want one thing from a woman."

"I want everything! I want her love. I want her laughter. I want her to hold me when I have lost a friend in battle. And she wants things from me. She wants a home, children, I give them to her. But I have my revolution! For me, time with a woman is hard to find, so we must take what time we have." Realizing he was waving his fork about like a sword, he calmed himself and resumed eating. "Because a man and a woman must be apart much of the time, does this mean they should not love each other when they can?"

Victoria had no reply to this. Villa accepted her silence as consent for his unconventional marital arrangements, and he became the genial host once more. He refilled her glass and turned the talk back to the Alamo, and old Sam Houston's clever retreat following Santa Ana's victory there. Houston fell back, waiting for Santa Ana to make a mistake. When he made it, Houston pounced, taking the Mexicans by surprise at San Jacinto during their afternoon siesta.

"I am like your General Houston," Villa told Victoria. "I am waiting for my enemies to make a mistake. When they do, I will be ready, and then I will follow Santa Ana as president of *Méjico*."

He went on like that, building himself up, hoping Victoria would remember what he had said earlier, about men and women and the ways of love.

While Victoria was wining and dining in comfort, the only other Americans in the vicinity were playing a nine-handed game of freeze-out up on the ridge overlooking Villa's camp. The desert may be hot in the daytime, but this was the month of January, and the gibbous moon seemed to shine its cold rays upon us as if determined to make up for all the warmth the sun had blessed us with during the day.

"They got men on the trail up and down from the camp," Chief John informed us when he and Redeye returned from a silent scout of Villa's stronghold. John was seized by a spasm of coughing and he held his mouth with his hands to stifle the sound. We had moved down the ridge as far as we dared, taking shelter behind a clump of pines that overlooked the camp. Seeing the glow of the fires more clearly made us all the colder.

"There's a couple more guards off to the sides there, in the rocks," Redeye said. He grinned. "We saw 'em lighting cigarettes. Don't never set out a guard who smokes."

Leroy didn't take much notice of the scouts' report. He remained where he had been the whole time they were gone, hunkered down holding Sonny's reins, watching the camp. I hadn't seen him like that before, all serious and alert like a wolf on the hunt.

"It won't be easy getting in there," I said.

"Maybe not for the rest of you," Leroy said. He got suddenly to his feet. "Pancho's expecting me."

I had been searching for some sly way to get into the camp when the easy way was as plain as the nose on my face. Pancho's friend "Roberto" might be welcome. The reception he would receive depended on what had brought Victoria to the insurgent camp, and there was only one way to find out what that was.

Of course we couldn't know that Victoria was about to take matters into her own hands.

Villa ate lightly and drank not at all. As Victoria ate heartily he entertained her with stories of his life, but he grew more serious as he touched on the subject of her "movie picture."

"It is a grand story, señorita," he said, "but it is not true."

"Not true?"

"I would never do anything so foolish as to attack the United States."

"What about Columbus, three years ago?"

"It was the Carranzistas who made the attack, not I! When they were captured, they said they were Villistas! They did it to throw the blame on me, and it worked. Your President Wilson turned against me and recognized Carranza as president of *Méjico*."

He shook his head ruefully. "Many Americans fought beside me in the early days of the revolution. 'Soldiers of fortune' your newspapers called them, as if they did not care which side they fought on, only that they must be paid. Some were like that, but many believed in the revolution. Since the attack on Columbus, there are few Americans to help me."

He sighed, but then he brightened. "Roberto was one of those who believed. He and his friend Harry, they stayed with me when I could not pay them."

This was what Victoria had been waiting for. She had been looking for a way to steer the talk toward Leroy, and now Villa had done it for her.

"Was he with you long?" she asked, as if she were only making polite conversation.

"Six months. Maybe seven. He was married then, but he left his wife in New *Méjico* and came to fight with me."

Even at this, Victoria gave no sign of interest.

"It was a marriage of convenience, not of the heart," Villa went on, reminiscing. He seemed to speak more to himself than to Victoria, but he knew what she wanted to hear.

"His name was Robert Parker. We called him Capitán Roberto. When he left me, his friend Harry went with him. Later, Harry returned and fought by my side for two years. His woman became a *soldadera*. Roberto always said he would come back. And now he has."

Victoria was perplexed. "Robert Parker?"

She had looked at the posters in my study dozens of times over the years, first in Santa Fe and later in Hollywood, but there in Villa's tent she never thought for a moment to match the name Villa told her with the wanted flier for Butch Cassidy.

"He has another name," Villa admitted.

Victoria's face grew dark as the hurt returned. "He lied to me. He lied about his name and he didn't tell me he was married. I won't be lied to!"

"He is a man who would rather live with the truth, but the truth is dangerous to him," Villa said. "His other name is dangerous to him, even now, after so many years."

"Tell me what it is."

Villa smiled. "For the price of a song. If you will sing to me, I will tell you the other name." He called to the guard at the entrance of the tent and ordered him to bring a guitar.

"Sing for me, and I will tell you everything," Villa said. "I owe him nothing. He has made you angry, so he is no longer my friend."

"Do you always abandon your friends so easily?"

"I never abandon a friend!" Villa was outraged at the thought. "I only said that to please you. But I will tell you his name, for the price of a song. You should know the name of the man you love."

Now it was Victoria's turn to be outraged. "Love him! I would sooner love you!"

Villa smiled broadly. "Love me then, and forget the song." Seeing Victoria stiffen, he shrugged. "I only wished you to sing *Las Mañanitas,* for my birthday."

The guard appeared in the entrance. Villa motioned him to give the guitar to Victoria, then waved him out.

"Is today your birthday?" Victoria asked. Birthdays, along with weddings, funerals and babies, make her sentimental and easily swayed.

"My birthday is in June, but I will carry the song in my heart."

"I don't think I trust you. Tell me his name first. Then I'll sing for you." Instinctively, her hands were tuning the strings.

And so he told her.

Victoria's eyes opened wide. Her hands grew still. The confusion Pancho's revelation aroused in her made it seem that until that moment all her feelings had marched in perfect harmony. Half a dozen emotions competed for her attention, milling about in her breast like longhorns spooked by lightning.

But perhaps because she is a detective's daughter, she brought her feelings under control sooner than another woman might have done. She already knew that Leroy had come to Mexico to stay, because he told her so. Now, hearing his real name, she guessed at once that he had come here because he wanted to live as Butch Cassidy again. He had kept his identity from her, and finally tried to drive her off by telling her the truth about his family back in the States, all to protect her.

If that were so, what better proof could there be that his feelings for her were genuine, and just as strong as hers for him?

Thus a woman's mind works, arriving at a conclusion opposite from the one intended, but often more true.

Victoria finished tuning the guitar and began to sing the plaintive Mexican birthday song, eager now to end her visit and return to Delgado, never imagining that the object of her affections was even then riding up the trail to the camp.

"*¡Alto!*" commanded the officer of the guard, stepping into the trail with his pistol at the ready. "*¿Quién vive?*" This challenge means "Who lives?" which is the Mexican equivalent of "Who goes there?"

"*Gente buena,*" Leroy replied, proclaiming himself "good people," and therefore a friend. He identified himself as Captain Roberto, and added that General Villa was expecting him.

"Come closer," said the guard, still in Spanish. "Yes, I know you. Welcome, Captain. I am Lieutenant Alarcón. Luís!"

At this, a soldier stepped into sight on the opposite side of the trail.

"Tell Colonel Ortega that Captain Roberto wishes to see General Villa." Off went Luís. Leroy made as if to follow him, but Alarcón put out a hand, indicating that Leroy should remain where he was.

Lieutenant Alarcón was being a prudent fellow. He knew that Victoria was with General Villa. Well aware of the general's taste for pretty women, he may have imagined that interruptions would not be welcome. And so he invited Leroy to stay with him, where they would recall the glories of bygone campaigns until Luís returned to conduct Leroy into camp.

In Villa's tent, Victoria's song came to an end. Villa's head was resting against the back of his chair and his eyes were closed.

"Who can say where I will be in June," he said in a voice that longed to be far from the revolution and all its concerns. "I would like to be with a woman I love on my birthday." He opened his eyes and looked at her. "A woman like you."

Victoria was at once on her guard, but Pancho appeared not to notice. "Yes," he said, "I could love you, if you would permit it."

Victoria rose and stepped back from the table. "If you lay a hand on me—"

"I would never dishonor a guest," Villa protested, getting to his feet. "This is not an insolent proposal, señorita! Naturally, I would marry you."

"Marry me!"

"I would ask very little. Only that you come to see me once or twice a year, between the movie pictures. The rest of the time will be your own. You could have another husband, an American, if you wish."

"You can't be serious!"

"I have a priest in my army to give absolution to the dying, to pray for the dead. It will make him joyful to perform a marriage."

Victoria couldn't find the words to reply to such an affront, but Villa feigned to see only a bashful girl stunned by his offer.

"Of course you are free to choose," he said. "When you choose to marry me, you may return to your friends."

Victoria felt the beginnings of fear. She had come to learn more about Leroy, never for a moment considering what Villa might want from her.

"Do you mean I am your prisoner?"

"Is it so much to ask, a few weeks of companionship now and then for a man who bears such a burden? I have a revolution to make!"

"And I have a picture to make!"

"I adore your movie pictures! Always you play a brave woman. But I must be brave for all of *Méjico*! Since Carranza murdered Emiliano Zapata, I am the revolution!" Villa spread his arms wide, as if to show that he held the fate of *Méjico* in his arms, but then he calmed himself.

"Who was to know we would fall in love in a few short hours? Of course it was you yourself who gave me the idea."

"*I* gave you the idea?!" Victoria was reduced to repeating Villa's new affronts as he spoke each one.

"In your movie picture. Here we have no camera, but the story is the same. We are alone together and you surrender to me, as you wished to surrender in the movie picture."

His face lit up as if he was struck with the most wonderful idea since Eve bit the apple.

"Imagine it! We will show your movie pictures all over *Méjico*! When the people learn I am married to Rosa Cimarrona, they will flock to me and the revolution will be victorious! Say you will marry me! I will have my priest perform the ceremony tonight, and tomorrow my men and I will escort you to Delgado. We will guard you while you finish your movie picture, and then we will return to Chihuahua for our honeymoon!"

Victoria was by now so angry that she did not see the spark of mischief in Pancho's eyes, while he did not know her well enough to recognize that her anger was about to break its bonds. She had come to Villa's camp of her own free will, and now the revolutionist threatened to keep her prisoner until she married him! The very notion left her speechless with rage.

Villa took her silence for acceptance. He stepped to the entrance and spoke once more with the guard, ordering him to fetch the priest. While Villa's back was turned, Victoria took the wine bottle from the table. When the guard departed, she broke it over Villa's head and knocked him senseless. He went down like a poleaxed steer.

Chapter 24

VICTORIA WAS OUT of the tent and making for the horses before Villa hit the ground. It was past the middle of the long winter night and the camp was quiet, save for a sentry reporting to Colonel Ortega. This of course was Luís. Moments later he and Ortega walked together toward Villa's tent to tell him Captain Roberto was waiting to see him. Victoria had made her escape in the nick of time.

Ranger was where she had left him, tethered to a tree near the stream, beside the rope corral that contained the Villistas' horses. She tightened the cinch, mounted, and had the presence of mind to hold Ranger to a walk as he moved through the sleeping camp. She dared a trot as she left the tents behind. Seeing two men beside the trail, one on horseback, she thought at first that both were sentries. She forced herself to smile, preparing a few words to say in farewell, as if her visit with General Villa had gone pleasantly for both, but before she could speak, the alarm was raised behind her. Ortega and Luís had found Villa.

"¡Agarra la americana!" cried a voice, commanding anyone within hearing to seize the American woman. Victoria dug in her heels and crouched low in the saddle to present a smaller target.

Lieutenant Alarcón heard the alarm and drew his pistol as Victoria rode down upon him. He shouted to her to stop, but Leroy shifted Sonny sideways into Alarcón, knocking the officer to the ground. Putting spurs to Sonny, Leroy raced after Victoria as she headed down the trail at a dead run.

I had accompanied Leroy to the trail below the camp so I could come to his aid in a hurry if things went wrong. When I heard the shouting I made ready to charge in like Teddy Roosevelt at San Juan Hill, but just as Jake hit his stride I saw Leroy and Victoria heading my way. Being a good cow horse, Jake can turn on a dime, which he did now, just as happy to charge in the opposite direction.

"That was quick," I said as they overtook me.

"She got out on her own," Leroy said.

"That's her way," I told him. "She gets into trouble on her own and out of it too."

"Then why in hell did we come after her?" Leroy sounded genuinely puzzled, but he said it for Victoria's benefit.

"Just in case," I said. I gave Victoria a grin, but all I got in return was a look that said she would have plenty to say to me once we got out of our present fix.

And I had no doubt it was a fix. We trusted our horses to find their own way as we galloped up the rocky trail where it began to rise out of the little valley. As we climbed toward where the rest of the rescue party was waiting, we could hear shouted orders rising from the camp below. I looked back and saw the whole place aswarm with men and horses.

"What happened back there?" Leroy asked Victoria.

"Villa tried to keep me prisoner," she said. "I hit him over the head with a wine bottle. They must have found him." This brief explanation left aside why she had gone to Villa's camp in the first place, but there would be time for that later, if we got away.

When we reached the grove of trees where Leroy and I had left the others, I opened my mouth to tell them to get mounted up quick, but Leroy beat me to it.

"Mount up, boys," he said. "We've got the whole of Villa's army after us."

He took the lead as if he had left off running the Wild Bunch twenty days ago, instead of nearly twenty years. No one looked at me twice or thought it strange to hear Leroy giving the orders, and I will admit this bruised my pride. I was studying up a way to take charge again and let Leroy know I would have no more of his high-handed ways, but he was off and gone, heading up the trail, and all I could do was put my heels to Jake and go after him with Victoria beside me and the rest following close.

He led us over the ridge and down the other side, straight back along the trail we had followed to Villa's camp. As we reached the broad wash, I urged Jake alongside Sonny.

"We'd do better to get off this trail," I said. "That way we might lose 'em in the foothills. This way, all they've got to do is follow their own tracks."

"Your job is tracking people down, Charlie," Leroy said. "Mine is getting us all out of this in one piece."

That shut me up, for I saw the truth of what he said. All his life he had been a leader of men, but as our rescue party set out he had sided with me, backing my play because Victoria was my daughter. And I had done my job. I had tracked her down. Now Victoria's safety, and ours, would depend on whether we managed to shake off the Villista cavalry that even now was forming up behind us. If Victoria had hurt Pancho badly, they would be out for blood. And I couldn't think of any man better qualified to lead us out of danger than Butch Cassidy.

But that didn't do much to soothe the itch I felt at the back of my neck. He was used to having posses on his trail but I wasn't, and he saw my discomfort.

"Kind of different, isn't it?" he said cheerfully. "Being chased, I mean."

He gloried in it. Just as I had felt the years drop away from my shoulders when we started out after Victoria, he felt the same thing now, but it took having a bunch of armed men hot on his trail to make him young again.

"You get us all killed, you'll answer to me," I said.

As we continued along the wash, Leroy shifted Sonny over beside Gene Ortiz and spoke briefly with the vaquero. A few minutes later Leroy said, "This'll do," and reined in where the river took a sharp curve to the north. He led us up the bank and told us to dismount, all but Nate and Gene, and he sent Brian to take the rest of the horses out of sight.

"If you're figuring on an ambush, they'll just work around and come at us from behind," I said. The bank offered little cover, although its height would give us a brief advantage over the Villistas, who would be riding straight into our guns.

"You've got no faith, Charlie," Leroy said. There was no damping his high spirits. "You swap that coat of yours for Gene's serape," he told Victoria. "Give him your hat too."

While they were exchanging clothes, he told us his plan. An ambush was what he had in mind, all right, but it was a fake. To Villa's men, we would seem to be trying to hold them back while Victoria made good her escape with just one man to protect her. But what we really wanted was for them to follow her. Only they would be chasing Gene instead of Victoria. He and Victoria were of similar size, and from a distance no one could tell them apart. While Gene and Nate led Villa's cavalry on a wild goose chase, the rest of us would make straight for Delgado. If Villa's men were angry enough to take on the whole town, we would prepare a hot reception for them.

"Why should Gene risk his neck out there instead of me?" Victoria demanded when Leroy was done laying out his scheme. As always, she wanted to do her own stunts.

"How bad did you hurt Villa?" Leroy asked her.

"I don't know. I didn't mean to hit him too hard."

"But you hit him hard enough to knock him out. Maybe you hurt him worse. Either way, those Villistas know who did it. If they catch up with you, they'll probably kill you."

"If they catch up with Gene and Nate, they'll probably kill both of them when they find out they've been tricked," she shot back at him.

"Don't worry, they won't catch us," Nate said, all cocky and ready for adventure, just like Leroy.

"Gene knows the country like the back of his hand," Leroy said. "He figures he can stay ahead of them."

"For Señorita Hartford, I will gladly do this," said Gene, delivering himself of more American words than I had heard him speak before. He spoke in Mexican to Leroy then, pointing out a route that angled away from the wash. By following the westering moon, he said, the rest of us would arrive in Delgado in far less time than it had taken to make the outward journey.

"What if they don't all go off after Nate and Gene?" I asked when the chitchat was done.

"Then they'll work around and come at us from behind," Leroy said, flashing me that smile of his in the moonlight.

I saw now another reason why men would follow him anywhere. He was cheerful and sure of himself in the face of danger. A man who can demonstrate those qualities does much to shore up the confidence of his companions, so long as his plans work out. Leroy's present plan had a fair chance, but like any plan cooked up in the heat of a running chase we would have to wait to find out if it would work.

"We'll lead them to hell and gone," Nate said, raring to go.

"Not too far," Leroy cautioned him. "Just give us a little time, then head for town. Come straight to the hacienda. We'll be ready."

"They're coming," said Chief John, who was watching our back trail.

The Villista cavalry, fifty or more of them, were scrambling down the ridge, but it was too far for them to make us out yet, despite the moonlight. When they reached the bottom of the slope they disappeared into the wash.

"Get going," Leroy told Nate and Gene. "Start moving before they come into sight, and ride like hell when they see you."

The rest of us lay belly-down on the high river bank while Nate and Gene rode out onto the sandy bottom.

A moment later the cavalry came down the river like a flash flood, all abreast and jockeying for the lead. Nate and Gene spurred their horses from a trot into a gallop, and the cavalry saw them. The Villistas surged ahead, some of the riders letting off a few shots, charging straight for our hiding place.

"Shoot like you mean it, but don't hit 'em if you can help it," Leroy said calmly. "We don't want them coming for us."

"I sure hope you're right about this," I said.

"So do I." This time there was no grin.

Leroy shot first, firing over the heads of the cavalry, and the rest of us followed suit. If we had aimed to hit them, we would have done some damage. As it was, we might as well have tried to stop a stampede with a slingshot. The Villistas saw our muzzle flashes and swung away from us, up onto the far bank, but they kept on down the wash, hot after Nate and Gene. A moment later they were gone, all but the dust.

"You were right," Chief John said to Leroy.

By the look that Victoria gave Leroy as we got to our feet, she expected him to be right every step of the way from now on.

Brian led the horses forward and we mounted up, not quite believing it had been that easy. Leroy looked for all the world as if the whole thing was a game and he was winning. He was happier than I had seen him since we set foot in Mexico.

"That was Ortega," Buddy Johnston observed as we started off. I had seen Villa's second in command too, out in front of the rest. Something about the way he rode told me he had murder on his mind. What if my daughter had killed Pancho Villa? His men wouldn't rest until their *jefe* was avenged.

Leroy set the pace at a steady trot, so as not to wear out the horses in case we needed to run for it before we reached the town. With the moon as our guide we left the mountains behind and made our way through the foothills, and soon we were riding once more on the open grassland of the plateau. There Leroy let the horses stretch out into an easy lope. We kept our eyes peeled and our ears pricked up, but we had the countryside to ourselves. We were careless of disturbing the cattle now, our main concern being to get to Delgado as quickly as we could in order to prepare a warm welcome for the Villistas.

Victoria stuck close to Leroy and me throughout our journey. Cloaked in Gene's serape, with his hat pulled low, she observed Leroy closely, especially when his attention was elsewhere. There was something approaching awe in the way she looked at him now, and she didn't say a word from the time we left the ambush site until we were a mile or two from Delgado.

We were crossing a patch of rocky ground when Jake stumbled and shied sideways, almost bumping into Leroy and Sonny.

"Whoa, Sundance," Leroy said, calming the sorrel. That was how I learned that the horse's name was Sunny, not Sonny, as I had believed from the start, and it pleased me to know that Leroy, like me, had named his mount for a former companion.

Perhaps speaking his old friend's name reminded Leroy of times gone by, for he turned to me and said, "Say, Charlie, is it true that Joe LaFors almost got you killed once?"

"He called me by name up in Rawlins, when I was with some of the Hole-in-the-Wall bunch. I had quite a time convincing the boys old Joe was wrong about me."

Leroy grinned. "The same thing happened to me in a restaurant in Denver. Elza Lay called me by name with three deputies sitting at the next table."

Victoria did not take kindly to being left out of this conversation, so she got in with both feet. "I wouldn't want to make the same mistake," she said. "Should I call you Bob or Robert? Or do you prefer Butch?"

"Hush, girl," I cautioned her. We were beyond the hearing of the others, but not by much.

The extent of Victoria's knowledge took both of us by surprise, and Leroy at once suspected me. "Somebody's been blabbing," he said, giving me a look.

"It wasn't Charlie," Victoria said.

Leroy nodded, remembering the time she had spent with Villa. "Pancho never could keep his mouth shut around a pretty woman."

"Well?" she demanded.

"We started with Leroy," he said. "We better keep to it."

"This small talk is fine, but it'll be light in a while," I said, hoping to get their thoughts back to the problem at hand. "Along about then, Nate and Gene will lead Ortega and his bunch into our trap. Only we don't have a trap."

"The hacienda's not a bad place to defend," Leroy said. "I figure we hole up there until Pancho's boys get tired of being shot at and go home to Chihuahua."

"The trouble is, we don't know how bad old Pancho's hurt," I said. It was time to face the facts. "If Victoria killed him, they might not quit. Or they might take it out on the town."

"I didn't hit him that hard," Victoria protested, but I could see from her expression that she understood the danger of our situation, maybe fully appreciating it for the first time.

Just then we had to rein in to keep from trampling Chief John and Redeye, who had stopped ahead of us. We were atop a low swell in the prairie. In the distance we could make out lights twinkling in the dark. The moon was low in the west, nearing a bank of clouds moving in from that direction. The breeze was freshening and there was a change in the air. Before long we would lose the moon, and the countryside would be pitch dark for a time before the eastern sky brightened.

"Something's not right," Redeye said.

"It looks quiet enough to me," I said. "Let's get going."

But Redeye held out an arm. "Look there."

He was pointing to the north of town. From somewhere beyond the edge of the plateau a dark column of smoke rose into the sky, where it was dispersed by the freshening wind.

Chapter 25

OUR FRIENDS IN the hacienda gave no thought to sleep once our rescue party set out, but despite their wakefulness, the *federales* caught them napping. The soldiers arrived by train, the troops on flatcars and the horses in boxcars. Forewarned about the break in the tracks, the train approached Delgado cautiously, otherwise it would have derailed and wrecked and events might have taken a different turn. As it was, the engineer braked to a stop at the site of the explosion, the eighty-odd soldiers unloaded their horses and mounted up, and silently they entered the town. One by one, startled *delgadeños* awoke to find armed *federales* standing over their beds.

The first warning those in the hacienda had that anything was amiss was when a dozen soldiers galloped into the courtyard. Before those inside could do anything to defend themselves, the soldiers burst into the big hall with rifles ready and bayonets fixed.

Most of the household was gathered in the hall to await our rescue party's return. Gerald was tied to a chair, watching Jack Whistler play cards with Bob Elderberg and Charlie Noble. Gerald had long since ceased his protests and was passing the time plotting revenge on those who had manhandled him. Señora Delgado, always the thoughtful hostess, had ordered the servants to prepare a late supper. This layout, sufficient to feed half of Sonora, was set on the dining tables for any to partake of as they wished.

Behind the soldiers came two officers—a captain and a lieutenant—with pistols drawn. Six soldiers moved quickly off to search the house while the others remained to guard those present. Outside, more soldiers were searching the outbuildings and the wagons.

In short order, all who were found in other parts of the hacienda—vaqueros and servants and a few Americans—were hustled into the big room. Willie Two Horse was brought down from upstairs, where the soldiers had found him sound asleep on my bed. His head was bowed in shame and he wouldn't meet anyone's eyes.

No one there blamed Willie as hard as he blamed himself. For an old warrior like Willie, his promise to "keep an eye on things" had the force of a sacred obligation. He had sworn to protect his tribe from danger. That night his "tribe" was everyone in the hacienda. He had climbed the ladder to the roof and for a time he sat there looking in all directions, determined that nothing larger than a field mouse would escape his detection. But the night was quiet, the town was asleep, and danger seemed to be far away. Willie took a chill and removed himself to my bedroom, where he could look from time to time toward the east, the direction we had taken and from whence we would no doubt return. Eventually he fell asleep and that's how the *federales* found him.

With the household thoroughly under his control, the captain of the *federales* directed a string of rapid-fire questions at Rafael Delgado.

As Villa had proclaimed when he intended to shoot the Delgados, they had supported Carranza since the start of the revolution, but the federal captain's attitude was hardly one of deference toward the town's *patrón*. The soldiers kept their weapons at the ready and the young lieutenant did not holster his pistol. Jack Whistler, who naturally speaks a good deal of Mexican, having grown up a stone's throw from the border, noticed that the captain wasted no time asking who the *yanquis* might be. The presence of the Americans was clearly no surprise to him. He inspected them disdainfully before turning to the Delgados, and then all his questions concerned Villa. When did he leave? Which direction did he go? Where was he now?

Señor Delgado opened his mouth to answer, but his wife beat him to it.

"We know nothing," she informed the captain in a tremulous voice. "The insurgent pigs molested us and robbed us. When they left, I think they went to the west. I myself was violated by the cursed Villa, may he suffer the torments of the damned."

"Lies!" the captain shot back at her. "We know the bandit Villa was received in this hacienda. We know he celebrated the new year with you. We know you made no effort to resist him. We know the *gringos* put him in their moving picture!"

Magdalena Delgado stepped back, clutching her children to her skirts.

The captain and his men had already learned a great deal about the events of recent days. When the soldiers awakened Señor Garza, the ardent Carranzista stationmaster, he demanded to be taken at once to the officer in charge, proclaiming that he himself was responsible for summoning the *federales* thither. He had managed to get off a telegraph message before Villa's men cut the wires, he told the captain when he was ushered into his own railroad station. The captain had made the station his temporary headquarters, perhaps because it was the only building in town, besides the hacienda, equipped with electric lights.

"What took you so long!" Señor Garza demanded to know.

The captain explained that the message had been relayed to Agua Prieta and Nogales, and then to Hermosillo, a hundred and fifty miles to the south, before reaching someone of sufficient authority to act on it. The captain and his men had been dispatched from Nogales by train, but the Nogales-to-Douglas line runs north of the American border for the last thirty miles before reaching Douglas, and the *federales* were obliged to disembark at the border—the Yankee border guards being unwilling to permit armed Mexican troops to pass across American soil in view of the unsettled relations caused by the Jenkins affair. The captain and his company had to march to Agua Prieta overland, before finally proceeding south along the Nacozari branch line to Delgado.

"I assure you, Señor Garza," the captain said, "we have come as quickly as possible."

Somewhat appeased, Señor Garza volunteered everything he knew about what had happened in Delgado in recent days. He related the exact number of Villa's force, when the Villistas had arrived, when they had left, and which direction they had taken. Then, pointing toward the hacienda, he gleefully informed the captain that the *gringos* had been very friendly with General Villa. Yes, indeed. Particularly the one called Leroy Roberts. It was said he had fought in Villa's army some years ago as a soldier of fortune. Garza concluded by describing in detail the New Year's Eve festivities at the hacienda.

This accounted for the captain's bad humor when he questioned the Delgados. Now, faced with Señora Delgado's lies, he raised a hand as if to strike her, but Rafael stepped in front of his wife. Settling for this sacrificial lamb, the captain slapped Rafael Delgado twice across the face.

"Where is Rosa Cimarrona?" he demanded. "Which one is Leroy Roberts? Where is the bandit Villa?"

For all the captain knew, Garza might have lied to him. He wanted to scare the Delgados into confirming Villa's departure and the direction he took, and anything else they could add that might be of use.

"I do not know where Villa is," Señor Delgado said. "Señorita Hartford disappeared. Señor Roberts and some others went to search for her."

He told the truth, but it didn't satisfy the captain. His hand was raised to strike Rafael Delgado again, when Gerald Ball spoke up.

"General Villa left here yesterday, about midafternoon."

Living with a Mexican wife, Gerald had picked up a smattering of Spanish, perhaps more than he let on. Maybe he had followed the talk up to then, maybe not. It didn't take a genius to figure out what the captain wanted to know.

"What did he say?" the captain demanded of Rafael Delgado.

Rafael shrugged.

The captain hit him in the face with a closed fist, causing Rafael to stagger. Blood ran from his nose.

"Tell him what he wants to know, dear," Magdalena Delgado pleaded.

And so Rafael translated for Gerald. The first thing Gerald wanted was to be untied, but the captain put a swift stop to any bargaining. With a nod of his head he ordered his lieutenant to make Gerald talk.

Just seeing the officer coming his way was enough for Gerald. He spoke rapidly, repeating that Villa had left the previous afternoon, and that he went east toward the mountains.

"*Ya lo sabemos,*" the captain said. We already know this. He dismissed Gerald with a wave of the hand, but Gerald spoke again.

"I know where his camp is."

That got the captain's attention.

"He is camped beneath a mountain that looks like a gunsight," Gerald went on. "He said he would stay there three days waiting for Mr. Roberts."

When Rafael translated these words into Spanish, one of the soldiers spoke up excitedly. He knew the mountain, he said. He was from this part of Sonora and used to work as a vaquero for a hacienda not far to the south. He assured the captain that the valley below the mountain was no more than a three-hour ride.

The captain directed one of the guards to cut Gerald's bonds with his bayonet. Turning to the Delgados, he addressed them sternly.

"With your lies, you have proven yourselves enemies of the government." To the room at large he said, "You will all remain here. When we have captured the bandit Villa I will decide what to do with you."

Leaving two soldiers in the hall to guard the prisoners, he ordered four guards to remain outside the hacienda walls to keep the household in and all others out.

"If anyone tries to leave, shoot him," the lieutenant told the guards as he followed the captain out the door.

Gerald stood up, rubbing his wrists where the ropes had chafed them, while Jack translated the officers' final orders. Jack looked at Gerald like he wished Gerald would try to leave so the guards would shoot him dead. Gerald decided not to press his luck and sat back down.

It was fortunate for me that the captain and his men left the hacienda when they did, as I was about to approach the main building just then and would have stepped straight into their guns had they departed a few moments later.

We had scouted the town and the hacienda and were acquainted with the situation by now. In town, lights were on in many houses, and Leroy and I saw one man being beaten by federal soldiers while his wife cried pitifully in the doorway of their little shack. Chief John and Redeye, in the meantime, had scouted to the north of town and found the *federales'* train deserted but for the engineer and fireman. They were keeping up a head of steam, which accounted for the column of smoke that had alerted us to the train's presence.

Following our scout, we rendezvoused with Victoria and Brian and Karen in an arroyo near the burned sets of our movie "town." We exchanged information and held a quick council of war, fearful for our friends in the hacienda. We knew the *federales* would learn that Villa and his men had celebrated the new year with us, and we knew that in the hard days of the revolution, towns had been wiped out for lesser offenses against the government. If we were Villa's friends, we were President Carranza's enemies, Americans or not. It was as simple as that. Woodrow Wilson had thrown his weight on Carranza's side, but in the Sonoran desert a federal captain might kill some meddlesome *gringos* in a "shootout" with Pancho Villa and cause only a flurry of telegraphed protests by his carelessness.

"We don't have a vast lot of time here," I said, as Leroy considered what to do. "Nate and Gene will be along pretty quick, and Ortega right behind them. If we don't figure up a plan, they'll ride straight into those *federales*."

"Hush, Charlie," Victoria said. "Let him think."

But Leroy was smiling at me. "Charlie, if I'd known you Pinkertons had all the answers for me, my whole life would have been different."

Chief John and the others took some notice of his words, but he didn't give them time to unlimber their curiosity. Once again he had come up with a scheme to get us out of our ticklish predicament and he laid it out in very few words.

All we had to do was get into the hacienda. He had told Nate and Gene to come straight there, planning to fend off Ortega and his men from behind the thick adobe walls. With luck, our two decoys would follow orders. Only now, instead of having to fend off Ortega ourselves, the *federales* would do it for us. Ortega's men would charge smack into the federal cavalry while we sat on the sidelines and watched them whip each other to a froth.

Recalling my many years of slipping unnoticed into the lion's den for William and Robert Pinkerton, Leroy assigned me the task of scouting the hacienda and getting inside if I could. Before setting out on this job I swapped my coat to Victoria for Gene's serape and traded Chief John for his floppy-brim hat. This was as close as I could come on short notice to disguising myself as a Mexican, but it would have to do.

Clouds covered the sky by now, all but the far eastern rim of it, over by the mountains. The wind was cold and the night dark. This suited me perfectly. The sentries at the four corners of the hacienda huddled close to the wall and tried, like turtles, to pull their heads down into their uniforms. Keeping warm was the first and last thing on their minds in the cold hour just before dawn.

I watched from behind one of the McQuain & Vickery wagons as the captain and his men rode down toward the town. When they were out of sight I approached the closest guard, walking with a list to starboard and a stagger in my step, humming a Mexican ditty under my breath. This was a trick I had used many times in my detective career. Most men are not suspicious of a drunk, but whether I could pass myself off as a Mexican drunk was another matter. In my hand was an unlit cigarette I had borrowed from Brian Hill.

"Hello there, young soldier," I greeted the guard in my best Mexican. I waved the cigarette about. "Do you have matches?"

The guard didn't stop to wonder what an old man was doing wandering about drunk. Perhaps he thought it natural that someone would get drunk to celebrate the *federales*' arrival. He fumbled in his jacket, looking for a match, and while he was thus occupied I drew my Peacemaker from beneath the serape and cracked him on the head.

Knocking a man out with a gun is a precarious business. Hit him in the wrong place, you'll kill him. Not hard enough, and he'll go down but not out. But I had some practice at this art. The guard dropped hard and stayed down, and I hastened along the wall toward the east corner of the hacienda.

"Hey, there," I said, once I saw the soldier posted there. "Your friend is sick."

This speech was not much longer than the first, and once again I hoped the way I slurred my words would hide my Texas accent.

Once again I was in luck. The second guard followed me like a lamb over to where the first one lay on the ground. As he bent over to shake the fallen man, I put my six-shooter in his ribs and relieved him of his weapons.

Seeing this, Leroy and the others sprang from where they were hidden among the wagons. Reckoning that we had better not push our luck with the drunk-Mexican trick, Leroy had Redeye dress in one of the guards' uniforms. The Indian approached the two remaining soldiers in turn, leveling a pistol while Buddy Johnston stepped out of the dark from the guard's other side with his Springfield rifle at the ready. Neither guard was inclined to argue with the two determined men.

We left the guards bound and gagged and watched over by Victoria and Karen, each armed with a Colt's revolver, while the rest of us crept through the courtyard and peered into the big room from the darkness of the veranda.

The federal captain expected no trouble from a bunch of *gringo* movie folks, nor did the two guards he left inside the hacienda. Grateful not to be chasing the fearsome Pancho Villa through the foothills, they had settled themselves into a pair of armchairs from which they could keep an eye on the room, and were lighting two of Rafael Delgado's Cuban cigars at the moment of our appearance.

On Leroy's signal the six of us stepped through the French doors as one, our guns leveled at the two *federales*. Very slowly they raised their hands. Very quickly Leroy and I stepped forward and disarmed them.

"As easy as ABC," I said, feeling pleased with myself.

"Don't count your chickens," said Leroy.

Chapter 26

NATURALLY, OUR FRIENDS were overjoyed to see us, all the more so because Victoria was safe and sound. They thronged around us, wanting to know every detail of our nighttime adventures, but Leroy put a stop to that.

"Nate and Gene will be along soon. We better get ready for them."

He explained our situation briefly to those in the hacienda, and under his direction we made ready to defend ourselves from *federales* and Villistas alike if the need arose. As had been the case with our rescue party, no one in the hacienda hesitated to take orders from Leroy. It was more like they had just been waiting for him to speak up and take his rightful place, all except for Gerald, who didn't easily take orders from anyone.

"Now see here—" he protested, as Leroy was assigning tasks to one and all.

"You hush up and stay out of the way or I'll gag you myself," I told him. Jack Whistler had apprised us of Gerald's willingness to tell the captain where to look for Villa.

So it might appear that the federal guards were still on duty outside the hacienda, Charlie Noble and Jim Ray Thompson and Luke Fister and Tommy Fear donned the guards' uniforms. Tommy wore the one Redeye had used temporarily, as Leroy wanted Redeye free for other duties.

The biggest risk we took was bringing the horses into the courtyard. Bob Elderberg and I and a few of the Delgado vaqueros rode the rescue party's horses and brought the McQuain & Vickery and Delgado mounts from the pasture, knowing there was no way to disguise what we were doing. But the *federales* were apparently busy down in the town and none spied the dust from our brief activity outside the hacienda walls. I couldn't help feeling that our luck was too good to be true, and I wondered when it would fail us.

While we rounded up the horses, Willie Two Horse and Jack Whistler fetched the guns from the wagons, all those that had escaped the *federales'* hasty search. Willie was almost pathetically eager to accept any duty passed his way and to perform it well, hoping in some small way to redeem his poor job of keeping a lookout while we were gone.

Once we were back inside the hacienda walls, the courtyard gates were closed. The animals our rescue party had ridden were unsaddled and the saddles transferred to fresh horses. A few more were saddled for good measure, against the chance that we might have to make a sortie for one reason or another.

In the meantime, Leroy posted gunners at all the windows and atop the walls, until the Delgado hacienda resembled a small fortress. Victoria and Karen and the rest of our cowgirls were among the defenders, all those who were familiar with firearms, while the women and the servants of the household were to help reload if things got hot.

Through it all, George Bleumel was filming with his portable Aeroscope, concentrating on Randall and Victoria and those in our hero "Tom's" band, no doubt thinking he might use some of what he filmed in *The Trail of Pancho Villa.* When the preparations were complete and there was nothing left to do but wait, Leroy offered George a gun and a chance to man a window, but George declined.

"I went through the war without firing a gun," he said. "I'd just as leave keep it that way."

Leroy did not protest George's decision. After a final check to assure himself that the hacienda was ready to defend itself against all comers, he led Chief John and Redeye and myself to the second floor and thence up a ladder to the roof, where we crouched behind the adobe wall that surrounded it like a low battlement. From this vantage point we could scan the desert all the way to the foothills as well as keeping an eye on the town.

In the east, the mountains were silhouetted by the first light of dawn. Already we could make out the landscape around us far better than when I played my drunk scene for the guards.

"Looks like the *federales* are getting ready to pull out," Redeye said. Down in the town, the federal cavalry was forming up along the railroad avenue. But as time passed and the light in the east grew stronger the column remained where it was, the men standing beside their horses while the officers came and went from the station, where the electric lights shone brightly.

On any other morning the townsfolk would have been up and about before the sun, but today they stayed prudently indoors.

"Might be he's still questioning people," Chief John ventured.

"He knows what he needs to know," said Leroy.

"Could be he'd rather not go looking for Pancho Villa until it's proper daylight," I said. A similar caution on the part of many federal commanders was one reason they had so rarely brought Villa to bay.

"What if they pull out before Nate and Gene show up?" Redeye said.

"Then we'll hold off Ortega by ourselves," Leroy replied.

I had been in many similar situations over the years. So had Leroy. No one knew better than we two that sometimes you just have to wait to see what other men will do, knowing your life will depend on how quickly you react once someone makes the first move.

So far, Leroy's plan was working like a charm. The real test of his leadership would come when something went wrong.

"There." Redeye pointed to the north.

At first I could see nothing, Redeye's vision outstripping mine. But then I saw it too, a small trail of dust, and two horsemen riding hard. Behind them came a larger dust cloud. It looked as if a whirlwind was hell-bent on catching the two riders and sweeping them up.

Dawn had a firm grip on the countryside now. The long winter night had protected us when we needed it most, giving us a helping hand in taking the hacienda, but it could offer no help to Nate and Gene.

"The soldiers are on the move," said Chief John.

The captain had given orders at last. The column of federal cavalry was moving away from the station, heading up the road to the plateau. If it is true that all the world's a stage and we are only players, on this occasion the Director was ordering everyone onstage at once.

Leroy leaned over the edge of the roof and called softly to Charlie Noble. "Charlie, you and the others get inside now."

The captain might notice that his guards were missing, but in a few moments the masquerade would be over anyway.

Nate and Gene had played their hand well, sometimes holding back to be sure Ortega was still on their trail, but always keeping a good lead on him. Gene chose a cautious route, not straying too far from a straight line toward Delgado, which might have given Ortega to suspect he was being intentionally led astray. Now that they had the town in sight they rode flat out, heading for the hacienda.

"They see 'em now," said Chief John, who was keeping track of the *federales*. The head of the column had reached the edge of the plateau.

The captain put a hand up, halting the column while he peered at the oncoming riders. Now he motioned his men forward at a trot. When the whole column was on the flat, he motioned to the left and halted again, this time with his men in a line facing the riders. From the roof of the hacienda, we could hear the captain's shouted orders clearly.

Nate and Gene were less than half a mile away. The *federales* had their carbines at the ready but they made no move to fire. Two men posed no threat to the soldiers. What the captain wanted to know was who was chasing them. The riders changed course slightly, making for the east end of the *federales'* line, evidently intending to slip past the soldiers and head for the hacienda. That's when Gene's horse tripped in a gopher hole and went down, and thus an innocent gopher turned our luck from good to bad.

The horse screamed as its leg broke. Gene jumped free and rolled twice before staggering to his feet, stunned and disoriented. Ortega and his men were coming on fast, heedless of the waiting soldiers.

Nate didn't think twice about what to do. He wheeled Buster around, removed his foot from the near-side stirrup and held out a hand to Gene, knowing they would get one try at it. One of the more common stunts performed by the McQuain & Vickery boys is a man on horseback picking up a man afoot. It is simple enough, once learned, but even a simple feat is another matter when a life depends on executing it successfully.

Gene had seen the trick practiced by the Americans and had the presence of mind to know what was expected of him. He tensed himself, caught Nate's hand, found the stirrup and swung up behind him, clinging to Nate's waist. Buster turned as only a cow pony can turn, and headed for the *federales* at a dead run.

The fall had cost our friends precious time. With Buster carrying double, Ortega was gaining fast. The Villistas were still out of carbine range, just barely, but that didn't stop them from burning some powder in the hope they might get lucky. Bullets began to kick up dust around Buster's feet. Ahead, the *federales* leveled their weapons.

Nate did the smart thing. He socked spurs to Buster, reined him hard to the right and hauled his freight for town as fast as he could, his objective being to get out from between Ortega and the *federales* and behind some kind of cover.

Buster was a credit to the mustang race. He had run half the night without rest, but he didn't slow down a bit as he reached the edge of the plateau. Over the lip he went, down the slope, through the town's northernmost shacks, sending chickens and dogs running for their lives.

From atop the hacienda, we saw Buster and his two riders disappear into the far end of town and then we saw them no more, while up on the plateau the festivities were just beginning.

Ortega realized he would have to deal with the *federales* before pursuing his quarry further. At his command the Villistas spread out in a line, neither slackening their pace nor changing direction. They were half as many as the *federales*, but they came on as if they outnumbered the foe ten to one.

The *federales* wavered. The captain shouted an order and the line grew straight again. Another order carried above the rumble of the Villistas' hooves and the *federales* loosed a volley of shots at the charging insurgents. Ortega's men fired back, more raggedly, and it was Ortega's line that broke. With a shout and a sweep of his hand he ordered his men to the right and led them over the lip of the plateau and down into the town, not far from where Nate and Gene had vanished.

With a shout from many throats, the *federales* were after them, breaking into bunches, dashing down the slope. Shots rang out and the fight was on, with Nate and Gene somewhere in the middle of it.

"Okay, boys, let's go," Leroy said. He scrambled down the ladder with John and Redeye and me close behind him. John broke out coughing as we ran through the house. He was still coughing when we reached the big hall on the ground floor, where Victoria and Karen and Katie Elderberg stood guard at the west windows, and Leroy saw that he was in no shape to accompany us after Nate and Gene.

"You look after things while we're gone," Leroy told him. "Keep everyone here and get ready to let us in if we come back in a hurry." John nodded, still struggling to control the spasms that shook his barrel chest.

As Redeye and I followed Leroy out to the courtyard, my eyes met Victoria's and she formed two silent words with her lips. *Be careful.*

In another moment the three of us were mounted and out the gate, Leroy leading a spare horse for Gene Ortiz. As we approached the town it appeared to be deserted. There was not a living soul in evidence, not even a dog. Apparently even the town mutts knew when to lay low. Only the sporadic sound of gunfire revealed the presence of the Villistas and *federales*, who were creeping among the buildings, taking potshots at one another. It was a stalking game now, but it could turn into a proper war at any moment.

Leroy led us at a gallop down the road to the railroad avenue. Along the tracks we went toward the station, heading for the north end of town where Gene and Nate had disappeared. As we passed the Avenida Central I looked toward the plaza, but the street and plaza were both empty.

"Hey, look there!" cried Redeye suddenly, reining back. Up ahead, Buster trotted out from between two houses. Nate and Gene were grinning to beat the band.

"Who in hell was that other bunch?" Nate wanted to know as Gene hopped down from Buster's rump and mounted the spare horse.

"*Federales* came by train, took the town in the night," I said, telling him the essentials in a few words.

There were hoofbeats from behind us. Leroy pulled his Colt's as he turned, and I discovered that my .45 had found its way into my hand when I wasn't looking.

The new arrivals were Victoria and Karen. They reined in as they reached us, looking very pleased with themselves. They both wore pants and had their hair coiled beneath their hats. Victoria's matched set of Cimarron Rose Peacemakers was strapped to her waist and Karen carried a Winchester. Karen was plainly cheered by the sight of Nate whole and sound.

"You've got more damn luck," Karen said.

"Yeah, I guess I have," Nate agreed.

"Doesn't anybody around here do what we tell 'em?" I wondered aloud.

"Hush, Charlie," said Victoria. "We're here and we're staying."

"There's no need to stay," Leroy said. "We've got what we came for."

As we reined around to start back for the hacienda, half a dozen *federales* rode into view from between the houses beyond the Avenida Central. They started shooting as soon as they saw us. We kicked our horses and scattered, making for the cover of the nearby houses. Leroy and I ended up behind the same whitewashed wall, but the others were out of sight. I was so mad at the *federales* for shooting at us that I jumped off my horse, stuck my pistol around the corner of the house and emptied it in the direction of the soldiers, driving them out of the street and back amongst the houses whence they had come.

"They've got no business shooting at peaceable Americans!" I said, feeling a little better. "Where have the others got to?"

"There's Victoria," Leroy said. She was behind us, and she was alone. Leroy reined his horse around to join her and I followed him on foot, trying to hold my reins and my pistol with one hand while fumbling for more cartridges with the other. Before leaving the hacienda I had stuck my shotgun in the rifle scabbard attached to my saddle, but with surprises popping up on all sides I felt better with a six-shooter in my hand.

As I have said, Delgado has a very slim layout of proper streets. Behind the houses facing the railroad avenue there were vegetable patches and pigpens, and more houses arranged in no particular pattern. As I stepped from the alley where Leroy and I had taken shelter, a shot boomed from somewhere off to my left. Victoria's horse reared and pitched over, throwing Victoria from the saddle. She fell on her back, knocking the wind out of her. I turned and saw Colonel Ortega approaching on horseback. He

was trotting through a patch of dry corn stalks, closing at last on the
quarry he believed he had chased through the night, utterly unaware of
the heroic decoy role played by Eugenio Ortiz.

The huge Remington Army pistol in Ortega's hand was pointed at Victoria, but before he could fire again, Leroy rode between them. Leroy had
his .44 in his hand, but he seemed to be having trouble with his horse.
Sunny had been unsaddled after our nightlong ride and Leroy was now on
Jack Whistler's gray stallion, Buck. The stallion skittered about like a half-
broke mustang. It appeared that Leroy had no idea how to handle such a
spirited creature, but I soon saw that it was he who was keeping the horse
off balance, guiding him with his legs, first one way and then the other,
while all the time appearing unable to control the animal.

Of course he was doing this to draw Ortega's attention from Victoria,
who was gasping for breath and struggling to sit up. Ortega hesitated and
frowned, but his indecision lasted only for a moment. He brought his
Remington to bear on Leroy, and Leroy snapped a shot at him.

Ortega's horse buckled at the knees and fell. Without ever taking his
eyes from Leroy, Ortega stepped off the horse as it went down, landed on
his feet, and fired once.

Leroy slumped in the saddle.

"No!" Victoria screamed. She was up now and running toward him,
but I grabbed her, dropping my pistol in the process and scattering cartridges in the dust.

It is a strange thing, but nine men out of ten, perhaps ninety-nine out of
a hundred, having shot a man once, will not shoot again until they see
how badly he is wounded. Like the rest of those ninety-nine, Ortega was
fascinated by his own handiwork. He watched with his pistol held high as
Leroy pitched forward, but now something slowed Leroy's fall. His left
hand was gripping the horse's mane as if in a desperate effort to remain in
the saddle. His forward motion carried him under the horse's neck and
only in the split second before he brought it up to fire did I see that his .44
was still in his hand.

Leroy's shot flung Ortega backward like a rag doll. He fell to the
ground and lay still.

When Victoria and I reached Leroy's side he was off his horse and
bending over Ortega, feeling for a pulse, but a glance at Ortega's chest was
all anyone needed to see that the Mexican's heart would never beat
again. Leroy's shot took him square in the breastbone, shattering lungs
and heart and killing Ortega while he was still standing.

Leroy was sound as a dollar. He had only pretended to be hit to make
Ortega drop his guard. Victoria reached out to touch him, as if to reassure
herself that he was all right.

Leroy straightened up. "He was a good soldier," he said. "He was with Villa right from the start."

That was why he hadn't dropped Ortega from his saddle as soon as he saw him. Right up until the end he had hoped to avoid killing him. Ortega was Villa's right-hand man, and Villa was Leroy's friend. But it came down to kill or be killed, and Ortega lost out.

Chapter 27

ORTEGA'S HORSE WAS dead and Victoria's was foaming bloody froth at the mouth, struggling in its death throes. One thing the moving pictures do not portray accurately is the rate at which horses are killed in battle. In this one instance I would not like to see life depicted on the silver screen as it really is.

I finished reloading my Peacemaker and put the wounded horse out of its agony. As the shot echoed off the surrounding houses, Nate and Karen and Gene Ortiz appeared behind us.

"Here they are," said Nate.

Just then four young Villistas came running on foot around the corner of a nearby house and stopped dead in their tracks.

"¡Los gringos!" said one.

"¡La americana!" said another, but they made no move to raise their weapons.

The Villistas were younger than Nate, scarcely more than boys. They looked at Ortega's body, took in the six of us armed to the teeth, and lit out running in the other direction, faster than they had come.

"Where's Redeye?" Leroy asked, once the youths were gone.

"We were separated when the federales shot at us," Karen said.

Around us, the firing was increasing. Apparently the Villistas and federales were done pussyfooting and intended to start fighting in earnest.

"You got the *federales* and Ortega's boys set against each other, all right," I said to Leroy. "The trouble is, we're caught in the middle."

"We'll be okay if we can get back to the hacienda," he said.

"What about Redeye?" Nate protested as Leroy started off on foot, leading his horse.

"He'll find his way," Karen said, but she too was looking all around, wishing the Indian would show up.

I have never been a soldier, but I have been in battles all the same. The closest I came to something like the fight for Delgado that day was back in '92 when the striking union miners in Gem, Idaho, besieged the mine owners in their own mines. I was behind the strikers' lines, but suspicions against me were running high and I thought it wise to get myself up to the mines before some unionist decided to ventilate my hide. I scampered across no man's land and made it to the other side with some help from Lady Luck, but that was a stroll in the country compared with trying to get from one side of Delgado to the other on the second day of January, 1920.

Leroy led us through the town's crooked back alleys, keeping near the railroad avenue. So far the fighting was all uphill from us. The Villistas had advanced from the north side of town while the *federales* came up from the south. By the sound of it, they had joined battle in the vicinity of the plaza. Many of the Mexicans were burning black powder, and even where we were the air was hazy with smoke. It appeared we might have a chance to sneak back along the western edge of town, staying close to the railroad, but as we neared the Avenida Central we could hear bullets chipping adobe from the walls of the nearby buildings.

We stopped behind a house that faced the avenida. I took a quick peek around the corner of the house.

"What do you think?" Leroy said.

I thought that the avenida looked as wide as the Brazos River in flood, but I didn't say so. Across the street *federales* were moving among the houses, some on horseback but most on foot, extending their line toward the railroad. One saw me and at once took a shot at me.

"*¡Cabrón insurrecto!*" he shouted as I ducked back.

"You do look kind of like one of Pancho's boys in those duds," Leroy observed with a grin. Apparently having hot lead thrown his way made him cheerful.

"We're between the devil and the deep blue sea, and you're making smart remarks," I said. "How about coming up with one of your smart ideas instead."

These words were scarcely out of my mouth when hoofbeats sounded close at hand. We looked around and saw a horseman charging toward us from between the houses, coming from the direction of the plaza. Karen swung her carbine in his direction, but Nate knocked the barrel aside.

"It's Redeye!"

Karen was shamefaced, but Redeye wasted no time with recriminations.

"The Villistas are getting whipped," he said as he reined in beside us. "They're falling back from the plaza. The federals will cross the street pretty soon."

"We better find some cover," Leroy said. "If we can hide out while the federals move past us, we might make a run for the hacienda."

"Whatever we're going to do, we better do it quick." Nate was peering out across the avenida. "Those boys are getting set to move."

"Let's make 'em think there's a bunch of Villistas over here," I said. "That'll give us a little time."

We sent a volley of shots across the street, then pulled back the way we had come, looking for someplace to hide, and before long we found it. The first shelter that presented itself was a barn, although I do not mean to suggest anything like what American readers will imagine when they see this word. It was a ramshackle piece of furniture, made of twisted mesquite poles and odd planks and a sparsely thatched roof that would stop maybe one raindrop in ten. But it was large enough to hold us and our horses, and Leroy made for it the moment he saw it.

The barn contained three sheep and a pair of pigs. These are animals I do not customarily associate with, but this was no time to be particular. As we entered, the pigs trotted over in a friendly manner, evidently hoping we had come to feed them.

With all of us safely inside, we took a moment to catch our breath while we peered between the poles of the wall. Outside, it was fully light now. Before long the sun would come up.

Our hideout adjoined a house that faced the railroad avenue. From within the barn's flimsy walls we could see in three directions, including a piece of the railroad avenue and the stockyards, without being seen ourselves.

"The soldiers are coming," said Gene Ortiz.

The *federales* were on foot, some moving along the avenue while others passed among the houses. Their captain was a smart man. A cavalryman hates to get off his horse, but fighting through the streets of a town is no job for a mounted man. He's up too high and a horse makes a tempting target. The soldiers had left their horses somewhere in the rear. They advanced cautiously but steadily. The firing was still uphill from us, but the federal line was sweeping across the full breadth of the town to be certain no Villistas remained behind them before driving Ortega's men into the northeast corner of town, under the edge of the plateau.

We stood stock-still with our hands over our horses' nostrils while four soldiers passed within twenty feet of our hiding place. When they and their companions were out of sight, we began to breathe again.

"Those federals outnumber Ortega's boys two to one," Redeye said. "They'll likely push 'em out of town directly."

Leroy gave Redeye a look like he wished Redeye would shut up, and I knew what he was thinking. The four young Villistas had informed their *compadres* that Ortega was dead. Without Ortega, the Villistas didn't stand a chance. Soon they would run out of places to take cover. Once they were forced into the open, the *federales* would cut them down.

"The *federales* might hit the hacienda once they're done with Ortega," I said. "We best get back up there."

From within the fortress walls of the hacienda, we could stand off either party, and now that the *federales* had passed us by we stood a chance of regaining our sanctuary. I started for the barn door, but Leroy put out a hand for quiet.

There was a rumble of hoofbeats from the railroad avenue. By peering between the houses we could see the *federales'* horses, all in a herd, being driven toward the stockyards. Thanks to the Villistas' dynamiting, the trains were not running at present, and all the stock pens were empty. The horse guards drove the animals into a large holding pen. With their mounts safely confined in what was now their rear area, more of the *federales* were freed to join the fighting. As best we could make out, four guards remained with the horses while the rest rode off toward the north end of town.

"You reckon those horse guards will give us any trouble?" I said.

"There's only one way to find out," Leroy said. "You let us go out first so they don't shoot you for a Villista."

"There's more soldiers," Redeye hissed.

Where he was pointing we saw first two men, then five more, moving on foot behind the houses that fronted on the road.

"*Son villistas*," said Gene Ortiz.

"I'll bet they're after the horses," Nate said.

"That's Alarcón," Leroy said.

From my hiding place near Villa's camp in the hills, I had seen Leroy chatting with Alarcón while waiting for Luís, the other sentry, to return. It was this same officer who commanded the little party of insurgents now. Somehow they had made their way through the *federales*, or maybe they had seen the *federales* coming and laid low while the soldiers passed them by, just as we had done.

The Villistas moved cautiously in our direction, pausing at every alley to look toward the stockyards. What they had in mind was clear enough. If they could run off the *federales'* horses, their enemies would be left afoot and maybe the tide of battle could be turned.

Alarcón stopped his patrol fifty yards away and conferred quickly with his men. There was no way to sneak across the road and he knew it. He raised a hand and dropped it forward, and as one the Villistas charged out of sight.

"They seen 'em!" said Redeye, who was watching the horse guards from the other side of the barn. I joined him, and I could see two of the horse guards firing, but I couldn't see the Villistas. The gunfire from the street was fast and furious.

"Uh oh," said Leroy. "Here come reinforcements."

Attracted by the gunfire, a federal officer and five men appeared where we had first seen the Villistas. They ran forward and nearly collided with the retreating revolutionists. Only four of the Villistas returned from the street. Alarcón and another man were supporting a wounded comrade between them. The abruptness of their appearance startled the *federales* and saved the Villistas from being shot down at once.

Alarcón dropped his weapon and threw up his hands, commanding his men to do the same. The wounded man slumped to the ground. One of the *federales* poked him with his carbine and ordered him to get up, but the officer called the soldier off.

The officer was looking closely at one of the Villistas. He lifted the insurgent's felt hat and a mass of hair uncoiled and fell to the revolutionist's shoulders. It was a *soldadera*. Like Victoria and Karen, she had thought it wise to conceal her sex so her enemies would not single her out for special attention. With her hair down, I recognized the girlfriend of the Villista balladeer who had sung in the hacienda on New Year's Eve. That festive evening was barely thirty-six hours in the past, but it seemed like much longer.

The federal soldiers howled with glee upon discovering a *soldadera* in their midst. One man grabbed her uniform blouse and ripped it open, exposing her womanhood for all to see. The *soldadera* spat in his face. The soldier raised a fist to strike her, but the officer pushed him away, cursing him and saying something else I could not make out. Now the soldiers all spoke at once, arguing with him, plainly demanding that they be allowed to take their pleasure on the unfortunate *soldadera,* but the officer put a sudden end to the dispute.

He had been holding his pistol in his hand all the while. Now he turned, raised the pistol, and shot the four Villistas in the head, the *soldadera* first, then the others, saving Alarcón for last.

It was over in the space of a breath.

Chapter 28

"OH, GOD," SAID Victoria.

There was a pounding in my head and I felt as if someone was choking me.

Before I knew it, Leroy was pulling his horse out of the barn and mounting up, and I was moving to follow him. We were on the far side of the barn from the soldiers. They wouldn't see us until we rode out into the open.

"You look after the women," I threw over my shoulder to Nate. Then I was in my saddle and off after Leroy, charging around the corner of the barn and making straight for the *federales*.

Seeing Alarcón and his helpless companions shot down like dogs was the last straw for Leroy. The Villistas were leaderless because of him. He felt responsible for their fate. Rushing out there alone didn't make any sense, nor did my jumping aboard my horse to follow him, but I couldn't let him go alone. If he met his last reward amidst the pigpens of Delgado, I would be right beside him.

He had a lead on me, but I pounded my horse's ribs with my heels and let him run. Ahead of us the *federales* turned to see two madmen bearing down on them.

Leroy's first shot dropped the officer. The second took down the soldier beside him, the one who had ripped the *soldadera's* blouse open. Some of the others got off a few shots, but the ferocity of our attack unnerved them and they scattered out of our way, running for cover.

I was drawing even with Leroy now. He looked my way and threw a shot so close in front of me that it nicked the flapping serape. Out of the corner of my eye I saw a man spin out of an alley on my right, throwing up his arms and sending his rifle flying.

On we went, our pace never slackening as we raced along parallel to the railroad avenue, behind the neat row of houses. Other soldiers appeared as we overtook the rear of the federal line, which was still sweeping northward and eastward through the town. A bullet passed so close to my head that I heard the wind, but I paid it no more attention than I might have given a butterfly on a summer's day. My blood was up and fear was not part of my constitution.

Directly in front of me, one soldier stood his ground. He was working the bolt of his rifle, evidently having shot at me already. I fired at him and he fell as I galloped past him.

We passed by a house that was on fire. Some men were trying to extinguish the blaze with water from a horse trough while the fighting raged around them.

And then we were out in the open and there was nothing before us but railroad tracks and chaparral. We turned to the left, swinging around the last house, and reined to a halt at the end of the railroad avenue. Before we came to a full stop, both of us were reloading our pistols.

Leroy seemed surprised that he was still alive, but this look was quickly replaced by the exhilaration a man feels when he has ridden into the jaws of death and lived to tell about it.

"Now what?" I said, feeling chipper myself and ready for anything.

"We hit the federals in the rear," he said. "They'll turn back on us."

Even as he spoke, we were fired on again. As we rode for shelter behind the nearest house we saw a handful of soldiers step out onto the railroad avenue. Leroy was right. Our reckless charge along the rear of the federal line had shown the soldiers how vulnerable they were to attack from that direction, and they were turning to meet the threat.

We looked back the way we had come, through the alleys behind the houses, but already that locality was swarming with soldiers. We were cut off.

"We're in for it now," I said.

"At least we took some of the heat off the Villistas."

"Those soldiers get horseback, they'll make short work of us."

"We could make a run for the river," Leroy suggested, looking around for other choices.

There was a new outbreak of shooting from the railroad avenue, and I dared a quick look. No one shot at me, and then I saw why. The *federales* in the road were facing the other way, and charging down from the hacienda like the Light Brigade of poetic renown was a pack of riders, firing at the *federales* as they came. Fifty yards behind them came the Delgados' Model T.

"That's our boys!" Leroy said.

The riders were on McQuain & Vickery horses and I had no doubt that they had come charging out of the hacienda to save our bacon, or Victoria and Karen's more likely, when we failed to return. As they drew nearer I began to make them out by their clothing and the way they rode. Jack Whistler and Chief John and Willie Two Horse were at the head of the pack. Close on their heels came Bob Elderberg and Tommy Fear and some others. The largest rider could only be Buddy Johnston. It was a sight to see, but as our cowboys charged along the road they raced into federal guns.

Fortunately the ragged barrage that greeted them quickly filled the roadway with smoke, and the soldiers' marksmanship suffered as a result. Were it not for the black powder with which Carranza's army loaded most of its cartridges, our boys would have suffered grievously. They were caught out in the open by an enemy with good cover, and with a few exceptions the cowboys were not fighting men. To give them their due, they burned some powder of their own as they retreated, but retreat was the only course open to them and they took it, making for the adobe station house and the shelter offered by its thick walls. When whoever was driving the Model T saw where the cowboys were headed, he swerved the machine and vanished behind the station.

Leroy and I lost sight of the cowboys as they pulled back, thanks to the gunsmoke in the roadway, but then to our amazement we saw that one rider had not changed course.

It was Randall Steele. He had his reins in his teeth and his shiny Colt's revolvers in his hands, riding hell-bent-for-leather just as audiences far and wide have seen him in the movies. He was clear out of the smoke before he realized that his friends were no longer with him.

"That boy could use some help," Leroy said, and once more we were off and running.

"Get back!" I shouted to Randall, but my voice was drowned out in the volley of shots the *federales* directed at him.

Leroy and I began shooting at the soldiers we could see, hoping to spoil their aim. The horse guards, who were closest to Randall, were still engaged in driving the rest of the cowboys back to the station and didn't notice him, but Randall's horse was not one of those trained to perform calmly in the face of gunfire. The noise in the street had made the animal half crazy with fear and it reared up now, nearly unseating Randall. At that moment two bullets struck the horse.

It dropped to its haunches and fell sideways, pinning Randall's leg. Leroy and I were still fifty yards away, but that was close enough to give Randall some cover. My pistol was empty, so I pulled my shotgun and cut loose with both barrels, driving the nearest soldiers back into an alley between two houses.

Luckily for Randall, his horse was not dead. It struggled to get up, and Randall pulled his leg free. Somehow the wounded beast lurched to its feet and staggered off, while Randall took advantage of the new smoke screen provided by the *federales*. He ran for the stockyards, where he scrambled over the fence into a vacant pen and crouched behind the plank wall of a loading chute.

Leroy and I saw his dim form reach this hiding place, but we had worries of our own. The rest of the cowboys had gained the railroad station, taking their horses right inside with them, which left us as the only handy targets for the *federales* on our end of the line. Once they recovered from the surprise of our charge they commenced throwing lead at us in a businesslike manner, so we reined around to head back the way we had come, not wishing to run the gauntlet between our present position and the station.

We no sooner changed direction than I felt my horse stagger. An instant later, Leroy grunted and grabbed his arm. A second bullet grazed my horse on the haunch and he began to pitch like a wolf, trying to shake the hot pain in his hindquarters. As Leroy pulled up beside me, a shot lifted Chief John's floppy-brim hat from my head and another hit Buck. The gray went down, blowing blood and life from his chest all in a great *whoosh* that tore my heart to hear it. He went down so fast that he caught Leroy with his foot still in the stirrup, just as Randall had been pinned a moment before. All the while I was making like the bronc-riding champion of Sonora. From the federal positions came shouts which roughly translated as "Ride 'em, cowboy," even as the soldiers continued shooting at me.

The bullets began to come closer and I judged that I had put on enough of a show for one morning. I doubled the pony hard to his left, spinning him in a circle and making him stop his bucking. As soon as he quit I was out of the saddle and ducking for cover behind Buck's body with Leroy, while my wounded horse lit out for the open range.

"You've got some cowboy left in you, Charlie," Leroy said. He managed a grin, but I could see he was hurting. Where he had hold of his arm, blood ran between his fingers.

"You gonna live?" I asked.

"It's not bad."

As he said this, I became aware that for the moment at least, federal bullets were no longer striking around us. There was shooting from behind the closest houses, but it was not directed at us. Just then, two *federales* burst from an alley into the street. One fell as he reached the road, and lay still. The other cast a worried glance at Leroy and me, but he ran off toward the north end of town without even taking the opportunity to throw some lead our way.

Before the soldier was halfway up the street, Victoria ducked out of the same alley, closely followed by Redeye, Nate and Karen, and Gene Ortiz. All of them had guns in their hands, apparently having used them to chase the *federales* out of that vicinity.

"Charlie!" she shouted. "Are you all right?"

"We're okay!" I called in reply. We were clear across the wide roadway from the little band and I had no wish for them to expose themselves to the fire of the *federales* who were still lurking up and down the street. As if to emphasize the danger, one shot and then another came our way from farther along the row of houses facing the avenue. Down the road there was a lively exchange of insults in progress between our boys in the station and the *federales* across the way.

"We're going to cover you!" Victoria said. "Get going now!"

Without waiting for a reply, she and her companions sprinted along the line of houses toward the station, firing into each alley as they came to it. The suddenness of their appearance took the *federales* off guard, and in their haste to defend themselves they forgot about me and Leroy.

"We'd best move along, unless you'd like to homestead this section," I said.

"You get me loose, I'll run like a panther," he promised.

I braced my boots against the saddle and shoved at the dead horse while I heaved on Leroy. His leg slipped free. He wiggled his foot to see if it still worked. "You all right?" he asked.

"Never mind about me," I said. "Let's hoof it."

He needed no urging. We lit out for the railroad, both of us running like younger men.

"I feel bad about that horse," Leroy said as we ran.

How many men, running for their lives, would pause to mourn a horse? When I was young most people dealt with animals daily, as commerce or transportation or simply as a source of food, but these modern times are changing all that. The bankers have abandoned their thoroughbreds for Oldsmobile phaetons or Mercer Raceabouts, the farmers are trading their draft animals for tractors, and working men in our burgeoning cities ride to and from work on streetcars driven by electric motors. Only the cowboy works in much the same manner as fifty years before and has the same regard for animals. I don't mean to suggest that Leroy reflected on any of this as he noted Buck's passing. It is just that hearing him voice my own sentiments in those simple words gave rise in me to a strong sense of kinship with the man who ran at my side.

While I was sharing this tender moment with Leroy, he unaware of my feelings and both of us running like chicken thieves to save our skins, I was keeping an eye on Victoria and her friends. The cowboys in the station had seen them and at once set up a fearsome covering fire. As Leroy and I reached the railroad tracks, the little band arrived at the station and ducked inside. The sight made me so happy that I didn't even mind when some eagle-eyed *federales* spied us and bullets began to fly our way once more.

We cleared the tracks and flopped down on the far side of the embankment, both of us panting from our short sprint and me coughing to beat the band from breathing all that smoke and dust. Between spasms I took the opportunity to reload my pistol and shotgun.

"Looks like we picked sides in this fight," Leroy said. "The *federales* aren't going to forget that."

In town the firing was louder than before. It occurred to me that with the *federales* now fighting on two flanks, the Villistas might be holding their own. I was wondering what our next move should be when I noticed that everything around us was glowing. For a moment I thought my eyes were failing me, but Leroy too had noticed the change in the light. To the west, beyond the bench and the river, the desert was turning red as if lit by some enormous fire.

We turned and saw that the sun was rising over the eastern mountains. The clouds that had been moving lazily from west to east covered the whole sky now, save for a thin band of blue above the mountaintops. Into this space the sun rose majestically, silhouetting the jagged peaks of the sierra, casting the rosy light of the new day across the foothills and the broad plateau and down upon the town. It tinged the smoke that drifted past us and bathed everything around us in a radiant glow.

"Listen," said Leroy.

As if in response to the warm light of the sun, the battlefield had fallen silent. From a hundred yards away, we could hear the federal horses snorting and stamping in their pen.

"Look there," I said. There was movement at the edge of the plateau. Horseback figures rose into the blinding disk of the sun, drawing nearer. In the town, several houses were on fire now, and the smoke from these conflagrations mingled with the cloud of dust and gunsmoke that hung over everything. Seen through this nightmarish haze, the riders looked like the vanguard of Lucifer's legions. In the unnatural silence we could hear the rumble of their horses' hooves as they swept over the edge of the plateau and down the slope. Brandishing rifles and pistols they charged through the outlying houses, straight into the rear of the Villista positions.

And then from that region a mighty cheer arose, but it was impossible to tell which side in the battle welcomed the newcomers' arrival. Even as the cheer echoed through the streets, gunfire broke out all along the western edge of town, ending the unplanned cease-fire, and fresh smoke rose into the air.

"If that's more *federales,* we're in big trouble," Leroy said.

"Whoever it is, they've still got a fight on their hands. Maybe they'll let us be for a while." I was trying to look on the bright side.

"No such luck." Leroy pointed to shadowy figures moving toward us through the smoke. There were eight of them, and they were clearly looking for us. Something about the young officer leading the squad was familiar to me.

"I've seen that officer before," I said, trying to get a better look at him. "He was with that bunch that came out of the hacienda. Must be that lieutenant they told us about."

"We'll need a bigger piece of cover," Leroy said.

"That shed oughta do." The stockyards were between us and the railroad station. At the near end of the stock pens there was a long storage shed. It was a good fifty yards away. I let off four shots and scrambled to my feet. Leroy fired twice and then I heard the sound of his boots pounding along the graveled embankment behind me.

We were on the downhill side of the tracks. The embankment was high enough to hide us as we ran, but we would have to expose ourselves to the soldiers' view in order to get to the shed. Judging that surprise was our best advantage, I scrambled up the embankment as soon as we were even with the shed, but as I crossed the tracks I caught a boot heel between two close-set ties. My foot was held as if in a vise, and the *federales* saw us at the same moment. As if I needed more incentive to free myself, a bullet whizzed past my head. Leroy was beside me now, firing at the *federales* and shouting at me to get unstuck. I gave my leg a wrench, ripping the heel clean off my boot, which caused me to fall to one knee, but I was up in a flash and diving behind the corner of the shed with Leroy right behind me as bullets chopped splinters from the boards.

In addition to losing my boot heel, I had skinned my knee and torn my pants leg, but I made no complaint in view of Leroy's more serious wound.

"You shoot, I'm reloading," he said.

I looked around the corner. The smoke in the roadway was thinning. The *federales* made good targets now. I fired once. A soldier screamed and went down. I thumbed back the hammer again, but this time it dropped on an empty chamber.

"Reloading," I said.

Leroy took my place at the corner. "It's all right. They're falling back."

He sat back against the planks, breathing heavily while I plugged new cartridges into my .45.

"You think they'll let us be?" I asked.

"No," he said. "They don't like crossing that open space, but pretty soon that lieutenant will get 'em going again."

"Thanks for being such an optimist."

When I was done reloading my pistol, I had a look at Leroy's arm. The bullet had missed the bone in his upper arm, but he had a nasty flesh wound. I cut the sleeve off his shirt with my Barlow pocketknife and used my silk bandanna to bind the folded sleeve in place over the wound as a makeshift bandage.

"Let's get inside," he said as I tied the knot.

On the side of the shed facing the tracks there were long double doors hung on overhead rails. We heaved on one of the doors and it slid open with a groan.

Shafts of sunlight slanted through the cracks in the shed's east wall, illuminating the gloom of the windowless structure. The shed had a dirt floor and a high peaked roof like an American barn, and it was empty. There was not so much as a stack of hay to shield us from federal bullets.

"Looks like the freighting business has come on hard times," Leroy observed.

We pushed the door shut behind us and moved to the north end of the shed. We peered through the knotholes, which were in plentiful supply, just in time to see the young lieutenant and his soldiers cross the road in a crouching run. Two of the soldiers carried small boxes, while two more were carrying an awkward piece of machinery between them as if it were a man on a stretcher.

Leroy craned about for a better look. "What the hell is that thing?"

When the soldiers reached the tracks they took up positions around a small switchman's shack. Those carrying the strange device crouched over it, working at it feverishly under the lieutenant's orders.

Leroy sat down against the wall and I joined him, glad of a chance to rest for a moment. I wondered how we would get out of the shed alive. From their new position, the squad of *federales* would see us if we tried to escape by the way we had come in, and the doors on the opposite side of the shed faced the street, which was exposed to other federal guns.

"Dammit," said Leroy, as much to himself as to me. "I promised myself I'd never get in another fix like this one."

"You been here before?"

"Something like it. The last time I didn't get shot so early in the game."

"If you got out of that scrape in one piece, you're just the fellow to get us out of this one."

"You do wonders for my confidence, Charlie." He got to his knees and peered out at our *federales,* who were still working over their mysterious contraption.

"What the hell is that thing?" he wondered again. Then a thought struck him. "I hope it's not a Gatling gun."

This prompted me to take a look. "It's too small for a Gatling gun."

"Good. For a minute there I thought we were in trouble."

He sat down against the wall once more, holding his wounded arm with his gun hand. As I dropped back down beside him, a fearful din cut loose from up the tracks and a stream of bullets bored through the planks above our heads, showering us with splinters. We threw ourselves flat on the dirt floor of the shed, wishing there was a deep hole handy. The barrage lasted for only a few seconds, but it seemed like an eternity. When it stopped, three of the planks were cut clean through.

"Holy shit!" Leroy exclaimed.

"I hope you don't use that kind of language around my daughter."

"This is no time to worry about Victoria's morals."

"Meaning it's too late?"

"Dammit, Charlie, we've done nothing to be ashamed of!"

Once more the infernal din began and once more we hugged the ground. A new string of holes danced across the wall at the height of a man's waist.

"What the hell is that thing?" Leroy demanded when the racket stopped.

I took another look, staying low to the ground, and this time I recognized the device. "I saw something like it in a war picture," I said. "I think it's one of those Maxim guns. That and the tank have revolutionized warfare, they say."

Leroy got to his knees and looked through the holes the bullets had drilled in the planks. "If they show up with a tank, I'm going to surrender. Hey, look there."

Thirty yards or more behind the Maxim gun, half a dozen federal soldiers ran across the railroad avenue, jumped the tracks, and took cover behind the embankment, as Leroy and I had done not long before. Moments later, three more men crossed the street and joined their comrades. It appeared that at least some of the *federales* were looking for a way out of town.

"You don't suppose that new bunch was Villistas?" I said.

The lieutenant's soldiers looked over their shoulders as more soldiers ran across the roadway. One man pointed at the fleeing *federales,* but the lieutenant spoke angrily, waving his hand toward our shed. Four soldiers started forward—reluctantly, it seemed—with carbines at the ready. We threw a few shots at them to let them know we were alive and kicking, then ran to the far end of the shed, where we huddled as more bullets raked the full width of the north wall, low down. Most of the missiles embedded themselves in the dirt, but a few ricocheted and struck the planks above our heads.

When the firing stopped, we peered through the cracks in the south wall. The nearest pens were close against the shed, but the *federales'* horses were at the far end of the stockyards, near the station. Between the horse pen and the station was fifty feet of open ground. Across the avenue, the soldiers among the houses were no longer firing at the station, but to their own rear, away from the street.

"They're getting pushed back, all right," Leroy said. "They'll come for their horses soon."

"They get the horses, they still might turn this thing around."

We were not the only ones who reached this conclusion. In the stock pens, Randall Steele emerged from his hiding place and crept cautiously along a fence toward the pen where the federal horses were confined.

"What's he up to?" Leroy wondered.

Randall reached the horses' pen and slipped between the fence rails. He moved stealthily among the animals, doing his best not to alarm them, making for the gate that led to the street. The four horse guards were all on the side of the pen nearest the railroad station. Now and then they threw a shot at our friends' stronghold but mostly they kept their heads down. I saw movement in one of the station windows, a figure in a strange position, and I realized it was a man cranking a moving-picture camera on a tripod.

"That's George!" I said. "He must have seen Randall."

"Or Randall saw him," Leroy said.

George was back a few feet from the window, out of the horse guards' line of sight, but just barely.

Randall was almost at the gate now. "By God, I think he's got a chance," I said under my breath.

"Not if that lieutenant sees what he's up to," Leroy said. He ran to the far end of the shed and emptied his pistol at the soldiers there. The shed was between them and the horse pen, but they would only have to move their Maxim gun a handful of yards to command the entire avenue.

Leroy was reloading as he returned to my side. "They were coming for us again. A couple of them were packing up that damn gun. I sent them looking for cover, but they won't stay down for long."

There were so many holes in the north wall, the *federales* could stick their carbines into the shed and shoot us like fish in a barrel, but I was more concerned for Randall. He was at the gate now. Crouching low, he pushed the gate open as wide as it would go. The rusty hinges squeaked, and gave him away to the horse guards. Three of them climbed up on the fence to get a shot at him over the horses' backs, but the cowboys in the station had been waiting for them to expose themselves. Rifles cracked, and two of the guards dropped from the fence while the third dove to the ground. I made out Buddy Johnston crouching at the same window where George was filming, and Dusty Clark at the window next to theirs. Each of the sharpshooters had a rifle in his hands.

Across the avenue the *federales* saw the horses beginning to trot into the street. *"¡Los gringos están robando nuestros caballos!"* someone cried. The gringos are stealing our horses!

A few shots sounded, and splinters flew from the gatepost as Randall dodged back among the horses, but covering fire erupted at once from the station, driving the soldiers back to cover. This encouraged George to risk moving his camera closer to the window. He resumed cranking at once, in time to capture a brave horse guard jumping onto the fence at the rear of the horse pen. The guard fired at Randall, but Randall whipped out both his pistols with the fast draw that has made him famous. He let off half a dozen shots, and the guard fell.

Randall gave George a grin and a wave before beginning to make his way through the horses. By these actions he confirmed Leroy's guess. The actor was well aware that he was being filmed, and I wondered how much of a hand that knowledge had played in moving him to leave his hiding place and play the hero's role.

A moment later I spied the sole remaining guard creeping along the stockyard fence beside the tracks. He was coming toward our shed, apparently having had his fill of the cowboy sharpshooters in the station. I poked my Peacemaker through a knothole and fired twice, missing the guard on purpose but surprising him mightily. As I had smokeless powder, I had not revealed our position and he had no idea who was shooting at him. Leroy fired once, kicking up dirt at the guard's feet and sending him running off across the tracks even faster than Leroy and I had run to gain the safety of the shed.

By now Randall had made his way to the rear of the pen, where he mounted a sturdy bay mare and began shouting and waving his hat, pushing the horses ahead of him. They needed little urging to find the gate and take to the roadway.

Near panic, the *federales* fired into the air in a futile effort to drive the animals back, but the gunfire only served to frighten the horses and send them running south along the railroad avenue with Randall in their midst, clinging to the bay mare's neck. As he galloped past the station he straightened in the saddle and waved his hat to his friends, grinning jubilantly. Federal bullets chased him, but once Randall and the horses were out of the way, the cowboys resumed their covering fire, forcing the soldiers back into the alleys.

As if on cue, the last sliver of the red sun vanished behind the clouds, the golden glow faded, and as Randall and the horses raced up the street, the light on the scene dimmed to a somber gray.

Chapter 29

"THOSE FEDERAL BOYS are in a fix," Leroy said.

"So are we, in case you forgot," I reminded him. Through the bullet holes in the far end of the shed I could see the soldiers moving toward us.

"Let's get over by the doors," he said. Because the big doors hung on the outside of the shed, the door frame offered some slim shelter. It wasn't much, but we took what we could get. Together we tried to squeeze behind a six-by-six post while we kept watch on the walls of the shed and strained our ears for the sound of soldiers creeping up on our door.

Oddly, the absence of my boot heel bothered me more at this moment than the danger I was in. I was sure I looked foolish hobbling about, and I felt like a cripple.

"We get out of this," I said, "you owe me a pair of boots for the ones I ruined when your mule Ikey left me stranded."

Leroy looked at me as if I was crazy. "After twenty years? I didn't figure you for the sort to hold a grudge that long, Charlie."

"You could have trained that mule to stand still when a man was trying to hunt his supper."

"Hell, I tried, but he was damn near as stubborn as you are. The two of you together must have been quite a pair."

As he spoke these last words we made out the sound of running feet on gravel. We raised our guns, preparing to sell our lives dearly. But instead of attacking our hiding place the federal lieutenant and his men ran past the shed as fast as their legs could carry them, tearing along the tracks, making for the stockyards.

"Where the hell are they going?" Leroy said, as if he suspected some sort of trick.

The running feet kept on until the sound was drowned out by the din of battle, which was growing louder. Judging by the firing from the village, the Villistas were pushing the *federales* steadily toward the railroad.

Leroy pushed the door open and popped his head out, then pulled it back quickly. When no shots came our way we opened the door wider and both looked out. To the north, where the Maxim gun had been, more *federales* were scampering across the tracks in twos and threes, then running along behind the embankment, apparently making for where their train stood waiting to the north of town, beyond the break in the rails. In the other direction, toward the stockyards, we could see no one. The lieutenant and his men had disappeared.

"Where'd they go?" I wondered aloud.

"Come on," said Leroy. We stepped through the door and moved along the side of the shed to the corner nearest the stockyards. Once again he popped his head out. This time a shot slammed into the corner post almost before he could pull it back.

"They're in a bull pen," Leroy said. "That lieutenant's probably setting his gun up to cover the street. He's got men watching his rear too."

I stuck my hat out up high, then peeked out down low, and got a look at the stockyards for myself as a shot poked a hole in my Stetson. One quick look was enough to confirm what Leroy had guessed. The federal officer had seen a chance to help his captain regain the upper hand, and he took it. By setting up his Maxim gun behind the gate of the bull pen he could rake the roadway with deadly fire. Except for the gate, the round pen was made of solid logs, giving the soldiers good protection from all sides but the front, which faced on the street. When the Villistas gained the street the Maxim gun would cut them down like ripe corn, and the *federales* would have a chance to regroup.

Even as I was calculating how the lieutenant's move might change the odds, four Villistas rode down the Avenida Central and out into the railroad avenue. Shots from the bull pen killed one horse and sent all the Villistas running back for cover, but the Maxim gun did not get into the fray, no doubt because it was not yet reassembled and loaded. While the soldiers were occupied with the enemies to their front, Leroy and I looked out to see what was going on, and we saw the Villistas retreat.

"Now what?" I asked.

"We run out there and pray," he said.

"That's the best you can come up with?"

Before he could make some smart reply there were more hoofbeats from the Avenida Central. A larger group of Villistas charged out, this time heading straight for the bull pen. They had seen the *federales* there and thought they could easily overwhelm the small force, but they reckoned without the Maxim gun. It came to life as soon as they appeared and the Villistas went down as if felled by an invisible scythe, horses and men dying in a roar of explosions that drowned out their cries of pain.

"Now," said Leroy. He left the shelter of the shed and sprinted along the ends of the crossties as nimbly as a gandy dancer. I was right behind him, not as surefooted thanks to my missing heel, but I clumped along just as fast. I figured I had a good fifty-yard dash in me, seeing as my life depended on it. For the second time in half an hour I was running into the face of death, wondering if this was the day my name would be called on the roll Up Yonder, but the thought was unaccompanied by any fear. The fever of battle rises quickly in the blood and leads men to do dangerous things.

While their comrades were occupied murdering Villistas, the two *federales* posted to protect the bull pen's rear were on their toes. I had run some distance before I realized they were shooting at us and Leroy was shooting back. The bull pen was on the side of the stockyards farthest from the tracks. The closest we could come to it on our present course was about fifteen yards. I let fly with one barrel of buckshot and the *federales* ducked, and then we jumped off the trackbed and ran close beside the stockyard fence, coming even with the bull pen and moving beyond it, heading for the shelter of a plank chute.

"Reloading," Leroy said as he crouched beside the chute.

I hunkered by his side and replaced the spent shell in my shotgun. Across the street there was increased gunfire among the houses. Obviously the Villistas were attacking the *federales* there from the rear, but with what luck we couldn't tell. From the Avenida Central and the houses to its south, Villistas continued shooting at the bull pen, but whenever they showed themselves the Maxim threw a few pounds of lead their way and they ducked back quick. It seemed that the Villistas held the whole south side of town, but so long as the gun was in operation, the roadway was a deadly no man's land.

When Leroy was done reloading he flexed his gun hand wide, clenched it, stretched it again, then shook his arm, and finally I recognized this mannerism for what it was—a gunman's habit, a way of loosening up his most vital limb before he depended on it for his life.

"Ready," he said as the Maxim commenced another of its ugly coughing fits. Up we jumped, dodging around the loading chute and running along an alley between two large holding pens, coming up on what we hoped was the bull pen's blind side. Although we hadn't discussed it, I understood Leroy's plan. With any luck, the *federales* would figure we had kept on going to join our fellow Americans in the station and wouldn't be expecting us.

There was a cold feeling in my gut now. The pause to reload had given my fear time to raise its ugly little head, but I kept going. One foot ahead of the other. I felt like I was running in deep mud. My heart was pounding and I prayed it would keep on beating. One heartbeat and then the next. That's all I wanted. I was aware of Leroy running beside me, the bull pen, and the Maxim gun. The rest of the world was trifling business.

There was spirited firing from the station now. It ceased as we reached the bull pen, but the fusillade had prevented those within from noticing our approach. When we reached the round structure we did not hesitate. Leroy motioned me to the right while he turned to the left. We would come over the walls on opposite sides of the pen, so those within would have to defend themselves on both flanks. Using the railings of the adjoining pens to climb on, we scrambled up, hoping the suddenness of our appearance would let us get off the first shots.

But Willie Two Horse beat us to it, and he saved our lives. As it turned out, he saw us coming.

Ever since the *federales* took the hacienda and caught him napping, Willie had been looking for an opportunity to recover his lost honor. When the cowboys were forced to take cover in the railroad station, Willie kept his eyes open for his chance, and he saw it. After Randall made off with the horses and the horse guards were disposed of, there were no *federales* between the station and the stockyards. When the Villistas charged the Maxim gun, Willie took advantage of the action to slip out of the station with his Winchester carbine in his hand. Chief John saw him go and didn't try to stop him, knowing that Willie would rather die in battle than live with his shame. But John posted Dusty Clark and Buddy Johnston in the windows overlooking the stockyards to give Willie some cover, and the three of them were responsible for helping make the soldiers in the bull pen keep their heads down.

Chanting his spirit song under his breath, Willie crawled through the railings of one stock pen after another, staying against the fences near the tracks and keeping one eye always on the bull pen. He was in the shelter of its wall, girding himself for his attack, when he saw Leroy and me coming along the alley, and he wasn't about to let us steal his thunder. As we came pounding up on the rear of the pen, he ran around and came at the *federales* from the front, stepping right out in front of the gate.

The last thing the Maxim gunner saw was a squat, gray-haired Indian throwing down on him with a Winchester carbine, and then Willie shot the gunner through the heart. The two-hundred-grain bullet threw the

soldier flat on his back, deader than the dirt he lay on. The shot startled
the other *federales*, but one soldier jumped for the Maxim as soon as he
saw his comrade fall. His hand was already on the trigger when Willie shot
him, but he managed to squeeze it anyway. The Maxim roared. The
soldier fell on top of the gun, swinging the barrel from left to right across
the gate, and Willie went down.

I gave a Comanche yell as I cleared the top of the bull pen wall, hoping
to startle the defenders, but my shout was just one more sound in the
cacophony of cries and gunfire prompted by Willie's attack. Willie shot
the second gunner just as we appeared. We saw him die and we saw Willie
fall. The Maxim kept shooting for several seconds, gouging splinters from
the logs as the dead soldier's hand clenched the trigger. When he finally
rolled off the gun he pulled it around and cut another soldier nearly in half
just as the Maxim ran out of cartridges.

The remaining *federales* were not idle. Even before the Maxim fell silent the young lieutenant shot at me, taking the fuzz off my left ear and
putting a second bullet hole in my Stetson. I fired one barrel of the shotgun, shifted it a hair and fired the other. Then there were just three
federales standing and I was reaching for my pistol.

Maybe the memory of killing Ortega made Leroy hesitate. Or maybe
he just figured Willie and I had everything under control. But when
he saw Willie down and me drop my shotgun, he didn't wait any longer.
He emptied his gun at the remaining soldiers, and his handful of shots
sounded like one. I have seen two or three men shoot faster, Clay Allison
for one, but he was a cold-blooded killer, not an amiable cowboy bandit.

Leroy looked around like a man in a trance, his six-shooter scanning
the scene, searching for any remaining danger. Finding none, he tucked it
back in his belt.

We looked at each other, but found nothing to say. We had fought
together and lived through it. That said it all.

Within the town the gunfire was still spirited, but the railroad avenue
was empty and quiet. Any *federales* who saw the fight for the bull pen had
no doubt lost their nerve and skedaddled, making their way through town
on foot as most of their *compadres* were apparently doing, heading for
their train. Judging by the steady stream of soldiers running along the
tracks from the north end of town, the federal retreat was becoming a
rout.

I became aware of shouting behind me and turned to see our cowboy
friends pouring out of the station, Victoria and Karen among them.

Leroy swung over the wall and dropped into the bull pen. The lieutenant and his seven men looked strangely peaceful where they lay, but
Leroy wasn't concerned for them. He made for the gate, and then I remembered Willie.

Willie lay on his side in the street, his shirt soaked with blood. When we rolled him on his back, he opened his eyes.

"You fellas all right?" he inquired.

We both nodded.

He smiled like that was the best news he'd had in some time. "That's good." His eyes closed again.

Leroy felt Willie's wrist for a pulse and found one. "He's a tough old bird."

The crowd from the station arrived. As Victoria knelt by Willie's side she gave me and Leroy a quick look to see if we were all right.

Brian was there, he and George having followed the charging cowboys in the Model T, not wanting to miss out on the excitement and never dreaming they were running into a real war.

"How is he?" Brian wanted to know, but when I told him Willie was hurt bad he shook his head and pointed to his ears. "I can't hear a thing. All that gunfire." He was deaf as a stump.

"You're not going to believe the film I got," George said to me as he arrived with his tripod in his arms, but his usual exuberance was missing as he looked down at Willie, who was being tended by Victoria and Karen.

"You and Nate get a car or wagon to carry Willie in," Victoria told Red-eye Hawk. "We've got to get him to the hacienda."

"Fetch that Model T from the station," Jack Whistler said.

Victoria opened Willie's shirt and began to examine his wounds, accepting the half-dozen bandannas that were offered her by the cowboys. Chief John knelt beside her, coughing from the smoke and dust.

George set up his tripod to one side of the gathering and was looking around for something to film when there came a rumble of hooves from the Avenida Central. A band of Villistas burst from the street and turned along the railroad avenue toward the retreating *federales*. I was astonished to see that it was Pancho Villa himself in the vanguard, his head wrapped in a bloody bandage. As he and his men swept past, Villa gave us a wave and a smile, and I had the peculiar impression that the smile was directed at Victoria. It seemed he harbored no grudge for the wound she had dealt him.

Villa's presence explained the great cheer that the revolutionists had raised when they saw the demonic riders enter the fray at sunrise. With their leader in command once more, they were invincible, even though outnumbered. Now, when the few *federales* who were still holding their ground at the north end of town found themselves faced with Pancho Villa and his cavalry, most ran, some fought back, and some died.

Naturally, George did not miss this chance to capture Villa in action. He followed them with his camera, and when the riders grew small in the distance George turned the camera toward the bodies in the bull pen, cranking all the while, as Nate and Redeye sputtered up in the Model T. The car had been wounded in the battle. Its windshield was shattered and there were bullet holes in one of the doors.

Leroy and I stepped out of the way as the cowboys moved to pick Willie up. Leroy was holding his wounded arm.

"You ever been shot before?" I asked him.

He nodded. "Once. In Bolivia. It hurt a lot worse than this."

"Sometimes it hurts right off, sometimes later. It'll likely bother you a good deal tomorrow."

"You're no end of encouragement, Charlie."

I myself took a large caliber bullet in the knee when I was a mere lad of nineteen, a rancher of my acquaintance having sent a Negro gunman after me because he believed I was scorching his mavericks with my own brand. A gunshot in the knee hurts both now and later, more than any other wound I ever had.

Around us the town was coming to life. Several clouds of smoke showed where houses were still on fire. With so much powder being burned, it was a wonder the whole community did not go up in flames. The men of Delgado had shown great bravery in trying to bring these conflagrations under control, running hither and yon with buckets of water while the fighting continued around them. Now there were women in the streets too, and everyone was talking. Shouting was more like it. Somewhere a woman was crying, and the dogs were back. Where they hid, I can't imagine. They were running every which way, all barking at once, as if they had stored up a morning's allotment of barks while hiding from the fighting and just had to get them out before they burst.

Overhead, clouds covered the whole sky and the wind had picked up. It was a gray winter's day, cool but not cold. Up the road, people were running down from the hacienda on foot, Katie Elderberg and Dottie Thompson and Gerald Ball in the lead.

A loud *bang* came from behind us. The cowboys had Willie in the Model T, and at first I thought the car had backfired, but then I saw George Bleumel. There was an expression of great surprise on his face as he looked down at a red spot on his chest. He toppled sideways, knocking over his camera as he fell. His porkpie hat hit the ground and rolled on its brim, finally coming to a stop ten feet away.

"George!" Brian screamed.

In the bull pen the lieutenant was up on one elbow. His hand held a smoking gun that was swinging in my direction.

My own hands were empty. Before I could think about reaching for my Peacemaker, Leroy's gun was already out. But the hammer fell on a spent cartridge. He hadn't reloaded.

The lieutenant's automatic was pointing at us by the time I belatedly grabbed my pistol. Leroy ducked down as if to get out of the line of fire and at that moment the lieutenant's gun went off. I felt something hit my forearm like the glancing kick of a mule. It spun me around and I fell, dropping my six-shooter. Even as I went through these gyrations I noticed that Leroy's hands were clawing at his boot. I couldn't make any sense of his actions until I saw one hand come up holding his derringer.

Pop! went the little Remington, twice: *Pop! pop!* And down went the lieutenant for the last time.

Chapter 30

THE BATTLE FOR Delgado may find no place in the history books. It was small potatoes compared to the bloody slaughters of the late war, and the Mexican revolution offered more glorious victories for Pancho Villa. But for those who died in Delgado on the second day of January, 1920, the result was just as final.

We buried George Bleumel in the town cemetery. The services were held the morning after the battle. The day was as gray and cool as the one before, and there were a few drops of rain at dawn, just enough to settle the dust.

Others were buried that morning. Besides Colonel Ortega, there were eight dead Villistas and fifteen *federales,* including their captain. With the captain dead and his lieutenant pursuing Leroy and me, the *federales* were leaderless, which explained why they had lost heart so thoroughly when Villa showed up.

Three townspeople had died as well. One of the caskets was very small. A child had run into a cross fire.

The priest prayed over George in Latin and Spanish and I found myself making the sign of the Cross and murmuring the prayers along with him, my Catholicism reborn, for the moment, as I contemplated the Lord's mysterious ways. Like many a pioneer of earlier generations, George Bleumel willingly faced great dangers to follow his dream. In middle life, it seemed he had survived them. Then, having spent years on far-flung battlefields and lived to tell about it, he came to Mexico to film a make-believe battle and died in a real one. He tempted Fate, perhaps, and in the end she got even.

Victoria stood between Leroy and me during the service, clutching our hands in her own. These were our sound arms, Leroy being wounded in the left arm and I in the right one. Both of us wore slings. My wound pained me some, but far less than a bullet in the knee.

Like Brian Hill, who stood beside us, Victoria's cheeks were wet with tears, and from time to time her breath came in short sobs during the burial. She felt that she was partly to blame for George's fate, reasoning that if she and Karen had not left the hacienda to come help Leroy and me, the rest might have stayed there as well and George would be alive and with us still. I told her, and Brian told her, and Leroy and everyone else told her, that she was not to blame. I pointed out that if she hadn't run out there, Leroy and I and Willie might not have been nearby when the Maxim gun came into play and maybe the *federales* would have slaughtered the Villistas. Maybe they would have cut down us *gringos* too, just for good measure, I said, and this notion reassured her somewhat. What's done is done, I told her, and there's no one to blame. Either that, or we were all guilty. In the heat of the moment we all did what we thought was right, George included.

Brian was grieving as much as Victoria, worse maybe, because he didn't have the chance to think how he might have prevented George's death. One minute his friend was there, the next he was gone, while Brian stood by watching. Brian had never seen a dead person before, let alone a friend killed before his eyes. It helped him to comfort Victoria, and I think it was comforting him that got her through the worst moments.

Randall told us that if he had not seen George filming from the station window, he never would have had the nerve to turn the *federales'* horses loose. Like a true gentleman, Randall tried to give George all the credit. He shrugged off the congratulations we heaped on him when the battle was over, but Randall Steele was the man of the hour. Not only had he left the *federales* afoot and thus insured the Villistas' victory, it was he who inspired the cowboys to charge out of the hacienda in the first place. When they found that Victoria and Karen were missing, they held a council of war in the big hall. Chief John reminded them that Leroy had said to stay where they were and be ready to let us in when we came back. That's when Randall stepped into the middle of the crowd and took off his hat. "Boys," he said. "You all know how I feel about Victoria. I can't ask you to come with me, but I'm going after her."

As it happened, this was exactly what Tom said to his pards after Evangelina was kidnapped in *The Trail of Pancho Villa*, but there in the hacienda Randall meant every word he said and the boys knew it. As he started for the door, Charlie Noble went with him, ready to play the faithful sidekick for real, and that was all Willie Two Horse needed. "I'm goin' too," he announced. After that there was no holding the rest back.

Randall did not tell this story, but it was volunteered readily enough by the others. And they gloried in recounting what happened when Bob Elderberg and Tommy Fear found Randall up on the plateau after the battle, still guarding the *federales'* horses. When they relieved him, Randall finally thought to reload his pistols. "Hey, those are blanks," Tommy observed. Randall looked down, saw that cartridges in his hand were indeed blanks, and he fainted dead away. He had never made the distinction between loading up for a scene in a picture and loading up for real. Maybe imagining the whole battle as playacting was all that enabled him to do what he did, but knowing he had faced the federal guns unarmed made his feat all the more extraordinary.

Later, it occurred to him to wonder why the horse guard he shot had fallen down, and he learned that it was Dusty Clark who had picked off the unlucky soldier while Randall blazed away with his six-shooters.

Celebrating Randall's heroics did much to help us bear our grief over losing George. Even as we stood there in the graveyard, first one person and then another would glance at Randall and sometimes they would smile, taking pride in the knowledge that our movie star was a real live hero.

Villa's cavalry sat their horses in a line facing the burying ground. When the priest was done praying over Colonel Ortega and the rest of their fallen comrades, they fired a ragged volley into the air.

As we filed from the graveyard General Villa took Victoria by the arm. He drew her aside and walked with her apart from the rest of us, his head bowed, talking earnestly. This sight brought murmurs of approval from his soldiers. For the Villistas, Victoria was a true heroine. They had heard how she fought the *federales* to help Leroy and me when we were pinned down in the street, and they saw that Villa himself wished her no harm, although she had knocked him senseless. He had regained consciousness not long after Victoria escaped from his camp, and when he learned that Ortega was pursuing her he gathered his remaining men and set off after Ortega to prevent him from harming her, which is how he happened to enter the battle at the crucial moment. As he saw it, Victoria was responsible for his victory, and he had commanded the Villista balladeer, who was in mourning for his *soldadera* girlfriend, to compose a *corrido* honoring both her and the *soldadera yanqui*.

Villa and Victoria walked and talked for some time. As they rejoined us at last, Villa took something small from his pocket and slipped it into her hand. Whatever it was, she tucked it away in a pocket of her own before taking Leroy's arm.

"I'm sorry about Ortega," Leroy said. "He was a good soldier."

"It is best this way," said Villa. "He would never have agreed to surrender."

"Surrender?" Leroy's surprise was apparent.

"Carranza will not last long," Villa said. "Someone will kill him like the dog that he is. Then I will make peace with the government."

"What about the revolution?" Leroy asked.

"When you and Harry were by my side, the revolution was a joyful thing. Now—" He shrugged. "Seeing you, I felt young again. But I am alone. It is too much for one man. I am the revolution, and I am tired. To sleep for just one night without thinking of the revolution, that would be heaven."

He closed his eyes for a moment as if he might take a nap right there on the spot. Then he looked at Leroy again. He seemed older now, a man weary of war.

"My army has killed more than forty thousand of my people," he said. "They were *my people*. Who knows how many more have died?" He shook his head. "It is time for the killing to end. Soon the *federales* will forget about this." He waved a hand at the graves and the town, indicating the battle and its aftermath. "That is why I did not kill them all, so they would forget sooner."

Villa's mercy toward the fleeing *federales* had been a puzzle to us all. He could easily have wiped them out, but instead he and his men chased the surviving soldiers to their train, herding them along like cattle, and let them escape. He even turned loose the four guards we had taken captive at the hacienda, providing them with horses and sending them on their way. Two of the four were so grateful that they joined the revolutionists on the spot.

Now I understood Villa's purpose in sparing his enemies. He didn't add that if he had wiped out a company of federal cavalry, the government might have retaliated by burning the town of Delgado and killing all its inhabitants, but I was sure that too was part of his reason.

"We'll both go with you if you need us," Victoria told Villa, and my heart skipped a beat.

"You see how brave this woman is?" Villa said to Leroy. "When she came to me in the night I thought she loved me. I asked her to marry me, but she refused. She almost broke my head."

He smiled fleetingly, and his eyes moved to Victoria. "I have won the battle but I am losing the war. Go home and love this man while you can."

The revolutionists were in high spirits as they set out. They were exhilarated by their victory. They had horses, guns and gold. They even had two new women, *delgadeñas* who had fallen under the spell of young Villistas. Pancho had not yet told his men that the revolution was over. He would tell them when he had struck his deal with whatever government followed Carranza, and it would have to be one he could trust to honor a guarantee of amnesty for his men as well as himself.

Brian Hill filmed the departure of Villa's ragtag army. "George wouldn't have missed this shot," he said to no one in particular.

As the column grew smaller in the distance, Villa drew his horse aside and gave us a parting wave.

WE LEFT DELGADO an hour after the Villistas. Just as Gerald had demanded two days earlier, we would travel home to the States by wagon. When Victoria and Rosa and Gerald made their farewells to the Delgados and their household, the parting grew so emotional it seemed it might never end. Gerald stood apart from the tears and embracing, embarrassed by all the Latin sentiment.

We had no choice about staying or going. We had sided with Pancho Villa against the *federales*. If more *federales* showed up, as they were bound to do when word of the fight got out, they would make short work of any *gringo* adventurers they found loitering about. And no one had the heart for trying to finish the movie within sight of our fallen comrade's grave.

Finally Chief John stepped up to Leroy. "We're ready to pull out any time you say."

It was like that from the start of the journey, everyone looking to Leroy to tell them what to do.

In a short time the order of march was laid out just as if we had all traveled by wagon train many times before. Buddy Johnston rode with Redeye in advance of the wagons, his Springfield rifle held across his saddle the way the old mountain men used to ride, ready for whatever might come. Jack Whistler and Bob Elderberg kept the wagons together and kept them moving. Chief John posted scouts around the wagons in a protective ring. If the horsemen of War and Death should ride nearby, we would not be caught unawares again. So long as we were in Mexico we would regard any armed men as hostile, whether they were *federales* or *rurales,* or others less blessed by government sanction.

Every few hours John or Jack or one of the others would find Leroy and let him know that everything was going all right. He never acted like a boss, never gave what you could call an order, but he was the one who knew where everyone was and what they were doing. He looked to me for advice and spoke with me often, giving me every chance to get my two cents in. He made it plain that I was his partner now, just as I had been when we faced the federal guns together, but there was no doubt who was really running the show.

I felt no resentment, for I understood far better than the others why he was so at home in the role and I was not. Throughout my detective career I had sometimes worked with a partner, but more often acted alone. I kept my thoughts and plans to myself while putting up a false front for the rest of the world to see. If things got too hot, I could cut my suspenders and go straight up, leaving my outlaw friends to wonder what had become of me. I had more than my share of natural talents for surviving dangerous predicaments, but I was not a leader and Leroy was. He had an uncanny way of binding those around him into a group, arousing in them the willingness to do anything in the world for him simply because he asked it.

Of course the easy way he ran our traveling western show did not sit well with Gerald Ball. For a full day after we left Delgado, Gerald was as quiet as a mouse, but the next morning he was up to his old tricks. He descended from the wagon where he and Rosa slept, shaved himself, and set about issuing orders as if there had been no Villa, no battle, no moment in the past week when he was not fully in charge.

The men and women of the company looked at him as if he had gone mad.

"Here, Brian," he said as Brian chanced to pass him by. "I want you to see that—"

"Sorry, Gerald," Brian said without slowing down. "I've got to find Bob Elderberg for Leroy."

With no luck in that quarter, Gerald stepped up to me. "Good morning, Charles. If you'll come along with me, you can—"

"Shut up, Gerald," I said without raising my voice.

He shut up.

"That's better," I told him. "The next time you open your face to give an order, I'll tie you up and stuff a gag in your mouth."

Despite my harsh tone, Gerald seemed almost relieved, for these were the first words anyone had spoken to him since the battle. His attempt to betray Villa to the *federales* had come to naught, or we might have meted out a harsher punishment. Then, too, the fact that he distracted the federal captain from beating Rafael Delgado further weighed in Gerald's favor. But he had volunteered more than he had to about Villa's whereabouts, and denying him any acknowledgment of his presence for a day or two was our way of slapping him on the wrist.

"Gerald!" Rosa called him from the wagon. "Come over here and stop bothering Charles."

After that, Gerald gave us no trouble, and gradually he was readmitted to the company, albeit at the bottom of the totem pole, so to speak.

For the first part of our journey, the memory of George's death hung over the caravan like a shroud. Chief John sang his songs of power softly under his breath, mourning a brave man's passing in his own way. The white folks, having no such custom, were very quiet. Perhaps like Randall some of the others had forgotten themselves in the excitement of battle and imagined that it was only make-believe, but George's death and the graveside services for the victims of war had brought the grim reality home to them.

In the midst of all this mourning, there were a few bright spots. The Indian songs that came from Willie Two Horse's wagon, where he lay swathed in bandages, carried a note of victory. A red man's sense of honor is a powerful thing, and Willie had regained his honor in spades. He had redeemed himself for letting the *federales* sneak up on the hacienda without a peep of warning, and the knowledge brought him joy.

Karen Valdez and Nate Dicenzo were another ray of sunshine, cheering everyone who caught them casting sheep's eyes at each other. In the midst of the battle, Nate had proposed marriage to Karen and she had accepted. It happened after the two of them, along with Victoria and Redeye and Gene Ortiz, made their mad charge along the railroad avenue, giving me and Leroy time to get out from behind poor Buck's dead body and off the street. Once they were safely in the station, Nate had said to Karen, "Okay, you win." "Win what?" Karen asked. "If we get out of this in one piece, you pick the day and I'll say 'I do,'" Nate replied. By the look of them now, riding side by side all day long, it would be quite a while before we had to put up with any more lovers' spats.

Leroy was happy too. I don't mean to suggest he didn't grieve for George as much as the others. He spoke softly to one and all and went out of his way to console Brian. The lad's hearing was gradually returning, but he was still bowed down with grief over the loss of George. Leroy had a word with Chief John on our first day of travel, and that night Brian was put in charge of the guards. Leroy used him as an intermediary when he wanted to pass along some suggestion to members of the crew, and within a few days Brian was more like himself, although he would never again be the young innocent he was when we set out for Mexico.

Gradually Leroy broadened his healing efforts to include the whole caravan. He would ride on one wagon, chatting with the driver, then move to another, then climb aboard Sunny and ride up and down the length of the little train whistling softly to himself, stopping to say a few words here and there. In the midst of a general sorrow, he was a calming presence. His agreeable nature did much to perk up those who were feeling low, and underneath it all he was full of life.

The reason was obvious to me. He was Butch Cassidy again. He had found a band of comrades who accepted him readily among them. In a crisis, they had looked to him for leadership. He knew he still had what it took when the chips were down.

On top of that, he had the love of a rare woman and the silent approval of her father, who had put aside his misgivings about their union. On the night after the battle, Victoria had abandoned her bed in the hacienda to join Leroy where he slept in his wagon. She had stopped in the doorway of my room with her blankets in her arms. I knew where she was going, but I didn't lift a finger to stop her. Things had gone too far for that, and as one who had loved unconventionally for so many years, I could hardly forbid my daughter to do the same.

Once on the trail for the border, she and Leroy laid out their bedrolls together, apart from the wagons, and I could not ignore the fact that Victoria was happier than I had ever seen her before. She shared Leroy's high spirits. She knew he had come to Mexico intending to remain there, and that she was partly responsible for changing his mind. Whether she understood the rest of it, I was not certain, but I think she suspected the truth: He had come to Mexico to die. He was going home to live.

Around our campfires at night, Leroy led the older men—Jack Whistler and Bob Elderberg and me, along with Chief John and the other Indians—into remembering stories from our younger days. Like most men who have known danger in their lives, we recalled the happy times and retold jokes and pranks we had pulled to bedevil our comrades. Our laughter drew the others like a magnet. When we ran out of stories, the guitars appeared and often Victoria would be called on to sing. Before long everyone was joining in the talk and the songs, rediscovering the delight of being alive. The lesson of death's sudden and irrevocable nature would stay with each and every one, but Leroy helped us through the mourning period by reminding us of the comfort there is to be had in friendship shared.

As spirits improved, the journey became something of a lark for many of the company. We were a band of pioneers moving through an unfamiliar land, although we were returning to our mother country, not seeking a new one. The young cowboys and Indians who had joined the wild west outfit to recapture the life of frontier days in make-believe now found themselves living it for real. Unlike the battle, this experience was a pleasure, and an education too. They learned how to tend the stock in rope corrals at night and how to get a wagon train under way in the morning while they were half-asleep. They became acquainted with the delights of sleeping under the stars. For me, it was both a return to my youth and a taste of life from an even earlier period on the western plains, and I enjoyed myself thoroughly once I recovered from all my exertions during the battle.

For the first week, we scarcely saw a living soul. While the moon was full we traveled a good deal at night, especially when we were near the towns along the railroad. We kept our distance, skirting around them in the dark, and no one challenged us. When the waning moon rose later, we stopped early in the evening to graze the stock and allow the people to rest, resuming our march after the moon was up. Each time we got under way, Leroy would ride back down our trail to be sure we were not followed. When he slept, he placed his bedroll so his back was to a cutbank or a large rock so he could not be taken by surprise. These were outlaw habits that I knew well, for I had adopted them myself in my detective days. But save for the occasional vaquero or shepherd tending his four-footed charges, we had the country to ourselves.

Even with the long hours of march, we made only fifteen miles or so on a good day, less on the hard ones. It was rugged country, although it grew gentler as we neared the border.

There is not much to do but talk while wagons and beasts and people are plodding along. From the start, Leroy and I would fall in beside each other and ride a while, when one or both of us weren't seeing that all was well up and down the train, and Victoria was often with us. She did her share of the work, of course. She helped Anna tend Willie Two Horse, and she helped with the cooking and the scouting too, but she was rarely long from Leroy's side.

I already knew I would want to write down this story some day, so when he and I were alone, I asked him to recall various incidents from recent weeks, to get his version of the facts. At other times, we recalled further episodes from the old days as a way of passing the time. But while Leroy spoke openly about his past, he said not a word about his future. If he and Victoria discussed such matters at night, in the privacy of their bedrolls, they said nothing about it to me. On our seventh day from Delgado, I approached the matter in a roundabout way as the two of us ranged together out in front of the wagons.

"You figure you'll need a room for a while when we get back?" I asked him.

He gave a little shrug. "No idea, Charlie. None at all."

Those words, accompanied by his gesture, the expression on his face and the tone of his voice, spoke volumes. We were out of touch with the world, moving between the end of our Mexican sojourn and whatever lay before us. When we got back to California, we would pick up our lives and go on as best we could. Until then, we were living outside of ordinary time.

Victoria was riding in front with the scouts, but shortly after this brief exchange, she stopped beside the trail and waited for us to overtake her, falling in beside us when we reached her. While she conveyed to Leroy the outriders' reports on the country ahead, I kept to myself the fact that I was just as concerned about my own future as Leroy's. The picture was not finished, and the allotted month was over. No one had said a word about it, not Victoria, not Brian, not even Gerald. But I had seen Gerald look in my direction from time to time. Although his expression revealed no emotion, I imagined that he was smiling inside, happy to know that he would get back at me for opposing him down in Delgado and again on our wagon trek. Had I known of Victoria and Brian risking their salaries, I would not have thought it would make any difference to the fate of the Bunk House. All I knew for certain was that I would lose my place, and with each day I became firmer in my resolve that I would not stay on to manage it for that upstart British pipsqueak. As for what I might do instead, I had wrestled with that question more than once since leaving Delgado, and I got no closer to an answer today than I had on those previous occasions.

To put my cares aside, I turned to Leroy. "I've got one for you," I said. "Is it true you liked to put on shooting exhibitions for policemen?"

He knew at once which policemen I had in mind, and he grinned at the memory. "Those Argentines got quite a surprise."

Victoria was waiting for one of us to let her in on the secret. She had missed my storytelling on Christmas Eve, so I explained how Butch Cassidy and the Sundance Kid and Etta Place had led a peaceful life as stock raisers in rural Argentina until a former Wyoming lawman put the local constables onto them.

"The first thing we know, there's a squad of frontier police at our door," Leroy picked up the story. "*Buenos días,* says Etta. She spoke the best Spanish, and she hoped they'd think she was something besides an American. But they knew who we were, all right. They were very polite. Asked us to go into town with them until our identities could be investigated. So Sundance and I told them to stand back, and we did a little shooting for them. We threw rocks in the air and shot them. We walked stones across the yard. Sundance even shot his initials in the side of our barn. The policemen remembered some pressing business in other parts, but there was no way we could stay there after that."

He had grown sober in the telling. "They won't let you go straight, Charlie. Not if they know who you are and where to find you. There's always someone who'll put the law on you."

We rode in silence for a few moments, but then he brightened. "Well, at least we got some fun out of it. You should have seen their faces when Sundance shot his initials in the barn. *Adiós, señores,* they said. *Muchas gracias.*"

"What's that dust?" Victoria pointed to a low haze rising from the country dead ahead. That brought us back to the present in a hurry. The day was calm, with no wind to raise such a cloud. In minutes we had the wagons stopped and drawn up in a square, with armed men posted all around, even before Redeye came galloping back to report.

"It's a bunch of cattle," he said. "Maybe fifteen hundred. Just a dozen or so vaqueros."

Leroy and I accompanied Redeye up to the herd.

"*Buenos días, señores,*" said the head vaquero. You could see he was surprised to run into our outfit, but he never let on. He and his compadres hailed from just south of Agua Prieta. There were *muchos federales* in that region, he said. The soldiers were preparing to move south in force, having heard that Pancho Villa was raiding into Sonora.

Up to that point we had been shadowing the railroad line, but after we ran onto those vaqueros and their bovine charges we turned toward the west across the open grassland and made for a deserted stretch of border. That night Leroy increased the number of night guards, and the next day he sent the scouts farther ahead of the wagons.

We reached the border on the tenth of January. There was no line drawn through the chaparral, of course. The Arizona border is not like Texas, where the Rio Grande marks the boundary. We did not know for certain when we left Mexico behind, but we were fairly sure we were on American soil when we saw four riders approaching at a good clip. Once again we drew in the scouts and made ready to receive visitors, although there was no need to box the wagons for just four men.

The riders were American border guards. They reined in when they reached the lead wagon and looked at us as if we must be a mirage or hallucination. A wagon train? Indian scouts? Homer, the heat's got to me at last.

Finally one of them cleared his throat and said, "I guess you'd have to be Americans."

Chief John nodded.

"Got anything to declare?"

John shook his head.

"We'll have to search the wagons."

That's when Gerald stepped in. Or rode in, since he was on horseback. Since our little tête-à-tête, he had been Mr. Wells's invisible man. He would lend a hand to push a wagon that was stuck in the sand, and once he had volunteered to stand a watch at night, but he never tried to tell another soul what to do and he rarely spoke unless you spoke to him first.

Sometime that morning he had cleaned himself up, perhaps in anticipation of such an encounter. When he rode forward to greet the guards he looked like a British lord on holiday, somewhat embarrassed to be found in the company of the rough-and-ready Americans who surrounded him. The dust was knocked off his jodhpurs and his boots were gleaming.

"Officer," he said to the man who had spoken, "I am Sir Gerald Ball. This is my motion picture company. We would appreciate it very much if you would let us proceed without delay. We buried one man in Mexico, and the rest of us are lucky to get out with our lives. We are all American citizens and most anxious to get home to Los Angeles."

The four guards chewed over this mouthful in silence, looking at each other, back at Gerald, once more at Leroy and myself and Chief John and Redeye, where we sat our horses. Redeye had found a dead hawk a few days before. He had plucked the wing and tail feathers and now had one long feather stuck in the cotton bandanna he had tied around his head. If he had been indistinguishable from the rest of the cowboys when we entered Mexico, he was pure three-quarter now.

"You run into trouble down there?" a second guard asked, unnecessarily, I thought.

"Had a little set-to with Pancho Villa," Redeye said without changing his expression, which was none at all.

The guards' eyes widened.

"We taught him a lesson too," Randall put in. He was on the seat of the lead wagon, the reins in his hands, looking as if he had been driving wagons all his life.

The second guard looked at the wagon driver closely. "Say, you're Randall Steele!"

Randall gave his famous smile and nodded toward the dusty cowgirl seated beside him. "May I present Miss Victoria Hartford, better known as Cimarron Rose?"

"Holy smoke!" the first guard said. "I'm sure proud to meet you Miss Hartford."

After that it was old home week. Nothing would do but that the border guards should become personally acquainted with everyone in the caravan and hear of our hairsbreadth escape from the clutches of the dastardly Villa. We did pretty well at keeping our story straight, supporting Redeye's claim that we had fought Villa, this being far simpler than explaining why we had helped him whip a company of *federales*. We made it up as we went along, everyone putting in their own part in the heroics as the spirit moved them, and about the time we began to contradict ourselves, Gerald pointed out that we should be moving along if we ever hoped to get back to Los Angeles.

The guards fell all over themselves being helpful, telling us of a spur railroad line that would save us a day of wagon travel and promising that they would telephone the railroad to expect us. Gerald accepted this assistance as if it were no more than his due, tipped his hat to the border guards, and rode up and down the line ordering the folks back into the wagons. In no time, the train was rolling again.

I looked at Leroy and he looked at me. "It's his outfit," he said. He was smiling, and I couldn't help smiling too. We turned our horses around and fell in behind the last wagon, riding drag, two old cowboys eating dust together as if we had done it for years.

You see, unlike Gerald, Leroy had no need to be in charge of things all the time. Down in Delgado he had gathered the crew around him for the pleasure of the companionship they shared, and to see if he still had the knack. By chance, a man with his abilities was needed, and so he took charge. Once we were back in the States, Gerald's abilities would do to get us home.

FROM THEN ON Gerald rode out in front of the wagons. He asked Chief John to pick the camping place that night, and when we reached the railroad spur on the following day he oversaw the loading of the half-dozen flatcars and boxcars that were waiting to receive us, and the joining of our cars with a whistle-stop passenger train that took the remainder of the day and half the night to deliver us to Los Angeles.

Boarding the train and seeing the other passengers in their modern clothes was a shock to all of us. Down in Sonora we had been transported to an earlier time, but this yanked us back to the present. Even the youngsters in our outfit found the jolt a bit much to take all at once, and for the most part we kept to our own cars. During the afternoon, while the others lounged on the flatcars or rode in the wagons, Leroy and Victoria and I watched the passing countryside from atop one of the livestock cars. We sat at the front of the car with our legs dangling over the edge, enjoying the wind in our faces. Before long Nate and Karen joined us there for some leisurely "car dancing," as Nate called it, this activity being his favorite pastime during the wild west show's travels by rail. To music only he and Karen could hear, they waltzed along the top of the car as the train made its leisurely way across the desert.

Leroy had been uncommonly quiet all day. I suspected he might be regretting his decision to let Gerald resume command of the outfit, but I was soon disabused of this trifling thought.

"Cat got your tongue?" Victoria said after a long silence.

When Leroy answered, he spoke to me. "You were one cool son of a bitch back there."

I knew he was thinking of the battle. "Me? I was quaking in my boots. I thought you were the cool one."

We rolled past half a mile of desert.

"I never killed a man before, Charlie," he said, unconsciously flexing his gun hand.

I remembered him in action, so quick you couldn't follow it with the eye, the movements smooth and sure, instilled by a lifetime of practice, all in the expectation that one day it would come down to kill or be killed. I remembered the look of the men who had fallen to his gun, and mine.

"Neither did I," I said.

I was feeling what he was feeling, wondering why it ever had to come down to taking another man's life and knowing there was no good answer. I pondered the twist of fate that had allowed the two of us to go so long without killing, although we had lived among killers and seen other men cut down in their prime. Through it all we had honed a skill with firearms we hoped never to use for real, and now fate had brought us together and made murderers of us on the same day.

I became aware that Victoria was holding my hand, and Leroy's, binding the two of us together, helping to soothe the troubles we were feeling.

Leroy got to his feet. "You know what I didn't like about it most?" he said as he helped Victoria up.

I nodded. "A man could get used to it."

Leroy took Victoria in his arms and twirled off with her, moving along the roof of the car to join Nate and Karen.

I stayed where I was, the warmth of the afternoon sun pleasant on my face, while behind me the two couples danced away the miles. On either side of the train, the joshua trees raised their arms in astonishment at such a sight.

Chapter 31

WE RETURNED TO a world that was like something out of a fairy tale. While we were still beset by thoughts of life and death, the people of Los Angeles were enjoying the sunshine and fretting about such matters as Harry Carey's divorce, and whether or not Harvard's victory over Oregon on New Year's Day in Pasadena had nevertheless been a moral triumph for western football.

In the midst of such frivolity we were voyagers from a distant land, and so we did the only thing we felt up to: we got back to work. Within three days of returning to Hollywood we had filmed everything that was needed to make our picture story whole. In the evenings Brian edited the scenes into their proper order as soon as the film was back from the laboratory. When the filming was done he worked around the clock to show us a rough cut before the cast party, which was to be held on Friday the 16th of January, in the final hours before Prohibition seized the nation in its desiccating grip.

At Friday noon we gathered in a projection room Brian had borrowed from Jesse Lasky, and for the next hour and a half we were spellbound. The picture was a humdinger. The on-screen titles had not been prepared yet, so Brian supplied them out loud, and most of the dialogue too. Before long, Victoria and Randall and the others began saying their own lines, with Chief John speaking Villa's part.

No dialogue was needed when we got to the battle. Brian had managed to use most of what George filmed, and the pictures were every bit as vivid as newsreels of the Great War. It would not be going too far to say that the work of both men was touched by genius. What had impelled George to leave the hacienda in the first place was the new scenario we had cooked up for the showdown of our picture, where Tom and Evangelina and their cowboy pals take refuge in a Mexican town and defeat Villa with the help of the brave townsfolk. George had said as much to Brian in the station. Filming the real battle, he had our movie story in mind all the time, and Brian had done his best to honor George's great sacrifice. The acted scenes were edited together with those from the battle to make it seem that Tom and Evangelina and their cowboy pards were fighting an overwhelming force of Villistas. Many of the enemy soldiers were *federales,* of course, but you would never guess it from seeing the film.

Near the end of the battle, Brian had combined pictures of Willie Two Horse creeping through the stockyards with those of Leroy and myself assaulting the bull pen, together with close-ups of Randall and Charlie Noble and some of our movie bandits, to produce the impression that there were Villistas in the bull pen instead of *federales,* and that they were vanquished by Tom and his pard in the final moments of the conflict.

As the smoke cleared, we saw the somber images of the dead men in the bull pen. But then one of the corpses moved. The "dead man's" hand came up and seemed to aim his pistol straight at the camera. There was a puff of smoke and the screen went black.

"There's a filler shot that goes there," Brian said softly. "I didn't have the heart to put it in yet. We go to one of the cowboys falling over, then Randall shooting, and cut back to the body."

Had George too been lost in a dream of make-believe? Because he was looking through the camera lens, did he fail to see the danger when the federal lieutenant brought up his pistol? Or did he know it was real and keep on cranking anyway? These questions haunt me still, but George took the answers with him to the grave.

As the picture drew to a close, the vanquished revolutionists rode off toward the mountains. And as he had done in real life, Villa turned to give a parting salute, but now he appeared to be acknowledging that he had met his match in Tom and his fearless chums. In the foreground, Evangelina stood with her arm around Tom, watching the Villistas ride away. It was really Victoria and Leroy, but only we would know it was Leroy, as the couple was seen from the back. In the final image of the film Randall Steele and Victoria appeared in close-up, seen from the front. They turned to look lovingly at each other as the flickering picture faded to "Finis."

We sat in silence as Brian switched off the projector and Orville turned on the lights. Gerald, as always, was the first to speak, but even he needed a few moments to gather himself, so moved was he by what he had seen.

"It is splendid," he said, without his usual bombast. "Absolutely splendid."

Gerald had been subdued since our return, and like many others in the company he seemed changed by our experience. In his dealings with members of the crew he was more considerate, less inclined to lord it over anyone. And now it was he who found a way to honor the memory of George Bleumel.

"What would you say to a title at the beginning dedicating the picture to George?" he proposed to the room at large.

"Oh, Gerald, that's a wonderful idea!" Victoria said.

"I will want to arrange a showing for Mr. Laemmle as soon as possible," Gerald told Brian.

"It's only a rough job, Sir Gerald," Brian said hesitantly, deferential once more when addressing his producer. "I would prefer not to show it to anyone else until I've had more time to polish it."

Gerald acceded to Brian's request with a wave of his hand. "I leave all that up to you. But let me know as soon as you're ready for him to see it. He must be the first one." He turned to Victoria. "It is everything you said it would be, and more. Your reputation will gain a great deal from this picture."

It went without saying that Sir Gerald Ball's reputation would not suffer from the picture's release. Already the newspapers were trumpeting our daring encounter with Villa and the tragic death of George Bleumel. By the time the picture was released, half the nation would be frothing at the mouth to see it.

"And now I must get to my bank," Gerald said, "or no one will be paid this evening. Charles, will you and Leroy accompany me? It will be the last of your guard duties."

It was a brisk day with a few clouds drifting in from the sea, but the sun was warm and Gerald drove with the top down. People in the street turned to stare at Leroy and me. With our western hats and getup they probably took us for movie stars.

"Nice bank," Leroy observed as we followed Gerald into the imposing granite edifice of Gerald's bank on Vine Street. Inside, the customers' footsteps echoed off the marble floor.

"I bank here myself," I said, swelling up with pride as Leroy gazed about like a rustic just off the ranch. I had picked this bank because when it came to entrusting his money to others I figured Gerald would choose with care, and also because it was the most solid-looking bank in Hollywood.

"Kind of fancy for a small town," Leroy said.

"Small but growing fast," said Gerald. "In time our business district will be second to none, you mark my words."

Gerald received our payroll directly from the bank president while Leroy and I looked on. Here too we were regarded with curiosity. We acknowledged this attention with smiles and nods, letting the customers think what they liked, but of course they never dreamed we had loaded six-shooters under our coats.

THAT EVENING THE payroll was disbursed in the Bunk House dining room as the guests arrived for the party. And although they didn't carry their salaries off in greenbacks like the rest, Brian and Victoria were paid as well, for Gerald proved himself to be magnanimous in victory. "We have all been through a great deal," he told Victoria when she finally raised the matter of their agreement. "Everyone will be paid, including the director and the star."

Victoria informed me of this generosity as the company gathered, and that was how I finally learned just how much she had risked to get her feature picture made. She was still obliged to make two more Cimarron Rose serials with Gerald, but that seemed to her a small enough price to pay for *The Trail of Pancho Villa*. The unfairness of Gerald's dealings with the two of us festered inside me, but I wouldn't spoil Victoria's evening by revealing that I too had risked something, and lost. Although Gerald hadn't said a word about the Bunk House since we returned to California, I was sure he wouldn't wait much longer.

The party that night topped all of Victoria's previous cast parties. It began joyfully with Nate and Karen's wedding, which was held in the parlor. Willie Two Horse was carried in by Bob Elderberg and Jack Whistler and propped in an easy chair to observe the ceremony. Chief John gave Karen away, and all of us bunched around the nervous groom to give him no chance to escape.

Anne Hartford was present, although Jay was not, his health having taken a turn for the worse. Anne had fretted for Victoria's safety when she learned that the telephone lines to Delgado were mysteriously silent, and she nearly had a fit when she was told of the scrapes we had come through. Even though Victoria was safe and sound, Anne needed constant reassuring, so she had hired a private nurse to sit with Jay for the evening. She stood beside me during the wedding, and like me she noticed that Victoria held Leroy's hand throughout the service.

Dancing and general merriment followed the "I do"s. The band struck up a tune and Leroy and Victoria were among the first to take the floor. Someone had fashioned a sign saying "Eat, DRINK and BE Merry. PROHIBITION STartS at MIDnight!" but we gave little thought to that piece of legislative foolishness. If some government revenue agent wanted to put a premature end to our celebrations, he was welcome to try. And when memories of George sobered us now and again, others may have reflected, as I did, that surely George would have rejoiced for Nate and Karen. We had mourned him in private thoughts during our journey home, and if there was any mourning left to be done, it was now fitting to celebrate his memory in the style of an Irish wake.

As I led Anne into the dining room, where the tables were pushed back to provide a small dance floor, she glanced fretfully at Leroy and Victoria. The car dancing had made Leroy light on his feet and Victoria was dancing on air.

"I'm worried about her, Charlie," Anne said. She held me close when I took her in my arms.

"She's happy," I said.

"I suppose I wanted a more conventional happiness for her."

"So did I, but you take what you can get, the way we did."

Anne knew of Victoria's love for Leroy, and knew he had been a wanted man in the old century. She did not know he was Butch Cassidy. The decision to keep this intelligence just between the three of us was Victoria's.

When the musicians took a short rest, Gerald approached us and inquired graciously if he might have a moment of my time. He offered me a glass of my own whiskey and suggested we go to my study to talk over a few trifling matters.

"You haven't forgotten our wager?" he said as soon as I turned on the light.

My tongue was already loosened by John Barleycorn. "It doesn't seem right, you making deals with Victoria and Brian and me too, never letting on."

"Protecting myself as best I can is simply good business, Charles. You wouldn't go back on our agreement now?"

"I'm a man of my word, you know that."

"And so am I. Once I own the Bunk House, you will continue to live here and manage it. Nothing will change."

He looked about the study, noting the paper strewn all over my desk and writing table, covered with my scrawl. I had been busy as a bee since our return from Mexico. There was a half-written page in the typewriter and a small pile of typescript beside the machine.

"What's that you're writing?" he inquired.

"My next book. All about making pictures in Mexico and running into Pancho Villa."

"You're telling the true story?"

"That's what I do, Gerald."

He smiled condescendingly. "You see, we all come out of it with something." No doubt he was imagining that my book would get folks all the more het up to see his picture. I didn't tell him I had no intention of publishing it until both of us were dead and buried.

"Just don't forget you got a week to come up with the money or the deal's off," I said. That week had begun when the last scene of the picture was filmed, two days earlier.

"You can have your money first thing on Monday. I thought you would prefer I not take over until after the party."

That took the wind out of my sails. "I'm grateful for that," I said, somewhat grudgingly, and then a thought struck me. "What if the picture came in on time? What were Victoria's terms?"

"I suppose there's no harm in telling you. She would have received an increase in salary on future serials, and one third of the profits on *The Trail of Pancho Villa*."

I was getting the beginnings of an idea. If I couldn't get out of my own hot water, I might improve Victoria's lot just a bit.

"Of course, you know she's going to hit the roof when she learns how I lost this place," I said. "She thinks a lot like I do. She won't like you taking bets with both of us and keeping quiet about it."

I could tell that he saw my point, and I pressed my advantage. When Sir Gerald Ball gives you an inch, you take a yard and a half or he'll have you by the short hairs.

"Now if you were to give her some time off, say a month's vacation so she could go somewhere and take it easy, when she got back the whole thing would be over and done with."

He thought this over and finally nodded. "All right, I'll tell her tonight. One month vacation."

"With the crew on half wages."

"Oh, come now, Charles!"

"You want her to swallow a bitter pill, you give her some soothing syrup to help it go down. This picture's going to make you a bundle and you know it."

"Very well. Half wages for the crew."

"Even so, she's got a temper," I said, scratching my head as if unsure whether these concessions would go halfway to controlling Victoria's Irish. "If I was to talk with her, I could make her see things my way."

"You would do that?"

"For the right consideration."

"Which is?"

"You give Victoria that one third of the profits."

"I won our wager fair and square! She knew my terms. An act of God or Pancho Villa, it doesn't matter. The picture is late."

"Well, I just thought I'd ask. It seems only right that she should get a

share, considering she brought Brian Hill on board and the story was his
idea. But I suppose she'll settle down in time, even without me talking to
her. Oh, and by the way, you do recall that you've got to pay me in cash.
I'll want to start looking for a new place right away."

"New place? Whatever are you talking about?"

I really had him going now. When you're breaking a horse, the trick is
to keep him so busy he's got no time to study up new devilment to spring
on you.

"The fact is, Gerald, I just can't see myself managing the Bunk House
knowing another man owns it. I thought I'd find another place and start
over. It wouldn't be as grand as this, not for what you're paying me, but it'll
be my place and that's what counts. The boys and I get along. They'll
spread the word. It might be some of them will come along with me."

"They are my crew and they will stay where I tell them!"

"Nobody hates taking orders worse than a cowboy, Gerald, except
maybe an Indian."

He took a deep breath like he was about to give me what for, but he let
it all go in a whoosh, his cheeks puffing out and the fight going out of him
along with the wind.

"If I agree, will you stay on here?"

I nodded. "I'll stay."

Back on our wagon trek, I was bitter about losing my place to Gerald
and couldn't imagine running it for him, but if staying on for a while would
benefit Victoria, I would make that sacrifice. Besides, I was accustomed
to writing in my study here, and I had a book to finish.

"One thing," I added. "I run this place my own way, like I always have." I
wasn't about to have him coming around every day with orders and regulations.

"Very well," he said. "But you will speak with Victoria when she comes
back from her holiday? You will make her accept things and keep to her
bargain?"

"She's free, white and twenty-eight, but I'll do what I can."

"All right. I will tell her about her holiday, and her share of the profits. I
will simply say that our travel time can't be counted in the production,
and so we finished the picture within the allotted month."

"If she gets stubborn and tries to turn you down, you might suggest
that she can share her profits with Brian, and George's widow. She won't
miss a chance to help them out."

When we returned to the parlor Gerald cut in on Jack Whistler, who
was dancing with Victoria in the dining room. Gerald spoke to her as they
danced, and I could see Victoria growing excited. When the dance was
done she ran to tell Leroy the good news, and a short time later they
approached me arm in arm, Victoria all aglow. Gerald was a good man at

heart, she said, so forgiving. It was enough to gag a goat, but I smiled and nodded, because seeing her happy made me happy too.

"We'll be leaving in the morning," Victoria said. "We're going camping."

"We'll put the horses in a boxcar and take a train to New Mexico," Leroy said. "From there we'll ride north so long as the weather holds out."

That was enough to let me know where they were headed. Leroy was going to show her the haunts of his younger days, beginning at the southern end of the Outlaw Trail.

"Could you get away for a couple of hours?" Victoria said. "I mean right now, this evening?"

Her request took me by surprise, but I said, "I don't know why not. It's my place." I didn't want either one of them to smell a rat until after the Bunk House was deeded over to Gerald.

"We'd like Mother to come too," Victoria said.

Anne was as mystified as I was by this request, but she telephoned her home to tell the nurse she might be late, and together we followed Leroy and Victoria as they led us out behind the Bunk House. Parked there was a 1917 Buick phaeton as sleek and shiny as a racehorse. Leroy ushered the ladies into the rear seat and indicated that I was to sit beside him up front. He set the controls and pushed the self-starter, urging the motor to life as if managing the intricacies of automobiles was something he did every day.

"Hang on, Charlie," he said, and off we went.

I am of the opinion that no one should drive a motor car and talk at the same time, but Leroy pulled it off. He kept up a steady stream of chatter about nothing very important while driving fast enough to keep me hanging on for dear life.

"Aren't you going to tell us where we're going?" Anne asked at the outset, but Victoria just told her to be patient and she would see.

We headed south and east, as best I could make out on the moonless night. We skirted downtown Los Angeles, passing through a corner of the Liquor Zone, where it appeared that all the inhabitants of the metropolis were in one saloon or another, taking on every intoxicating beverage in sight in preparation for the sober years to come. Then we plunged into the country again. Low clouds had crept in off the ocean at sundown and the night was cool. The moist air brought us the scent of eucalyptus and manzanita and live oaks when we passed through patches of woods along our route.

The perilous journey lasted for almost an hour and took us to a truck-farm district populated mostly by Mexicans. As we neared our destination, Victoria referred often to a scrap of paper in her hand and gave Leroy directions such as "Turn right by the big oak tree," or "Go left where you see the sign for Pico Rivera," until at last we stopped in front of a small adobe church. Victoria gave Leroy the scrap of paper as he got out of the car, and when he had vanished in the darkness she told Anne and me why we had come to this humble outpost of Catholicism.

"The priest in this church is a Villista. General Villa gave me a note for him, asking him to marry us."

Anne's breath caught in her throat, but Victoria rushed on.

"That last morning in Delgado, General Villa said I must stand up before God and tell Him of my love for this man. He said it is a rare thing for a man and a woman to love each other, and that God does not favor those who let the chance pass by."

"But Leroy is already married, dear," Anne protested.

"General Villa said God would understand, even if the Church doesn't," Victoria said. "He said that God didn't recognize Leroy's first marriage because he gave a false name and because he married to live a false life. Anyway, you were married when you fell in love with Charlie."

"And I have carried that burden ever since," Anne said.

Victoria took her mother's hand in her own. "But if you hadn't loved him, I would never have been born."

"It seems you are your father's daughter," Anne said. "And mine as well. You're just as headstrong as the two of us put together. I don't suppose anything I say will change your mind."

Leroy was waving to us from the door of the church, where lights now showed in the windows. As we got out of the car Anne said, "Help me, Charlie. Tell me it's all right."

"At least there's no one to be hurt by what they're doing," I offered.

"I resisted every lecher in the picture business and now I'm marrying a cowboy," Victoria said, trying to be lighthearted. "What more do you want?"

"What I wanted for you—" Anne began, but then she stopped, because what a mother wants for her daughter is idle dreaming.

"It would mean a great deal to us to have your blessing," Victoria said, serious now.

Anne took Victoria's face in her hands. "You have had my blessing since the day you were born, my darling. Besides, it's too late for my salvation now. Condoning one more sin won't tip the scales any further. I give you my blessing. And I will pray that General Villa was right about God's understanding."

Inside the church we met the priest, one Padre Candelaria. He was surprised and a little afraid to be waked in the middle of the night by four *gringos*. He trotted hither and yon, lighting candles, looking over his shoulder as if he thought the bishop of Los Angeles was about to inspect the parish. But when every candle was lit and the interior of the church shone with the warm light, he turned to us with a smile on his face.

"Everything is ready," he said in Spanish. "Let us proceed to marry the friends of General Villa."

Then I realized it was Villa, not some trifling bishop, who had caused the good padre's nervousness. The great Pancho Villa had called on him for a favor and he did not care to be found wanting. I suppose the power of Villa's name, even beyond Mexico's borders, should not have surprised me. From the start of the revolution he has inspired much devotion in the hearts of the common people, and I found myself remembering what he said after the battle, when he and his men stood looking at the bodies of the *federales* in the bull pen.

"It is better that you killed them," he said. "Despite the uniform, they are my brothers."

Even in battle his love for *Méjico* was stronger than his hatred for the enemy. Perhaps, unlike most of the others who have fought so hard to lead that unfortunate land, Pancho Villa thinks sometimes of his country first and his own glory second. They say Benito Juarez was such a man. The Abe Lincoln of his day, I guess, although it has taken me a lifetime to grant old Abe the respect he deserves.

For the second time in one evening, Anne and I stood side by side to watch a marriage ceremony, but this time my feelings were more complicated. In the Bunk House I had looked on with fatherly benevolence as Nate and Karen tied the knot. Here, I was the real father of the bride, and still not certain she was doing the right thing. I had come to California to be a better father, thinking that I might teach her some of what I had learned in my hard years on the western frontier, and I wanted her to know that she could count on me through thick and thin. Now I would have no chance to prove my worth to her.

I became aware that everyone was looking at me. Padre Candelaria asked in Spanish, obviously for a second time, who gave this woman in marriage.

I squared my shoulders and spoke up in a clear voice. "I do," I said. As I spoke the words I felt a weight lift from my shoulders, and I found myself smiling as the ceremony resumed.

Like the priest in Delgado, who had so moved me during the burial services, Padre Candelaria spoke in Spanish and Latin. He required some assistance from the couple when it came to pronouncing their names as he led them through the vows. Victoria's did not prove too great an obstacle, but he struggled over Leroy's.

"Robert Leroy Parker," he managed at last. Hearing him speak this name sent a chill up my spine, and I felt a surge of hope. Maybe General Villa was right. Maybe God would understand, and perhaps the Church would as well, although I doubted it would ever be called upon to judge the matter. I recalled a Texas outlaw of my acquaintance, who had married a Mormon girl in the Blue Mountains of Utah under an assumed name. Later, when he told her the truth about himself, she arranged for the local bishop to marry them again, by the right names this time, her intention being to assure their offspring a place in the shady side of heaven instead of the sunny side of Hades. I wasn't certain how the Roman clergy viewed such situations, but it was possible they saw eye to eye with the Mormons. It was of no consequence, of course. What mattered to me was that as Victoria and Leroy exchanged their vows, I understood the true import of what I was witnessing.

It was not a married man who had courted my daughter. It was Robert Leroy Parker, who had never settled down, never been tamed, never been married under his christened name. Now he put his life in my daughter's hands of his own free will, standing in the sight of God. And by giving her himself, he gave her all I had hoped to give her, and more.

A few short weeks ago I had done my best to prevent him from courting her. But even then I was coming to know him. All his life he had been self-reliant. By going to Mexico, perhaps to die, he was striving to be true to himself. And I knew for certain I could entrust him with my life. These were the very traits I wanted to pass along belatedly to my daughter, but perhaps she already knew and valued them. I prayed that they were the reason she loved him. She had scorned the Hollywood dandies, who lacked these attributes, and she held out for a man who measured up to her standards. Now she had found him, and she was willing to risk everything to plight him her troth. That was more than enough reason for me to give her my wholehearted blessing.

Anne understands less Spanish than the rest of us, but she hung on Padre Candelaria's every word, clinging to my hand all the while. When he got to the part where the couple promised to love each other forever, she squeezed even tighter. When the service was over she touched her lips quickly to my cheek when no one was looking, taking this opportunity to do as Victoria had done, to stand before God and declare her love, asking His understanding and forgiveness. In my own heart I said a silent prayer in support of hers, adding my hope that Victoria should know as much happiness as Anne and I had shared.

Chapter 32

LEROY HAD SEQUESTERED two bottles of champagne in the car. On our way back to Hollywood we drank warm champagne and he drove like a wild man. Victoria now sat beside him in front, so Anne and I clung to each other in the rear seat.

The wind had freshened while we were in the little church. It carried a few drops of rain, but we were snug beneath the Buick's canvas top. Leroy had even thought to provide lap robes. Traveling in such style, we became very jolly. Thanks to the champagne, we also became lost.

"I think we should go left here," said Victoria, who had taken less of the bubbly than our driver.

"Left it is," he said, pouring on the gas. We careened around a bend and plunged headlong into a creek. By good fortune, and the late coming of the winter rains, there was only a foot of water in the little stream, but we were stuck hard and the motor had quit. Leroy and I heaved and hauled, becoming thoroughly soaked in the process. We were somewhat impeded in these efforts by our wounded arms, which were not yet fully healed.

"We'll help," said Anne, preparing to step into the water.

"Now hold on," I cautioned her. She has always been game, but she is no longer a spring chicken.

"Hey, Charlie, look there." Leroy was pointing at a young cow that had appeared on the creek bank to see what the humans were up to now.

"By golly, it's a cow," I said.

"It's not just any cow. It's a beef cow." He sounded as pleased with himself as if he had just discovered the principle of gravity. "Where there's beef cows, there's horses."

He was right, too. Not far away we found a small ranch. In answer to our knocking the rancher appeared in a longhandled union suit, with a kerosene lantern in one hand and a shotgun in the other, looking like a figure from our past. He was understandably reluctant at first to lend us his horses. We were in city clothes, and none too steady on our feet. To prove our competence, Leroy took a rope from the tack room and dropped it neatly over the head of a black gelding in the corral. I followed suit and the rancher allowed as how we seemed to know what we were doing, so he would go back to sleep.

It tickled us pink that we needed horses and lariats to extricate our horseless carriage from the creek, and we laughed more or less throughout this operation. When we returned the horses to the ranch, Leroy left a twenty-dollar gold piece on his saddle before we tiptoed from the barn.

There was still the problem of the lifeless motor, but Leroy opened up the hood and performed some magic with his bandanna, drying this and that, and shortly we were on our way again, just as jolly as before, Leroy and I now wrapped in the lap robes like Egyptian mummies so we wouldn't catch our death of cold. Victoria and Anne gave each other meaningful glances, as if to say "Boys will be boys."

Light was breaking in the east when we arrived back in Hollywood. We left Anne and Victoria at the Hartford home so Victoria could pack her things for their journey while Leroy did the same at the Bunk House after returning the Buick, which he had rented.

"It's the coming thing," he said. "You don't have to buy a car, you just rent it for however long you need it."

"Hmmph," I replied, unable in my present condition to keep up with the newfangled age.

Leroy took a roundabout route back to the Bunk House, straying beyond the settled districts of town and looking down every side road as if searching for something. When he spied a small road house and café, he turned sharply and made for it. The proprietor of the establishment stood on the front steps, throwing bottles one by one into the ditch. Judging by the pile of broken glass he had built up, he had been at this task for some time. As we drew to a stop in front of him I caught the tantalizing aroma of illegal liquor.

"Until today I could pay the cops to look the other way," he told us dolefully. "Now they say the government boys will be on the case."

"We'll take one of those bottles off your hands," Leroy offered. "How about five bucks?"

"I wouldn't take your money, friend," the proprietor said, handing over a bottle of bourbon. "Drink it in good health, and the government be damned."

I was expecting some watered-down fourteen-percent swill, but my first taste from the bottle took my breath away. "Holy smoke! That's the real McCoy," I exclaimed, offering the bottle to Leroy.

The taste of the whiskey brought me to mind of another jolly journey, so I related to Leroy the tale of my stagecoach trip when I departed Alma, New Mexico, and abandoned my best shot at catching up with Butch Cassidy, alias Jim Lowe.

"You'll recall that your friend Blake Graham was on board that stage," I told him. "But you probably don't know he had a quart of whiskey in his satchel. Not only that, but the driver of the stage was Bill Kelly. I knew old Bill when he was called the LS Kid down in Texas, so we got pretty chummy. We poured Bill full of whiskey and he sang us cowboy songs all the way to Silver City. My favorite went like this."

I proceeded to warble Bill's song, which he claimed to have originated during his cowboy days. I am not much of a songbird, but my Dutch courage gave me a voice like a nightingale on this occasion.

> *My lover is a cowboy*
> *He's kind, he's brave and true;*
> *He rides the Spanish pony*
> *And throws the lasso, too;*
> *And when he comes to see me*
> *And our vows we have redeemed*
> *He puts his arms around me*
> *And then begins to sing:*
>
> *Oh, I am a jolly cowboy*
> *From Texas now I hail*
> *Give me my saddle and pony*
> *And I'm ready for the trail.*
> *I love the rolling prairie*
> *Where we are free from care and strife*
> *And behind a herd of longhorns*
> *I will journey all my life.*

In no time at all, Leroy had caught the pleasant tune, and as we navigated a rambling course back to the Bunk House we drank half the bottle and sang innumerable verses of Bill Kelly's cowboy ditty. In the midst of an especially rousing refrain, Leroy was moved to celebrate in the cowboy manner. He pulled his Colt's Frontier from its shoulder scabbard and made as if to fire through the Buick's canvas top, but I put a hand on his wrist to stop him.

"We did that too," I said. By now I was having some difficulty forming my words. "We emptied our six-shooters through the roof of the stagecoach. Shot the luggage full of holes and set the canvas on fire."

"You burned up the stagecoach?"

"Just the roof. We put it out, all right, but we pulled into Silver City without a buggy top, and the liquor all gone."

Leroy grinned at the thought of this pretty picture. "If I had known you Pinkertons had so much fun, I'd of joined up," he said. Then a new thought occurred to him. "Hey, Charlie, how come you took off like that, anyway? You knew where I was. Why didn't you come after me?"

"Frank Murray said Jim Lowe was a swell fellow. He said to leave him alone and haul my carcass back to Denver."

"So that's what you did."

"Followed orders like a good soldier. Good thing for you I did." A moment later I added, "Good thing for both of us, I guess."

A steady drizzle was falling when we finally pulled to a stop in front of the Bunk House. Leroy shut off the motor but he made no move to get out. "I hate for this night to end," he said.

"It ain't over yet," said Tommy Fear, who was sitting with Jim Ray Thompson and Redeye Hawk on the front steps of the boardinghouse.

"Hold on now, I'll get the door for you two fancy dudes," Jim Ray said. He rose to his feet and fell down the steps. Redeye, who alone among the three of them was sober, helped him up, and together we all entered the Bunk House, where a few of our friends were still awake.

"Good Lord, what happened to you two?" Jack Whistler inquired when he saw our wet and muddy clothes. I related our adventures while Leroy changed into dry clothes before setting off to return the car. I managed to make the tale so entertaining that no one thought to inquire why we had been motoring about in the middle of the night in the first place. I said nothing about the wedding, which was to remain a secret among the four of us who were there and Padre Candelaria, at least for now.

Leroy was gone for an hour and a half. When he returned he was riding Sunny, having left the gelding wherever it was he rented the Buick. Not long after that, Anne arrived with Victoria in the Hartfords' Model T and Josefa insisted we should all have an early lunch before Leroy and Victoria set out. This put off the farewells a while longer, but finally we were done eating and it was time for them to leave.

"Take care of her," I said to Leroy.

"I'll do that," he promised.

Anne kissed Victoria and they shed a few tears.

Jack Whistler and Buddy Johnston's little brother George had loaded

Sunny and Ranger and Leroy's pack horse in one of the McQuain & Vickery trucks. When the truck finally pulled out, with Jack at the wheel and Leroy and Victoria sitting beside him, a handful of the cowboys gave a cheer and a wave. None of them saw anything so unusual in Leroy and Victoria going off together. They knew the two lovers were fond of each other, and they were glad that Victoria had held out for a man of such high caliber. With these requirements met, they were unconcerned for the social niceties.

Soon afterwards, Anne went home to Jay, the cowboys went off to sleep, and I was left alone. I felt somewhat abandoned, but I perked up when I went to my study. There on my writing table was a brand new pair of boots. They were fancy ones, with tooled leather tops and lots of stitching, and they were just my size. I looked down at the old boots on my feet and I remembered another battered pair I had worn out twenty years before, the ones I had ruined chasing an outlaw mule.

EARLY IN THE afternoon it commenced raining in a serious manner, signaling that winter had arrived at last in sunny California. The Bunk House was quiet as a church. Some of the lodgers were asleep and the rest were nursing hangovers. I built a fire in my little Ben Franklin stove to ward off the chill that had settled in my bones as a result of our nighttime escapades. To soothe my tender nerves I sipped from a teacup and listened to Caruso's "My Little Posy" on the Victrola, expecting that at any moment Gerald Ball would show up to claim his rooming house.

I caught up on the newspapers, which were full of the Harry New verdict—guilty in the second degree—and the onset of Prohibition. To find proof that this measure was pure folly, however well-intentioned, I had to look no farther than an item reporting that the California congressional delegation had requested one hundred thousand dollars from the House Agricultural Committee for "agricultural experiments" to find a new use for the California wine grape. But what really brought a smile to my face was reading that in the Chicago rail yards, four bandits had tied up the yard master and four members of a freight train's crew, broke into two cars, and escaped with seventy-five barrels of liquor valued at one hundred thousand dollars.

It struck me that this would be a very promising line of work for the nation's holdup artists, and I made a note to show the paper to Leroy the next time I saw him, as I was sure he would get a kick out of it. This in turn sent my thoughts back to our Sonoran adventures, which caused me to pick up my writing tablet and jot down a number of ideas about telling the story, lest they be lost in my presently befuddled brain.

About three o'clock I heard a shout. "Charlie!"

The front door slammed and footsteps pounded through the house. Outside, it was raining to beat the band.

"Charlie?" The voice was closer now, coming down the hall. A moment later Brian Hill burst into the study.

"There you are! My God, Charlie, you're not going to believe it! Someone cleaned out Sir Gerald's bank this morning. Kidnapped the banker from his home at gunpoint and made him open the safe."

Brian was dripping wet. He had on a cowboy's slicker and the John B. Stetson hat he bought before we left for Mexico, the hat having acquired a good deal of character in the interim. He wore faded denims and the same boots he had worn all the time we were in Delgado, which were unpolished since then. All in all he looked fairly authentic, but it wasn't just the outfit. He wore the cowboy clothes naturally, as if he belonged in them. You wouldn't have taken him for a dude.

I regret to say that my first reaction to his news was a selfish one. "I guess that takes care of my nest egg," I said. "Not that it was much to speak of."

"My gosh, I forgot you banked there too," Brian said. "I'm sorry."

I had been counting on adding that nest egg, such as it was, to the money Gerald would pay me for the Bunk House. The size of my new place dwindled to little more than a shanty in my mind, and then I remembered that Gerald was cleaned out too.

"I imagine this was quite a blow for Gerald," I said.

"Oh, he's as mad as can be. But it's not as though he's lost everything. Neither have you, for that matter. All the robber took was cash on hand. The bank says by the end of next week they'll make good on all deposits."

It struck me that next week would be after the deadline for Gerald to buy the Bunk House. One week to pay cash on the barrelhead or the deal was off, those were the terms. God or Pancho Villa, it didn't matter.

While I was mulling this over, Brian shucked out of his wet hat and slicker and hung them on the coat rack by the door before putting his backside toward the stove. He fished a pack of Lucky Strikes from his shirt pocket and lit up, having switched from Pall Malls when he ran out of his own cigarettes during our wagon trek from Delgado. I think the fact that Gerald smoked Pall Malls may have had something to do with why Brian stuck to the cowboys' store-bought brand once we got home.

"Gerald would still be rich even if his bank account was wiped out," Brian said. "That last Cimarron Rose serial is doing record business and we'll have the feature out before long. Did he tell you Mr. Laemmle has sold over thirty thousand dollars in rentals? The picture has already made money!"

I don't like to profit by another man's misfortune, but I was already over feeling sorry for Gerald, and I saw now that the robbery was quite a stroke of luck for me. I was cash poor, but I still had the Bunk House, unless Gerald had a bundle of greenbacks hidden away in a cookie jar somewhere.

"You best have something to warm you up." I offered my teacup to Brian. He sipped at it and nearly choked.

"It's mescal!"

"It'll put hair on your chest." I took the cup back and refilled it from the bottle I had stashed in a desk drawer.

"This brand of tea will prove popular from now on, or I miss my guess," I observed as he drank again, more heartily this time. "Now tell me about this robbery."

"The robber drove up to Mr. Packworth's house—that's the bank president—and when Packworth stepped out to see who it was, the robber pulled a gun on him. 'Please get in,' he said. Isn't that a corker? 'Please get in.' He was very polite, Packworth said. He drove to the bank, made Packworth open the back door, and then the safe. He cleaned the place out in five minutes. The police think it was kind of a spur of the moment thing, someone celebrating Prohibition. The banker said there was liquor on the robber's breath, but that's not the best part. He was all dressed up like a cowboy in a hat and slicker! He had a bandanna pulled up to hide his face, just like something out of the Old West. The newspapers will have a field day with this one."

"Can the police trace the car?"

"Oh, sure. When the robber was done at the bank he took Packworth back home, then he drove away. Packworth was on the telephone in two minutes. He gave a perfect description of the car. He even got the license number. But the car was rented! They found it half a mile from Packworth's house, where the robber had a horse waiting. The rain wiped out the tracks and the robber gave a false name when he rented the car. The police haven't a clue who he was, but they figure he's from Hollywood. Packworth said he knew all the streets like the back of his hand."

My brain was turning record laps around the old racetrack, you can bet. "There's not much chance of catching one man, not unless he makes a habit of bank robbery," I said. I gave a wave at the fliers on the walls around us and added, "There's not a lone bank bandit in this whole crowd."

I tried to keep the hopeful tone out of my voice, but it was the simple truth. My Pinkerton colleagues and I had little luck catching bank robbers, unless they committed several holdups in a row or were part of a gang.

My gesture had directed Brian's attention to the fliers, and suddenly he went stiff with surprise. When I saw where he was looking I wished I had thought twice before pinning Butch Cassidy's flier back in its old place.

"My God, Charlie, it's Leroy!"

I didn't trust myself to speak. Brian looked at me, back at the flier, then at me again. I was taken so unawares that he saw the truth in my eyes before I could think of a way to hide it.

Brian sat down in my swivel chair. "It can't be. Butch Cassidy's dead, isn't he?"

"Dead and buried, as far as the rest of the world's concerned. And best for everyone if he stays that way."

"You knew, right from the beginning?"

"Not right off."

"God, I can't believe it. For the last month I've been working alongside Butch Cassidy!" He calmed himself and held up a hand. "Don't worry, I won't tell a soul. I wouldn't hurt him for the world. Where is he now?"

"Long gone." I didn't add that Victoria was with him, thinking that side of the story might be more than young Brian could digest at one sitting.

He fished out another Lucky and lit it from the butt of the first, nodding slowly to himself. I could almost hear the wheels turning inside his brain. I hoped learning who Leroy was had driven all thoughts of the bank robbery from his head, and I was relieved when he said, "You let him go for the same reason you and he helped Villa. You're the same kind of men."

I had underestimated Brian. He understood.

"You're the kind of men I read about when I was a boy. You're the ones I want to make pictures about. I tried to tell Gerald about it while we were in Mexico, but he didn't understand. All he thinks about is business and money. I told him it was no accident that just a few years after Americans tamed a continent we won the biggest war the world has ever known. It's the frontier spirit that gives us our strength, Charlie. Men like you and Leroy, out there on your own, you represented us all and showed us the way. You showed what free men can accomplish. That's what I want to put in my pictures."

He brightened. "Victoria and I have a new picture in mind for when she's done with the serials. You'll help us, won't you?"

"Be glad to," I said.

For the first time, Brian noticed the writing pad on my desk and the pages strewn around the typing machine.

"I'm sorry to bust in on you like this when you're working." He tossed off the last of the mescal and got to his feet. He put on his slicker and settled his hat on his head before looking for a final time at Butch's flier. "What you and Leroy have in common, that's more important than the law, I guess. It's funny how things change."

I couldn't have put it better myself, so I didn't try. When he was gone, I removed the flier from the wall and read it one last time before I crumpled it up and put it in the stove.

Chapter 33

THAT IS HOW my daughter married Butch Cassidy and how he pulled his last stickup. More than a year has passed since then. Today, as I pound at my typewriter, I can raise my eyes from the page and see the yard of my Sunny Slope ranch. I am back in Santa Fe, having sold the Bunk House to Rosa Ball not long after Leroy and Victoria departed for their honeymoon on the Outlaw Trail. But before I tell how this came about, I will relate some news of the others.

McQuain & Vickery's Wild West is no more. Jim McQuain and Walt Vickery had to pull teeth and wring blood out of rocks to get enough money to make one final swing around the country this past summer. Knowing it was their last hurrah, everyone worked hard to go out in style. Gerald tried to keep Victoria in Hollywood to finish up the latest Cimarron Rose serial, but she told him the serial would just have to wait, and she appeared in each and every performance of the tour. Leroy even joined the company for a few weeks when they were in the Northwest. He rode in the grand entry but otherwise he stayed in the background, helping out, and enjoying the gabfests late into the night.

Now the intrepid crew has scattered. Many are still working in pictures, and many still reside at the Bunk House, which at last report is thriving under Rosa's ownership.

Bob and Katie Elderberg went home to Wyoming hoping to buy a ranch, and as best I can determine, Jack Whistler and Willie Two Horse have just plain disappeared. As for Redeye Hawk, he is called Redtail now, which was his real name all along. Having given up firewater for good—so he promised—he felt the nickname was no longer appropriate. He has gone with Chief John to the Apache reservation to continue learning Indian lore from the old warrior, so long as John's health permits. John has tuberculosis. His coughing grew steadily worse during the summer's tour, and finally he went to a white medicine man in Los Angeles who gave him the bad news. Upon returning to his own people, he was made a real chief at last, as they judged his spirit had grown sufficiently large to justify his ruling in peace as well as war.

And so the moving pictures and the organized stampedes—they call them "rodeos" now—have brought an end to the old wild west shows. I guess each generation has to lose something it holds dear. The cattle drives of my youth scarcely lasted twenty years. The wild west shows Bill Cody started have been around for twice that long, but few survived the war, and soon there will be none. Not so long ago, it was those very shows that awoke the dream of the fading frontier in many a young man's breast and sent him out to celebrate the cowboy's way of life. But as happens so often in modern times, the old has been forced to give way to the new, and it falls now to these new entertainments—the movies and the rodeos—to see if they can do as good a job of preserving the traditions of the Old West.

Fortunately, those nearest and dearest to me are taking full advantage of the movies' booming popularity. *The Trail of Pancho Villa* was a smash. Although Brian has not been brought into the public spotlight as much as Victoria by its success, his career is running at a 2:40 gait and he now commands a weekly salary that many an old cowboy would accept for a year's work. After the two serials Victoria was compelled to make for Gerald, she and Brian made another feature, for Carl Laemmle this time. As promised, I went back to Hollywood to help with the scenario, and I am glad to report that both the serials and the feature are doing well.

Randall Steele has gained new prominence too, although for some reason he took it into his head that Randall is no name for a cowboy hero. He is billed as Bob Steele now. Like Victoria and Brian he is at Universal, and of course Victoria had him in her second feature, once more as the daring hero. Such was the interest in this film while it was in production, who should stop by the lot one day but Tom Mix himself. Mix was a personable fellow, Victoria said, but my, has he got a lively imagination. Between scenes he was regaling the crew with stories of his deeds. For half of them to be true, he'd have to be older than Methuselah. Besides claiming to have been a famous Texas Ranger—one this Texas boy never heard of— he fought in the war with Spain, the Boer War, and the rebellion in the Philippines, as well as making it to China in time for the Boxer Uprising.

As if that weren't enough, he says he sided with General Villa early in the revolution, and claims to be old Pancho's blood brother. While Tom expanded on these stories during the lunch break, Randall winked at Victoria behind Tom's back and sauntered off to see that his horse was fed. The two of them could have traded Mix tale for tale, but like so many who have endured life-or-death experiences and come through them changed, Victoria and Randall (and Brian too) tend to keep their stories to themselves.

On that day over a year ago when Brian told me about Gerald's bank being robbed, I had plenty to keep quiet about, and a few days later I was heartily glad I had thought to burn Leroy's wanted flier, for I received an unexpected visitor.

"My name is James Tolliver," the young man introduced himself. "I am with Pinkerton's National Detective Agency, and I wonder if you might spare me a few moments of your time."

He looked more like a clerk than the sort of detective I was familiar with, but I ushered him into my study and offered him a seat. When he set his morning paper on my desk I could see at a glance that the exploits of "the mystery outlaw," as the newspapers had dubbed him, were still front-page news.

"*A Cowboy Detective* is kind of like a bible to me," young Tolliver said, by way of explaining his visit. "Just knowing you helped break up Butch Cassidy's gang, well, I want to say it's an honor to meet you. I was hoping you might give me some advice about this bank robbery case. Frankly, it's got us stumped."

By the unabashed admiration he showed me, I guessed he had not read my *Two Evil Isms*, in which I detailed my complaints against the Agency. But so long as he looked up to me as some kind of hero, I figured I might as well play the part for what it was worth, and my first concern was to put a stop to the rampant practice of mentioning Butch Cassidy and the robbery of Gerald's bank in the same breath.

"You'll find a different sort of bandit nowadays," I said, leaning back in my swivel chair and putting on the air of a man who knew his stuff. "They aren't professionals. Not like the men I chased. From what I hear, this robbery was a spur of the moment deal."

Tolliver nodded sagely. "We think so. Actually, my other reason for coming to see you is because you know many of the men who act in western movies. My superintendent thinks the robber may have been an actor. I mean, who else would have picked an old-time western getup like that?"

From there on it was easy. I encouraged Tolliver in his line of reasoning, I scratched my head and said I couldn't think of anyone desperate or crazy enough to pull such a stunt, and finally I sent him on his way like a hound searching for a trail, while the fox enjoyed his mountain holiday. But even though I had misled the Pinkertons for the moment, I was still worried for Victoria and angry with Leroy for straying so recklessly from the straight and narrow.

Victoria herself had no hint that anything was wrong until they reached the small robber's roost "Jim Lowe" had set up in the mountains near Alma, New Mexico, all those years ago. The weather being unseasonably warm, they took the opportunity to swim in a small lake. Victoria gave Leroy the swimming lesson she had promised him down in Delgado, and Leroy proved to be an apt pupil. While he lingered in the water to splash about in his new swimming costume, Victoria went looking for a towel in their saddlebags.

"Not that one!" Leroy shouted, seeing her open the wrong bag. But it was too late. Inside the saddlebag were canvas money sacks overflowing with gold and silver coins.

She turned to him, aghast. "Leroy! What have you done?"

The look of fearful concern on her face reminded Leroy of the way his parents had looked when the Circleville sheriff came to inquire about a pair of overalls taken from the general store. He remembered the pain his youthful wildness had caused his family, and he wanted Victoria to suffer no similar discomfort just because of a prank he had pulled to help a friend. He built a fire and made camp by the lake, and as the twilight dimmed he told Victoria about how he had overheard Gerald and me talking on the night of her most recent cast party.

He had been on his way to the privy when he recognized Gerald's voice coming from my study. He stood outside my door and heard how Gerald had won the Bunk House from me, and it made his blood boil. As soon as my study was empty, he used the telephone to learn where the president of Gerald's bank lived. Then, after our little trip to see Padre Candelaria and after he had dropped me back at the Bunk House, Leroy had gone to fetch the banker and rob the bank.

When he had told her all this, Victoria understood his reasons, but she was still afraid for him. "They'll be after you now," she said. "How will we—"

It was Leroy's turn to be aghast. "I'm not going to keep the money!" he protested. "I lived twenty years on the run and that was enough. If I want to live to see my grandchildren, I've got to keep a low profile."

"Then what—"

"I only took the money so Charlie could hang onto the Bunk House. I figured to send it back."

"If you knew you were going to send it back, you might have taken greenbacks!" She was angry and relieved and happy all at the same time. And she had a point. But of course he had taken the greenbacks too, his intention being to clean out the bank. All in all, the loot weighed nearly a hundred pounds.

They returned it by Railway Express. This choice of a carrier tickled Leroy's fancy and restored Victoria's high spirits.

"It'll go out this afternoon on the Limited," the express agent told them as he handed Leroy his receipt.

"Are you sure it's safe?" Victoria asked demurely.

The agent puffed himself up, all full of pride in his job and the whole Railway Express Agency. "Little lady," he assured her, "Railway Express hasn't lost a package since nineteen-ought-one, when Butch Cassidy held up the Great Northern Coast Flyer."

I learned of these happenings from the two of them in letters posted the same day they sent the loot back. The papers made a big to-do about the money being returned, but with the cash back in the safe the bank saw no reason to pay Pinkerton's to chase a man who had merely taken out a short loan, so they dropped the case. In no time the story of the "mystery outlaw" faded to the back pages of the newspapers and then disappeared entirely.

Close on the heels of that happy development, my own plans for the future took a turn toward the wide open spaces. Since our return from Mexico, I had found myself longing for the Rocky Mountains and my Santa Fe ranch. Having given over to another man the task of passing on to Victoria the frontier values I admire, I saw no reason to linger in civilized parts while further adventures might await me back in the real West. These sentiments were what first prompted my thoughts of selling the Bunk House, but I didn't want to sell to Gerald, who had come so close to buying it against my will. Then, as if Lady Luck had only been waiting for the idea of returning to Santa Fe to take root in my two-by-four brain, another party expressed interest.

When the week in which Gerald might have bought the place had expired without his handing over the cash, and after the furor caused by the bank robbery had died down, Rosa Ball came to see me.

"I am happy for you, Charles," she said, after first telling me how Gerald had gloated to her over the prospect of owning the Bunk House. I could see that her expression of good will was genuine, but I guessed that she had not dropped by just to wish me well, and I told her so.

"As always, Charles, you are perceptive." She allowed herself a small smile. We were sitting in the parlor, Rosa sipping a cup of coffee Josefa brought for her, and I a cup of genuine tea.

"I know how attached you are to the Bunk House," she went on, "but if you ever wished to sell it, I wanted you to know that I would be interested in buying it myself. I would like to have a business of my own, and this is so close to our home. I could be near the children."

Never one to beat around the bush, I told her I was homesick for Santa Fe and we concluded the deal then and there. The amount we agreed upon was less than Gerald would have paid me under the terms of our agreement, although Rosa would gladly have paid more. As I have said, she brought the lion's share of wealth into her marriage with Gerald. But I insisted on making her a bargain price, taking much enjoyment in imagining how Gerald would burn up when he heard what his wife had paid.

I came out short on the deal, but I have never been very good at holding on to money. That is a cowboy trait if ever there was one. But what I didn't get out of the Bunk House in cash, I took in the form of satisfaction.

Naturally I arranged to stay on until Victoria and Leroy returned from their honeymoon, but when the allotted month was over Victoria came back alone, and she was in no mood to share my good news. Besides their fun and games, she and Leroy had done a good deal of talking on their journey. And try as they might, they could see no way to be together for the time being. In Hollywood, Leroy would attract too much attention if he suddenly appeared as Victoria's swain, or husband. He would go from being the mystery outlaw to the mystery husband, and inquisitive reporters would pry into his past. Nor could Victoria quit pictures and leave Hollywood to be with him, or those same reporters would want to know why, and again they would turn their questions on Leroy.

So Leroy had taken the course that would attract the least attention, returning to the false life he thought he had left behind for good, while Victoria came back to Hollywood. Only now her life in pictures would be a false life too, a public distraction she kept up to divert attention from the private life she must keep hidden at all costs.

Hearing this sad news, I began to turn dark with the righteous wrath of a father whose daughter has been wronged, but Victoria nipped my anger in the bud.

"General Villa told me it would be like this, Charlie. I didn't want to believe him at first, but he was telling the truth." She told me what else had passed between herself and Villa on our last morning in Delgado. Even as he gave her Padre Candelaria's name and urged her to declare her love for Leroy before God, Pancho had given her a warning.

"Do not let this man destroy himself for you," he said.

That surprised Victoria. "What do you mean? Why should he destroy himself?"

"For years he has lived in safety with a false name. He gave it up because he had no friends, no one he could trust completely. Now he has you. You love him for who he truly is. But only in his false life is he safe."

Victoria shook her head. "I don't understand."

"As Robert Parker, even as Leroy Roberts, his old life is still dangerous to him. If he tries to return to it, it will catch up with him."

Pancho spoke to her softly, but with an intensity Victoria had not seen in him before. "One day the life I have lived will catch up with me and it will destroy me. For me, there is no other way. But Roberto has a chance. He must keep to this new life he has made, or the troubles of the old one will find him and they will destroy him."

The joy Victoria felt within herself withered and threatened to die. "What can I do?" She was not simply asking. She was pleading for some way to save her happiness.

"You must both love him and let him go. The false life is safe, but from time to time he must be himself again. In those times he will have much need for a woman who knows him as he truly is."

"I didn't know what to do, Charlie," she said as she related the story to me. "Then I thought of you and mother. You've been happy, haven't you? Even though you haven't been together all the time?"

I didn't answer right away, but finally I nodded. "Yes. My feelings for your mother, and knowing she returns them, have made me happy."

"And if you had it to do over—?" She let the question hang in the air.

"Oh, I'd be as big a fool the second time around, I imagine." How could I feel otherwise, with Anne Hartford watching me through my daughter's eyes?

Since that bittersweet conversation another New Year's holiday has come and gone, far more peaceful for Victoria and me and our friends than the last. More peaceful for Mexico too. Just six months after his final raid into Sonora, General Francisco Villa surrendered, ringing down the curtain on his lonely revolution. As Villa predicted, President Carranza suffered a fatal dose of lead poisoning. It was the followers of Obregón who did the deed, and Obregón with whom Villa made his peace.

Obregón is president now. Villa has a large ranch near Parral, in his home state of Chihuahua. The government will pay him a million pesos a year so long as he keeps the peace. Villa himself wrote Victoria of this in a letter not long ago. He also renewed his plea that she marry him, but he let on that the offer was made just to show his high regard for her.

Since Villa's surrender, a number of graying *federales* have claimed they could have had him any day, but let him go because they always had a soft spot in their hearts for old Pancho, even though they wore the government's uniform.

The news of Villa's surrender has had a considerable effect on Leroy. Victoria spends as much time with him as she can between pictures, and I went to visit them in their cozy mountain cabin over Labor Day, barely a month after Villa made his deal with Obregón. Leroy couldn't seem to get Villa off his mind. As he pointed out to me down in Sonora, he and Villa are much alike. Because of that similarity, he sees Villa's fate as closely linked with his own. I think he took Pancho's surrender as proof that the modern world doesn't have room for the outlaw life, even in Mexico, and it has strengthened his resolve to lay low. He has Victoria to think about now, and their time together is precious to him.

Like many a proud father, I wanted my daughter to lead a different life from my own. I thought she deserved finer things than I had, and a life less fraught with danger. But Victoria has grown up to be every bit as strong-willed and contrary-minded as I am. Observing our similarities makes me wonder if perhaps Mr. Darwin may not be right about heredity, which gives me no comfort. I do take some solace in the hope that he may be right about survival of the fittest. I think I may stand as example of that principle, and hope that I have passed this trait on to Victoria along with my bad ones, so she may survive her hardships as I have survived mine.

Whether she and Leroy will find a way to spend more time together in the years to come, I cannot say. It is too early to tell. They have chosen a difficult road. I have given them my prayers and my blessing, but I can do no more.

WHICH LEAVES YOUR humble servant sitting in his Sunny Slope ranch house, looking for new thrills to add to those already under his belt. The ranch is still mortgaged to the hilt and I cannot publish the book I have worked on all year—this one—but I am wolf-wild and free as the wind, and that's what matters most. There is no fool like an old fool, they say.

I take much satisfaction, and no doubt more pride than I ought, from my memories of our Sonoran sojourn. Except for poor George, our adventure was not an ending, but a turning point from which we have gone on to live our separate lives. For most, it was a turn for the better, I believe. For my part, I discovered that I, like Leroy, still have what it takes when the chips are down. This in itself should be enough to help any man face life's smaller problems. But I take even more encouragement from another discovery. When all our lives were up for grabs, the young men and women of our company displayed every bit as much courage as I once took for granted in my cowboy companions of fifty years ago, and I saw that they have the same fearless willingness to face up to the risks and dangers, great and small, that stand between themselves and their dreams. I thought these qualities had died with the passing of the frontier, but I see now that only the nature of the challenges has changed. And so for the first time since my headstrong youth, when I imagined that my pards and I were the very finest specimens of manhood the Earth had yet produced, I feel that the future of our nation is in good hands, even though today's young people live in a world very different from the one I grew up in.

San Francisco
May 25, 1988

Mr. G. Gregory Tobin
Senior Editor
Bantam Books, Inc.
666 Fifth Avenue
New York, N.Y. 10103

Dear Mr. Tobin:

As we agreed when we spoke yesterday on the phone, I am enclosing the letter I told you about, written by my mother in 1941 when she and I were on a car trip through the western states. It has been kept with my grandfather's manuscript ever since Mother wrote it, and I am very glad you may use it as an afterword to South of the Border.

Also, as you requested, this letter will constitute my formal permission for Bantam to proceed with publication of South of the Border, contingent upon your keeping my true identity confidential. With the recent death of my mother, the last of those who took part in these adventures is now gone, to the best of my knowledge, and I believe no one will be hurt by revealing the secrets my grandfather and mother and I have kept for so long. As you are aware, some have already been told by my father's sister Lula, in her book Butch Cassidy, My Brother.

My husband's name is the only one I have changed. This was done to spare myself and our children too much public attention when the story is published. Apart from this liberty, the manuscript and letter are just as they were when Mother entrusted them to me.

Sincerely yours,

Martha Anne Hill

Martha Anne "Hill"

THE CRABTREE HOTEL

JACKSON, WYOMING

"Right On The Town Square"

Jackson, Wyoming
July 4th, 1941

Oh, Charlie, dear Charlie,

You understood so much, so long ago.

I have just finished rereading South of the Border *for the first time in several years. Writing this letter helps me to preserve the feeling of being close to you. I may throw it away when I'm done, but for now it's the writing that matters.*

Marty and I have been away from home for over two months, travel-ing by car through the western states. It is our first proper vacation to-gether. She said she wanted to know more about her father, so we have been driving all through the country he loved. She has been a wonderful companion, coming alive, as I do, each time we stop in some place he knew as a young man. Most nights we sleep beside the car in our small tent and cook for ourselves on the compressed-gas camp stove Leroy used for so many years. Reading a few pages of your manuscript each night after Marty was asleep has kept you in my thoughts all along the way.

We began our journey as Leroy did when he came to Los Angeles in 1919, although we sometimes traveled as far in a day as he did in a week. In May we spent five days in northern Sonora and two nights in Delgado. Rafael Delgado is dead, I'm sorry to say, but Magdalena pre-

sides over the hacienda with as much authority as ever. Gene Ortiz is the foreman now. He is older, of course, but looks much the same. The Delgado children are grown and have families of their own, and that made me feel old. The town has grown too, but you would recognize it easily. Progress is not so rapid in that country as in this one, even though the revolution is long in the past. Magdalena and I spent hours reminiscing about our adventures of twenty years ago, and Marty's eyes fairly popped out of her head when she heard of our battle with the federales.

From Sonora we came north, stopping in Alma and Telluride before turning west into Utah and north to Wyoming, passing through Brown's Park and Baggs. It is rugged country, but not too bad for travel by car in the spring, before the summer heat. We carry canteens of extra water for when the car boils over on the mountain passes.

As you have guessed, I am taking Marty along the Outlaw Trail, although I have not told her that.

Nor have I told her yet who Leroy really was. But I will. Not right away, but soon.

We took a detour to South Dakota to see the likenesses of the presidents on Mt. Rushmore, and to visit Redtail Hawk. He is greatly changed, Charlie. As you know, Redtail returned to the Sioux when Chief John died, determined that he would become a teacher among his people, helping them to preserve their ancient ways while bettering their lot. But from the start it has been an uphill battle. The government has been so preoccupied with fighting this Depression, it has almost totally neglected the Indians, and I am afraid Redtail has grown discouraged. He tried to put on a cheerful face for Marty and me, but I smelled drink on his breath and he looks old beyond his years.

To balance this sad news, I will add that I have some recent tidings of our other McQuain & Vickery friends. All are doing well. Nate and Karen are still living in the San Fernando Valley, raising children and stunt horses for the movies (that sounds as if they are raising their children for the movies too, but you know what I mean). Karen reports that Buddy Johnston reenlisted in the army when the current buildup began and is now stationed at Fort Ord, near Monterey, training recruits. Buddy's mother passed away some years ago, but his father is still fit and lives in a small house in Seaside, to be near Buddy. Hollywood is booming and real estate values are sky high, Karen says. The lot where the Bunk House once stood would bring you a fortune today, but she adds that she doubts you would want to live there.

From the Black Hills, Marty and I turned west toward Sheridan, where we hired horses and rode into the Hole-in-the-Wall. We were accompanied by an old man who claims to have been in the posse that finally drove the gang from that hideout. It may be that he told the truth, for he had his facts right. "Butch Cassidy wasn't part of the outfit yet, not then," he told us. "Kid Curry was the boss of that bunch. A mean sort, the Kid was. But Butch, now there was a man. He ain't dead, y' know. He's as alive as you and me, livin' somewhere in the mountains, they say."

How I wish that were so.

The summer heat came into its own while we were in Sheridan so we didn't linger there. The Big Horn and Wind River valleys were hot as well, and our car boiled over twice on the way over Togwotee Pass. The second time, Marty and I had to carry water from a stream in our canteens to refill the radiator, but the effort was well worth it. What a view of the Tetons when you enter Jackson's Hole from that direction! We felt very much as the pioneers must have felt when they came into this wondrous valley for the first time.

You would be so proud of Marty, Charlie. She grows more beautiful with each passing year, and she has never forgotten you. "Where's Grandpa?" she would ask, out of the blue, long after you died, until she was old enough to understand that you weren't coming back. Tonight she is out on her first date, which is how I happen to be alone with South of the Border *and you. We are in the Crabtree Hotel, where Leroy once stayed, although I didn't tell Marty that. I felt we deserved a night in a real bed after many nights camping beside the road.*

The Independence Day parade this morning was a lively event. With the new war in Europe, patriotism is very high, and at least here in Jackson it manifests itself on July 4th as an outpouring of all kinds of wild but good-natured behavior. Afterwards we went to the community luncheon in the park, where for one dollar you could eat as much as you wished of barbecued beef and all the trimmings. One young cowboy—he can't be more than eighteen—couldn't keep his eyes off Marty. Finally he got up his courage and introduced himself. "I'm Martha Anne Roberts," Marty said, sounding so grown-up and sure of herself. She introduced me, and when we went to the rodeo the young man, whose name is Hardeman, accompanied us. During the rodeo he kept up a running patter all about the various events. He took us for city slickers and I said nothing to disabuse him, but Marty let on that I knew a thing or two about rodeos, having performed for many years in a wild west show, and he was properly impressed.

As we left the rodeo grounds, young Mr. Hardeman invited Marty to go with him to a barn dance that is only one of the evening's events, as the holiday celebrations continue into the night. My first impulse was to forbid Marty to go. Then I remembered you, and how you let me go off with Leroy despite your misgivings. You gave me your approval, without reservations, even though I chose a course you would not have picked for me if it had been up to you. That was a great gift, and I can't tell you how much it meant to me over the years. You had your doubts, but you trusted me. So I followed your example and let Marty go to the dance with young Mr. Hardeman, once I was assured it would be properly chaperoned.

Did you know that Matt Warner and Tom McCarty honeymooned in Jackson's Hole with their Mormon wives? That was just a year after they held up the Telluride bank with Leroy. At the time, their wives had no notion they were married to outlaws! Matt said the Hole was "the greatest robber hide-out in the West outside of Robbers' Roost," and it is easy to see why. The place is ringed by mountains and getting in or out in the winter is still very chancy, they say. The town is respectable now, although many of the older families don't talk much about their past, which is one reason I like it here.

Matt Warner tells about this and other adventures in his book The Last of the Bandit Riders, *which came out a few years ago. There are more and more books about the Old West, and I read them all. You would think me foolish for indulging in this nostalgia, but the stories take me back to you and Leroy.*

While Marty and I were in Utah I learned that Matt Warner died a few years ago. After his prison term at the turn of the century, he went straight for more than thirty years. He even became sheriff of Price, Utah, and later he was appointed tax collector! If only Leroy had been given a chance like that.

I came here hoping to meet Bert Charter, the friend of the Wild Bunch whom you mentioned several times in A Cowboy Detective. *He had a ranch a few miles outside of town in a place called Spring Gulch. Leroy spent some time there in the summer of 1925, when I was pregnant with Marty. But when I asked for directions to the Charter place I learned that Bert died two years ago.*

First you, then Leroy, now Matt Warner and Bert Charter. I feel so lonely as one by one you "old-timers" drop from sight like the tallest and finest trees in the forest going down before the winds of time. When Leroy died I missed you more than ever, Charlie. I wanted to talk to you about how much it hurt me not to be with him at the end. But I guess you know all about that now. I take comfort from imagining you and him together, wherever it is the old cowboys go.

I wanted even more to talk with you about the rest of his life, the ten years we had together after you were gone. It still hurts me to think that we might have managed to make a home together, as we always wanted, if only I had quit the movies a few years earlier. But the money helped Mother take care of Jay, and I thought to provide us a nest egg. Just a few more years, I told myself, but I hadn't counted on General Villa dying. You remember what a blow that was for Leroy. I have never seen him so shaken as when we got the news. Villa predicted that his old life would catch him and destroy him, and it happened far sooner than any of us expected. Because he was a public figure he had no chance to fade into obscurity when he made his peace with Obregón. He lived publicly as Pancho Villa and died just as publicly, shot full of holes in his Dodge touring car (which was identical to the Delgados', judging from the photographs) in the middle of Parral in broad daylight. Leroy took his death as proof that Pancho's advice to him—to keep to his false identity—was advice he could ignore only at his peril. He was never afraid of peril, but he was in love with life once more, and it seemed unfair to him that his past might try to sneak up on him and cut him down, the way Pancho's had done.

Before that, we had even thought a day might come when Leroy could come out of hiding altogether and live as Butch Cassidy again—or at least as Robert Leroy Parker. He planned to reside in Wyoming long enough to extinguish the statute of limitations there before revealing himself. We hoped that people would be so fascinated to learn of his return that no one would think of prosecuting him for his long-ago crimes. And we thought too that my being his wife, and learning that we had been married for some years, would work to his favor.

But General Villa's death put a stop to that talk. We put off trying to start a new life together and I kept on making movies. I'm so glad you were back in Hollywood then, Charlie. You were there when I needed you the most. The hardest time for me was when I was pregnant and had to stop working, and couldn't be with Leroy. I would come over to your "den," and we would tell each other stories about Mexico to keep my spirits up when I was lonely for him. "To hell with 'em," you said, as my movie "friends" looked knowingly at one another and talked behind my back. So I said to hell with them too.

It was the right time for me to quit the business anyway. More and more the women in westerns were being portrayed as wilting violets just waiting around for some man to rescue them, and I wouldn't play those parts.

Then sound came along and offered us hope from an unexpected quarter. You scoffed at the talking pictures, but you would have been amazed at how quickly they took over the business. You and I saw (and heard!) Jolson sing together, but you didn't live to see the silents relegated to film history. Within just a couple of years they were gone, and most of the actors and actresses who didn't make the transition to sound were soon forgotten, Victoria Hartford right along with the rest. Then Leroy and I dared hope we might live together at last. We had our hearts set on some small town on the California coast, or maybe up in Oregon, and our hopes rose further in the spring of 1930 when a man named Arthur Chapman wrote a long article on Butch Cassidy and the Wild Bunch for Elks

Magazine. He traced the history of their outlaw escapades, more or less accurately, and stated as a fact that both Butch and the Sundance Kid died in San Vicente, Bolivia, more than twenty years before.

Of course this story came from Percy Seibert. Leroy was gleeful at first. "God bless old Percy," he said. He told me all about what a good friend Percy had been to him and Sundance. He knew they wanted to quit their outlaw lives more than anything in the world. Covering up their tracks by misidentifying those bodies the Bolivians showed him was a final act of friendship. And having the story repeated in Mr. Chapman's article seemed like the greatest good luck we could possibly have asked for. But we soon saw that it was a silver cloud with a dark lining.

Until the Chapman article appeared, Butch Cassidy's reputation had been slowly fading. As you relate in South of the Border, there were many conflicting stories that purported to tell how he died. And like other men from the frontier period he belonged to a time that was dead and gone. Even people who knew nothing of the controversy simply assumed he was buried in some lonely grave like all the rest. Then suddenly his name was on everyone's lips, and friends Leroy had visited in the twenties (sometimes with me) began to talk. Rumors flew all over Wyoming and Utah. "Hell," some old-timer would say, "old Butch, he ain't dead. Why, he stopped by to see me just three or four years ago."

So while my star set, Leroy's rose again, making it necessary for us to be even more cautious in our travels and our visits together. Leroy was glad that he had never told his old friends and acquaintances anything about his false identity. He went by various names when we traveled in the twenties and he kept to them in the thirties, using the names of real men and imaginary ones in a way that would make it hard for anyone ever to trace his movements even long after he was dead.

So as you see, our life did not improve much. I think the longest we were ever together at one stretch was six months. But I don't want this to sound like a lament for what was not to be. Our times together were all the more precious to us because of the times apart. We did have happy times, and one of the happiest was in the summer of 1932 when Brian Hill met us in Wyoming for a month-long camping trip. We rode into the Wind River Mountains, just the four of us. Marty was nearly seven that summer, and what a rider she was already. I think she put twice as many miles on her horse as the rest of us, and having Brian along was icing on the cake for her. More than once she fell asleep against his shoulder or in his lap as we sat around the fire after supper.

We hunted and fished, and we spent several days trying to find a cache of gold Leroy and his friends buried beneath a lightning-scarred tree before the turn of the century. At last we found the tree, but the gold was gone, all but six double eagles. They were wrapped in a bit of paper left inside the old money sack. On the paper someone wrote "Sorry, boys, but I needed it bad." He didn't sign his name. Leroy gave three of the coins to Brian for a souvenir and we kept the others. Sixty dollars for three days' work seemed like very little, but many earn far less in this Depression. (On other occasions Leroy was more fortunate. The few caches he recovered helped us through some tough times after the Crash. He chuckled when he remembered you asking if he had ever put anything away against a rainy day.)

We three grown-ups scarcely got any sleep, what with talking for hours over the campfire. We got in the habit of taking naps in the afternoon, after a strenuous bout of hunting or fishing. It was during one such siesta that a rider came in sight of our camping place. We hoped he would ride past, but he made straight for our tents. As he drew near, Leroy got abruptly to his feet. He took a few steps forward and stood there as the man dismounted, and they looked at each other for a long time. The look on Leroy's face reminded me of someone else, in another place, and finally I realized I was thinking of General Villa, when he recognized Leroy among our crew down in Delgado.

At last the man stepped forward and put out his hand.

"Butch," he said.

"Harry," said Leroy.

It was Harry Longabaugh, the Sundance Kid. I still get chills when I remember the moment I realized who he was. We were camped in a place where Leroy and Harry had camped with their friend Elza Lay long ago. Like Leroy, Harry was revisiting old haunts, and like Leroy he came to look for the very same buried cache we had dug up.

"When I found that note, I thought you took it," Leroy told him.

"Wasn't me," Harry said.

He was somewhat ill at ease around Marty and me and Brian at first, but when he saw that Leroy trusted us, he accepted us. After supper was cleaned up and Marty was asleep, Brian and I were as quiet as bumps on a log while Leroy and Harry talked.

Harry too had been more careful since Mr. Chapman's article appeared, but it was easier for him. There are fewer photos of him and he has changed more. He is a moody sort, not much like Leroy, and they didn't relive the old times as I thought they might. They would mention some event from bygone days, but they would pass it over with a nod or a few words. Harry had a bottle with him and Leroy took a small glass to be sociable, but Harry threatened to become morose as he drank the rest. The one time he grew animated was when Leroy told him about seeing General Villa again, and our adventures in Mexico. Harry seemed almost envious.

It was still well before midnight when he rose to go to his bed, but he stopped just at the edge of the firelight and turned back to Leroy.

"It's not like it was," he said.

Leroy shook his head. "No, it's not like it was."

As Harry walked off, Leroy smiled and said, "Still, we're doing all right for dead men." I don't know if Harry heard him or not.

In the morning I was wakened at first light by the footfalls of a horse. It was Harry riding off. He looked back once, and seeing my head raised, he gave me a small wave of the hand.

Marty is back now, and sound asleep. She came in a few minutes after eleven, very flushed in the cheeks. She had a wonderful time at the dance, she said, and told me nothing more. She is growing up fast, but when she is asleep she reminds me of herself as a baby, when Leroy and I watched over her together.

As I kissed her good night I felt that I must not wait much longer to tell her the whole truth. And in that moment I decided that just as you and Mother told me the facts of my birth on my eighteenth birthday, so Marty will learn the truth on hers. I will let her read your manuscript, and perhaps this letter too. That would be a good reason to keep it.

Then she will know everything. But what will I say if she asks me—as I have so often asked myself—whether I would do it all over again? Will I be able to say, as you said to me, "I'd be as big a fool the second time around"? And did you still feel that way about your life as it neared its end? Oh, I know you would say, "I had my chances and I took 'em." To your dying day you were proud of who you were, willing to take the blame and credit for everything you did, and Leroy was just the same. He may have had a bit more to regret, for the heartache he caused his family and for letting his adventurous spirit push him across the line into the outlaw life for a time, but even there he was respected and admired, and he was proud of that. As Matt Warner put it in his book, "No Western cowboy bandit was ever loved more by the outlaw element than Butch Cassidy."

Is there really nothing you would change if by some miracle you had the power? Wouldn't you do something to spare yourself the constant fighting with the Pinkertons over your books? You were bound and determined to tell the whole truth, but it cost you so much! The legal fees ate up your royalties and finally took your Sunny Slope ranch. Between that and the money you lost selling the Bunk House to Rosa, you ended up almost as poor as the cowboy companions of your youth, living in that shack you called "Siringo's Den" behind Linder Stafford's house in Hollywood. When you were sick you let me nurse you, but you would hardly take any money from me at all. Back then I could afford it! I wish you had let me buy or at least rent a proper home for you in your last years. But Siringo's Den suited you just fine, you said, and I know you were happy much of the time, especially after you met Bill Hart and had the chance to help him with his scenarios.

If you wouldn't wish for money or fancy houses, what about more time with Mother? No, I know your answer to that one already. Jay outlived you, and that was how it was meant to be, you would say. I know you wouldn't change that even if you were God Himself.

All right, I can hear that stubborn tone coming into your voice. You took your chances and wouldn't change a thing, except maybe the next time around you would accept that dinner invitation from Will Rogers so you would have had a chance to meet "the only cowboy able to throw a loop large enough to circle the globe," as you called him in Riata and Spurs. I wish you could have seen the telegram Mr. Rogers and Bill Hart sent me when you died. Any time I'm feeling blue I read it again, along with the letter Bill wrote you, the one you used on the flyleaf of Riata and Spurs, where he says "My Lord, with Western stuff being written by Soda Jerkers and Manicure Girls, there must be millions that would like to read the straight facts if they only knew which one it was,—so this is to tell the world that yours is 'It.'"

I always get a laugh out of that part about soda jerkers and manicure girls.

Well, I am teasing you now. You see how this one-sided conversation has raised my spirits? Like everyone else I may have moments of doubt, but when I look back on my life I remember the good times, and I wouldn't change a thing. How could I, when all I have to do is turn my head to see Marty sleeping peacefully? If I falter, I look at her and remember the example set for me by my father and my husband.

Our time in Mexico was more than a turning point for me, Charlie. It was a moment that shaped the rest of my life. You discovered that you still had what it took and Leroy discovered the joy of being himself again, and I saw you both as you were in your prime. I learned more from you two in a month than most women learn in a lifetime. So I will use what I have learned. I will live as you taught me, taking each day as it comes, ready for anything. I will take my chances. I will become a rambunctious old woman, and I hope I have a dozen grandchildren so I can tell them tall tales about their Great-Grandpa Charlie and their Grandpa Leroy.

I will never forget you.

Good night, dear Charlie.

> *Your loving daughter,*
> *VICTORIA*

Author's Note

South of the Border is fiction—a romance, in the broader meaning of that term—but Butch Cassidy, Charlie Siringo, and Pancho Villa were real men, and with a few small exceptions I have tried to depict their lives prior to the start of this story accurately.

Charlie Siringo wrote the books mentioned in this one and did the things he speaks of doing. The facts of his Pinkerton career and his pursuit of the Wild Bunch are factual. Charlie's marriage to his first wife Mamie occurred as I have related, but Anne, Jay, and Victoria Hartford are wholly fictional, and I have left aside other facts about Charlie's real marriages and offspring. In *South of the Border* I have made his California sojourn a brief one, in between longer stretches of living on his Sunny Slope ranch, which is consistent with the fact that he was often away from the ranch for months at a time on one adventure or another, but did not sell Sunny Slope and move to California for good until late 1922. He died in Hollywood in October 1928. (Wyatt Earp died a few miles away, just three months later. The presence of Wyatt, Emmett Dalton, and other famous frontier figures in Hollywood at this time is factual, and the news story Charlie reads about Bill Carlisle's capture in Wyoming is taken verbatim from the Los Angeles *Evening Herald* of December 3, 1919.)

Charlie Siringo's life was as significant as those of many more-celebrated frontier figures, and he deserves to be better known. It's my hope that this novel, together with forthcoming biographies by Professor

Howard Lamar of Yale University, and Ben Penginot may achieve something toward that end.

Pancho Villa remains an enigmatic figure sixty-five years after his death. Among recent works about his life some proclaim his butchery and lechery, while others extoll his patriotism and humanity. It was not within the scope of my story to attempt a fully rounded portrait of Mexico's last great revolutionary leader, but at least some of his contemporaries saw him as I have portrayed him here. For my purposes it was enough to assure myself that I was presenting one aspect of the real man. He did have American film cameramen with him early in the revolution, he did once delay an attack at an American cameraman's request, and he did appear in at least one fictional film as himself.

As for Butch Cassidy, there is much broader agreement about what sort of man he was, and continuing controversy about his ultimate fate. The facts of his outlaw career and the widely held estimate of his character by his contemporaries were as presented in *South of the Border*. The varied reports of his death given in the story are also factual, and the intervening years have provided no certain proof of when and where he died. It is possible that he was killed in a gun battle with Bolivian soldiers, as was so vividly enacted in William Goldman's film *Butch Cassidy and the Sundance Kid*. It is also possible that he survived his South American adventures and returned to the U.S. There have been many reports from many different sources claiming that he revisited his outlaw haunts in the 20s and 30s. Some of these stories have been supported by people who knew Butch during his outlaw career and swore they saw him again many years later. The most thorough attempt to date to document the evidence for Butch's return was made by Larry Pointer in his *In Search of Butch Cassidy* (University of Oklahoma Press, Norman, 1977). But despite Pointer's persuasive suggestion that Cassidy lived as William T. Phillips in Spokane, Washington, from 1910 until his death in 1937, and repeatedly visited Wyoming in the 20s and 30s using that name, other Cassidy investigators are equally convinced that he lived elsewhere, under other identities, while yet others believe that he died in South America after all.

Butch's sister, Lula Parker Betenson, says in her *Butch Cassidy, My Brother* (Brigham Young University Press, Provo, 1975), that he returned to Utah and visited his family in 1925, but she refused to divulge what name he used or where he lived, when he died, or where he is buried, saying, "Where he is buried and under what name is our secret. Dad said, 'All his life he was chased. Now he has a chance to rest in peace, and that's the way it must be.' Revealing his burial place would furnish clues for the curious to crack that secret. *I* wouldn't be a Parker if I broke my word."[*]

Pinkerton's National Detective Agency kept an open file for many years on Cassidy, the Sundance Kid, and other Wild Bunch members whose deaths were not verified. Correspondence within the Pinkerton organization shows that they believed Butch and Sundance to be alive as late as the teens.

I did not write *South of the Border* to support any faction in this lively controversy. The story came about because I was fascinated by the possibility that Butch might have returned to the U.S. from South America, which led me to wonder what his later life would have been like. Butch was well-liked, had many friends, and came from a loving family, but to live under an assumed name he would have had to cut himself off from friends and family and trust no one completely. I was convinced that such a man would be unhappy in those circumstances. And so I wrote a story that suggests how he might have abandoned his false identity and sought to regain his own, and I placed it in the context of another fascination of mine: the extraordinary grouping of frontier figures who converged on Hollywood in the teens and twenties. These men seemed to be aware that they had lived through an important period in American history. Many apparently saw in the movies both a way to relive their frontier adventures and to preserve those exploits for posterity. Since Charlie Siringo was already in Hollywood (or soon would be), I thought, what could be better than to bring these two men together at last? And isn't it about time Butch got the girl?

John Byrne Cooke
Jackson Hole, Wyoming

[*]Betenson, Lula Parker, as told to Dora Flack, *Butch Cassidy, My Brother,* p. 195.

Acknowledgments

A writer is sometimes helped by almost as many people in preparing a novel as he might be in writing a nonfiction work about the same time and place. This has been the case with *South of the Border*.

Above all, I owe a great debt to Charles Angelo Siringo, just for being who he was and writing as he did. He was not formally educated, but he had good natural intelligence and a grand sense of humor. He was the first of the cowboy autobiographers, and with more than a hundred similar books published since *A Texas Cow Boy*, it is still the best. If some of Charlie's favorite expressions have crept into *South of the Border* (and they have), I have borrowed them openly and aboveboard as a tribute to Charlie.

Among the others who have helped me I especially want to thank Andy Leonard, who was there in the beginning, and who offered patient and thoughtful suggestions throughout the story's development.

Professor Howard Lamar of Yale University and Philip Garvin of Norac, Inc., in Denver, gave me helpful information and made available to me their film *Siringo*, shown as part of *The Westerners* series some years ago on PBS.

Several of my colleagues in the Western Writers of America provided generous assistance: Dee Marvine gave me detailed information on the then-rapidly-changing styles of dress women wore for riding horseback at the time of the story; Professor L. D. Clark of the University of Arizona offered words and music to revolutionary *corridos;* the late St. George Cooke provided information on many aspects of Mexican popular culture; and my good friend and singing partner Professor W. C. Jameson of the University of Central Arkansas pointed me toward Haldeen Braddy's *The Paradox of Pancho Villa* and gave me helpful facts concerning the flora and fauna of the Sonoran Desert.

I am indebted to the staff of the Teton County Library, Jackson, Wyoming, and especially to Nancy Effinger and Susan Blackstone, for assisting me in my continuing search for obscure facts and for helping me obtain many books and other materials through inter-library loan. I am also grateful to the research librarians at the Ocean Park and Fairview branch libraries in Santa Monica, California, for their help while I was there.

Others in the Jackson Hole community who assisted me are Manuel Lopez, of Snow King Resort, who reviewed my rusty Spanish and offered many helpful suggestions, and Bob Rudd, of the Teton County Historical Center, for information on Butch Cassidy and on Jackson hotels.

Gene Gressley, of the University of Wyoming, gave me important leads to sources on Siringo and Cassidy early in my research.

Jim Dullenty, of the National Association for Outlaw and Lawman History, steered me to helpful reference sources on Butch Cassidy and threatened to break my budget with his offerings of books on the Wild Bunch.

Anne Coe, Kathryn Coe, and Matt Cartsonis were perfect companions for my short research trip into Sonora, and I am grateful to Matt's father for lending us his car.

I owe special thanks to George O'Neill, Assistant Vice President of Pinkerton's Inc., who made it possible for me to see Pinkerton's files on the Wild Bunch, to attorney Sean Cassidy of Santa Monica, California, for valuable research regarding the western states' statutes of limitations in 1919, and to my friend Hal Kant for referring my request to Sean. (Hal also provided important encouragement at a turning point in the development of my first novel, *The Snowblind Moon*, which through an oversight on my part went unacknowledged at the time.)

Cassidy scholars Daniel Buck and Anne Meadows of Washington, D.C. provided articles and information about the current state of the Did-Butch-Die-in-South-America controversy. In a time when many historians keep their own counsel until they publish, Buck & Meadows wrote me, "We eschew turning outlaw history into a secrecy-cloaked treasure hunt. Whatever anecdotes we harvest we are more than happy to pass along." I applaud their generous attitude and thank them for it.

Finally, I am indebted to Larry Pointer for *In Search of Butch Cassidy,* which was largely responsible for starting me thinking about what Butch's life must have been like if he came back alive from South America.

To others whose help I may have overlooked here, I offer my thanks and apologies. Naturally any factual errors that may remain in the historical background of *South of the Border* are my responsibility.

J.B.C.